THE
Best
AMERICAN
SHORT STORIES
1954

THE
Best
AMERICAN
SHORT STORIES
1954

and The Yearbook of the American Short Story

Edited by
MARTHA FOLEY

19 54

HOUGHTON MIFFLIN COMPANY · BOSTON

The Riverside Press Cambridge

"A Great Reckoning in a Little Room," by Geoffrey Bush. Copyright, 1953, by The Atlantic Monthly Company, Boston 16, Massachusetts.

"A Beautiful Night for Orion," by Richard Clay. Copyright, 1953, by The Hudson Review, Inc. Reprinted from The Hudson Review, Vol. V, No. 4, Winter 1953, by permission of The Hudson Review, Inc.

"The Sense That in the Scene Delights," by Benjamin DeMott. Copyright, 1953, by *Partisan Review*.

"A Stop on the Way to Texas," by Ward Dorrance. Copyright, 1953, by The Atlantic Monthly Company, Boston 16, Massachusetts.

"The Firebird," by LeGarde S. Doughty. Copyright, 1953, by The University of Nebraska Press. Reprinted from *Prairie Schooner*.

"Apple Seed and Apple Thorn," by Elizabeth Enright. Copyright, 1953, by Street & Smith Publications, Inc. Reprinted from *Mademoiselle*.

"My Brother Down There," by Steve Frazee. Copyright, 1953, by Mercury Publications, Inc. Reprinted by permission of the author and *Ellery Queen's Mystery Magazine*.

"A Change of Air," by Ivan Gold, first appeared in *The Columbia Review*, an undergraduate magazine, and was later included in *New World Writing, Fourth Mentor Selection*, published by The New American Library of World Literature, Inc.

"Farewell, Sweet Love," by Priscilla Heath. Copyright, 1953, by *The Western Review*.

"The House on the Esplanade," by Anne Hébert. Copyright, 1953, by Anne Hébert. Reprinted from *Queen's Quarterly*.

"Char on Raven's Bench," by Frank Holwerda. Copyright, 1953, by *Accent*.

"Gertrude and Sidney," by Randall Jarrell. Copyright, 1953, by Randall Jarrell. First published in *The Sewanee Review*, Autumn 1953, and later included in *Pictures From an Institution* by Randall Jarrell, is reprinted here by permission of the publishers, Alfred A. Knopf, Inc.

"No Way Down," by Almet Jenks. Copyright, 1953, by The Curtis Publishing Company.

"The Latter End," by George Loveridge. Copyright, 1953, by the Yale University Press. Reprinted from *The Yale Review*.

"The Game," by Frances Gray Patton. Copyright, 1953, by The New Yorker Magazine, Inc.

"The Red Mountain," by Robert Payne. Copyright, 1953, by Harper & Brothers.

"The Mango Tree," by Rosanne Smith Robinson. Copyright, 1953, by Rosanne Smith Robinson.

"In the French Style," by Irwin Shaw. Copyright, 1953, by The New Yorker Magazine, Inc.

"The Shorn Lamb," by Jean Stafford. Copyright, 1953, by The New Yorker Magazine, Inc.

"The Pale Green Fishes," by Kressmann Taylor. Copyright, 1953, by Kressmann Taylor. Reprinted by permission of *Woman's Day*, the A & P Magazine.

"The Third Guest," by B. Traven. Copyright, 1953, by Ziff-Davis Publishing Company.

"The Man in Gray," by Christine Weston. Copyright, 1953, by *The Virginia Quarterly Review*, University of Virginia.

"The Indomitable Blue," by Ira Wolfert. Copyright, 1953, by Ira Wolfert.

"The Rock," by Vurrell Yentzen. Copyright, 1953, by *Quarto* Magazine.

The Riverside Press
CAMBRIDGE · MASSACHUSETTS
PRINTED IN THE U.S.A.

TO
ELIZABETH ENRIGHT

ACKNOWLEDGMENT

GRATEFUL ACKNOWLEDGMENT for permission to reprint the stories in this volume is made to the following:

To the Editors of *Accent, The Atlantic Monthly, The Columbia Review, Ellery Queen's Mystery Magazine, Esquire, Fantastic, Harper's Bazaar, Harper's Magazine, The Hudson Review,* Alfred A. Knopf, Inc., *Mademoiselle, New World Writing, The New Yorker, Partisan Review, Prairie Schooner, Quarto, Queen's Quarterly, The Saturday Evening Post, The Sewanee Review, The Virginia Quarterly Review, The Western Review, Woman's Day, The Yale Review;* and to Geoffrey Bush, Richard Clay, Benjamin DeMott, Ward A. Dorrance, LeGarde S. Doughty, Elizabeth Enright, Steve Frazee, Ivan Gold, Priscilla Heath, Anne Hébert, Frank Holwerda, Randall Jarrell, Almet Jenks, George Loveridge, Frances Gray Patton, Robert Payne, Rosanne Smith Robinson, Irwin Shaw, Jean Stafford, Kressmann Taylor, B. Traven, Christine Weston, Ira Wolfert, and Vurrell Yentzen.

FOREWORD

*T*HIS BOOK is intended for enjoyment by intelligent readers. In it they will find a broad cross section of short stories ranging from historical fiction to adventure, from fantasy to problems of contemporary life and love. The variety of the stories shows that American literary talent is as wide as the continent itself.

It has been said many times and by many persons that in no other country and in no other period of history has the short story been so loved a form of writing as it is in America today. Some of the reasons given have been derogatory, such as that we are in too much of a hurry to spare time for long works or that our culture is still fragmentary and not yet full-blown. To this editor, however, it seems fitting that the oldest form of literature, the tale, should be the most popular in the newest of great nations.

In 1942, when I first started editing this volume, I told a French friend how much I dreaded the bloodshed and suffering that was to come in the war only just then beginning to be fought. Out of the wisdom of her greater age and older civilization, she said, "I am more worried about what will happen afterwards." I did not know then what she meant but I believe everyone in this period which so often has been called "The Age of Anxiety" now understands her statement.

And, as I have been reading the thousands of short stories published during the past year to find those that should go into this collection, I have thought of the difficulties under which their authors have written them. For there is no ivory tower where a fiction writer or a poet may retreat in peace, safe from tensions and dissensions, to create the magic that should be in his work. Nor was there ever from the time of the ancients onward.

Shakespeare, the Englishman, and Cervantes, the Spaniard, lived at the same time and on opposite sides of the Armada. The battles between their countries have been almost forgotten but not Hamlet and not Don Quixote. Even Jane Austen, whom so many seem to think of as living a placid life amid the people she so wittily and profoundly depicted in quiet villages, was writing against a background of the Napoleonic Wars. We remember Jane but who knows the Admiral, her brother?

In the nineteenth century, the most powerful explosive ever discovered up to that time was made known to the world. It was called "Giant Powder" and when Americans learned that its inventor, a would-be poet, of all things, was coming to this country to raise money to finance it, there was near panic. Outraged citizens demanded that laws be passed against it and newspaper editorials cried that the maker should not be permitted to land. But land he did, the money was raised and the Giant Powder made. He was Alfred Nobel and his invention, dynamite, became a part of the world's routine, used to blast not only in war but in the construction of peaceful buildings and roadways.

The sound of all those blasts is not as loud or earth-moving or permanent as the great literature written since dynamite was invented. And so, I believe, it will be even with atom and hydrogen and cobalt bombs. We shall learn to live with them and create in spite of them.

No, there is no ivory tower for the writer. There is only an ivory tower for the reader. He can open a book and find there delights either of adventure or of new kinds of recognition.

When I was a small girl my home was broken up by the illness of both my parents. With my brother I was sent to stay for a time with people who either did not like or did not understand children. It was a harsh and brutal period in my life. Fortunately, my parents' library — the kind assembled by a former schoolteacher and a doctor — accompanied us.

All the old-fashioned, uniformly bound sets of the classics were there. Dickens and Thackeray, Hugo and de Maupassant, Shakespeare and Tolstoy, Jane Austen and George Eliot, along with Wordsworth and Tennyson and Keats. There were individual volumes of Melville, Hardy and the Brontës and many, many others. Those books became home to me, the only home I was to know for a long time. Looking back across the years, I see myself lying on the Brussels-carpeted floor of a New England parlor, a book open before me and lost in such utter joy that it was of no importance at all that surely, some time during the day, I would be wrongly whipped for something I had not done. At night, before sleep came, I could lie thinking of the people in those books and know that I might be only a little girl who was very unhappy in many ways but that there was another world beside the one in which I lived and to which I could always flee for refuge.

Somehow, I recognized even then that the books which were giving me so much happiness were often made out of the unhappiness of their authors. That they, too, once had been children and that they knew what it was to be unhappy and helpless not only when they were young but when they were older, and that they had the great courage so to transform their own small lives that many people could share in their joys and agonies and find strength.

So every time I edit a book like this, it is a little like paying back a bit of what the little girl who was myself once received. I am hoping it will quicken the life and pleasure of readers whoever and wherever they are, and upset though they may be by whatever stress of today's living.

Perennially, the question is put to me, what trend did you notice most in your reading of stories this year. As always, it is a difficult question to answer. Literary trends are long-term movements not to be gauged in twelve months. What did impress me most was that all kind of magazines, from the pulp level to the literary quarterlies, published the largest number of stories about children and old people I ever have encountered. And this in spite of the fact that editors and agents have been saying for some years now, "Please! No stories about children and the aged!"

I have tried to understand the reason for so many stories of this kind and have failed. All I can do is report the fact.

Another trend seems to be that so much editing of stories is being done that the editors' hands are becoming too apparent. That is true of both literary and popular magazines. Once writers submitted their stories to magazines, editors chose those they liked and with, perhaps, a few changes in grammar, spelling or punctuation, off they went to press. There is a great deal of other work besides reading and accepting manuscripts to be done in any editorial office. Planning has to be taken care of, along with conferences, layouts, working with printers, budgeting and correspondence, among other things, and editors work hard.

Now such a frenzy of revision and rewriting is going on in many magazine offices that overassiduous editors are interfering with communication between writers and readers. What they are achieving with all their smoothing out and contriving is about as lifeless and tasteless as most chain-store bread. Or most Hollywood moving pictures and television programs which long have undergone the same procedure.

It seems silly to say that writers should be able and permitted to do their own writing. But what sensible person would not be shocked if he were asked to look at a painting as a good piece of work and then told that, of course, the painter didn't paint it that way? A lot of critics and gallery managers touched it up here and there for him.

Happily, many good, original short stories are being written and are being published. From them I have chosen this anthology. The original meaning of anthology is "bouquet." Some of the stories here may have thorns for some readers but I hope they also find a lot of roses.

I wish to thank Joyce Hartman for her assistance during the early part of the year and to thank David Burnett for the help he has given me, especially in regard to fantasy and science fiction. Also my gratitude goes to all the editors of the various magazines published in this country for sending me copies of their publications.

Finally, I wish to recall that this anthology was founded and continued for many years by the late Edward J. O'Brien, to whom the writers of America long will be indebted.

MARTHA FOLEY

CONTENTS

THE
Best
AMERICAN
SHORT STORIES
1954

(From the Atlantic Monthly)

A GREAT RECKONING
IN A LITTLE ROOM

BY GEOFFREY BUSH

*T*O THE Most High, Mighty, & Magnificent Elizabeth, by the
Grace of God Queen of England, Ireland, & Virginia, Her
Most Humble Servant Sir Thomas Walsingham Wishes Peace
on Earth and Eternal Peace in Heaven:

May it please your Majesty to know that your will has been accomplished: the one you know of is dead.

At two hours after sundown of this day, the 30th of May, the judgment of Heaven was performed upon him at Deptford in a quarrel over a tavern reckoning. His body lies with friends, and the instrument of judgment has been conveyed to France. My lady, the late danger to true religion is removed, the right and lovely order of the commonwealth is restored: thus does God, the true executioner of divine justice, work the end of his enemies. May Heaven bless your kingdom here and hereafter with an everlasting Peace.

The manner of his taking-off is known to only five; in the generations to come it shall be known to no one. The four with me in this work were these:

Nicholas Kyrse, sometimes Skeres, tall, ragged, twice imprisoned; with him Robert Poley, employed formerly to this as a spy upon Babington and the false Mary.

Ingram Frizer, gentleman, thin of body, white-faced and red-eyed, to be known by a knife scar on the right cheek and a cough.

Ephraim Cudworth, old, fat, and drunken, without fixed abode.

Skeres and Poley spied out the movements of the one we speak of during these latter two weeks; Frizer struck at the last; and Cudworth has witnessed and testified to the manifest guilt of the one who is dead concerning the doctrines of the only true Religion. At this hour Skeres and Poley are riding under guard toward Scotland, Frizer is in France, mortally wounded, and Cudworth lies drunk in a tavern near Oxford.

There are those whose sight, in these disturbed days, may be blinded by a weak natural affection to the justice of this work, done in obedience to a higher command than human love. By your leave, therefore, I here append the several documents of this undertaking: Cudworth's witnessed proofs of the dead one's guilt; Skeres' and Poley's account of the last three days; a catalogue of the papers found afterward in his rooms, the poor trivial things he shored against eternity; and lastly his own Journal of the final three days until his departure for Deptford. One of his papers I must beg leave to keep, a foolish trifle of no importance but to him and me.

My Lady, your kingdom has been cleansed of the devil of Scepticism, Doubt, and vain Reasoning. An enemy to God and to yourself has taken leave of his mortal life, and he was one who allowed himself few hopes of a life immortal. He has lost it now forever; he died unconfessed, his guilt unacknowledged. May God have mercy on his soul: in God's name was this work done.

Whether he recognized me, I cannot tell, but his look has been before me these five hours.

6 Proofs of the Vile & Filthy Atheism of C. M., Truly Witnessed & Faithfully Set Out by E. Cudworth on this 30th Day of May:

1. While drinking M. said that in his belief Moses was no more than a Juggler and Aaron a Magician at a Carnival.
2. M. said that the latest doings of the Lord Chief Justice were a sore trial of the established faith in a Divine Providence.
3. M. said the first beginning of Religion was only to keep men's minds in comfort.
4. M. said he could hardly believe God's love was so infinite as to forgive the guilt of the human race.
5. M. swore 7 times by the name of the Blessed Mary and 2 times by the name of Him who rescued us from Death.

6. M. said that he knew not whether there were a God or no, and the doubt was like a shadow or a bad dream, and never in this life to be resolved.

A Report of the Actions of C. M. from the 28th to the 30th Day of May, Observed & Attested by N. Skeres and R. Poley:

May 28. — M. rose at noon, having the night caroused with the witness Ephraim Cudworth and the Queen's agent Sir Thomas Walsingham. Walked north from his rooms and drank 2 pts. of ale. Swore several times and said he would be damned if he drank again. Returned to his rooms and in the afternoon wrote for 2 hrs. in his Journal.

At nightfall M. studied for 3 hrs. by candlelight. At 10 o'clock as appointed he met the witness and the Queen's agent at the Red Boar, Cheapside. He caught sight of Skeres by lamplight but seemed to take no note of it. At the Red Boar Skeres and Poley sat in a far corner. M. in high spirits argued blasphemously the existence of Our Lord. The witness Cudworth noted all that was said. The Queen's agent Sir Thomas Walsingham spoke seldom, but looked at his hands where they lay on the table.

In appearance the condemned is middling tall, slender, and fair-haired; he dresses fashionably, walks nobly, sings well, laughs often, and as often retreats within himself while others talk around him. He speaks first soft and then loud, and alters suddenly from one mood to its opposite. He shows no sign that he recognizes his guilt.

May 29. — The Queen's agent instructed Poley to discover the witness, who had disappeared during the night following the assignation at the Red Boar. The witness was found at 11 o'clock, in a room above the Crown & Thistle by the river, lying in bed sweating and thrashing and regarding a picture of the Virgin Mary. He was in a fever and was attended by the woman of the house. Poley asked the witness to tell what it was that troubled him. Cudworth said in reply that he refused to bear witness. He then looked at the ceiling and asserted several times in a loud voice that he saw the Archangel Michael with a flaming sword. Poley sent away the woman of the house and said to Cudworth that there was no one in the room but himself, Poley, and Skeres. Cudworth laughed violently and said that the room was his own conscience, that someone had put out the light and he heard nothing but confused noise. Thereupon he began to cry weakly and said he was betraying the sweetest young gentleman in London, and what did it matter whether there were a God or no, there remained love among men.

Poley and Skeres restored the witness, who promised to be at Deptford at the appointed hour on May the 30th.

May 30. — On the day of execution the condemned rose early and walked through the City, seeming listless and depressed. Once or twice he looked behind him. In the afternoon he wrote in his Journal and began a letter to a Lady which he did not finish. At 9 o'clock he descended to the street. He wore a sword and appeared excited and elated. He took a water ferry to Deptford and went to the Bull & Baby as appointed. There were already at the Bull & Baby the Queen's agent, Cudworth, and another, with a white face and a cough. M. spoke jokingly to Cudworth and drank 2 pts of ale. At 20 minutes past 10 o'clock the execution was accomplished, a difference having arisen over the reckoning. M. died at once of two knife wounds.

The costs of this surveillance are £2, 4s., and 11d.

A Catalogue of Papers Found in the Rooms of C. M. Following His Accidental Death at Deptford:

1. A demonstration, derived from the miserable estate of the world and the natural guilt of man, that there can be no God.
2. A copy of your Majesty's letter to the University of Cambridge six years previous, when M. was engaged secretly in state affairs, to the effect that he had done your Majesty good service, and that it was not your Majesty's pleasure that anyone employed as he had been in matters touching the benefit of his country should be defamed or refused his degree by those ignorant of the business he went about.
3. Manuscripts of plays, entitled *Edward II, The Jew of Malta, Tamburlaine,* and *Doctor Faustus.*
4. A long poem, unfinished, entitled *Hero and Leander.*
5. A letter begun to a Lady, and broken off.

And lastly, your Majesty, there was a paper that for these ten years I had altogether forgot, but that he had remembered and preserved, and that I must sue to preserve also. It is a slight youthful thing I wrote myself, when we were both lads at Cambridge, that means nothing to anyone except one or two foolish people:

6. *A Masque of Love,* Written in Celebration of the Nineteenth Birthday of Christopher Marlowe, by Thomas Walsingham.

CHRISTOPHER MARLOWE TO MARY L.

May 30, at Sundown

MY ONCE DEAREST MARY:

The reason why I should write to you, after so many months, I know not, and the reason why I should hope that you may read what is written, I know less. I could go on with more false antitheses, but I have no heart for them. I fear there is something amiss, but whether in the world or in my mind, I cannot tell. Mary, I am heartsick. I have not spent these seven months with women, but with philosophers, reading and writing and pondering till my head reeled. The voices of philosophers are more shrill, jealous, and various than women's ever were; the winds of doctrine have swept through my mind till it is blown to tatters. I know not whether there be Reason in Heaven, Reason in the world or any Reason at all in this poor life of mine. I know only that at this shadowy hour of sundown I have a sudden longing for the regard of another human heart. This same silly presentiment in my mind, like a child's fear, bids me tell you that there is a thing I would have you know: though I betrayed the certain simplicity of your affection for the doubts and perplexities of reasoning, I loved you, Mary, and I love you still.

I have been watched these two weeks by a pair of curious eager villains, the one short and the other tall, who rush forward, fall back, scratch their heads, frown and whisper, and pretend an intense interest in objects invisible to others. The shorter now awaits me in the street below my window, disguised as a paving stone. In forty minutes I must keep a rendezvous at Deptford. There is a plot forward: by someone I am deemed guilty of I know not what. The powers of the state are in motion — from my simple service six years ago I am familiar with the gait of their approaches: but I shall meet them like old friends, and so, Mary, shall I condemn their judgment and redden their hands with their own guilt. There is one notion I have found in my philosophy, that redeems all: had I time to speak further —

THE JOURNAL OF CHRISTOPHER MARLOWE

May 28. — Rose late this morning, having caroused till two o'clock with Tom. The talk was of the ways of God, but though we gave the matter our full attention for the space of two hours, we reached no conclusion. There was a third with us, an odd friend of Tom's, entitled Cuthbert or Cudwart or some similar cowlike name, a fat fellow with white hair and a pious watery bovine eye who spoke no more than to ejaculate "Ah!" or "Oh!" or "Do you so?" or "Is not the green grass, in respect not only of its greenness, but of its grassiness, a marvelous proof of God's wonderful workmanship of the world?" While he uttered these religious sentences with a profound piety he drank seven pints of ale in half an hour.

I fear I offended Tom with some silly joke of Moses and Aaron. He turned pale, looked at Cudwart, and back to me as if he wished I had not said it for all the world. In the six years since we left the University, Tom has become a respectable man, a husband, a father, and a servant of the Queen; he has no longer this childish undergraduate trick of joking and arguing of mysteries, but knows the Prayer Book and the Articles and where he hung his socks; says "Yes, quite," and "An interesting position," and smiles not once. I have not seen Tom smile for a fortnight. He is so weighed down with affairs of state and Heaven that he speaks like a man of sixty. But I would cut off my right hand rather than offend him; I must hold my tongue firmer; for this Cudwart, he can break his neck on his religious grass and drown in his religious beer, but if Tom will be respectable, let him be respectable, and I will love his respectability.

Now I am twenty-nine; next year I shall be thirty; and so the great world decays, every year a year older. This philosophy will unhinge me wholly. I can moralize on the natural guilt of my left foot, with classical examples from Achilles to King Oedipus. I am afflicted today with the spectacle of Time and Age, and the desire to consider my life. What have I accomplished in this marvelous long life?

I have played with boats and cried to go to bed; I have been to University though my father has not; I have made love to a girl whose lower lip would break your heart, who loved me with the awe of a daughter, came when I called, talked when I talked, laughed when I laughed, was silent when I was silent, and I sent her home; I have written a handful of verses so light they would fly upward had I not chained them in a desk drawer, a bushel of treatises on Heaven and Hell so foolish they would make the most inferior devil laugh in his torments, and half a dozen plays of so little volume they would not fill the grave of a field mouse — no, nor my grave either.

The fault cannot be my nurture; my father is an honest man. He has made shoes for thirty years, an honest man in an honest trade, thanking Heaven for an honest wife, giving thanks in the morning for breakfast and in the evening for supper, praising God for good fortune that he may feed his family, and for adversity that he may educate his soul. He speaks little and that roughly, thinks less, and reads nothing. He sent his son to University, and when that same son returned for Christmas, filled with fashion and Aristotle, he looked at his son with amazement and pride while the son sat sullenly in a corner of the kitchen in a new doublet. "A long journey?" said the father presently. "Middling long," said the son out of his discontented silence. "Cold?" said the father. "Reasonable cold," said the son.

My father has worked long and hard to one end, and that end is to work hard. Here am I, all beginning and no end whatever, that change color with every breeze, not laboring from poverty to prosperity, but launched at full sail. I can go where I please and think what I will; I have a chart of the whole world, but I wander confused in the middle of the sea. For a week I can be a pair of pagan lovers; for two weeks I can be an Asiatic conqueror scorning heaven; for two weeks more I can be a learned doctor in terror of damnation. I have doubts that unseat the stars, and I resolve nothing. I have served the Queen, as Tom does now, but it was no more than a plaything with which to busy the hands while the mind wandered still. I can advocate a case today and its opposite tomorrow, with equal fervor. This tree of knowledge will damn me always: under this curse of thinking I can here spend an hour of God's sunlight in a small dark room recollecting a short and aimless life while Cuthbert improves the day with drinking. I must soon say that this searching intellect, this divine lamp of reason that includes within itself the thousand judgments and betrayals that men have ever conceived, is a light to lead us to drowning. Is a man who thinks a thing of nothing? I shall meet Tom tonight and discuss the proposition, and Tom will say, "Yes, indeed, yes, an interesting opinion."

May 29. — Supped and talked with Tom, and ever with us was the zealous Cudwart. I shall inquire of Tom who this rascal is. I fear he is one of the twelve apostles disguised as a drunken old man, for he will bear witness to the handiwork of the Lord ten times in five minutes, and a falser witness he never had. "Witness the hand of God," Cuthbert cries in his religious chant, "in the delicate decorum of nature, angels before men, men before beasts, locusts before pismires." Yet I begin to have a strange fondness for this Cuthbert, a kind of amiable fascination, despite myself, in this pious monster, though he has looked me in the face not once.

The talk was once more of Heaven and Providence: there are those, and one of them is I, who will vex themselves into their graves with notions, loudly arguing with philosophers two thousand years dead, arming resolutely against shadows, expounding mists, and tilting with reflections. The wretched Codberry drank all in and cast up holy examples with the regularity of a Roman Emperor. Tom, thank Heaven, is grown sensible; he and I have talked from a late dusk to an early dawn at Cambridge, but these vain philosophies trouble him no longer. What lies within the reach of his arm, he discovers and orders; what lies beyond, he cares not for. I have a meloncholy voice in my head that says we shall grow still farther apart; we are on different roads, he and I, and obey different commands. This is a sad thought, that boys are warm and pliable, and soon friends, but men harden into themselves.

At Cambridge Tom was as reckless as anyone in mind and hand. He is so no longer; and I might have seen the signs before, when once or twice he held back from an enterprise. He has hardened into a man of property: he speaks with the gravity of his grandfather; he jokes no more; he keeps accounts; he owns lands; he maintains a wife; he is a model to his son. When he walks into the air after supper he says, "A fine night, Christopher; a lovely night, Kit," as one says to a wife, "A fine gown, my dear, an excellent choice" — speaking with the quiet kindly pride of one who knows that although God made the night, yet he, Tom, must admire it, and though his wife chose the gown, yet he, Tom, paid for it. Then he pulls on his fur gloves and turns up the collar of his cloak and observes with satisfaction that the stars are exactly where he placed them the night before.

And still there is something in Tom which I cannot name, and which I fear in its anonymity, something almost ruthless in that sweet and reasonable friend. I think beyond all things Tom prizes Peace: the established doctrines of religion, the established order of the kingdom, and the due propriety of the family. The necessity is so strong in him for peace and order that sometimes I fear he would betray his own conscience and condemn his own heart. There is a strange irrational violence confined within that respectable Tom, from some terrible dread of disorder; I would give the rest of my life to let it loose harmlessly.

Its marks are on his face. While I and Codfish rattled on with the ways of God, Tom said "Oh" and "Ah" and looked at his hands, betraying nothing. His face was as strained and gray as the Tower of London in a mist from the river. I caught his eye but once in three hours, and in that one look there was a pleading beyond description. If he could only utter what is in his heart, I think he should be saved. I could argue no further; there was that in his look which killed my words.

These are uneasy times. There is a Catholic in every chimney; if a girl drop a handkerchief there is a popish plot. All that a man may talk of in safety is the price of hay, and that only of English hay. Spanish lace is a sly reference to a second Armada; seven old ladies reading aloud the Psalms are disguised Cardinals plotting to overthrow the government and establish all in common. We hunt out priests and atheists, with fine impartiality, as we hunt witches. In courts and street corners, public houses and court balls, there is fear of war. Ministers are condemned; friends are suspected; families are quarrelsome. At our most glorious hour, when we hold in our hand the peace of the world, we condemn ourselves, and in the name of God: in sixteen hundred years what things have been done by the unhappy human race in their betrayal of that name.

This minute I caught a glimpse from my window of the fellow who walked behind me in the morning. There must soon come an end to this. I am as uneasy as the times. When Tom looked at me imploring, I had a fancy there was one word I might speak to redeem all and save us both: if I knew that word —

May 30. — I write now at sundown. This morning the City was radiant in a white mist: such a mist, no doubt, as surrounds the city of Heaven. Why I think of that second city, and see it so simply and sweetly in my mind's eye, like a child, I know not. I must cheer myself; for a letter pushed beneath my door summons me to meet with Tom in two hours' time at Deptford.

I could bear thinking were it not for the one thought which returns to me daily: that there is no tenant in Heaven, but an empty void, a deserted room, that would mock us to our deaths were it anything more than a great Nothing. In these troubled years I dare say this to none but friends; yet the thought is with me ever, and it stops my heart: that there is no God; that my father labors and thanks Heaven and when he dies will receive Nothing; that the articles of Tom's respectability rest securely on Nothing; that Cudworth shall on the last day march triumphantly into an abyss of Nothing; and that my father's son has spent twenty-nine years thinking of Nothing, to no purpose. These are wild and foolish words; I am shamed to set them down; I would I might go to Church on Sunday and sleep at night the other six days without dreaming. I would I were my father, and an honest man.

I have finished walking in the garden ten minutes and have cooled off somewhat. I think I see my way: if reason is my only instrument, if I have not the honest skill to cut leather nor the true simplicity to worship, I must employ that instrument as well as I may. I shall study further in these matters and resolve myself. If at length there seem indeed to be a Divine Providence, I shall fall down and weep for joy; if there seem to be none, no Reason in the world and no Reason in our short unhappy lives, why, men have looked that emptiness in the face before this, and stared it down and lived honorably. Philosophy is almost as honest a trade as any other; I shall follow it, and not despair.

And yet I have a weariness that stings my eyes. Perhaps before the highest court I am guilty indeed. The streets are darkening, as if this night were the last night of all, and there is no one come to light the lamps. I pray God there is One to light a lamp on that last night; for I cannot find my way alone.

In my folly I tried to write a letter to Mary, and could not finish it. I see no particular cause why she should go so far as to remember my name. It was a silly weakness moved me, but I confess I am calmer to find that natural affection has not altogether died within me. It may happen I shall be forgiven, for having loved truly.

I must set off for Deptford. My watcher awaits me below. I might not go: there is a kind of unease in my mind, such as would trouble a woman. Yet I am ready. Whoever they are that come toward me, I can do no less in politeness than go to meet them halfway.

I put on my sword this instant, that has not slapped my leg in two years. I think that doubts shall end this night.

Your Majesty, he reached Deptford at half-past nine o'clock. The stars were clear and the moon was rising. There was a summer wind from the river and water lapped the barges.

In the tavern Cudworth and Frizer sat together. I waited in an alcove behind a curtain. A dozen laboring men were drinking and singing. The room was thick with tobacco smoke and the smell of ale — the place of judgment, dark, confined, and confused with voices. Your Majesty, it was the small perplexed room of a man's conscience.

He entered armed, looked about him in the smoke and noise, saw Cudworth, and sat down beside him. Cudworth told him I would come before long. Christopher clapped him on the back and laughed — I had not seen him laugh so happily in a month — and said, "Inform me of the condition of your soul tonight, Cudbelly; for Cudbelly, I love you, and I joy to see you, and I delight in your soul, and I can think of no other reason but that I wish to see you saved on the last night." Cudworth wiped his mouth, looked at Christopher, but not full in the face, and said, "These are grave matters, Master

Marlowe." "None graver, Master Cuthbert, none graver," Christopher said, and all the while Frizer regarded him carefully and coldly, inspecting the white hollow of his neck as a lover studies a woman.

"Will you buy me an ale, Master Cuthbert?" Christopher said. He drank it in three swallows and turned suddenly to Frizer. "Do I know this gentleman, Codberry?" Christopher said, addressing Cudworth but his eye not leaving Frizer, who returned that look but so blankly there was no more expression in it than in a knife blade. "Master Marlowe, Master Frizer," Cudworth said. "God save you, Master Frizer," Christopher said, and looked at him long and hard, as though he recognized his opponent.

Then Christopher turned as suddenly back to Cudworth and said, "Buy me a second ale, Master Codfish, I think we shall have a carousel this night to put a stop to all our healths." He drank it and laughed and said, "What think you of the works of men, Cudworth?" Cudworth answered, "They shall vanish from the face of the earth." Christopher laughed again, from pure pleasure, and said, "No, not all, Cudworth, not all, there are one or two shall remain." "What are they?" Cudworth said. "Shall I tell you?" Christopher said; and leaned forward as if to whisper, but instead said loudly, "I say that the work of Master Frizer shall be remembered for generations."

Frizer half rose, his hand over his dagger; but Christopher moved not a hair, smiling sweetly at him, and the laborers sang still. "Shall I resolve you upon the question of Providence?" Christopher said to Cudworth. "Do so," said Cudworth. "There shall be a God," Christopher said, "so long as men believe in him." "Ah," said Cudworth, wiping his mouth once more, "you say that God is a mere imagining of mankind." "I say that they imagined him for love," Christopher said softly, "and that that love shall redeem us all."

At this moment the host of the tavern came to them saying there were two ales yet to be paid for. Christopher looked up at him and said, "Master Cudworth has paid for these two." But Cudworth shook his head. I saw Frizer move his hand toward his knife, draw his chair slowly backward, and gather his feet beneath him. "Shall we quarrel over a reckoning?" Christopher said. "We do all await a greater reckoning than this.

"Friend," he began, and there was something in that single human word that moved me more than religion. I stepped out, but I could go no further. "If I am guilty, though I know not how," Christopher said, "I shall pay my account." Frizer was up, his chair fallen backward and his knife shining. "And Heaven permitting I shall pay yours also," Christopher cried. Frizer leapt upon him, stabbing twice. Frizer stumbled back, and we saw that Christopher's sword was through his stomach. There was no sound in that small room but the two of them separating from that sudden embrace, Christopher turning and falling, and Frizer stumbling back into a table and coughing. The lights were put out and the room was filled with a confused grappling and shouting. He died without a word; but as he fell his head was bowed, like one who sinks to pray on a summer Sunday.

I can write to the Queen no longer. He lies tonight with angels. When he turned he looked full upon me: whether he saw me, I cannot tell, but I shall see that look forever. We are all guilty. I loved him. *God have mercy on us all.*

(From the Hudson Review)

A BEAUTIFUL NIGHT FOR ORION

BY RICHARD CLAY

*A*S DIANA SCHUYLER hunched herself in the corner of the front seat she saw the windshield wiper sweeping the snow from the dark glass with a whick-whack sound that seemed to her as cruel and persistent as if it were slapping her tear-stained cheeks from side to side.

"Worst storm this winter," said Harvey, and she started at the sound of his grating voice. "I'm sorry you were tired of the party, Diana, but maybe it's a good thing we left so early. This blizzard's going to make the driving pretty rough in a few more hours. I'll be glad to get home before the roads are blocked."

"Don't just make conversation, please. I've asked you before."

There was a short silence that seemed to her a blessing until she heard and almost felt the terrible clanking of those chains and until he started up again like an alarm that won't shut off.

"I hope you're not brooding some more. That's one of your bad points you'll have to get over, Diana. You're making a mountain out of a molehill."

"Shut up, please."

"Okay, if that's the way you feel. But I think you're acting very nervous. I hope it's not about the storm, because we'll get through okay. You can count on that. I always do get through, don't I?"

She felt the bitter draft around the door of the business coupé and tightened the leopard coat around her waist.

"Don't I?" he asked.

She noticed over the grinding of the chains that the door was rattling, and a sudden picture came to her mind of the door flying open and her falling out under those horrible chains.

"Don't I," he said.

She slid herself carefully away from the door but not so far that there was any danger of touching him. Then she grasped the cold door handle in her bare hands and pulled it, straining until something sharp happened, and she felt herself falling back against him so that the car lurched and threw her the other way again.

"My God, Diana. What the devil are you trying to do!"

"It came off," she cried, staring at the object in her hands. "It came off. Your damned door handle." She threw it on the seat between them, and it bounced to the floor.

"Owoo —" He reached down, and the car lurched again. "Did you throw that at me? Did you deliberately throw that at me, Diana?"

"Throw it? — deliberately throw? Oh —" and then that seemed to her to be absolutely too much, and she felt the laughter coming up and the tears running down her cheeks again silently but openly with laughter so she could snap open her gold kidskin bag and fumble in it and find the laced edged hankie and mop her eyes this time.

"You and your wonderful car," she said. "What a team. Driving me home. Getting me through."

"With no help from you."

"That's enough of that sort of talk, Harvey Trimmer. We've had just about enough of it tonight. Now listen. This door is dangerous. Stop the car and close it right now."

"I can't understand it," he complained. "It's a brand new car."

"I don't care how new it is. The door has to be fixed at once."

"I just bought it three weeks ago. You know that."

"Of course I know it. What are you telling me that for? What on earth has — oh you're being stubborn, are you?" There was a pause as she heard the door rattling, and she went on. "But I mean it, Harvey. It frightens me. Won't you please stop and fix it."

"Be glad to," he said briskly.

She felt the car swing off the road and watched him get right out in his galoshes. He left the motor idling. She could hear it very soft and hear the windshield wiper ticking like a friendly little metronome in a small room and see the green lights on the dash and the broad white beam out front pouring light through the swirls of snow and see the two — what were they out front? — like jack o'lanterns — what could they be? — oh my, oh MY, it was her gate, her gateposts, her very own place, her home. They were home. It was the carved lion gateposts and the wrought iron lights from Grandfather's time. How wonderful they looked, how priceless in the snow like two Santa Clauses with their caps of snow and their lighted faces and their beards of snow. She would have to tell him that. And the little evergreens that were planted last spring were standing like waiters with their arms full of snow dumplings. She would have to tell him that — or could she? Could she ever hope to make —

He opened her door suddenly. "Watch out," he said, and slammed it.

And then, thinking irrationally that Harvey was doing it in anger although she knew better at once, she felt herself and the car being jerked forward helplessly, so that her head snapped back against the seat as she heard the metallic clash slightly muffled by the snow and realized that the car had been hit from behind quite hard.

After that she heard Harvey shouting several times in his bossy voice and heard a door slam and another close less violently. As she scrambled up on her knees to look out the back window she saw the big dim moons of the lights of the other car behind them shining close as if to embrace their spare tire, although the lights did not seem to be tilted or the glass broken or damaged in any way. She saw the three black shapes in the reflected light to one side of the fender, dark and rather grim at first in the driving snow, until it parted in an eddy and showed them huddled in a circle, one of them obviously Harvey in his top hat, and the other two strangers, one of the two small, not much bigger than she was, and the other even bigger than Harvey. The big man seemed to bend over the other two as if to protect them in a fatherly way, so that she was surprised when the matchlight flared in his face and showed him to be so young, no older than Parmalee. The yellow light flickered on the soft curve of his cheek and the straight shadowed line of his nose and a curling lock of his hair that had strayed over a corner of his forehead because he wore no hat. The match glow was passed in cupped hands to the small man, who leaned towards the light so she could see that his face was wizened like a monkey and full of wrinkles like Daddy's face only younger, more like — "Oh, my goodness," she said aloud, "it *is* Parmalee."

She twisted around and leaned hard on the horn button, hearing the rich trumpet sound as she pushed it one — two — three — four times in her excitement. When she turned again to the rear window the three dark figures were facing her with their mouths open like a Christmas tableau of carolers in the snow about to sing a sacred song, except that the presence of Harvey's top hat cast a ribald doubt on their purpose, as if they might start with "We Three Kings" and suddenly shift to "The Whiffenpoof Song." She felt a sudden shivering from the cold and from a sense of merriment that was intense, private, and as clear to her as the stroke of a bell.

Harvey detached himself and disappeared from sight by the corner of the window a second before he opened her door, leaning in, bringing stray flakes of snow whirling around his shoulders.

"It's some crazy college boys," he announced. "They're probably drunk. They skidded into us, but they only dented the tire cover. Look, they gave me twenty dollars to fix it." He showed her the bill in his fist triumphantly as if it was retribution exacted for the wildness of young men and perhaps for door handles that came off.

"It's Parmalee. Isn't it Parmalee?" She pushed at his chest.

"Parmalee? Your brother? I've never met —"

"Well, get out of my way." She squirmed around on the seat and threw her legs over the side and out the door, grateful for the fur-lined boots as her feet touched the snow. "Puff," she called. "Puff, it's me."

The small dark figure dropped the red streak of his cigarette in the snow and came hurrying toward her.

"Danny? Is that you, Danny?" And then she knew it was her brother by the name given her and by the squeaky voice. As he embraced her she heard him murmuring in her ear, and she felt his wiry arms around her coat while her eyes watched over his shoulder as his tall companion ambled toward them until he was close enough so she could see his smile and the way he brushed the snowflakes off his hair. Then she turned her eyes away from him and kissed Parmalee quickly on his wrinkled cheek and said gaily, "It's gorgeous fun to have you home again, Puff."

She backed away from him, holding his arms as if to look him over, feeling almost as if she was acting again in one of those plays at school. "What on earth do you do with yourself these days?" she asked. "You never come home for weekends any more."

"We've had to work like the devil. This year's much tougher than last."

"Is it? I suppose that's why you never bring that fabulous roommate of yours to Philadelphia." She sighed and cocked her head, letting her eyes glance quickly beyond his shoulder and back to him again.

"We're here now," Parmalee said mockingly. He turned his head and spoke away from her so that she was forced to look at the tall man standing just behind him. "Sis, this is my roommate, Harold Stroud. He's staying with us for a few days. Harold, this is my sister, Diana."

She was prepared to shake hands graciously, as she had always been taught, and perhaps with some extra warmth because he seemed almost a relative, being her only brother's most admired friend at Princeton. She was even prepared to take both his hands in open welcome because she knew that Harvey was scowling and watching over her jealously and possessively. But she was not at all prepared for him when he stepped toward her and put his arms around her impulsively and hugged her like a bear crushing her to his chest, kissing her warmly on both cheeks and speaking into her ear with a low pleasant voice.

"Greetings, Diana," he said in such a friendly way. "I feel I already know you awfully well from what Jocko has told me. But I didn't know you would use words like fabulous. It sounds like a New York word. Where does it come from?" He held her tight, and she noticed that his arms were under her coat and around her bare back, which was not unpleasant except that she felt trapped for a moment until she remembered that he was almost in the family, and was very nice besides.

She reached up on her tiptoes and kissed him on his cheeks, first on one cheek and then on the other. "I'm so glad you've come to visit," she whispered. "You're just in time for my party tomorrow."

"Am I?" he asked. "Fine. But I should warn you that I don't talk to people who use words like fabulous about me. I give them a look of disbelief and bite their ears off. I never go to their parties. Never."

"Oh," she said, "they're the only ears I have, after all."

And then he laughed, and she laughed, although it seemed to her that neither of them knew quite why.

He let her go suddenly, as if remembering that the others were there watching. She introduced Harvey to him and to Parmalee with a sinking sensation of guilt that everything she had done was wrong. The knowledge of Harvey's disapproval filled her with trepidation about even such a lovely simple harmless thing as kissing someone new and nice on the cheeks. On the cheeks, and that was all. She felt nothing for him. He was just a friend of her brother's; a big, amiable guy who had kissed her because he saw Parmalee do it and thought it was the right thing. And if that didn't quite ring true the only other answer was that he liked her for some reason, perhaps from the photographs that Parmalee had, or perhaps from something else like the tone of her voice or something she had said, so that he responded to her mood at once before she even knew what it was herself, since she only knew that she had a merry feeling at the sight of them like carolers and at the absurd picture of the Santa Claus gateposts and the evergreen waiters in the snow. She had been frightened until then, frightened of the storm and the chains and the door handle coming off and of the fight with Harvey at the Thorntons' party, frightened of something that Harvey came from, some kind of living that made demands which she grew weary of meeting simply because there was no pleasure in them and because she couldn't be at home in that world, no matter how she tried. Now she realized that what she felt was not a sense of guilt at all but a sweet sense of relief because she had decided to break off with Harvey and take her chances in spite of the way that everyone would be shocked and in spite of not being in love when she had always been in love as long as she could possibly remember. Always in love. To be not in love would present a new sensation, but perhaps she needed it. And Harold, a complete stranger, had noticed everything at once in a flash; Harvey's top hat, the early hour to be coming home, and her forced mood, and had been able to put it all together instantly and understand more about her than she had known about herself until he came along with his fresh and rough and friendly bear hug.

Harvey closed her door and got in his side without a word. As the car entered the gate and began the long climb up her driveway she could see the green light from the dash reflected on his scowling face, making it look unhealthy and unhappy. She turned her eyes away toward the falling snow which had practically stopped now in spite of all his talk about several more hours of it. There was a glow, a pale darkness over the countryside, as the snow thinned out. This pale reflected light seemed to cling to her in a private way that made her feel more enclosed and more removed than when she had been sitting in the little closed-in room of the car with the thick snow all around. She sighed and relaxed in the seat and listened without concern to the pleasant muffled chewing of the chains in the snow.

"I'm sorry about it all," she offered. "It hasn't been your night."

"Is that my fault?" Harvey asked acidly, so that she was happy that he hadn't decided to be contrite just yet.

"I'm not talking about whose fault anything is," she said impatiently. "I'm talking about all the little things I've done, and all the big things you've done. In a way, I'm sorry for both of us that it hasn't worked out."

"Are you apologizing, Diana?"

"*Apologizing*," she cried. "What an incredible word to use."

"It's a good word."

She shrugged her shoulders, feeling the silk straps of her evening dress move over her skin. "I'm telling you it's all over, Harvey. There's been something wrong with us for weeks. You've known it too. Let's be civilized about it."

"You're being emotional and nervous because you're tired, Diana. You know perfectly well that there's nothing important wrong with us. Ask your mother and father." He spoke with a smug assurance that made her wince because she could remember how long she had admired it and found shelter under it.

"They don't always know what's best for me," she replied, admitting their authority and denying it in the same breath.

"You don't know what you want, Diana," he said with a labored patience. "You think you want excitement and some kind of Hollywood romance full of bogus emotions."

"Oh, don't be so stuffy."

"Well, it's true."

"Harvey, I've asked you before. Please save all that for your insurance prospects. I think it's indecent."

"Indecent! I'd like to know what's indecent about being sensible," he demanded. "I'd like to know what right you have to call me indecent."

"Yes, you are. You're positively indecent. You're cold-blooded and selfish and insensitive about other people except on the surface. Like that time you boasted to me about selling more insurance than your father, even though it was his company."

"What in hell is wrong with that? He's a semi-invalid from the war. He should have retired long ago, and he admits it himself. Hell, he's proud of me."

"Oh, of course. I'm sure he's proud of you. So why talk about it? — even if you did outsell him. Why talk about it to me, even to me? What good does it do you? What makes you need to take things from other people?"

"I don't. That's a lie."

"You do — do — DO. What about that twenty dollars you took from Parmalee for a silly little dent that won't cost you five dollars to fix?"

"I didn't take it from your brother, damn it. That other fellow, what's his name, was driving. He offered it to me. I didn't ask for it. I guess he was damned glad to get off so cheap, when I could have taken him into court."

"Oh, how vile, how indecent. All this talk about courts — "

"Diana, stop it. You don't know what the word decency means. I suppose, for the Lord's sake, I suppose you thought you were decent when you and that what's-his-name were hugging and kissing like a couple of moonstruck kids. You never saw him before, did you? What kind of behavior is that? Is that being decent?"

She looked away from him out of the window, lacing her fingers together in her lap and clenching them until she could feel her arms tremble. The pale snow-reflecting darkness heightened her isolation so that she felt for a moment that she might be two people, one of them far above in the night looking down on the other acting out this pitiful comedy like a tiny doll in a toy car way below.

"You know, Harvey," she said bitterly, "you have the most extraordinary ability to smudge even the nicest things."

Nothing further was said as they drove around the left turn by the garage and up the last rise to the house looming above them like a stone fortress with the terrace lights left on for her. When the car reached the steps and stopped there she said wryly, "You'll have to let me out, you know."

"Sorry. I forgot about the handle." He jumped out and came around quickly to open her door. She stepped down, refusing his arm as they walked up the steps together. She found her key easily and put it in the lock, setting the door on the latch as she opened it, so the others could get in.

"You go on now," she said.

He stood there. Finally he said, "I'm sorry about tonight."

"Of course you are. So am I. You go on now."

"I'll see you tomorrow night at your party, okay?"

"That's the way it's planned."

"Okay. I'll see you tomorrow night then."

"I suppose so."

As he left her she paused with her hand on the front door to watch him turn the car around and head it down the hill toward the garage, his strong white lights shining on the tire tracks that had been made coming up the drive and that looked like necklaces twined together and laid on a linen cover ahead of his lights, until the dark bulk of his car came between her and the tracks so that she could only see the white lights beyond the car through the rear window which grew smaller every minute as the red light blinked on and off with his braking the car around the sharp curve at the garage and heading it down beyond the trees, the white lights appearing between the trees like a flashing signal growing more distant as it flickered through the thick stand of hemlocks and among the bare branches of elms and chestnuts, all spidery in the faraway light.

She was holding her skirt up clear of the snow as she stood on her threshold and watched him go away from her and watched the dim light of Harold's car climbing the hill so slowly. And now a cold wind came up on the hilltop and whipped the snow around the corner of the house and around her skirt, the powdery wind-borne snow sweeping under her skirt against the fine silk mesh of her stockings, the light cold snow settling like diamond dust on her legs, melting as it touched her skin, tingling on her skin like a thousand tiny arrows shot by the pixies. The pixies — she hadn't thought of the pixies for years. She could remember her father reading in the soft light of the library long ago, and the pictures in the book, dark blue sky of night and snowflakes as big as cockleshells, and a little pixie man riding each snowflake down the wild north wind like a magic steed headed for some forgotten glory. She shivered, from the cold, or perhaps from some thin sense of the lost years so quickly gone, the brief time spent in dreams, such a short space back, and gone now.

As Diana entered the dim hallway of her home it reminded her again of another age, with the heavy chairs and tables, the umbrella stand, and the tall ugly clock that Mother couldn't bear to part with because it had belonged to her father, to Grandfather Rice, who had made his money from a carpet factory and had built this house early in the century when only rich men owned automobiles and could establish themselves in the Whitemarsh Valley, twenty or more miles from the city.

The solid ugliness of the furniture made her shiver as she walked toward the closet under the stairs, and then she laughed privately at the memory of Daddy's dismal and eternal joke about Grandfather's money being left to the clock with Mother as its guardian until it came of age. Daddy was often a tease, so she wasn't always sure what he meant or how serious he was.

In fact, it was Daddy's being a tease about her adolescent loves that had often shown her the weakness she came to see in each affair. She remembered in particular the night exactly a week ago

when he had spoken of Harvey several times as a "sound man,"
and then asked, "What more can you want of a man?" in such
a way that it had seemed to be praising Harvey and yet left the
question ringing around in her mind after she went to bed so that
she finally switched on the crystal lamp and made a list for herself.

Diana Rice Schuyler   Dec. 11, Friday — 1936

What I Want of Men:
1. To think the way I do.
2. To feel the way I do.
3. To like what I like.
4. To be bigger than me in every way so even if he doesn't
   think and feel the way I do he can be strong enough to make
   me want to think and feel the way he does.
5. To take care of all the big things and let me take care of all
   the little things.
6. To be willing to give up anything for me.

Several days later, when the excitement about the King and
Mrs. Simpson had died down, she crossed out the sixth require-
ment because of some wisdom that told her it was not of a piece
with the other five and that it was more than she could expect
of any other man in spite of the King, who had spoken on the
radio before supper on the night she made the list.

As she stood in the hall putting her leopard coat on the hanger
in the closet under the stairs she heard a voice or voices, one of
them like Daddy's, through the closed door of the Walnut Room.
Remembering that Mother would inspect the dress, she took a soft
old scarf from the closet and picked up the edge of the scarlet silk
skirt in her fingers, feeling it cool and hearing it rustle, as she
began to wipe at the wet spots, running the hem through her
fingers, blotting it dry where it had touched the snow. She let
the skirt drop, hearing it rustle again, and stood by the mirror,
straightening the waist and smoothing the drape of the scarlet
watered silk. She nodded to herself in the mirror, her brown eyes
following the curve of her neck as she feathered her hair with her

fingers, turning her small neat head from side to side to see the curls fitted close as a cap of golden fleece. And a big skirt because I'm small, she thought, pirouetting in front of the mirror, seeing the skirt flare like a scarlet bell, and hearing it rustle, and feeling the petticoat settle against her legs underneath.

She skipped to the front door and peeked out through the glass. Oh, Lord, she thought in panic, what's happened now? He's backing out. But as she watched the distant fan of light retreating down the drive it stopped and stood still a moment among the bare trees and started coming toward her again.

She ran her fingers lightly up her bare arms over the soft skin, turning the golden bracelets on her wrists for a moment and then touching her necklace, forming a loop of the pearls with her fingers to make the shape of a heart so she could see the white pearls in the glass of the door like a candy heart in the same shape as her face, a winsome face or rather a face that was just saved from being winsome by her long upper lip and her straight sharp nose.

The telephone rang, and she turned halfway from the door to answer it but stopped when she saw Annie hurrying from the Walnut Room in her plum-colored uniform. She glanced out at the lights coming up the drive and looked back at Annie bowed low over the phone. And then, for no reason, she put her hands on her ribs and arched her back slightly, standing in the front hall, waiting a minute for Annie. And then she ran her hands up over her ribs slowly until her palms and fingers were splayed over her breasts feeling warm through the silk. And she lifted her breasts, squeezing them a little. "Oh my," she said out loud, and then she spun away down the hall, dancing and whirling, her arms held out, settling like a nesting bird, smoothing the scarlet silk, sedate, walking nonchalantly into the Walnut Room ahead of Annie.

"Here I am," she sang.

There was no sound except the voice on the radio droning in the corner. She looked around the overfurnished room at the leather chairs and Mother's dove-gray sofa and Daddy's thousands of books and the ornate lamps on the endless tables, but the room was empty except for the voice, which she now recognized and heard more clearly, although it was strained through a fine crackling of transatlantic static as it said: " — tell you that I have found it impossible to carry the heavy burden of responsibility and to discharge my duties as King as I would wish, without the help and support of the woman I love. And I want you to know that the decision I have made has been mine and mine alone. This was a thing I had to judge entirely for myself."

As the voice hesitated she turned back to Annie. "Where are Daddy and Mummy?" she asked. "I thought they were here."

"They went to the theatre, Miss Diana. Didn't they tell you?"

"Oh yes, of course. But who's listening to the radio?"

"If you please, Miss, I didn't know you would be home so early. It's a record on a station in Germantown."

"Haven't you heard it often enough to know it by heart now?"

"No, miss, I'm always called away. I never can hear it straight through."

She was a plain dark-haired girl with a faint mustache on her upper lip and with no figure but with fine dark eyes sunk in a face that seemed too lined and wan for twenty-five. Diana had a sharp and depressing vision of Annie's present and future on this hill stranded in the valley with no family to make a match for her, no place to go on her day off but the movie palaces in Germantown. She probably sent a money order regularly to her family on the other side so she could not even afford the minor luxury of buying herself fine underwear. And there was nothing for her to look forward to.

Diana placed a hand on Annie's arm. "Go listen to him," she said. "If the phone rings again I'll answer it. Was it anything important, Annie?"

"Only the op'rator, Miss Diana. She was trying to locate some gentleman for an out of town call. I wrote it on the pad."

"Go listen to your King," Diana said. "I'll take care of it."

She closed the door gently and walked to the telephone table. The pad was covered with a few loosely scrawled words. "Call from Southport, Connect-i-cut for Mr. Harold Stroud. Will call later."

She wandered toward the back of the hall and into the kitchen, thinking that she would make them something warm to eat. They should be there soon. She flicked on the overhead light and took the milk and eggs and butter and sausage meat out of the refrigerator. She had cut the sausage into small patties and beaten the eggs to a creamy froth when she heard the outside door pulled open behind her back and the squeaky voice say, "Hello, Penguin, it's cold outside," and the door slam shut, sending a gust of icy air around her as she waited for the other voice that didn't come. Parmalee went on, "The juggernaut quit on the hill with a dead battery, and I came up the drive. He had some snowshoes in back — God knows, he has everything in the back of that junk wagon. He decided to climb the hill in front. He said he felt it was a challenge, like Admiral Byrd climbing the Ross Ice Shelf. I guess he wanted to prove something to himself."

"Snowshoes?" she said, turning around quickly to find Parmalee bent over, perched on one foot as he pulled the heavy crusted boot off the other. "Snowshoes in Philadelphia," she said incredulously.

"That's the way he is."

"I think it's perfect," she said. "I really have to see it." And then she started toward the door to the hall before he stopped her.

"Wait a minute, Danny," he called. "I'd leave him alone."

"Why?" she asked impatiently.

"They've been phoning him from Connecticut all afternoon. His grandfather is pretty sick. He calls him Gran. He's all the family Harold ever had."

"Yes?"

"Harold's pretty upset. He'd never have come with me tonight if he hadn't promised for months."

"Oh. But what about the snowshoes?"

"That's the way he is, like some big hermit or something. I can't change him."

"But he must need help."

"*You* can't change him, Danny," he warned.

She looked at her brother's wrinkled face, so much like Daddy's when he pressed his lips together with such finality.

"I don't want to change him, Puff, but he needs help, and he

doesn't have anyone to help him, even you." She kissed him on
the cheek and went to the window aimlessly, feeling sad and almost like singing or perhaps dancing by herself, as if she could
hear faraway music while she whirled with her arms empty waiting for him.

"Now, now, Danny. Don't get any ideas."

"Dear Puff, straight from the shoulder." She smiled at him fondly.

"Well, I mean it, lay off this time." He stared at her for a
moment before he dropped his dark eyes from hers and noticed
the things on the table. "What's that?" he asked. "Are you making a snack?" He looked at her again. "That's swell of you,
Danny." He began to shake off his heavy coat as he talked. "Gosh,
I'm cold all the way through. I think I'll take a hot shower. I'll
be right back." He had his coat over his arm as he walked toward
the door. He stopped next to her and put his free hand on her
bare shoulder. "I'm sorry, sis. Forget it, will you."

She gave him a quick kiss on the cheek and pushed him toward
the door. After he'd gone she perched on the stool and went on
with her work. When she had everything ready she lifted two
heavy cast iron frying pans from under the stove and placed
them on two burners, which she lit and turned down low so that
the spiky rings of violet flame were beginning to flicker and two
or three of the pale little buds in each circle popped out completely before she turned the handle back up just enough to hold
the flame steady.

The eggs and sausage were simmering when she turned to look
up at the clock and saw Harold standing in the hall door. He
was not exactly what she had pictured in her mind from meeting
him in the dark. He was big, heavily built through the shoulders
and chest, which she knew already. But she couldn't imagine anyone in his right mind wearing saddle shoes and white flannels in
winter as he did. As for his jacket, it was a racy black and white
hound's-tooth pattern. The middle button was entirely missing
so that not even a thread was left hanging. And his tangled hair
was windblown and uncombed with a stray wisp partly falling
across one side of his wide forehead, just as she had first seen it in
the matchlight in the snow. And the greek nose was too sharp,

like hers, and the lean cheeks too thin, and the mouth too soft
until she saw it begin to smile, and saw the smile slip by an almost
imperceptible tautening of the skin across his cheeks in a soft
arc around his cheek bones to the corners of his emerald eyes and
to the dark centers of those, and she felt the blush hot on her
cheeks and all down her neck, knowing that he had caught her
spying on him and had turned away amused.

"Hello, Diana," he said.

"Hello, Harold. I'm making something to eat. Won't you sit
down."

"Thanks. This is very hospitable of you." He walked over
and stood directly in front of her as if there was something more
he wanted to say desperately if he could remember the words.

She twisted away suddenly, hearing her big skirt rustle as she
leaned over the stove to lift the sausages onto the plates, feeling
herself in a strange state of suspension, not knowing what to think
of him or what to say to him. She served all three plates, putting
Parmalee's back in the oven. He had wandered over to the window.

"The stars are out," he said.

"Yes," she said. "You can get a fork in that drawer. Do you
want a glass of milk? I didn't make any coffee."

"This is a beautiful clear night," he said, "now that the snow
has stopped. It's a beautiful night for Orion."

She was already seated at the enamel table when he walked back.

"Do you know about Orion?" he asked.

She finished a mouthful and looked at him as he sat down across
from her. "Orion?" she said. "The stars, you mean? The constellation?"

"Yes. It's all over the sky tonight. And yet, I don't exactly
mean the constellation," he explained, as he speared a piece of
sausage and began eating. "I mean the god in the myth; the god
who fell in love with the moon goddess, Artemis or Diana, when
they were hunting in the woods one night." And then quickly,
before she could say anything, he looked up from his plate with a
grin and said, "These eggs are almost as good as eggs Stroud. What
else do you make?"

"Simple things like omelets. I knew how to make a jelly roll once, but I'm out of practice. What are eggs Stroud?"

"Pure ambrosia. Louis de Bellancourt invented them for Gran."

"How fabulous — having eggs invented for you."

"For Gran — not me. And there's that New York word again."

"Fabulous? Oh, I forgot." She smiled. "Who is Louis de Bell-something? Should I know?"

"He was at the Ritz in Paris before he became our chef. He died last summer. He used to tell me that women would never make good cooks because they had to nourish men instead of exciting them. He gave me lessons and made me practise and practise. I never told Gran."

"So you're a cook, too?"

"In a way, but only of silly things like poulet à la reine. I never could master eggs Stroud. There was something wrong about my timing. But I'll bet you could do them perfectly."

She watched him as he removed a cigarette from the breast pocket of his outlandish jacket and searched for a match in the pockets of his flannels, finally getting up and taking a kitchen match from the stove. As he sat down and bent his head to the matchlight she caught a swift glance from his eyes that she knew she wasn't meant to see. It was serious and sober, without a speck of acting or flirtation. He blew out the match and turned away quickly. She looked down at her lap and at her hands, clasping them quietly together as she felt the impact of discovering something solid behind the many masks he put on so easily. She placed her elbows on the table and rested her chin on her palms as she looked up at him.

"Parmalee talks about you all the time," she said. "He thinks you're pretty wonderful."

"He talks about you, too, and he has all those pictures of you by the swimming pool last summer."

"Oh no!"

"But yes. Although none of them do you justice. Not half what that dress does for you. You look like Christmas candy."

"Thank you."

"Don't thank me. I'm off of women."

"What's that mean?"

"Simply that I have too much work to do. I'm on probation at college. My best subjects, English and Philosophy. I haven't scheduled my time right."

"Was it the same before? I mean, were you off of women even before you didn't schedule your time right?"

"Christ, yes. I've been off them all this year. Not like Freshman year. But you've got a pinched look so I can tell you don't want to hear a damned thing about Freshman year. By the way, that's a real dress you've got on."

"Yes. Thank you again. It's my favorite."

"I like the way it leaves your arms and shoulders bare and then fits like a sheath down around your waist and then spreads out like a waterfall in the fireworks on the Fourth of July. It makes you look like a celebration."

"It makes me feel like one, too," she said. "You know, it's a shame to wear it when I'm off of men."

"A crying shame."

"Men can't think of anything but sex," she said.

"Too true, the beasts, too true."

"You aren't like that, are you?"

"Perish the thought. In fact, I want you to know that I have only the highest and purest thoughts about things like Plato and the ethereal beauty of women and how very nice your eyes look now that you're smiling."

"You're smiling, too. Like the Cheshire cat."

"That's not what you think it is," he said. "I have a true feeling of heavenly benediction, as if I was getting the call. Perhaps I should go into a monastery."

"And leave me?"

"You could come, too."

"Oh, I'd like that. You could study philosophy or — what would you study?"

"Philosophy's all right. Diplomacy's better. I've always wanted to be a Prince of the Church like Cardinal Richelieu, and wield unseen power. We could meet at prayers and stand in line counting our beads and glancing at each other occasionally with all our bitter knowledge of the world."

"Yes, and I could illuminate your prayer books for you. You didn't know I was a painter, did you?"

"A painter with galleries and showings and things?"

"Oh, no. Just a little painter, just for myself. I've never shown them to anyone but my teacher."

"Aren't they any good?"

"Don't tease, Harold. This is important to me."

"Is it? Of course it is. Maybe too important. All nice sensitive young girls want to paint or write poetry."

"Is that so?" she asked. She stuck her tongue out at him. "I'm certainly glad you know everything we want to do, Mr. Stroud."

"I didn't say everything."

"Now, now. I can hear perfectly well. That's what you told me."

"In a sense it has some truth if you — "

"You're just floundering," she said.

"None of them are as beautiful as you."

"Thanks," she said.

He laughed with a deep warm laugh. "All right," he said, "maybe you are a painter. I don't know. I'd have to see."

"You can see right now if you want. Up in my room."

"Suppose I don't like them?" he asked.

"I wouldn't ask you unless I knew you would."

"But suppose I don't?"

"I'll have to burn them all and start over."

"Burn them? Listen, Diana, my opinion isn't worth that much. That's too dramatic. Why should you care what I — but you do care, don't you?"

"I'd burn them. Every last one."

"You know," he said, as he rose from his chair and loomed very large across from her and started around the table. "You know," he said, "I believe you would." He had just put one firm hand on her bare shoulder and was leaning over her as she tilted her head back to look up at him and watch his lips moving as he said again, "I believe you would," when they stopped suddenly, startled by the shouting.

It was Parmalee's voice from upstairs. The telephone was ringing. She jumped up and started for the hall as she heard the flip-flop of his slippers. He got there first and called for Harold while Annie went back to the Walnut Room. Diana returned to the kitchen and picked up the two plates to put them in the sink, letting the cold water run as she heard Parmalee come in behind her and clatter around getting his plate out of the stove. She peered out the window, squinting her eyes to see the stars, but she couldn't see Orion at all. And then she remembered that the window faced north, while Orion was always in the southern sky. A beautiful night for Orion indeed! Harold hadn't even seen Orion. She turned off the water to let the dishes soak and wiped her hands on the clean roller towel just as he came back.

He spoke quickly and urgently to her brother not looking towards her at all. "Jocko, we've got to get that car going again — even if I have to buy a new battery."

Parmalee was in the middle of eating his eggs. "Leave it there," he said. "Nobody's going to use the drive tonight."

"Jocko, c'mon. I mean it."

Parmalee put down his fork and looked up at him. "How bad do you mean it, boy?"

"Four alarm, Jocko. C'mon. I'll tell you."

Without another word her brother stood up and followed Harold into the hall, neither of them as much as glancing at her as they left. They had an air of being insulated in some private masculine world of problems whose importance she was incapable of understanding.

She heard their voices murmuring for a minute or two before Parmalee's slippers went flip-flopping up the stairs again. She was leaning back against the sink, humming to herself, leaning on her hands behind her on the cold metal of the sink, rocking back and forth slowly on her hands as she tried to remember the words from the Benny Goodman record. "Goodnight, my love," she sang softly, "the tired old moon is descending. Goodnight, my — " but there wasn't any moon. There wasn't any moon tonight. She looked down at her dress. Like a celebration, he'd said. Like fireworks on the Fourth of July. And then she felt herself beginning to run, bumping the table lightly as she passed it on the way to the hall.

Just as she expected he was already in his overcoat. It was a Chesterfield coat, new looking, draped down over his white flannels as he kneeled to buckle on the snowshoes.

"We have a battery charger in the garage," she cried, panting.

"I don't think that's the answer now," he said, leaning on his haunches and smiling up at her.

"I know how to work it."

"You don't understand," he said gently. "I haven't time now."

"Oh, you must have. You ought to try it."

He stood up, shaking the snowshoes to see that they were buckled tight. He looked down on her gravely as he buttoned his overcoat.

"You want to help, don't you, Diana?" he asked, but it was more a statement than a question. "I might have a try at your battery charger, even if I only get enough juice for one start. It might help. As for you," he said, "you come along with me. I guess I'm going to need you."

"I'll get my ski suit on," she said, still panting. "I'll meet you down by the car."

She heard him walking kalump-kalump toward the door as she tore up the stairs and down the hall to her room with her hands behind her undoing the buttons all the way. In a second she had wriggled out of the dress and the petticoat, letting them settle to the floor. She grabbed the ski suit from the rack in her closet and thrust her legs into the trim navy blue pants, one leg at a time, and slid the zipper up the side, her left side, up over the bump of her hips and — "Damn" — it was caught, caught, caught on her silk underpants, and there, free. Now the wool socks and then a sweater over her bra, and she was running again, running down the back stairs and through the kitchen, carrying her heavy studded boots in one hand and struggling into the jacket with the other. A moment was spent on the back steps with the boots and their rawhide laces, and then she was running breathless over the snow to the garage. She seized the poles and the skis, buckling the clamps tight before launching herself out on the crusted snow and swooping softly down the hill in the ghostly light, right by his dark and struggling shape, shouting at him, and on down and down and down until the car loomed ahead, and she slid to a stop by its side.

His car seemed very strange and foreign and sort of old-fashioned, composed as it was of queer box shapes and sudden jutting
planes. The hood and the windshield went straight up and the
roof was square and canvas and probably convertible and a luggage rack projected like a shelf from the rear. There was a muted
gleam of chrome in the starlight that reflected on the maze of
wire spokes in each enormous wheel and on the headlamps as big
as silver punchbowls and on little bright touches here and there
like the tire covers imbedded in each front fender and the metal
clef on the side near the rear, where she supposed it was part of
the folding mechanism for the roof. The very indistinctness of
the car in the night and the tiny lights of the reflections glinting
like diamonds gave her a strong impression of faded elegance,
although, as she took off her skis and stuck them in the snow and
circled curiously around it, the elegance appeared to evaporate
like a superficial film, leaving only the square brutal bulk of the
machine, ominous and broad and long and squat like some armored monster.

"It's quite a chariot, isn't it?" he asked, coming up behind her.
He must have stepped out of his snowshoes and run down the
slope after she passed him because he was carrying one of them in
each hand, swinging them loosely like tennis racquets. "It's my
first grown-up love," he said with a gentle mocking tone. "A
'twenty-nine La Salle phaeton with a Fleetwood body built spe-
cially for Dad just before he went off and got himself killed in
his plane flying up the Amazon. Gran had it put up on blocks in
the garage after that and had Frank polish it every month for
years until he gave it to me for my eighteenth birthday."

"That's odd, isn't it?" she said. "Why didn't he sell it or at least
trade it in on a new car?"

"Oh, Gran was always sentimental as hell about it, in a quiet
way, of course." Harold stopped and smacked the two snowshoes
together to knock the snow off, as if he was suddenly embarrassed
at the sound of his own voice but couldn't dam it up for long.
"This old stone crusher has meant an awful lot to several people,
including me, something like the way you feel about your paint-
ings because they're private and you don't give a damn what anyone else thinks of you as long as they leave that part of you alone

to yourself and don't ask to look at it. The only difference is that I don't care a hoot these days who looks at this buggy or what they say, though I used to terribly. And everyone has something to say about it. Even good old Parmalee says it's the gypsy caravan out of *The Wind in the Willows*."

"Isn't that just like Parmalee?"

"Exactly. Precise and fuzzy at the same time. No one else in the world could find that kind of whimsy in this old crate. I'd like to know what you think of it, Diana."

"To be perfectly honest," she replied, "I don't like it. I don't like it at all, and I've been trying to think why, and I believe it's because it reminds me of those dreadful cars in the gangster movies."

"Exactly the way I feel," he cried. "It's strictly a getaway car, something out of the twenties. If it hadn't been for Gran I think I would have sold it months ago and bought me a neat little Ford — and maybe I will now."

He opened the back door of the car and tossed the snowshoes on top of what seemed to be a tremendous heap of shadows and shapes, all of them in a confused convoluted mass that shivered with endless little shimmering movements as the snowshoes fell among them. She felt a piercing childish need to know what they were before he closed the door again, as if she realized that this was her only chance that would be lost forever if she let it go.

"Just a second," she said, laying her hand on his arm. "Let me see what you have in there. Is that all the loot from your last stick-up?"

"No," he laughed, and it seemed a very nice sort of laugh, infectious, and full of grace, and with more happiness than she would have expected from his somber thoughtful tone of a moment before. "It's just *things*," he said. "Things I've collected here and there for years and have been carrying around with me because I don't know what else to do with them. Most of them are unimportant, but I like things," he explained. "Parmalee says I kept several hock shops out of bankruptcy during the depression. Most of it's just junk now but let me show you one of the better gadgets."

He reached into the dark heap and produced a little box as if he had known just where it was all along or perhaps knew where everything was in there by touch. It was no bigger than a bedside alarm and had a little crank handle. When he cranked it there was a noise like pebbles being sloshed around in a flower vase and a dim red spark appeared behind a lens and grew orange and then yellow, spreading out in a bigger circle every second until she saw it was a bulb lighting up. When he had it really going it threw out a strong beam of white light on the snow and the car. Then he let the crank go so that the noise died slowly and the white light began to fade to yellow.

He was about to put it back when she laid her hand on his arm again and pleaded, "Won't you let me play with it for a while? I like things too."

"Sure, Diana. Here it is, and here's old Parmalee. Now we can get started." He closed the back door. "I think we flooded it before, Jocko," he said. "The choke is pretty tricky on this car. Don't pull it until you feel the motor really give a kick. All right?"

"All right. But I didn't flood it before. If you don't believe me you can get in and ride herd on your goddamned choke, and *I'll* do the cranking."

"Well, maybe it wasn't the choke," Harold said soothingly, "let me try it once on the battery and see if I can catch it." He climbed in, and after a moment she heard a noise like an old sleepy dog grumbling under the hood.

"No soap," he said, climbing out.

"What about it?" Parmalee asked. "Who's going to crank it?"

"Now, Jocko, you know very well that I count on you at the controls." She saw him put his arm around her brother's shoulders like the big bear and the little bear, and she thought, I believe he really loves him. And Harold turned to her, almost as if she'd spoken out loud to him, and said: "Will you help me, too?"

"Of course."

"Will you wind that thing and shine the light on me around here — " he was walking, and she followed. "Right here," he said. They were in front of the giant radiator. She began to wind the light, hearing the pebbly noises as she saw him lean over and put the crank handle into the car and begin pulling it around, bobbing up and down slowly in the complete darkness that diminished as her light warmed up, so that she realized with a pleasant but jolting shock that he had done this many times in utter darkness and had no need of her light, but had asked her anyway.

No matter what they did, and she saw him wipe his forehead several times in the cold night, there was no sign of real life from the motor. Once it coughed and almost seemed to catch, but that was followed by failure after failure until he straightened up and turned his back to the hood.

"I think it's flooded again," he whispered. "I guess I'll have to carry that damned battery up to your charger."

"Why don't we get the Packard from the garage and push you up the hill," she suggested.

"An excellent idea." He walked around the side of the car as she let the light fade out. "Jocko, I'm pooped from cranking, and Diana has a swell idea. Why don't you go and get the Packard and give me a push up the hill?"

"Oh, hell, let's leave the damned thing here and go to bed."

"Now, please, Jocko. I told you in the hall."

"And I told you, too."

"No, Jocko, no. It won't do. C'mon."

"All right, boy. You're sure jittery."

When Parmalee had gone his way up the drive. Harold climbed in behind the steering wheel and lit a cigarette. Her eyes had grown accustomed to the pale reflected light from the snow so that the bright flash of the match seemed to throw a segment of his face into such sharp and startling relief that she barely restrained her desire to reach out and touch his cheek.

"Would you like a cigarette, little sister of Parmalee?"

"Not this minute." She stood on one foot and then the other, and then she hunched her shoulders and tucked the lamp box under one arm in such a way that the crank wouldn't stick into her ribs while she clamped the box tight under her arm and dug her frozen hands into the pockets of her ski jacket.

"You remind me of a poem," he said playfully. " 'Ah, bitter

chill it was! The owl, for all his feathers, was a-cold.' Why are you standing there? Why don't you stop hopping around and get in beside me so you can be my gun moll?"

She ran around the front, slipping on the snow and almost losing her balance, but catching herself in time, and not even dropping the light as she got to the door with the big old handle and slid in beside him on the leather seat.

"I don't know *anything* about being a gun moll," she said, breathless and excited. "What do gun molls do? Oh, I'm sure I couldn't be one. I'm too much of a sissy. I was in such a hurry to get my ski suit on that I forgot to bring any — "

"Here, take mine. I've been wearing them, so they're warm."

"I couldn't. I couldn't."

"I've got an extra pair back there, coonskin. I'll get them when my hands are cold. Beside, I want to tell you what all this happy lark is about. You've probably been wondering."

"A little," she said. "But I think I know. Your grandfather is dying, and it's the end of something for you, and you have to get home."

"That's the general idea. He's had two heart attacks before, and he's over seventy. I'm afraid this is the last one. Parmalee says it's silly of me to go now. He says that either Gran is dying or he isn't dying, and if he is I won't be in time, and if he isn't I can go tomorrow. So let's go to bed. That's the way he talks."

"I always thought Parmalee should be a lawyer," she said.

"Exactly." He said it with a flat tone as if it was a reflex action. She looked at him, but there was not much to see in the dark. She moved closer. When he puffed on his cigarette the glow lighted up his nose and his eyes and the wisp of hair in the corner of his forehead.

"Where were you in your thoughts just now?" she asked.

"I think you know very well, Diana."

"Yes," she said. "You were home. You were home with him, probably holding his hand." She took off one glove and put her hand in his, feeling his long cold fingers closing around hers. "Personally, I think Parmalee should be spanked."

"Hell, no. That's just his way of trying to calm me down when he thinks I'm all broken up about something. He always says I'm too impetuous, and I probably am."

"You aren't," she said. "You mustn't believe anything like that. Not the way Parmalee means it, not in a bad way. Maybe you've just got more energy and excitement than he has. Maybe he envies you. Anyway, I like you the way you are."

"Do you," he said thoughtfully and squeezed her hand. "That's a real blessing, isn't it?"

"I guess so. I don't know anyone who would hug me the first time he meets me, shake my hand the second time, and give me a lecture on old cars the third. But you have to stop being Admiral Byrd and Cardinal Richelieu and Little Caesar driving this car and whoever else you are at other times. It's too much of a strain on me."

"I guess it is," he said. "But I can't stop all those things at once, Diana. The only thing I'll promise is that I'll get rid of this car as soon as I can."

"Good," she said, and then asked, "What did you mean when you said it was a blessing? Why? What's a blessing?"

And then he laughed, and she heard again that deep pleasure in the laugh as he squeezed her hand once more. "Diana," he said. "What a beautiful name. It fits you perfectly. I said it was a blessing because I have a feeling that I'm going to see a great deal more of you from now on. It made me happy to realize that, and that's all it was."

She moved her fingers in his, which were warm now and just the same temperature as hers. "I have the same feeling," she said, "and it also makes me very happy because I didn't expect anything like this. The best part of all is that it seems to keep getting nicer every minute."

She felt him uncurl his fingers, and she had a sudden panic that he was going to leave her until she realized that all he was doing was moving his hand so he could thread his fingers through hers and close his fingers, and she could fold hers and feel the hard tense cords on the back of his hand with the tips of her fingers.

"So that's the way it is," he said. "I'm certainly glad you told me. It isn't often in my life that I hear about something that gets nicer every minute. It sounds like people falling in love, doesn't it?"

"Heavens no! Everyone who has any sense knows that falling in love is a tremendously exciting thing that goes up and up and up like a skyrocket. This is much more comfortable, like going through a lot of rooms with each one better furnished than the one before."

"That sounds like the way I'd like it. Skyrockets are usually disappointing. At least, I think so, and I think I'm falling in love." She saw the bright arc of his cigarette as he spun it out the open window.

"It's getting stuffy in here," he said. "We need some air."

"Anything you say, dear," she replied.

She watched him as he reached up and unscrewed something above the windshield and half lifted himself from the seat, leaning over the back of the seat, pushing the top, folding it back and down, as far as he could reach.

"Well," he said, "look who's come to our party."

"Who?" She twisted around quickly. "Oh," she said, "just the old moon." She slid around and up on her knees beside him and put her arm through gently between his arm and his side, but he lifted his arm and swung it back and put it through between her arm and her ribs, where she could feel it when she pressed it, feel it hard against her ribs. He opened his palm in the full moonlight and held his pale silver fingers cupped until she laid her fist on his palm, and then he curled his fingers lightly, closing them on her small fist as if it was something immensely valuable and very breakable.

"Yes, it's just the old moon," he said. "It's always highly romantic at any other time of year, but never in winter. It's too cold then. The winter moon is frowned upon by all the poets, but I like the winter, even the moon in winter. I like everything about the winter. I like the fences sticking up out of the snow in the fields and the creaking of ice in the trees and the way everything feels on a still cold day with a little brook slowly freezing at sunset. I like to be cold and to look up at all those stars. It makes me feel like slapping my thighs."

"You're queer," she said, but she didn't move her hand in his. "I'd gladly spend the winter in Bermuda and never miss it once."

"You just don't know," he said. "You just don't understand that the wintertime has all the heat and growth and death of the rest of the year leashed and pent up and frozen inside it."

In the bright full moonlight she could see his frosty breath come out from his lips as he spoke.

"You're rather remarkable," she said, "but I don't quite understand winter the way you do."

"Most people don't," he said. He opened his hand quickly and pulled his arm out sharply from next to her ribs and turned himself on the seat so when she turned toward him she could see the long dark moon shadow from his nose and the smaller curling shadow from the lock of hair. She saw him raise one hand toward her face, and she felt his fingers touch her cheek. "There aren't too many people who understand what's trapped under the ice of winter that makes it so much more dramatic than any other season of the year."

"Dramatic? — under the ice?" she asked with some surprise.

And then she saw the smile beginning at his soft mouth in the full moonlight, and this time she knew very well that it wasn't amusement, and perhaps it hadn't been amusement before up in the house when he caught her spying on him at the kitchen door. Perhaps it had been a way of saying something to her, helping her to see something that was very real to him but was difficult to put in words.

"Don't you know what's caught under the winter ice, Diana?" he asked, and she felt now that she would believe anything he said. "Don't you know what's under the ice and under the rocks and under the frozen ground?" He spoke as if it were a litany. "It's all the heat from the red center of the earth. It's the molten heat that is under our feet just a little way down all the year round, but it seems closer and more horrible in winter when the mountains crack open in the long arctic night and pour red lava out on the crusted enamel of ice so that the glaciers melt and trickle away as if they were bleeding secretly from underneath — "

"Oh *my*," she interrupted. "I think I see."

"Yes, darling," he said. "I knew you would."

"Of course," she sang, and she closed her eyes and pressed his hand tight pressing it hard against her cheek. She opened her eyes and looked up and saw his eyes perfectly still looking into hers and the full moonlight around them and on his skin and on his lips. "Is that us, dear?" she asked. "Is that what you mean? Is that us with all that heat and pressure?"

He nodded. She could feel his breathing as he placed a palm on each of her cheeks and slid his fingers slowly under her ears and around her neck to the back of her head. She felt herself whispering words a long way off. "How do you know all these things?" she whispered. "How do you know all these wonderful things, darling?"

She could feel his hands firm at the back of her head and his cool nose touching hers, baffled for a moment until she moved her nose slightly to one side, and then his soft mouth on hers, cool and strange, everything feeling cool and strange as her head went back against his strong hands and her eyelids drooped and she felt her lips soften and her arms go around his big chest, pulling herself to him, pulling her breasts hard against him, feeling her heart begin to pump violently as his lips opened —

And then it stopped all at once as he raised his head and she heard — oh, lord in heaven — it was Parmalee coming down the hill, honking like mad, so that they fell apart quickly into their places on the seat.

After that she heard all the various distant metallic noises made by Parmalee driving the Packard past them and turning it around and getting in place behind them. She noticed that her hands were cold, and she put on his gloves again, the black leather gloves with the bunny rabbit lining. She was feeling a little tired and spent and rather annoyed at Parmalee, who seemed to be doing such a bumpy job of pushing them, so that he made her head roll back and forth on the gloves every time he bumped. From where she was resting her head on the gloves on the window frame she could watch Harold's strong hands on the steering wheel, and she could sometimes glance up quickly at his intent face as he reached out in the dark to pull at something, work something, probably adjusting that choke. The leather of the gloves began to feel warm and smooth against her cheek, and she noticed a faint smell from the gloves, something like oil or gasoline, so that all at once she had a picture in her mind of his working over the car in winter with these gloves on, fixing it up, getting it in shape. And it made her wonder idly what it was really like to be a gun moll or any kind of moll, and though she knew she was being romantic she persisted in it from some left over and unrelieved pressure, and she projected herself for a moment into a scene where a guy came home at night and said something very nice to her like: It's good to be home, or, What's for supper? or, It's time to go to bed, dear.

And then she noticed the light on the instrument panel warming up and getting brighter as she heard a noise like a motorboat racing and then slowing down as the light faded a little and as she watched him shift gears. As soon as they began to roll she sat up straight, looking out ahead at the dim yellow lights on the dark tire tracks in the snow. As they reached the long hill and started to climb, the car bucked several times before it stopped with the motor racing and the wheels spinning until he pulled the hand brake on and let the motor idle.

"Damn it," he said, "this is what happened before. I couldn't make this lousy hill without chains." Suddenly she heard the loud frightening noise of chains partly from earlier memory that evening and partly from the Packard coming up behind her.

He started to get out the door. "I'll ask Parmalee to push us," he said.

She watched him for a moment as he slid himself out of the seat. When he was standing up and about to move she called quickly, "Don't go away."

He stopped and looked back in at her. "I'm not going far, darling; I'll be right back."

"You want to get to Connecticut tonight, don't you?" she asked, feeling a terrible depression seeping through her. "You want to see your grandfather tonight, don't you? That's true, isn't it?"

"Yes," he said, and then he said, "of course," and in the reflected light on his face she saw an expression of intent ferocity that hardly had time to register on her before it blended into a smile of relief as he climbed back in, waving at Parmalee to stop his honking, and taking her hand in his. "Of course it's true. Did you think it wasn't?"

"Oh, I'm all mixed up." She began to shiver uncontrollably as she talked. "I'm so ashamed, Harold. I've been such a bitch. I should have told you before. That battery charger of our takes all night, and you can't hurry it up. There's no use going up there to the garage. I should have told you before, only I liked it so, and I didn't want you to go."

He moved his knees until they were touching hers, and he took off the gloves and held both her hands in both of his. "I know all about battery chargers, Diana," and when he said her name it sounded like a caress. "The truth is — we both liked it so. As for the battery, I passed a gas station down the road when we came in tonight. I can back out now and get a new one there."

"There you go again," she said, "always trying to help me, like asking me to hold the light for you. But it won't do now, Harold. I have to tell you the rest of it. I had a fight tonight with Harvey Trimmer. He's been my — oh, what can I call him that doesn't sound stupid? Mother calls him my beau, but that seems so creaky, I don't — "

"Why not call him your heart throb?"

"Heart throb! Oh, my goodness, what language! If you only knew Harvey."

"But I do know him."

"Oh, yes," she said. "Well, you only met him, you don't really know — but maybe you do know him, maybe you're right. Maybe he was my heart throb all along." She laughed a little and squeezed both his hands and went on quickly. "Anyway it's sort of final now, about Harvey, I mean, at least in my own mind, but I was upset about that, trying to decide. And then there's my party tomorrow night, and I've been thinking about that ever since I can remember. So you can see how it was when we met tonight. I was so full of something, I don't know what, excitement, tension, I don't know what. And I used you. That's the truth. I deliberately used you. I just chased you like some cheap common prostitute. That's the truth and I'm ashamed of myself. I just chased you like my name, like Diana and Artemis, like those huntresses like you said as if you know everything that's going on everywhere — "

She broke off and let go of his hands and picked up the gloves from her lap and the little lamp from the seat beside her.

"Here they are," she said. "You'll need them for the trip. Thanks for lending them to me. You'd better go now."

"Such cheap dramatics," he said. "And I think you enjoy it."

"What?" — she felt as if she had been slapped.

"You heard me."

"I did, I did. But I don't know what you mean. Are you trying to shock me?"

"You need a spanking worse than Parmalee," he said, although his voice didn't sound angry. "But not for what you think. All this childish talk about using me! Did you think you just discovered that, Diana? Did you think that no one ever used anyone else for anything in the whole history of the world until now? Hell."

She felt her skin flushing hot, but before she could answer there was a pounding noise along the side of the car, and Parmalee was standing by Harold's door.

"Sorry, folks," he said. "No all night parking allowed here."

"I'm leaving now, Jocko. If you'll move that lousy goddamned tank of yours I'll back out of here and be on my way. You can give your sister a ride up to the goddamned house."

She got out and slammed the door. "I'd rather walk," she said. "I have to get my skis, thank you."

Both of them were looking at her. Parmalee leaned his elbows on the window frame and put his chin in his hands. "Hold it folks," he said. "Before we all break out in happy boisterous farewells let me tell you what happened up at the garage. Annie saw the lights on and phoned from the house. She was trying to get you, boy. It seems there was another call from Southport just after we left; a guy named Loomis; I guess he's in charge because he gave Annie the message, and she wrote it all down. It seems that this Loomis was pretty riled because he'd just gotten hold of you, boy, and told you that your Gran died suddenly before supper tonight, and it seems that you hung up on him before he had a chance to talk to you about your plans. It seems that he wants to be sure that you're coming right home for the funeral and all that kind of stuff."

She put her hands on the door and felt the iron cold metal as she saw Harold turn his face away from her and toward her brother.

"Well, Jocko?" he asked.

"You didn't tell me he died, boy."

"I didn't tell myself until a couple of minutes ago."

Parmalee looked up at her, his sister, and then away toward Harold.

"So that's the way it was," he said. "All right." He started to walk away and stopped. "Do you need me now?" he asked.

"Not now, Jocko, except to call Loomis and say I've left."

"I'll call him, boy."

"Can I come after Christmas instead?"

"I'll be waiting for you."

After the Packard was gone she reached out a hand. "Lend me a hankie, Harold," she asked.

When he gave it to her he said, "You see, Diana, you gave me as much as you took, maybe more."

She took the white handkerchief out of his hand without touching him.

"I know," she said. "I just saw that," she said. "And I also saw how much more you've given me than I knew about before. Thank you, Harold."

"I hope it's a beautiful party tomorrow night," he said. "You deserve it. You deserve a fabulous party."

"It's going to be; it's got to be fabulous. Lots of old friends are coming; people I've known for years. I'm sorry you can't be there; but you have a long trip," she said.

"A very long one. It'll be dawn when I get there. Goodnight," he said.

"Goodnight."

After he had gone she went back to pick up her skis and her poles, and as she straightened up wearily she caught a glimpse, from the way her head was turned or from some trick of the mind, so that now she could see Orion standing up above the house in the winter sky, huge and a little dim in the moonlight it was true, but very easy to see when you knew where to look and knew that he would be there every night, so that she could see his outline even as she looked down again and tucked her skis and her poles under her arms, too weary to put them over her shoulder, as she went off up the drive for the last time that night and for the first time alone.

(From the Partisan Review)

THE SENSE THAT IN THE SCENE DELIGHTS

BY BENJAMIN DEMOTT

*F*OR MOST of the afternoon it was a soft spring rain that slipped lightly through the leaves and soundlessly drenched the earth. In the bunched heads of short grass and in the ruts that the car had gouged as it crossed to the grove, puddles filled and overflowed in quick eddies that vanished in the blackness of the lower marsh. Sometimes a squally wind bulled across the meadows and tossed itself noisily in this corridor of the forest, and then the rain swept in harder, and the branches of the small pines and the frail trunks of the weed-birches quavered, and the forest clutched its slick new greenness to itself. But at dusk the wind stilled and they noticed, as they sat in the police car with the windows shut, that the rain was thinning to mist.

There were only three of them here — the woman had returned to the village in the cab of the tow truck. The driver had refused to cross the marshy bottom that separated the cart road from the grove where the abandoned car was, so the Chief, after standing patiently in the rain and arguing with him, sent him back. Then the police officer named Charlie called the firehouse and asked for another truck. And now they were waiting — the finder, the Chief, and Charlie — for that truck, and also for the arrival of the doctor.

The soporific washing sounds of the rain in the leaves, and the gentle hum of the open radio band had eased them; they were almost startled when the finder spoke.

"Look, Chief," he began. He was a round-faced, light-complexioned man with close-cropped hair and an expression of uncomplicated earnestness; he was probably not thirty-five. He wore a gray tweed suit and a red and black striped tie.

The Chief raised his heavy chin slightly from his chest to acknowledge the voice, but he said nothing.

"I don't mean to butt in," the man proceeded diffidently, "but — what's to stop us from just driving it out ourselves?"

The Chief relighted his cigar. "Nothing," he said simply, waving the match that would not go out. "That what you want to do?"

In the back seat Charlie chuckled to himself.

But the man pressed on impatiently. "Oh I know the fire truck's coming but that does seem like more trouble . . . If we could just drive it out — it got in there without any trouble."

"Looks like it, don't it," the Chief said blankly, still without looking at him.

"Mister," Charlie said. The man in the front seat turned about politely. "I reckon the gas tank's empty, don't you know. And I reckon there ain't no spark. And I reckon Doc Bentley's got to do his business first, don't you know."

"I see," he said unhappily. He took off his hat and ran his palm lightly over his brushy hair and sighed. "Well, it's an awful thing, I'll say that much."

"It is, oh it is," Charlie admitted.

"The funny thing is why we were out here," he went on. "We don't come this way often — except the first walking Sundays. Grace likes to come here and hunt for trillium."

"Have to come regular now," the Chief observed, yawning.

He shook his head. "My God but it hits you. Grace — she was hysterical right up till a minute before you got here. Shook me up, too."

The Chief looked over at him sharply: "You should've kept your hands off that goddam paper box."

"I know it," he said. He raised one hand to his eyes and then, dropping it suddenly, he said very earnestly to the Chief:

"You haven't got any idea who it is?"

"What — that?" The Chief jerked his head back toward the grove, and shrugged. "Guess somebody from the hospital with that white uniform. I don't know. You know, Charlie?" he asked, glancing up at the mirror above the windshield.

"No idea, Chief," Charlie answered, lighting a cigarette. "Smoke, anybody?"

"Thanks no," the man said. "You see, what we do is go off right after dinner and leave the kids with Grace's folks. Grace takes that little trowel she had and the box and we go off through here looking for vines. Beautiful things they are."

"I imagine," Charlie said.

"And good Lord, the way it started out this morning — it couldn't have been better."

"Mighty nice," Charlie agreed. "Figured we'd catch some rain tonight, though."

"Yes," he said absently. He took off his hat again. "All I can say is what a terrible way to do it."

"Yeah," the Chief assented. "Pretty bad."

"I don't think I could do it," he pursued.

Frowning, the Chief leaned forward, pressed a button on the dashboard shutting the radio off.

"Charlie," he said then, "little blackjack?"

"Cards right here, Chief." Charlie tapped the finder on the shoulder. "Play a little cards, Mister? Might have a wait yet."

"Thanks I don't think so," he declined. "I'll kibitz if it's all right."

Charlie sat on the edge of the seat and dealt two cards face down on the level top of the back rest.

"Five and ten," the Chief said to him and, reaching through the steering wheel, he placed a handful of silver on the dashboard. Charlie handed some change to him and he arranged this in neat piles around the windshield wiper. They played in silence for a time, the Chief accepting or rejecting the proffered cards with gestures. The man watched restlessly and when the deck changed hands, he said:

"Mind if I open the window a bit? Thick in here all of a sudden."

"Go ahead," the Chief said.

He rolled the window down and, turning his back to it, he watched the Chief shuffle the deck on the seat.

"Why do you suppose he did it that way, Chief?" he asked when the game resumed.

"Who?" asked Charlie. "Oh, him. Dunno."

"Got enough?" the Chief asked Charlie. Charlie meditated.

"Didn't have no garage, simple as that," the Chief said briefly.

"He could have found one for that, I should think. You know more about it though . . ."

"Hit me once more light," said Charlie. "Oh-oh, too much is what she said."

The Chief added the nickels to his pile on the dashboard.

"Well you found him, Mister," he said, dealing again. "You looked him over close and there he was." He looked up at Charlie:

"Stick on two whores, huh? Mighty brave . . . Dammit, I got to cut the heat out of this deck."

"Sure, Chief," Charlie said.

"I guess he probably doped himself up first," the man reflected.

The Chief put the deck down in the seat. "Look Jack," he said abruptly, "it's a long day and the sun was out and now its raining, see what I mean?"

"Wh — ? I beg your pardon?"

"It's a long day."

The man considered this a minute. "Of course," he said then. "I'm sorry. I think — well, walking out after some flowers and coming on that. It makes you think, that's all."

"Sure it does," the Chief agreed. "What with pulling the box off and all."

"I'm sorry," he repeated. "I forget you people see this kind of thing all the — "

"Wait a minute wait a minute," the Chief interrupted. "Don't tell me what I see. Don't forget that, hear?"

Into the silence that followed Charlie said in a relaxed voice:

"Old man Bentley's probably asleep in the tub still, huh Chief?"

"He'll be along," the Chief assured him. He shifted his position behind the wheel, looked out the side window at the mist. "Used to be good hunting hereabouts," he said to no one. He turned up the bottom card. "Gus Baldwin used to choke that pickup of his with pheasant and let 'em go right back in there a ways."

"Grace and I didn't see any this afternoon."

"He don't bother around here any more," the Chief explained.

"That goddam development back there. Too close — they're all the time calling in. Every time a truck backfires on the pike they want the Guard out."

"Heinzie Kreuter bagged something out here last week, though, didn't he, Chief?"

The Chief nodded vaguely. But then he looked over at the finder and, with surprising animation, he laughed aloud. "He sure did," he said. "I was over there when he brought them in, I tell you."

"No," Charlie said.

"These two girls," the Chief said, still looking at the finder. "Out back there in the woods, playing with each other. Heinzie — state trooper runs the pike — Heinzie brought 'em in. He booked 'em with Gladys for unnatural and lascivious and this one of them, Leona her name was, with a big horse face and a leather jacket on and riding boots — she yells out, 'It is not, it is not. Oh my darling I can't live without you' and a lot more crap like that. Well, she's running on and finally Gladys just up and walks up to her and gives her a good crack across the face with the back of her hand."

"My God," the man said. "My God."

"Blood running through her teeth, way she hit her . . . And all the time they were waiting there, they were writing these love notes to each other."

"You see 'em, Chief?" Charlie asked.

The Chief ignored him. "Heinzie, that big boyo — he sneaked right in on them and grabbed up the paper and they were crying and shrieking around. He gave it to Gladys and Gladys gave it to the Magistrate."

"What'd he say?" Charlie asked.

The Chief paused a moment; he looked again at the finder.

"Nothing," he said finally. "He didn't even look at it. He give it back to them when they came up to the desk."

"Well," the man said, "I guess he knew they weren't there for writing letters."

Charlie picked up the cards. "Hell, it's like everything else," he said. "It's a goddam disease."

He was about to go on when they heard someone calling outside.

"Game's over," Charlie said.

"Chief?" the thin voice called again from the nearby ridge.

The Chief rolled down his window and peered out into the mist. "Down here, Doc, in the car," he answered in a loud voice. "Got your meatwagon?"

"They're coming around the other way," the bespectacled figure said as he came up to the car. He held an umbrella high above his head. "Where's my patient?" he asked.

"Back in the woods. Take you right back," the Chief said, opening the door and climbing out. "Come on, Mister," he said over his shoulder.

Charlie held the door open for the man in the front seat. He got out, walked straight to the Doctor, and stretched forth his hand. "Doctor Bentley," he said, "my wife and I were out for a walk and we just happened to stumble on this thing."

"Oh?" the Doctor said. He was a slight man, with a smooth, pale face, and nets of wrinkles at his throat. "Didn't catch the name?"

"Lives up Shady Oak Hill, Doc," the Chief said.

"Glad to meet you," the Doctor said mildly. "I'm deaf as that," he explained, rapping bony fingers on the fender.

"You want to watch you don't take cold, Doc," Charlie said solicitously.

The Doctor smiled at him. "Let's go make my rounds," he said.

The Chief led the way and although it was not yet dark, he kept the bright beam of his torch turned upon the path behind him for the Doctor. The spongy grass gushed under their feet; it was swept forward between the axle-deep tracks of the car. Ahead, a wire fence was rooted up, the poles overturned; the top wire had burst in two. They climbed over the wires and then before them, a few yards into the sparse birch grove, they could see the rear of the car, and beneath it, the body lying nearly supine.

One leg was drawn up slightly from the grass so that the white-clad knee touched and was soiled by the universal joint of the car above it. The left leg, hips, trunk, and neck pressed evenly into the grass that was growing through the iron spokes of the rear wheels of the car; the grass bent slightly under the great weight that had been lowered upon the axles as the tires, deflating slowly, sagged and split open upon the piercing rims.

The head was hidden from them. It rested upon an upended, misshapen cardboard packing box that was tilted toward them so that they could see the round hole in the upper flap. The box had been drawn back slightly from the car — the rusted end of the exhaust pipe was visible — and its outer layer had curled and shredded in the rain. Hanging heavily over the box from the branches of a springy pine was a mass of white, sheet-like material.

They waited for the Doctor just beyond the fence, Charlie and the Chief smoking under the umbrella; he came back to them quickly, pushing the branches away from him carefully to protect his glasses.

"Une charogne," he said, smiling at them.

"Don't give us that ginny talk, Doc," Charlie said, feinting at the Doctor's stomach. "Can we move now?"

"My wagon here?" the Doctor asked.

"In a minute," the Chief replied. He nodded at the finder. "Fellow here'll tell you anything you want about how it looked, you need that, Doc. Gave it a real good close going-over."

The man laughed shortly. "I wouldn't exactly set up as an expert on dead bodies, Doctor."

"Well, there's quite a lot of them you get to see," the Doctor said. "Ever see that French poem about a cadaver? Something. Not like the original though ... " He was shaking out the umbrella — then suddenly he turned back to the finder:

"You pull the box off that way, huh?"

"Why ... Well you see we just weren't sure and we wanted to — "

"Oh my Jesus," the Doctor interrupted in his weak reedy voice. "Let's go back and sit down. They're probably lost. I'm getting drowned here."

"Give you a hand through here, Doc," the Chief said.

At the Chief's car, they saw numberless, dancing points of light moving toward them in the meadows below. All four men gazed at them silently, and then the finder asked:

"Anything I can do?"

"No," the Chief said. "Stay where you are's best."

But he gestured at the approaching lights. "You don't want all those people up here, do you?"

"All right," the Chief said, "all right. You handle that, then. You tell them all to get out quick and mind their own cellar."

A moment later the Doctor's wagon pulled up before them and they heard the high grinding wail of the second tow truck swelling across the fields. The truck smashed down trees as it came swiftly over the ridge, and Charlie ran out to stop it. Then, when the Doctor's wagon backed away with its burden, he waved to the truck and it plunged backward into the marshy bottom, and the difficult labor began.

They worked for nearly an hour — the two firemen on the back of the truck, the driver, Charlie, and the Chief. And meantime from north and south, from the turnpike and from the development behind the forest, men and women, children and dogs, formed a widening arc behind them.

The Chief turned his car about so that its beams were trained upon the grove. Together with the pair of battery searchlights from the truck, they pushed a great drift of white through the mists toward the finder and others who had stepped out from the arc.

"Stay back there!" they were shouting to the crowd. "Somebody'll get hurt. Stay back!"

The broad rear tires sank deep into the mud, spun wildly, threw forth whirling, giant clods, slid backward finally over the wedged boards. While the motor throbbed muscularly and figures jerked across the lights preparing the next lunge, the arc of witnesses drew a few steps nearer. It advanced again when, with the chains of the tackle grinding against the steel pivot, the huge hooks were slowly let down crashing against the grille and the bumper of the car. But suddenly above the pivot the car was visible, gleaming in the light, its fenders quivering in the wet air, the scarred chrome grille dripping. And now the crowd stood motionless, fixed at the edge of the scene, glaring into the chaos of shadows and sounds before it. . . .

When the task was over and the forest was dark again save for the beams of the Chief's car, the Chief and Charlie circled the area to make certain that every observer had departed, and then returned to the car. The finder was seated on the running board awaiting them.

"You should've caught a ride back," the Chief said.

"It's all right," he answered. "Glad I could help out."

"Let's go," Charlie said.

The Chief drove rapidly along the cart road through the undulating potato fields and meadows, and then turned into the turnpike at the sign that read, ABC RUBBER WELDERS. The radio repeated, "702s, all 702s come in; 702s, all 702s, come home," until the Chief switched it off.

The finder took out a cigarette and offered his pack to Charlie.

"Little wet," Charlie said.

"Straight through to the skin," he answered, smiling. Then, serious again, he said to the Chief:

"What is it you suppose makes people come out into the rain through all that muck for? Damned if they'd listen — it's a miracle somebody didn't get buried back in there."

"Dunno," Charlie said.

"Turn here," he told the Chief. "I guess they just have to come out and see the worst, huh?"

"That's it," the Chief said, "that's so."

"But God it makes you — ashamed the way they were jamming and fighting to get back there. Hell, when the Doctor and the wagon pulled away with that thing, they — "

"Wasn't anything to see then anyway, was there?" Charlie loudly interrupted.

"If there was, I didn't — "

"Was no box with anything inside it there then, huh?" the Chief said, speaking very slowly, leaning toward him slightly.

"Couldn't pull it back and get a real eyeful then," Charlie said, moving forward on his seat.

"You — " the man started. "You've passed it. Let me off. Let me *out!*" He grabbed at the door handle.

"No puff-up face, no fat white — "

He threw open the door — the wheels wrenched off into the gutter, stopped. The car scraped savagely against the concrete curb. Standing, swaying, he said breathlessly,

"I don't have to — "

The Chief leaned far across the seat toward him. "You don't have to take anything, Mister," he said hoarsely. "You got all you want."

"You got the only closeup shot," Charlie said in an even tight voice. "He and 'Grace' got the real view of it — "

The door slammed shut and they saw him half running toward his porch. The Chief shot the car into second and then let it hang there while he swore:

"Dirty, lousy son of a bitch."

In high the car bounced swiftly down the wet hillside road toward the turnpike.

"It's like everything else," said Charlie calmly as they accelerated. "It's like everything, it's the same as this rain soaking us up — it's a goddam disease is all."

"All right then," the Chief said, slowing to a stop at the turnpike. "All right, all right, all right. A dirty, lousy son of a bitch."

"A curious sick son of a bitch," said Charlie. "A nosey bastard." He looked down the turnpike on his side. It was clear.

"All right," he told the Chief.

(From the Atlantic Monthly)

A STOP ON THE WAY TO TEXAS

BY WARD DORRANCE

*T*HE WHITE mares pulled the van into High Street and whinnied and shook their bells. Their driver sat up straight, and his gray eyes narrowed.

The ruts of High Street lay ahead of him in the melting snow. Women in poke bonnets and men in top hats were milling about among the farmers. All afternoon he had watched them stroll along the plank walks, nodding and smiling in the air's beady thaw. Now, just as the lamps were beginning to come on in the stores, and the people were about to return to their musty rooms, their eyes lit up to see the white team and the red wagon.

The driver reined the mares in until they pressed their chins to their breastbands. "Make it pretty!" he called to them, and when two lines of oval faces had gathered at the hitching rails, he laughed and gave the mares their heads.

They sprang forward in a trot. For all their grooved backs and big feet, they seemed to hang in the air an instant before they lit, sprinkling notes from the sleigh bells, and the stars on their blinkers and the knobs of their hames twinkled. The crowd laughed and yelled and tossed up hats, while the driver, pretending to dodge the children's snowballs, shook his whip. At the corner where the mares turned into a side street, he doffed his cap and showed his teeth in his dark beard.

"That was worth a dog fight," he said. He sat back on the box with a smile and let the team jog on through the empty street. At the end of it, where the road entered a cleft in the bluff and fell steeply to the river, he stopped and stood up on a hub. His eyes, which were as deep-set as a monkey's, darted into the drop below.

Three crows were flying between him and the depot and freight house, which lay down by the tracks along the river. One bird held itself apart, above the two beneath it, and their slow coasting flight made his knees tremble, as if, van and all, he were plunging into space. He ran his hand across his eyes and squinted downward, through his fingers. The frozen river looked narrow between its fringes of naked trees; and beyond it, the three miles of flat snow over to the bluffs on the other side seemed like a single field.

All day the whole town and the bluffs and the river had lain under clouds, and although the men back in High Street had said that it meant more snow, he noted that none had fallen. Instead, the air had mellowed, and dripping icicles had made holes in the drifts below the eaves. He looked back uncertainly into the cedars that grew on a ledge beside him, and grinned and felt of the air with his fingers.

At home the young leaves would be casting a shade. Frogs would be singing in the ditch water. But here, in this country, people ran out without their coats, looking up and wondering and chattering to one another at a little check in the cold. He bent down to get under the hood of the van, but halted halfway to glance back into the valley.

From both banks, a line of shallow fog was beginning to roll out on the ice. It twined within itself, idling, swelling out like pipe smoke, he thought, when a man takes a draw on the stem and leaves his mouth open. The crows wheeled over it, cawing.

He watched them until a cluster of lights came on, one by one, in a settlement across the river; then he nodded and picked up his reins.

The mares took the grade slowly. Limping, and halting while the single-trees pushed against their hocks, they made their way down through the wet brush that crowded into the trail. At the bottom, they turned left and trotted past a hut that sat against the base of the bluff.

The hut was small and its logs had settled. The door and the one window were squeezed out of shape, but the words *Depot Saloon*

appeared in white on the stone above the roof. At the window, in a
spot that had been rubbed in the steam on the pane, a hand was
waving.

The driver touched his hat, but glanced away and shut one eye
and scanned the river. Here by the tracks it looked its mile across.
The band of clear ice between the rolls of fog had shrunk. If the
two rolls met before he returned from taking the freight across to the
settlement, it would be up to the mares. He would have to sit, poised
to jump, while they remembered the snags and the air pockets. That,
he thought, will be worth a dog fight, too. His eyes lit up; then he
suddenly recalled the girl who had waved to him, and he moved to
the side of the box and looked back.

She had come out of the saloon to watch him by. Dimly lit by a
beam from the open door, she stood with her feet in the swirling
ground fog, as if she were walking on water. He was not sure that
she made him out, and he cracked his whip and would have called
back something jolly, but the mares were already jolting the van
across a spur of track into the freight yard.

They swept into a curve and stopped where he could back to the
platform, and he hopped out and sat down on the splintered boards,
with his shoulders to the freight house wall. A line of hogsheads,
capped with sooty snow, stood along the fence rails. The fence
stretched back to the bluff, and there the rock rose, black and dripping, like a prison wall. "It may be a thaw," he said, "but it's not
much to look at."

At the sound of voices inside, he turned toward the lamp-lit window. "Two for town," a man was saying, "and one for over the
river." A weight shook the floor and a second man repeated, "One
for over the river." After a while he added, "Where is Johnnie Reb?"

The driver smiled, but he sat still and let them have their joke.
The men were German, and in their accent they made of his name,
John Webb, something that sounded like John Reb. It made them
laugh. The civilian buttons on his butternut jacket were still new.

He watched the men through the dirty pane — Kurt with his pale
blue eyes and his nose that had no bridge; Helmut, with his hair
sticking out like straw from his leather cap. They were stooping and
rising and squinting at labels, as grave as two old women cleaning a
room. He yawned and looked back at the team.

The near mare was sniffing at the mist which crawled along the ground around her feet. She craned her head about when he whistled and, in the lamp light that fell from the window, walled her eyes at him, he thought, as she had done on the night he had met her.

Kurt and Helmut that night, leading the way to the stable with a lantern, had brought him past the van. It was long and bowed in the middle, and the canvas hood gleamed white. The polished bed — how well the civilians did themselves! — reflected their faces. He had supposed that a team which was fit to draw this must be stallions, but Kurt and Helmut, ahead of him, were talking about "them girls." "Tame as pigeons," Helmut said. "Them mares, they wouldn't hurt a baby."

At the box stall, John had stopped and let out a low whistle. "Where did you Yanks steal *them?*" he had asked. There the mares had stood; fat and white and matched, and as soft as glove leather; steaming, in the warm light, as if they had just broken out of the mold that had formed them. Each had looked around with hay between her lips and stared and, seeing the stranger, lowered her black lashes. They look like very fat women, whose faces happened to be pretty, and he had thrown back his head and laughed to hear that their names were Violet and Maud.

"So now you take the job?" Kurt had asked. He had stood, rubbing his hands together, until John wiped his eyes and said, "Sure. You fellows've sold me a ticket."

Now, while Violet looked back, and pensively studied him where he sat on the platform, Kurt spoke up inside the freight house. "I didn't hear Johnnie come up yet," he said.

"He's maybe hanging around Elsa at the saloon," Helmut suggested. He added something in German, and they both laughed. "But Elsa is a good girl, and smart," Kurt said sternly. "Wait and see what happens to her Pa's trade when she finds her man."

"Anyway," Helmut said, after a silence, "if that *Dumkopf* goes over the ice this evening, a shot of whiskey won't do him no harm."

John looked at the mare. "Do you hear that, Vi'?" he asked. "It's not a bad idea, is it?"

He jumped down from the platform and stopped beside her, and kneaded her plump, divided chest with his fingers. She swelled her nostrils and tried to lay her head across his shoulder, but he pushed her away and made off through the fog toward the lighted window of the saloon.

A round-bellied stove stood glowing on the sanded floor, inside. An old man with no teeth and a young one, in a fur cap with ear flaps, looked up from their drinks at a table in the center of the room. Behind the bar, a young woman wearing a black dress glanced back as she reached up to place a bottle on a shelf. "I thought you'd forgotten me," she said.

Her hair was cut into bangs above her startled blue eyes and drawn into a yellow knot at the back of her head. She turned around to face him, between the two lamps that shone to either side of the bar, and held out her hands. "Now what can I give you, Johnnie?" she asked.

He looked at her, pursing his lips, until she laughed. "I know," she said, and she whispered as she filled a shot glass, "Tell Mama hello."

He waved to a gray-haired woman who sat upright in a hard chair behind the bar. "Good evening, Mrs. Sensentaffer!" he called out, and she looked up from a piece of fancy work and nodded.

The girl was leaning on her elbows across from him, watching him drink. "You're not going out tonight," she said. "Kurt and Helmut say you shouldn't."

"Forget that," he told her. "Stand up and let me look at you."

She straightened up and threw her big shoulders back playfully. The blue stones in her earrings glittered. A gold crucifix, lying where her breasts came into a line above the yoke of her dress, lifted with her breath and caught the lamp light.

"You know what, Elsa," he said. "You're prettier than Vi'."

They laughed, but they both jumped when the old woman spoke. She dropped her crocheting in her lap and wagged the square comb that stood high in her hair, and began a speech in German.

John stared at Elsa until she blushed. "I thought you told me she was hard of hearing," he said.

"A deaf woman can hear some things," Elsa protested. "She says a nice boy shouldn't talk like that. You shouldn't call me a horse;

you should look at the bedspread she's making. A nice boy would like that."

The old woman watched him as Elsa spoke, and snatched up her work as if she were angry with it when he shook his head.

"They're all alike," he said softly. He held his glass up to the light and added, "Now, take my Ma . . . "

Elsa picked up a cloth and rubbed at the bar top. "You've got a mother, then," she asked.

"And a father," he said. "What did you think? They got me back out of the army, and right away they wanted to get me out to the field — and marry me off to the girl on the next place."

"I expect she was pretty," Elsa said.

"About like you. Yellow hair, but her eyes were brown. It wasn't her so much; it was my folks. They're all church and farm work." Elsa put her head to one side and watched him as he went on, "They had better luck with the older boys. The older boys were broke in before the War."

"Nice steady men," the old woman said in clear English. She lifted her needles to the light and examined her stitches. "My Elsa will get a section," she added. "Every acre of it cleared."

Elsa looked away. "Mama knows a little bit of English," she said. Her lips trembled and her lashes blinked, as if she were going to weep; then suddenly jolly, she thrust her plump hands toward him and called out, "Toss!"

She caught his glass and returned it, full. "Is it true, like Kurt says," she asked, tracing a figure with her thumb on the bar, "that you rode around the Union lines one night?"

"With Stuart, sure!" His loud voice startled him, and he added meekly, "It was just a bunch of us boys out burning some hay ricks."

He bolted the whiskey and held the glass out again, but she did not take it. "Not if you're going across tonight," she said. "You've had enough."

Seeing tears in her eyes, he glanced at the old woman and whispered, "We caught the Feds with their pants down."

Elsa did not smile. "I know why you have the job you've got," she said, and her voice grew tense. "Oh, I know why!"

"So do I," Mrs. Sensentaffer said. "He likes the red wagon." She tilted her head back and gave him a good look at her square cheek bones and her pale gray eyes. "With little boys it should always be the Fourth of July. He would like fire crackers, too."

Elsa was slowly shaking her head at him. "Not fire crackers," she said. "Guns is what you want. You wish you were back with those Rebels."

He met her gaze soberly. "Listen, Elsa," he said, and he moved his hand up and down before him. "I've told you before; now I'll tell you again. I left home to get out to Texas."

"Texas," the old woman cried. "That's big enough to hide in."

"You're right!" He grinned at her and looked back at Elsa. "At Natchez, I had to get a job on a boat. At Saint Louis, I heard about this work up here in the State capital. This job" — he raised his voice and pounded on the bar — "is just a little something to keep a man alive till spring."

"That's not true," she said simply. She hid her face in her apron a moment, then dropped the apron. "You wanted that job," she spat out, "*because* you may break your neck at it!"

He laughed and put up an elbow before his face. "Hey, wait," he said. "You act like I was a drunk. Or took dope, maybe."

She backed away from the bar and looked at him, wide-eyed. "In a way you do," she said.

"All right then," he said, and he stood up to go. "You know how those boys act."

"I do," Mrs. Sensentaffer broke in. "They double the dose," and Elsa said, "Mama's right. Just look behind you."

The young man with the ear flaps on his cap had gone. His old companion lay asleep, resting his head on the table. One of his eyes was partly open. His tongue protruded from his lips.

John turned away from the bar and strode past him to the door. "Much good may it do you," Mrs. Sensentaffer called, over Elsa's goodby. He did not answer them, but looked back with a smile at the threshold. Nobody saw him. The old mother had risen from her chair. The two women were walking past one another with their arms uplifted, shrilly disputing, between the lamps. He grinned and shrugged his shoulders and stepped out into the dusk to face the river.

Along the bank, the fog lay level at the height of his knees. Seeing that it hid his trail across the ice, he put his elbows to his sides and jogged back, at a dogtrot, past the van and up the steps and into the room where the men were still sorting parcels.

Helmut looked at him silently. Kurt, who was tacking on a label, put his hammer down. "It's warm outside, Johnnie," he said. "The ice is maybe soft?"

"Why talk to *him?*" Helmut asked when John did not speak. "If you're so afraid for him, you should see the agent, Kurt."

"I did it already," Kurt said. "The agent does like this." Kurt held his shoulders up to his earlobes. "He says, 'When the ferry don't run, I hire a man to cross the ice.'"

John stood with his feet wide apart, frowning at them. "You boys scared of something?" he asked. They looked at him and at one another, and dropped their hands to their sides. "If that's the way you feel about it," Kurt said, "come help us load up, then. This load ain't feathers."

When the last crate was roped down in the van, the men walked with John to the left front wheel. They went silently, in step, and crowded so close to him that he stopped and laughed at them. "You fellows deputies?" he asked. "Are you taking me in?" He shook off the hand which Kurt laid on his arm and leapt up to the box. Leaning over, so that they would see his smile, he said, "You grannies get back to your stove." He reached for the whip, and as the van lumbered over the rails toward the river, he yelled back, "Go knit me a bedspread!"

Then he slipped to the far side of the box, to be ready with a good-night for Elsa; but when the van drew abreast of the hut, the place was dark. The lamps on the bar had been put out.

The mares slid down the muddy bank and halted on the ice. He shook the reins, and at his cluck they trotted on, holding their noses above the fog as if they had been swimming. He gave them their heads for a few hundred yards, then stopped them, and looked back to see the town.

Upstream, high on the bluff, he found the State capitol building by its little galaxy of lights. Downstream, tiny tier on tier of lights pricked out the cell blocks in the penitentiary, and between the two big buildings a lamp here and a lantern there, some of them moving, flickered in the woods that hid the streets. The combined glow lit up the clouds, and as the clouds parted, showing the white dome of the State House, the town appeared to be burning.

Involuntarily, he looked back to the spot where he knew the landing was, behind the fog. It was quiet. No band of horsemen was out to take him, but his heart was pounding. He put both hands to his chest, and when the clouds roiled up about the dome again and hid it, he bore down in his boots as if they had been stirrups. "Get the son of a bitch!" he yelled. "Get the raider!"

"Raider!" the stone of the bluff repeated, and the mares, as if they had been spoken to, moved on. He sat down, breathing through his mouth, and stared at their weaving heads.

A short way before them the rolls of fog, which had been moving out from either bank, now met. They mingled, and rose into a bluff much higher than the one he had left, but at the top a narrow slit through the mist and clouds revealed a bit of the outer sky. He lifted his face to its clear, sunset pink — wondering at it, as if it were a thing he had once known and now, in a rush, recalled — and let the mares walk on.

They entered the high fog and drew the van into it after them. Their heads rocked from side to side as they plodded forward, and their ears, he thought, seemed oddly far from the buckboard. Once when a wheel scraped the side of the wagon, he realized that they were making an unfamiliar turn, but he sat back in the half dark, listening to their bells, and allowed them to choose the way.

When they pulled up short and stopped, he sat up alert. And when they would not start again, he leaned out and tried to see the ice beneath the wheels. Was the van resting in its old ruts, he wondered, and did horse sense tell the mares that the ice in the ruts would have melted first? He spoke to them, but they stood fast, and by the rattle of the bells he knew they were trembling. He reached for the whip, but they backed delicately into the traces.

"Well," he said, "we'll soon fix that." He jumped down to the ice and scuffed about it with his boot. He could not find the trail, even though he dropped to his hands and knees, but he saw that Maud had got a leg out of her chains. She shuddered when he struck her, and made him lift her foot. Vi' too, he saw, was shaking.

He walked around to her and pulled her head down by one ear, and kissed her warm skull. "What's the matter, girl?" he asked. "Did you lose the road?" He waited, but she kept her nose pointed tensely ahead. "I'll get you back on the trail," he said. "You watch," and he set off alone in the fog.

After a dozen steps he lost the team, but he stumbled on with his arms out before him. A sludge covered the ice, and here and there the water lay in pools. He could not see. He stopped, and stood still until he felt his socks grow wet. "Hell," he said. "We'll have to give it up."

He made a complete turn and walked back, but the spot where the team should have been was vacant. They made no answer when he called. He thrust out his left hand and shuffled after it until a slight tinkle of bells drew him over to the right. Presently his fingers touched the end-gate and he felt his way along the van. At the front wheel, he forced himself to crawl up slowly. "Don't *you* get scared," he told himself. "They'll smell it on you."

He sat silent a while. "All in God's world we can do," he said finally, "is make a dash for it." He cut the air with the whip, but the mares did not budge and he let them wait. If they went on willingly, and at a walk, all the better. Still, they weighed two tons apiece. The van, loaded, would double that, and meanwhile here the whole rig sat. If they did not get on, and keep off of one spot, a line of cleavage might flick around them. They would stand on a wobbling cake of ice. The team would go wild when it felt the "give."

While he held the whip poised again, a muffled shot rang out and a long ripping sound followed it. Somewhere close, the ice was pulling away from a log that was frozen in it, and though he saw that the mares had started off, his arm brought down the whip about their ears.

Their lunge knocked him down. His head struck the seat-back and he lay limp, smiling sleepily. The van hummed and swayed and whipped back into line. He listened to the spinning hubs and to the mares' feet, and he thought, You got away one more time. After a while a second thought occurred. You are galloping a team on ice, and he got up. He braced himself and found the reins and worked his wrists downward, alternately, upon the leather until they ached. But the mares ran on.

A common runaway, he thought. He let the reins slip through his fingers and forced himself to sit down. "Let them tire themselves a bit," he said. "There is time to turn them before we hit the bank."

But when a rear wheel bounced and shook the load, and the rope that held the crates in the van behind him snapped, he sprang up and jerked back with all his might upon the reins.

One of the mares screamed, but they both galloped on. They had come out of the high fog into a ground mist near a bank. In a wide curve, they were making for a row of lights that floated above a wall on the shore to the right. He gazed at the lights, open-mouthed. "There are too many of them," he said. He stood swaying as he counted them and added weakly, "They're on the wrong bank."

The mares' legs were moving like shuttles in the thinning mist, and he knew by their level pull on the bits that they would not stop. Meanwhile the shore line grew higher and darker. He watched the black rocks that jutted from it and thought, This is it.

He grasped the buckboard and sank on his knees to leap — then looked around. At the sight of the two white necks, fending the mist that rose from the ground fog, he drew back and sat down slowly. "I'm going to give you one more chance," he said.

It was Vi', on the outside of the curve, that he would have to turn. He sorted out her left rein, and lifted it and drew in a breath, then glanced out ahead of the team and yelled.

Fifty feet away, a log thrust its muzzle at the mares, pointing the blunt end up, like a mortar, out of the ice. They never saw it. It passed between them and missed the tongue, but splintered along the belly of the van and lifted it, knocking the load from side to side, and as if it had fired off a charge, it split the rear axle.

He was down on the ice, spinning forward on his chest. Maud was gone, but Vi' was sliding on her back, ahead. A wheel tottered and fell against her and he heard her cry out, then turned his eyes to the van. It was skidding, without its rear wheels, toward a ridge of ice that rose up before it. The ridge rolled onward a moment, rolled higher and stood like a fold of skin, and shot up in chunks when the tongue pierced it.

He fell into the pool where the van had sunk, and turned over. His head emerged, but when he tried to make for the solid ice, his arms would not move. He went under and slowly rode downward, sucking in his lips. For a long while the dark and the stillness, even the cold, made him drowsy, until finally his feet landed on the hood of the van, and his mind cleared. He felt his knees flex; his torso descended as if it were about to sit down. Then his hair, which had been erect, lay back. He was rising, in an updraft of bubbles from the van.

The bubbles seemed to draw him up, and to help them he forced himself to raise an arm. It, too, appeared to lift him faster, and he held it high until his hand struck an object above him and darted back, with a force that roused him.

The thing was cold and tough, and whatever it belonged to was making the water whirr about his head. He jack-knifed to dive, but as he thought, That was old Vi's bag! a rush of air from his mouth pulled him back.

She had lowered her feet around him. She was humping her back and wrenching herself from side to side; and the thing to do, he thought, was to feel along her to one end, and if he could miss her hooves, get out.

His hands on her stomach made her crazy. She twisted wildly and went limp and dropped her weight upon him. It bent his head down. The air in his gullet fought for room. He hiccoughed and let a stream of bubbles escape his lips. But he opened his eyes and blinked them as he thought, I am under a horse!

He said it again, and the thought so numbed his mind that the mare's shoe, when it hit his temple, did not hurt. It made his jaws spread slowly open, like a snake's. The cold water filled his throat and he was only conscious of a loud humming.

The humming went on as he slept, and dreamed that he lay under a blanket. The board beneath him felt like a table top, and now and then it seemed that the humming was trying to tell him something. He moaned and stirred, and after a while he asked, "Did somebody speak?"

"Do you hear me now, young man?" a voice answered.

He opened his eyes. Lanterns, in a wide, low room, were standing

about on packing boxes, lighting up a wall that was made of bread-
loaf stones and wet with seepage water. "It smells like tadpoles in
here," he said, and a second voice, as kind as an old Negro's, whispered at his hear. "Don't you study about no frogs. You just listen."
He tried to remember the Negroes on the place, but gave it up.
"Ask Pa to get the arnica," he told the man. "I think I'm hurt."
"That boy's ravin', Doc," a third voice said. "He thinks he's
home." The voice was wheedling. It would belong to a white man,
he thought, but to a thin one, with a weasel face. He lay still, and
rolled his eyes toward a stout man in black, who had moved into
view.

The lamp light caught the man's blond beard, and his blue eyes
and yellow lashes, as he leaned down to speak. "Young man," he
said, "you mistook our lights for those across the river. You were
headed downstream, not across. These men are convicts. With my
permission, they went out." He hesitated, and made as if to brush
something back from John's brow, and John asked, "Did they get
my team?"

"One of 'em's in. She's the off mare, by what's left of the harness."
It was the man with the fawning voice who had answered, and John
felt his eyes grow wet. "I scared her to death," he said. "Poor Vi'."

His chest shook as he heard the man in black go on, "You are in
the cellar of the State penitentiary, my boy. We must do what we
can for you here. You cannot be moved."

The voice trailed off. The doctor had turned around, and was
lifting an instrument from a satchel by one of the lanterns. It flashed
as he wiped it with a rag, and John sat up. He had time to see the
two men in striped clothes — the big Negro with gray hair, and
the little white man with the long nose and small eyes, who smiled
and drew back against the Negro. Before they could pull him back,
he put up a hand and felt a section of skin that hung down above
his eye.

"Jesus Christ!" he said. "Is it the bone, too, mister?"

"Takin' the Lord's name!" the Negro whispered. His breath was
hot on John's ear as he said, "Watch out!" Then he stood aside, with
his head bowed, while the doctor strode up to the table.

"Jace!" the doctor said, "did you let him up?"

"He was cussin', Doc," the other convict said. "He ain't got time."

John widened his eyes at him. "Some pickpockets," he tried to get out, "have got a lot to say." But his lips grew stiff. A film, that seemed to rise from a gust in his lungs, spread between him and the man, and he could not see.

The doctor shook the Negro by the arm. "Jace, you fool," he began, but he halted and for a long moment looked at the form beneath the blanket. Then he wheeled about and threw his scalpel into the bag and wiped his hands upon the cloth. "All right, Jace," he said. "It's your turn now."

The Negro dropped to his knees. He wagged his white head from side to side, nosing his face into his palms and talking hoarsely to himself.

The ferret-faced man glanced around, from lantern to lantern, about the room, and back at the ridge of toes under the blanket. Hearing the clasp of the satchel snap, he put a finger into his mouth and whimpered, and as if it hurt him, he got down to his knees, too. He did not move his lips, but he clasped his hands before his chest and stared at the wall, rapt, as if a fair shape were moving through its sweaty stones, outward, into the pure night air.

(From Prairie Schooner)

THE FIREBIRD

BY LEGARDE S. DOUGHTY

IT HAPPENED on Armistice Day, though Blink did not know Armistice Day from any other, unless he happened to walk into the parade.

Blink was dragging his own feet but somebody else's shoes. He was a scrawny man of medium height, and his "white folks" who passed on their old shoes to him must have all been right big men. His coat and pants were the same way, too big. The coat reminded you of a flag draped on a tombstone. The pants flapped at the knees with monotonous rhythm that inclined you to hum a silly tune whenever you saw Blink shuffling down the street.

Blink was just passing old man Thompson's seed store where the Salvation Army placard had been leaning, warped, splotched, and yellow, in the window for thirty-five years. Thirty-five years! *A Man May Be Down But He's Never Out.* That was what the placard said. But Blink did not know what it said. The benevolent phrase fitted him too, a lot better than his clothes did. But he did not know that either.

Mr. Jackson saw Blink coming, and Mr. Wall, talking to Mr. Jackson in front of the real estate office, turned his head just as Blink came to a stop a respectful distance away. Mr. Jackson knew that Blink wanted to have a word with him; he could tell that by the way Blink acted — just stopping and waiting for some signal to come up. Mr. Jackson frowned a little because Mr. Wall, a chain-store man from Chicago, had just about got to the point of deciding to buy a piece of business property down the street. If he did buy,

Mr. Jackson would make a commission of $2600, and he did not want to be bothered with any interruption.

Mr. Jackson looked at the brown bag in the crook of Blink's arm. It was Blink's usual bag of anything under God's sun from a hand-out of hard bread to a cast-off coffeepot. Some unidentified object of glass flicked on Mr. Jackson's mind, Blink was holding the bag so gently. But the fragile unknown thing flicked off Mr. Jackson's mind immediately. He could not be bothered with Blink now.

"Want to see me, eh, Blink?" Mr. Jackson said. "Guess you'd better come back tomorrow. Maybe the end of the week would be better. Too busy now. Come back another time, Blink." It was just a rapid slur of words, with hardly a glance at Blink.

The dubious expectancy on Blink's face flattened out. "Yassuh," he said. He took a back step, turned around, and shuffled off.

Mr. Wall had been looking more at Blink's eyes than anything else — the one good eye that was bloodshot so it looked like one of those five-cent marbles, and the blind eye that looked like the end of a boiled egg.

"Good Lord!" Mr. Wall said. "What sort of a creature is that?"

Mr. Jackson felt a little embarrassed. "Oh, that's Blink. He's an old-time darkey, about the only one left around here. Looks terrible, but he gets on all right. Used to do some handy-man jobs for us till we moved out to Bransford Heights. Lives in an alley back of our old house. Still works at odds and ends for folks in the old neighborhood." Mr. Jackson thought that was enough to say, but Mr. Wall was still watching Blink as he fanned his feet out along the sidewalk; so Mr. Jackson kept talking. "We're too far across town for Blink now. Don't see much of him. Good old faithful darkey, though. Comes by the office here now and then and I give him some sort of handout. A mighty fine darkey if he does look sorry."

Mr. Wall kept looking at Blink until he shuffled around the corner. There was an amused smile on his face. Mr. Jackson saw that Mr. Wall was still thinking about Blink because when he had gone around the corner Mr. Wall shook his head as if he could not quite make out how a man could look like that.

"Mighty good, faithful darkey," Mr. Jackson said again, sheepishly. He felt like a defense lawyer. Suddenly he was sorry he had not let Blink say what he had come to say; it would not have taken half a minute. "Used to take my —" He had started to tell how Blink used to take his son fishing when the boy was just getting up around twelve or thirteen. But he felt a tightening at his throat and cut the remark in a fake cough. Anyhow, Mr. Wall had turned around and was looking up to the next block in front of the building he was about to buy. He glanced at his watch and saw eleven o'clock.

"Lots of people pass there, just as you say."

"Hunh? — Oh! Right!" Mr. Jackson said. "And they'll be passing like that till five o'clock. Renovate the front and it'll be the best spot in town for a clothing store." But Mr. Jackson was thinking of his son, of Bob; was seeing Bob standing on the ragged lawn wet with early morning, waiting for Blink to come and take him to Briar Creek. They did not have much in those old days, but what, after all, did that matter? Mr. Jackson was seeing many years and many things in a sudden flare of memory. He was sorry he had turned old Blink away; it wouldn't have taken any time at all.

"Well, I guess I'm ready to sign," Mr. Wall said.

When Blink turned the corner he had made up his mind. It was only four blocks to his shack behind the old house. It was four miles to Bransford Heights. But maybe Mr. Jackson would be busy the next time too. Misser Tom's sho busy dese days, he was thinking. He reached into his coat pocket and pulled out a crumbly half of a jelly roll and smeared it into his mouth. His legs ached and his back too. But taint no tellin when I cn ketch Misser Tom, he was thinking. I cn ketch Miz Lucy right plumb now. Right *plumb* now, he thought again for emphasis.

When he came to the bus stop he put his fingers against the hard rim of the quarter in his pants pocket. Mr. Potter had given him the quarter that morning for taking ten scuttles of coal to the upper back porch.

Dat dair las scuttle neah bout pulled me right down dem steps wid it too, Blink thought, still pressing his fingers against the rim of the quarter.

But mostly he had his mind on the bus that would come along

soon. It would take him to the golf course, and that was just about half a mile from the Jacksons'.

Nawsuh, he told himself. Dat dair quarter'll buy me a piece of fatback and a nickel's wutha grits.

He did not fall in his temptation to spend a dime on the bus, not even when, by relation of ideas, his seven dollars in the fruit jar behind the sack of meal came to mind. That was eating money against hard days that might come any time.

When he crossed the next street he fixed his eye like a feeble beam along its colonnade of hackberry trees. The old house stood near the end of the second block down. It was the Potter's house now. He got a glimpse of the high steps that came right to the edge of the sidewalk. He looked toward the old house without realizing he was looking. He thought of the time Massa Bob caught his pants on a nail on top of the fence and hung there yelling till Blink came and took him down.

Heh-heh-heh. He uz hollerin like a houn dawg in a fox trap, Blink was thinking. But he cut off his chuckling suddenly, reproaching himself. He even looked around to be sure that nobody had heard him.

I sho ain't got nothin to laugh bout now, he resolved solemnly. But he kept on thinking for a while about Massa Bob hanging on the fence back of the house. So many years meant nothing to Blink. He had no way of thinking of it as fifteen years ago. He computed time in the manner of a sort of frayed-out patriarch: Hit sho uz a long time ago; *long* time ago, sho as de Lawd.

When Blink had got about halfway to Bransford Heights a tinker's truck turned into the street just ahead of him and was going his way. He recognized it by the way one side was skewed out. It was the truck Jim Bryant drove. He yelled Jim's name, but the truck was making too much noise, and Jim did not hear him.

He shuffled on, his legs hurting worse for the ride he had missed by an inch.

Um-um, de trials'n triberlashuns Gawd's chilluns has to beah, he thought with resignation. "Swing low, sweet chayut . . . " He began, half singing, half humming. It made him feel bad to sing it, though; so he stopped. He began thinking about the Bible, what he had learned long ago from Sam, who could read, and who used to preach sometimes in a regular church.

"De ways uv de Lawd is past all onnerstandin." He could hear Sam's lugubrious voice saying that; and he mumbled an awed response off his bluish lips: "Sho Lawd is."

Bransford Heights was a long new street on a long green slope. For blocks in the approach to it the houses were new and bright, and the closer you came to it the newer and better the houses were. The Jackson house was just beyond a slight curve in the street, up on a sort of knob by itself; and Blink could see the trim green terraces long before he came to the house.

Misser Tom sho been doin fine, sho been makin a heapa money, Blink was thinking. Yassuh, he sho been doin powful well. *Unhunh!*

It was twelve-thirty. Blink was getting hungry. It refreshed him to realize Miz Lucy would surely give him a good lunch and a piece of cake and some kind of fancy fruit out of a can. But he reproached himself again: Taint no time now to be studyin bout gittin favors fum muh white folks.

He came to the house number-plate with the name Jackson on it perched on a round of the lower terrace. It had gems of glass on it to catch automobile headlights. He felt a swell of pride for his white folks as he turned into the concrete driveway.

He knocked at the back door, and the cook came. The cook said she would go tell Mrs. Jackson, but before she left she gave Blink a high-flown look; and when she was safely gone Blink muttered: "Lissen heah, wid dat nose stickin up — I donh hafta take no sass off no yaller woman."

After a while Mrs. Jackson came. When she saw it was Blink her eyes went wide with surprise.

"Why, bless your soul, if it isn't old Blink," she said. "It's so good to see you, Blink."

"Yasm," Blink said. "I's proud to see you, Miz Lucy." But he thought she looked drawn and sad. Something besides surprise had gone over her face the minute she saw him. He had no way of thinking it out logically, but he somehow knew that she was remembering long ago. He felt suddenly as if all the strength had gone out of him, but he had a job to do, and he knew it would be harder if he just stood there saying nothing.

"Miz Lucy," he said, "it sho made me miserble to hyar Massa Bob got kilt in de war." He swallowed. "I been aimin to come ever since Miz Potter read me bout it out de paper. She showed me his picture in de paper too. And I uz mighty proud de way he look in dat soldier suit." Blink could see tears in Mrs. Jackson's eyes. He swallowed hard again and rubbed his mouth with the back of his hand. "I been aimin to come but I been had de rheumatism so bad I ain't been far fum muh dooh in neah bout a — neah bout since de las time I uz out dis way. And Misser Tom so busy I hates to go botherin him at de office."

Mrs. Jackson had turned her head, struggled to keep her mouth from twisting down. The streak of flame shot across the sky of her mind and vanished in smoke at the horizon. It was the only way she could think of Bob since . . . Korea . . . "killed in action while piloting an . . . " With effort she turned back to Blink.

"It has been a long time, Blink," she said. "You're a grand old friend to be thinking of us, Blink. — Why didn't you send word you were sick? We — "

Blink saw her lips tremble as if she wanted to say more but could not. He took the bag from under his arm into his claw of a hand.

"Massa Bob cyarved dis heah wid muh tools. Set right on muh dooh step and cyarved it out uv some crate strips'n odds'n ends. Took im neah bout two days. Den he jes went off'n forgot it. And it been settin on muh mantel shelf ever since."

Blink was fumbling with the bag as he spoke, but could not make up his mind to open it. He handed it to Mrs. Jackson.

She opened the bag and drew out its content, her wrist suddenly limp, like the neck of a dead goose. It was a beautifully modelled plane with wooden wings and a fuselage of cloth tight over wire ribs. She gazed at it wistfully. She could see the boy's hands scrupulously touching it to exquisite symmetry; could see him turning it critically to all angles, then, satisfied, smoothing on the scarlet paint; and then, the job accomplished, forgetting the thing that had kept his hands so busy.

"It's like dis, Miz Lucy," Blink was saying. "I figger Massa Bob ud want you'n Misser Tom to set it somewhar kinder like a . . . "

Blink stopped. He meant "memento" in the crude sureness of his mind but he knew no word to say for it. He said, "Turn it over, Missus."

She turned up the long shark-belly of the plane. Blink poked a thumb at the gilt lettering and peered at Mrs. Jackson. . . .

. . . No knowledge of written symbols — but understanding of his sacred rite more deep than knowing. He swallowed, hearing the words come wavering off Mrs. Jackson's lips. . . . *"Bob's Firebird."*

(From Mademoiselle)

APPLE SEED AND APPLE THORN

BY ELIZABETH ENRIGHT

*O*CTOBER SUNSHINE bathed the park with such a melting light that it had the dimmed, impressive look of a landscape by an old master. Leaves, one, two at a time, sidled down through the windless air. High up the treetops were perfectly still, but down below, on the walks and grass plots, all was a Saturday turmoil of barking dogs and ringing bells and shrieking children.

Barbara and Dickie, still new to the park, entered the playground tentatively. Everyone looked so well established, as if they needed no new friends. On the sunniest benches the mothers sat in a row surrounded by their possessions: baby carriages, toys, sand pails, market bags. They smoked, laughed, talked, yelled admonishment, paused to kiss the wounded. Here and there, since it was Saturday morning, a male parent wandered self-consciously beside a small child or sat and sunned his bald spot as he waited.

"What would you like to do, dear, swing?" suggested Barbara to her son. But Dickie did not hear. Used to country quiet, he stood amazed, pail in one hand, shovel in the other, staring at the scene before him. The place was a hive of activity. The sand pit seethed with infant life, the seesaws cawed and clanked, the swings flew.

The boys on tricycles made Barbara think of little centaurs, mechanized baby centaurs. There was something so lordly about their progress and their pauses. Magnificent in cowboy hats, heavily armed with gemmed weapons, they would suddenly convene in a group for as much as a minute at a time, boasting and vying, still in the saddle, and then at a signal or an impulse off they all wheeled together, their fat legs jigging above the pedals and their cap pistols snapping like popcorn. Yes, lordly; Dickie found them so. He stood beside her, quietly staring, too young to use pride as a mask or to know that it was ever used for this. He seemed very still and humble at her side.

"Maybe Dickie will get a bike too," Barbara suddenly said, although he had not asked for one.

"Maybe?" he said, and turned his face up to look at her, smiling his slow, perfect smile.

She put her hand under his chin. That's how it begins, she thought. Mothers begin it. What they've got you shall have too, they say; you're just as good as they are, honey, and I'll teach you to compete first thing.

Dickie gave one little jump, both feet together. "Maybe I get a bike?" he cried. "A really *bike*?"

"Probably not till Christmas time, my darling."

But Christmas was not a date to Dickie, it was a condition in which he would find the world one morning on awakening. There would be a pine tree smell and all things would have come true. Who knew when it would happen? It might be tomorrow.

"I'm going to have a bike too!" he shouted to a passing centaur, who responded with a stony glance and continued on his way.

"Watch out, sonny," warned a man of four, narrowly missing Dickie's toes as he rode by. Dickie shouted the news about the bike to his departing back.

"*Now* I swing," he said jubilantly, and thrust the pail and shovel into Barbara's hands.

At the swings she stood in front of him to push so that she could watch his face as it flew away and then came blooming toward her, alert and joyful. The reiterative motion, the occupation, brought to her mind an old count-out chant that she had not thought of in thirty years, and as she pushed her son she said it aloud, making it fit the rhythm of the swing.

> "*Intery, mintery, cutery, corn,*
> *Apple seed and apple thorn;*
> *Wire, briar, limber-lock,*
> *Three geese in a flock.*
> *One flew East and one flew West,*
> *And one flew over the cuckoo's nest.*"

The rhyme pleased Dickie, and Barbara sang it to him several times, making up a tune to match it. She felt contented, deeply satisfied, without a worry. The past and the future lay asleep like beasts in cages . . .

A voice beside them burst the spell, "You *dumb,* whaddaya wanna *do,* break open your head?" Barbara turned to see the child who had tried to stand up in the next swing being slapped into place by the raw, red hand of his mother. "My God, whadda I do? Turn my head, just, and here you are half outa the damn swing; you coulda broke your head open!" The scolding went on and on, loud and angry, and during it the rough hand continued to push the swing steadily, reached up to adjust a cap string, reached down to twitch a trouser cuff, busily caring for the baby as the voice railed. The baby sat impassive, staring at his mother, clad from top to toe in woolen garments although the day was mild. Under the ribbed edge of his cap his eyes, dark, Italian, were trimmed with lashes one inch long. His olive cheeks were smooth and fat, his lips red; he seemed well nourished on his diet of love and fury.

Roused from her trance, Barbara turned to look at the neighbors on her left: a woman and a little girl.

"Higher," the child was saying. "*Higher.* I said higher!" Her face was expressionless, without color, her hair hung limp into her collar. It was strange that anyone so young and pale could give such an impression of desperation.

Her mother was smiling determinedly and speaking through the smile.

"No, you don't need to go any higher. My arms are tired. It's time to go home anyway."

"I said higher," repeated the little girl tonelessly. "Damn you, I *told* you."

"So that's the way you're going to talk, is it?" said her mother with a sort of pleasure, as though some goal had been reached. "Very well then, swing yourself." She turned and started from the enclosure. Her child, watching her, gave a high, wild scream.

"Yes, scream," agreed her mother in a low, trembling voice, turning back for an instant. "Go on and scream." Then she walked away, out past the slides and past the railings, red in the face but still smiling, toward the other mothers on the benches.

"But I can't get down by myself!" shrieked the little girl. To and fro in lessening arcs she swung and screamed. Tears flashed dazzling from her cheeks.

"I'll help you down," Barbara offered.

"No, no. I want my mommy to."

"I guess she wants her mamma to," the mother of the wool-clad baby translated helpfully.

The little girl's swing came to a stop. She sat in it, a captive, her feet in black strapped slippers dangling, her face expressionless again, with tear tracks drying on her cheeks. She sat there for a long time.

"Would you like a push?" Barbara offered at last.

"No," said the child remotely.

The mother returned.

"Now are you ready to go home?"

"No. You push me. Push me high."

"Oh, Estelle! Please let's go *home*."

"You push me."

"Just once more then, understand? This time I mean it."

It was plain to see who was the victor, if such an outcome could be called a victory. The mother, her face sad and raddled with resentment, regarded her daughter without joy, and the child stared back, expressionless: a pair of enemies faced one another.

Barbara stopped Dickie in mid-air to press a kiss on his warm cheek. Life is so dangerous, she thought, people are so dangerous for each other, and love's so spotty.

Everywhere were signs of rage. In the swarming sand pit they were constantly on view: often as not a shovel was brought down upon a head; often as not a dimpled hand reached out to slap, and sand, a loose and handy weapon, was forever flying forth to sting the foe.

Now, as though her thoughts had been a prelude, she became aware of a commotion near the slides and turned to see two adults, two fathers, engaging in an argument. Their voices were suddenly rising, transcending the prosaic bounds of ordinary conversation.

One man she recognized, a European, small and dark and decent; the other she had never seen before, tall and heavy-set, with his wife beside him and two scared children clinging to his coat.

"Not *my* child," the little man was saying. "I do not permit any-one to lay a finger on *my* child! I do the disciplining!"

"Do it, then! Your kid comes up the ladder behind my kid and pushes him, a big push —"

"It was an accident, I tell you, he did not mean it."

"Accident, hell, he done it on purpose! I seen him, my wife seen him, and no kid's going to get away with that with my kid."

"Nevertheless they are children only. You had no right to slap my son!"

"I'd do it again —"

"You would have me to contend with, or the police!"

The little man was crimson with anger, the big one chalky-pale for the same reason; they seemed to tremble toward each other, closer and closer.

"You don't know what the hell you're talkin' about."

"On the contrary, I know *exactly* . . . "

The Italian woman at Barbara's right left her lump of wool and, smiling broadly, walked over to the rail of the enclosure and rested her arms on it, openly drinking in the sight. The woman at the left stopped arguing to listen. As for Barbara, though she frowned in distress, was it distress she felt or was it really pleasure? And she was listening as eagerly as any.

Then suddenly it was over. The big man, muttering, was stalking from the playground, his family hurrying beside him. The little foreigner, no longer crimson, seated himself on a bench and opened a newspaper, which quivered in his hands. Outrage had fatigued him; but for the onlookers the air had been mysteriously cleared.

"I thought the little fella was gonna hit the big fella," the Italian woman said to Barbara, happy and hearty. "Gee, I thought sure he was gonna knock'm down. Come on, Joe, we gotta go home and eat." Loving, maternal, she unloaded her baby from the swing, while at the left the little girl made no further objection when her mother lifted the bar; also refreshed, it seemed, she slipped down and skipped from the enclosure.

Now, as people departed and noise diminished, a stuttering sound of machinery came from across the park.

"Look, Dickie," said Barbara, stopping the swing. "I see a steam roller way over there."

"A steam roller!" Dickie was down in an instant and on his way, his red overalls flashing, and his mother jog-trotted in his wake along the concrete pathways to the far side of the park.

The roller, a squat orange machine, backed and bunted fussily on its carpet of wet tar. In its saddle sat the driver, lordly as any tricycle rider and lordly in exactly the same way. An audience admired him.

Nearby on the grass a bench had been constructed with a board and two sawhorses. Some workmen sat there with their lunch pails, a yellow-leafed bush spread out beyond them like a fan. One was drinking wine from a bottle wrapped in newspaper, one was slicing an onion onto some bread; the one on the end, finished with his meal, sat idle, his hands clasped loosely between his knees. He had stuck a pink paper carnation in his cap. The shoes, clothes, caps of all of them were dim and work-colored; their faces seemed relaxed and blank. In their short hour of repose they might have been the laborers of any century; Breughel had painted many like them.

The one with the carnation turned his head and looked at Dickie standing near. He held out his big shovel of a hand. Dickie inspected it warily and backed away, his own hands clasped behind him.

The man laughed and glanced at Barbara. He had white teeth and two broad, disarming dimples. His eyes seemed more mobile than other people's eyes, they rolled in his face like beautiful dark marbles: his expression was simple and benevolent and gay. Presently he turned away and spoke to his companions.

Dickie waited a moment or two and began cautiously to advance, paused, and seeing that nobody was going to coax him, climbed up on the end of the board bench and perched beside the man. Sudden pleasure and triumph were in the laborer's face; his great hand pulled Dickie close and then traveled up to stroke the little boy's cheek with a finger tough as kindling wood. From where she stood Barbara could hear the deep, masculine tones of his voice, then Dickie's piping treble in reply. She liked what she saw: the Breughel men, the golden bush, the paper flower, the friendship formed without a bond. After a while it was with reluctance that she approached.

"Come, Dickie, it's time for lunch."

"No," he frowned at her. "I like it here."

"But I'm afraid we must go."

"No. I don't want to."

The shovel hand pressed Dickie's shoulder and released it.

"Yes, yes," said the man. "You gotta do like Mamma says. Gotta go home, gotta eat, get strong to fighta da big guys, see? Gotta *fight*, see?" And he bowed out his elbows and made his mighty hands into two fists, with a smile as warm as sunshine.

Dickie accepted his advice and slipped down, walking backward to his mother, still watching his new friend with admiration. Halfway across the park he continued to turn and wave farewell.

But the sun was suddenly gone. Gray clouds had taken up the sky and a few large, separated drops of rain drove the last of the loiterers out of the playgrounds. All at once the park seemed darkened and desolate; the falling leaves as sad as rags.

Impervious to the weather, a fat old man in a billowing overcoat approached. He looked like a broken-down sofa with sagging springs and ripped upholstery covered all over with the keepsakes of past meals. In one hand he carried a paper bag; with the other he sowed the earth with scraps of bread, and down from the air above him came the pigeons. They covered the pavement around him in a piebald, mussy crowd. Here were the symbols of peace, waddling and gobbling in the dirt.

Where was that for which they stood, Barbara wondered? Where could she ever find it? Not in herself, alas, not in anyone she knew or had ever known. Perhaps it did not exist except in the imagination.

Yet even if only in the imagination . . .

"Go! Go! Fly!" cried Dickie, suddenly wild, galloping forward amongst the flock of pigeons and clapping his hands. The sound of their alarmed flight, heavy and cluttered, was like the flapping pages of telephone books. A few feathers fell, a few crumbs, and the old man in the overcoat glared down at Dickie.

"Now whatcha wanna go and do that for?"

"Come, Dickie," said Barbara, taking his hand in hers. "It's late and cold and raining. We must hurry home."

(*From Ellery Queen's Mystery Magazine*)

MY BROTHER DOWN THERE

BY STEVE FRAZEE

*N*OW THERE WERE three left. Here was the fourth, doubled up on his side at the edge of the meadow grass where the wind had scattered pine needles. His face was pinched and gray. Big black wood ants were backing away from the blood settling into the warm soil.

Jaynes turned the dead man over with his foot. "Which one is this?"

Holesworth, deputy warden of the State Penitentiary, gave Jaynes an odd look.

"Joseph Otto Weyerhauser," he said. "Life for murder."

Deputy Sheriff Bill Melvin was standing apart from the rest of the posse. He had been too deep in the timber to take part in the shooting. He watched the little green State patrol plane circling overhead. It was a windless day. The voice of the mountains spoke of peace and summer.

Joseph Otto Weyerhauser. Spoken that way, the words gave dignity to the fugitive who lay now on the earth in the pale green uniform that had been stolen from the wash lines of a little filling station a hundred miles away.

Sid Jaynes was a beefy man with dark eyes that glittered. Jaynes had not known who the convict was and he had not cared. The green pants and shirt, when Weyerhauser tried to run across the head of the little meadow, had been enough for him.

"He played it like a fool," Jaynes said. "He could have stayed in the timber."

"You made $12.50 with each one of those shots, Jaynes." The

deputy warden's voice ran slowly and deliberately.

"Let the State keep their twenty-five bucks," Jaynes said. "I didn't come along for that." His rifle was a beautiful instrument with a telescopic sight. The dead man lay beside a sawed-off shotgun and a .38 pistol taken from a guard he had slugged with a bar of soap in a sock. "Why didn't he stay in the timber, the damn fool?"

"They're all city boys," Warden Holesworth said. "He was heading for the highway."

It put you on the wrong side of your job to make a comparison between the dead man's short-range weapons and the rifles of the posse, Deputy Bill Melvin thought. Weyerhauser had been one of four prison escapees. He had taken his big chance with the others, and here the chance had ended.

That was all there was to it; but Melvin wished he did not have to look at Weyerhauser or hear any more from Jaynes, who was always the first man to reach the sheriff's office when the word went out that a manhunt was on. Jaynes, who ran a garage, never came when help was needed to find a lost hunter or a wrecked plane.

Sheriff Rudd spoke. Sheriff Rudd was a veteran of the open-range days of men and cattle. He stood like a rifle barrel, tall and spare. His face was bony, with a jutting nose.

"There's three more," the sheriff said. "All tougher than Weyerhauser." He squinted at the green plane, now circling lower in the trough of the mountains. "Call that flyer, Melvin. He's buzzing around this basin like a bee in a washtub. Tell him to get up in the air. Tell him about this and have him call the patrol station over the hill and see if anything has popped there."

Deputy Melvin started back to the horse with the radio gear. Jaynes called, "Ask him if he's spotted any of the other three."

Melvin paid no attention.

"One twenty, ground party, Stony Park."

"Ground party, go ahead."

"Get some altitude. You're making Sheriff Rudd nervous."

"What does Rudd think I am? There's a hell of a wind up here. What happened?"

"We got Weyerhauser. Dead. Call Scott and Studebaker on the road blocks."

"Stand by," the pilot said.

Melvin leaned against the mare. She moved a little, cropping grass, switching her tail at deer flies unconcernedly, while Melvin listened to the plane call across the mountains. Jaynes's sleeping bag was on the crosspieces of the pack saddle, put there to protect the radio from branches.

Jaynes walked over. "Has he spotted — ?"

"I didn't ask," said Melvin.

"Why not?"

"He would have said so if he had."

"Well, it won't hurt to ask. Maybe — "

"Go collect your twenty-five bucks, Jaynes."

"What do you mean by that?"

Jaynes did not understand. He never would.

"Ground party One twenty," the pilot said. "Negative on all road blocks and patrol cars."

"Thanks, One twenty. Call Studebaker again and have an ambulance meet us at the big spring, east side of Herald Pass, at one this afternoon."

"Okay." The plane began to climb. Melvin watched until it gained altitude and shot away across the timbered hump of Herald Pass.

"That's a hell of a note," Jaynes complained. "Guys like me come out here, taking time off from our business just to do what's right, and you don't even ask whether he's spotted the others or not."

Melvin pulled the canvas cover back over the radio. "Four times twenty-five makes a hundred, Jaynes. What are you going to buy with all that money?"

"I give it to the Red Cross, don't I!"

"You mean that first twenty-five you knocked down — that little forger? I remember him, Jaynes. He came out of a railroad culvert trying to get his hands up, scared to death, and you cut loose."

Jaynes was puzzled, not angry. He said, "You talk funny for a deputy sheriff, Melvin. You sound like you thought there was something nice about these stinking cons. What are we supposed to do with them?"

Melvin went back to the posse. Deputy Warden Holesworth had searched the dead man. On the ground was a pile. Candy bars, smeary and flattish from being carried in pockets; seven packs of cigarettes.

"One down and three to go," Jaynes said. "Where do we head now, Sheriff?"

Sheriff Rudd looked around the group. Two or three of the men sitting in the grass had already lost stomach. Rudd named them and said, "Take that sorrel that's started to limp and pack Weyerhauser up to the highway."

"At the big spring on the east side," Melvin said. "There'll be an ambulance there at 1 o'clock."

"I've got to get back myself," the deputy warden said. "Tomorrow I'll send a couple of guards out. We can fly in Blayden's hounds from up north —"

"I don't favor hounds," the sheriff said. "Keep your guards, too, Holesworth. The last time you sent guards we had to carry 'em out. You keep 'em sitting in those towers too much."

"That's what they get paid for, not for being Indian guides and cross-country men. To hell with you." They grinned at each other. Then Holesworth gave Jaynes another speculative glance and helped lift Weyerhauser onto the lame horse.

That left seven in the posse. They divided the cigarettes. Small ants went flying when someone gave the pile of candy bars a kick. One chocolate bar, undisturbed by the boot, was melting into the earth beside the other stain.

Two days later Sheriff Rudd cut the trail of three men whose heelprints showed *P* marks in the center. Rudd swung down and studied the tracks, and then he took the saddle off his gelding.

"What's the stall?" Jaynes asked. "That's the track of our meat, Rudd."

"A day and a half old, at least. Give your horse a rest." The sheriff sat down on a log and began to fill his pipe.

Melvin walked beside the footprints for several steps. He saw the wrapper of a candy bar lying on the ground. Four days on candy and desperation. The poor devils. Poor devils, hell; the candy had been stolen from the filling station where they had slugged a sixty-

year-old man, the desperation was their own, and they were asking
for the same as Weyerhauser.

Melvin looked up at the gray caps of the mountains. They ran
here in a semicircle, with only one trail over them, and that almost
unknown. If these tracks with the deep-cut marks in the heels continued up, the fugitives would be forced to the forgotten road that
led to Clover Basin. From there the trail went over the spine at
13,000 feet.

It was a terrible climb for men living on candy bars. Melvin
went back to the resting posse, saying nothing.

"Clover Basin, maybe?" Sheriff Rudd asked.

Melvin nodded.

"Why haven't the damn search planes seen them?" Jaynes asked.

"There's trees and rocks, and the sound of a plane engine carries
a long way ahead." Bud Pryor was a part-time deputy, here now
because he had been called to go. He was a barrel-chested man who
could stop a barroom fight by cracking heads together, but he didn't
care much for riding the mountains. And he didn't care at all for
Jaynes.

"Any other stupid questions, sharpshooter?" Bud Pryor asked
Jaynes.

The sheriff got up. "Let's go."

They rode into the first of the great fields of golden gaillardia at
the lower end of Clover Basin. The buildings of the Uncle Sam
Mine hung over the slope at the upper end like gray ghosts. Rudd
stopped his horse. The others crowded up behind him.

Motion started at the highest building and sent small points
out on the slide-rock trail. "Hey!" Jaynes cried. Both he and Melvin
put glasses on the tiny figures scrambling over the flat gray stones.
Two men in green uniforms. Two men who ran and fell and
crawled upward toward the harsh rise of Clover Mountain.

Jaynes let his binoculars fall on the cord around his neck. He
raised his rifle, sighting through the 'scope. Some sort of dedication
lay in his glittering eyes, some drive that made Melvin look away
from him and glance at the sheriff.

Rudd, however, without the aid of glasses, was watching the flee-
ing men on the eternal stones of Clover Mountain.

Jaynes kicked his horse ahead. "Come on!"

"Get off and lead that horse a while, Jaynes," the sheriff said. "You've knocked the guts out of him already the last few days."

"There they are!" Jaynes gestured with his rifle.

"And there they go," Rudd got down and began to lead his horse.

"Now what the hell!" Jaynes twisted his face. "They're getting away — farther out of range every second!"

"They're a mile airline. It'll take us the best part of two hours to reach the mine," Sheriff Rudd said with weary patience. "And then it will be dark. Go on, Jaynes, if you want to, but leave that horse behind."

"It's mine."

"You'll leave it behind, I said."

Jaynes looked through his 'scope and cursed.

"Three came in here," Bud Pryor said. "Go on up and kick that third one out, Jaynes. He's there."

"How do you know?" Jaynes's voice was not large.

Pryor's thick lips spread in a grin. He was still sweating from the last steep hill where they had led the horses. "Gets chilly mighty quick in these high places, don't it?"

Rudd started on, leading his horse. It was dusk when they closed in on the bunkhouse of the Uncle Sam Mine, working around from the rocks and coming closer in short rushes to the toe of the dump. Jaynes and Melvin went up the dump together until their heads were nearly level with the rusted rails that still held rotting chocks.

"I'll cover you from here," Jaynes said. "This 'scope gathers light so a man can't miss."

Melvin raised his head above the dump. An evening wind drove grouse feathers across the yellow waste toward him. He saw a rat scurry along the ledge of a broken window and then sit still, looking out. Inside, two or three others squealed as they raced across the floor.

Melvin scrabbled on up and walked into the bunkhouse. Two rats carrying grouse bones ducked through holes in the floor. One half of the roof was caved in but the other end, where the stove sat with its pipe reduced to lacy fragility, was still a shelter.

The stove was warm.

Here, for a time, three men had stayed. They were city-bred, and so this man-made shell seemed the natural place to take shelter.

No outdoorsman would have sought the rat-fouled place, but the escaped prisoners must have received some small comfort from it.

Instinctively they had huddled inside this pitiful ruin for the security that all pursued mankind must seek. And now, caught by the dusk and the silence, looking through a window at the mighty sweep of the high world, Bill Melvin was stirred by a feeling for the fugitives that sprang from depths far below the surface things called logic and understanding.

"What's in there?" Jaynes called.

Melvin stepped outside. "Nothing."

Jaynes cursed. He climbed to the dump level and stared at the dim slide-rock trail. He fondled his rifle.

Pryor's voice came from the lower buildings, high-pitched and clear, running out to the walls of the great basin and echoing back with ghostly mockery. "Nothing in any of these, Sheriff!"

"Let's get on the trail!" Jaynes yelled.

"Come down here," Sheriff Rudd said, and both their voices ran together on the darkening rocks around them.

Melvin and Jaynes rejoined the others. Melvin was dead-weary now, but Jaynes kept looking at the slide-rock, fretting.

"We can't get horses over that slide-rock at night," Rudd said. "And maybe not in daylight. We'll camp here tonight."

"And all that time they'll be moving," Jaynes objected. "Are you sure you want to catch them, Sheriff?"

"They'll be feeling their way down the worst switchbacks in these hills," Rudd said. "On empty stomachs."

"Like hell!" Jaynes said. "They've been living like kings on grouse."

"One grouse," Melvin said.

"They must be getting fat." Rudd pointed to the floor of the basin. "We'll camp down there and give the horses a chance to graze."

"And make this climb again in the morning," Jaynes said disgustedly.

Dew was gathering on the grass when they picketed the horses. All the chill of the high-country night seemed to have gathered in the enormous black hole. They ate almost the last of their food at a fire built from scrubby trees.

Jaynes cleaned his rifle before he ate. He rubbed the stock and admired the weapon, standing with the firelight glittering in his eyes.

"What will that pretty thing do that a good Krag won't?" Bud Pryor asked.

Jaynes smiled and let the answer gleam in the reflection of the flames.

"Somebody will have to start out tomorrow for grub," the sheriff said. "How about it, Jaynes?"

"I can live on the country," Jaynes said.

"Yeah." The sheriff unrolled his sleeping bag. "One hour each on guard tonight. Not at the fire, either. Stay out by the horses. I'll take it from three till dawn."

Jaynes peered into the darkness. "You think the third one is around in the rocks, huh?"

"I think the horses can get all tangled up. The third man went over the hill a long time ago," Rudd said.

"How do you know that?" Jaynes asked.

"Because I'm betting it was Marty Kaygo. He's the toughest and the smartest. He wouldn't sit in that eagle's nest up there, hoping somebody comes after him."

"Kaygo, huh? What was he in for?" Jaynes stared toward the gloomy crest of the mountain.

"He killed two cops." Rudd took off his boots, pulled his hat down tightly, and got into his sleeping bag. "He killed them with one shot each." The sheriff was asleep a few moments later.

Jaynes set his rifle on his sleeping bag and began to eat. "Who are the other two?"

"Don't you even know their names?" Melvin asked.

"What's the difference if I don't?"

Maybe Jaynes was right. It had to be done, one way or another; names merely made it harder. "Sam Castagna and Oro L. Strothers," Melvin said. "Castagna used to blow up rival gamblers for a syndicate. Strothers specialized in holding up banks."

"Ora L. That's nice and gentle, a con having a name like that," Jaynes said.

"Don't you give him the right to have a name?" Melvin asked.

"Don't you give him the right to be a human being?"

Jaynes looked blank at the anger in Melvin's voice. "What is it with you, anyway? You and Rudd both talk like it was a crime to send those bastards rolling in the grass."

Rolling in the grass. That was exactly what had happened to Weyerhauser when Jaynes's second shot ripped through his belly.

Melvin walked away from the fire suddenly, into the cold dark layers of the night. The possemen were sacking out. Jaynes squatted near the fire alone, eating, a puzzled expression on his face. Bud Pryor, stripped down to long underwear and his boots, came over and stood beside the flames for a few minutes, warming his hands.

Dislike of Jaynes and a sort of wonder mingled on Pryor's fleshy face. He parted his thick lips as if to speak. But then he left the fire and settled into his sleeping bag, grunting.

The night was large and silent. Up toward the knife edge of Clover Mountain two men had scrambled across the rocks, crawling where slides had filled the trail. Two men running for their lives.

Melvin kept seeing it over and over.

Castagna's sentence had been commuted to life just two days short of the gas chamber. Strothers had never killed a man, but he was cold and ruthless. Marty Kaygo, who must have gone across the hill before the others, was in debt to the law 180 years. This was his third escape from prison.

They were all no good, predators against society. But . . . In the solemn night, with the tremendous peace of the mountains upon him, Bill Melvin stared uneasily at the line which must run from crime to punishment.

Ordinarily, he did not allow himself to be disturbed like this; but Jaynes, scraping the last of his supper from a tin plate, had kicked over the little wall that divided what men must do from what they think.

"I'll take the first watch," Melvin said.

Jaynes came out from the fire. He spoke in a low voice. "It's only nine o'clock. Barker's got a flashlight. We could slip up on the slide-rock trail — there's patches of snow there — and see for sure if they all three crossed."

"Why?"

"If one is still here, he'll try to slip out of the basin tonight. We could lay out in that narrow place and nail him dead to rights."

"I'll take the first watch." Melvin walked deeper into the night, trembling from high-altitude fatigue, mouthing the sickening after-taste of Jayne's presence.

"Why not, Melvin?"

"Go to bed!"

Sometimes a healthy man does not sleep well at great altitudes, and so it was with Melvin this night. When Jaynes relieved him, Melvin heard the beefy hunter going down the basin past the horses. He knew that Jaynes would make for a place where he could command the narrow entrance to the basin, and that he would lie there, patiently, his rifle ready.

Melvin wondered if his eyes would glitter in the dark.

Jaynes stayed his watch, and the watch of the man he did not waken for relief.

Dawn slid across the peaks. Light was there when dew and gloom were still heavy in the basin. The sheriff and Pryor cooked the last of the bacon and opened the last two cans of beans.

Jaynes saddled up and led his horse toward the fire before he ate. "What kind of rifle was it this — what was his name, Kaygo? — stole at the filling station?"

"A 30–06," Rudd said. There were pouches under his eyes this morning, and he looked his years. He stared through the smoke at Jaynes. "New one. He took five boxes of shells, too, Jaynes. They're hunting cartridges."

"I've got a few expanding noses myself," Jaynes said. "Let's get started."

Rudd spat to one side. "You're like a hog going to war."

Bud Pryor laughed. The other manhunters stared at Jaynes or at the ground. They seemed ashamed now, Melvin thought, to be a part of this thing. Or a part of Jaynes.

Pryor said explosively, "I'll go in after chow today, Sheriff. Me and Jaynes."

"No!" Jaynes said. "I can live on the country. Me and Melvin can keep going when the rest of you have to run for a restaurant."

Rudd said to Pryor, "You and Barker, then. It's closer now to

Scott than it is to Studebaker, so we'll split up after we cross the hill. Try the radio again, Melvin. Maybe nobody will have to go in."

"No contact," Melvin said later. "When we get to the top, we can reach out and make it."

They took the slide-rock trail from the dump at the side of the bunkhouse. In passing, Melvin noticed that the grouse feathers were almost entirely blown away.

Seventy years before, jack trains had used the trail; but now the years had slid into it. The posse led their horses. Sparks from steel shoes in the stretches where the ledge still showed drill marks; a clattering and a scramble, with the horses rolling their eyes when they had to cross the spills of dry-slippery rocks.

In the snowbanks, the tracks of three men; and one man had gone about a day before the others.

There lay the ridge, half a mile ahead. On the left, where they traveled, the mountain ran down wildly to ledges where no human being would ever set foot.

They lost the little radio mare. She slipped and fell and then she was threshing over and the slide-rock ran with her. She struck a ledge and was gone. The rocks kept spilling down a thousand feet below.

Rudd patted the neck of his frightened gelding. "There went a damn good little mare."

Jaynes said, "They don't exactly give those radios away, either. My sleeping bag cost sixty-two bucks."

They came out on the wedge-top and went down three switchbacks to let the horses take a blow out of the wind. A dozen lakes were winking in the sunlight. The mountains on this side ran in a crazy pattern. Every major range in the United States runs north and south, with one exception; but from the pinpoints where a man must stand, the north-south coursing is often lost or does not exist at all.

There was no highway in sight, no smoke, just the vast expanse of timber with the gray-sharp slopes above and the shine of beaver meadows where little streams lay separated from each other by ridges eight thousand feet high.

"A regiment could hide out down there all summer," Rudd said.

"But these guys will most likely keep running downhill, hoping to hit a highway sooner or later."

Jaynes's rifle was in his hands, as usual when he was on foot. He pointed with it. "I know every inch of that country. I've fished and hunted all through it."

"Don't be a fool," Sheriff Rudd said. "I rode that country before you were born, and I discovered a new place every time I went out. And I could do the same for one hundred years." Rudd shook his head. "Every inch of it . . . !"

Jaynes said, "I can find any tenderfoot that tries to hide out down there." He patted the stock of his rifle.

"Goddamn you, Jaynes! I'm sick of you!" Melvin cried. "Keep your mouth shut!"

Jaynes was surprised. "Now what did I say? Have you got a biting ulcer or something, Melvin?"

"Let's go on down," Rudd said.

Melvin's stomach held a knot that eased off slowly. For a moment he had seen the land without a man in it, forgetting even himself as he stood there on the mountain. But Jaynes would never let a man forget himself for long.

In the middle of the morning the green plane came over and circled them. The pilot was calling, Melvin knew, but they had no way now to listen or call back. After a while the plane soared away over the green timber and drifted on toward Scott.

They struck the timber. Fallen trees lay across the trail, slowing the horses. There were still three men ahead.

"Planes, radios, horses — what the hell good are they?" Jaynes said irritably. "In the end it comes down to men on foot closing in on each other."

"Like you closed in on the Uncle Sam bunkhouse, huh?" Pryor asked. "Hand to hand, tooth and toenail."

"Strip down to a breechclout, Jaynes," Rudd said. "I'll give you my knife and you can go after Kaygo properly."

Barker said, "Yeah, why don't you do that, Jaynes? You big-mouthed bastard, you."

Barker had little imagination. He was a sullen man who would kill the fugitives as quickly as Jaynes. All that motivated Barker now, Melvin thought, was a desire to transfer the cause of his hunger and weariness to another human being. Jaynes had already been marked by him as a target.

"I don't understand you guys, so help me," Jaynes said.

Melvin felt a flash of pity for him; the man really did not understand. What made Jaynes tick probably was as obscure as the forces that had sent the men he so greatly wanted to kill into a life of crime. Somebody ought to be able to figure it out . . .

The big buck flashed across the narrow lane in a split second. The smaller one that followed an instant later was going just as fast. Jaynes brokes its neck with one shot.

The thought of fresh liver relieved some of Melvin's dislike of Jaynes. "Nice shooting, Jaynes."

"Thanks."

"I'll eat that thing without skinning it," Bud Pryor said. He had his knife out already and was trotting ahead.

Jaynes sat on a log and cleaned his rifle while Pryor and Melvin dressed the buck. Jaynes had merely glanced at it and turned away.

"He's larded up like first-class grass-fed beef," Pryor said. "Lucky shot, Jaynes."

"I seldom miss a running target." Jaynes spoke absently, looking ahead at the trees.

Pryor sent Melvin a helpless look. "It sure looked lucky to me."

"No luck at all," said Jaynes. "It's simple if you have the eye for it."

Pryor made a motion with his knife as if to cut his own throat. He and Melvin laughed. For a few moments Jaynes was no problem to them.

"Sling it on a horse," Sheriff Rudd said. "We can eat when we get to Struthers' sawmill set."

"Struthers? That's one of the men we want," Jaynes said.

"Different spelling," Rudd said. "Jumbo Struthers has been dead for forty years, and the sawmill hasn't run for fifty-two years."

"We could dig him up," Pryor said, grinning, "so Jaynes could shoot him."

For the first time Jaynes showed anger. "Why do you keep digging at me? What are we out here for, anyway? You act like there was something wrong in what we're doing!"

"We're here to bring back three men, dead *or* alive," Rudd said. "Let's go."

The trail expanded into a logging road, with live trees trying to close it out and dead trees trying to block it. Mosquitoes came singing in from a marsh on the left. Already tormented by the snags on fallen timber, the horses shook their heads as the insects buzzed their ears. Pryor kept swinging his hat at bowflies settling on the carcass of the deer. "The good old summertime," he said. "How'd you get me out here, Sheriff?"

"You were getting fat, so you volunteered."

The small talk irritated Jaynes. "We're not making much time," he said. Later, after a delay to lever aside a tangle of dead jackpines, he went ahead in a stooping posture for several steps. "One of the boys ain't doing so good all at once."

Melvin studied the tracks. One man had started to drag his leg; a second one was helping him. The third track was still older than these two. Farther down the road a punch mark appeared in the soil. One man was using a short pole as a cane.

Jaynes wanted to race away on the trail. "We'll have that one before long!"

"Hold up." The sheriff stopped to fill his pipe. "I'd say the fellow twisted a muscle or sprained his ankle trying to jump that tangle we just cleared out. The other one will leave him, that's sure."

"The old ranger lean-to in Boston Park must be pretty close," Jaynes said. "Half a mile, I'd say."

"About a mile," Rudd said.

Melvin knew about it, the big lean-to sometimes used by fishermen and hunters. Man had made it, and the fact would seem important to the men ahead. Considering the tracks of the injured fugitive, Melvin wondered whether the convict would last to Boston Park.

"If he's bunged up as bad as it looks, he's likely ready to quit," Rudd said.

"He won't give up," Jaynes said. "He'll make a stand."

The sheriff narrowed his eyes at Jaynes. "Why will he, if he's hurt?"

"If he's been left at that lean-to, he's the loneliest man in the world right now," Melvin put in.

"Yeah?" Jaynes kept edging ahead. "I'm not walking up on that hut to find out how lonely he is."

"Nobody is," Rudd said. "When we get close, two men will take the horses. The rest of us will cut off into the timber and come in from all sides of the lean-to. He may not be there at all."

The lean-to was set between two trees on high ground, clear of the swamp that edged the beaver ponds. Generations of outdoorsmen had piled boughs along the sides and on top until the shelter was a rust-brown mass. That it had not been burned by a careless match long ago spoke tersely of the nature of the men who came far into the mountains.

Melvin and Sheriff Rudd came to the edge of the trees a hundred yards apart. They waited for Pryor, on the right. Barker and Jaynes were to ease out of the trees on the left, Barker to cover the back of the shelter, Jaynes to prevent escape farther to the left.

There had been a fire recently among the blackened stones before the lean-to. Fine ashes stirred there, lifting to a little wind that rolled across the beaver ponds and whispered through the tall swamp grass.

Melvin saw Pryor come to the edge of the trees and signal with his hand. Barker slipped to the cover of a windfall behind the shelter. He wagged his rifle.

Inside the lean-to a man cleared his throat.

Melvin sank to one knee behind a log.

The sheriff said, "Come out of there! You're boxed. Walk out with your hands up!"

"I can't walk," a voice replied.

"Come out of there. We'll rip that place apart with bullets if I have to ask again."

The brittle needles scraped against each other. A chunky man whose face was black with beard came on hands and knees from the hut. He was wearing a soiled, torn green uniform, too small for him. One pants leg was gone below the knee.

"Toss your pistol away," Rudd ordered.

"No gun." The man clawed against one of the trees. He pulled himself erect. "No gun, you stinking, dirty —" He started to fall and made a quick grab at the crosspiece of the shelter.

A rifle blasted from the edge of the timber beyond Barker. The man at the lean-to fell. He was dead, Melvin was sure. "Watch him! Watch him!" Jaynes called. "It's just his arm!"

Melvin and the sheriff walked in then. The man had been shot through the left hand, a thick hand, by a soft-nosed hunting bullet. The palm was torn away and the fingers were spread like the spokes of a shattered wheel. The man rolled on his side and put his broken hand under his arm.

"My leg is cracked before." He cursed. "Now look at it!" The leg was really broken now; it had twisted under when the man fell. Melvin searched him and found two packs of cigarettes.

Barker came around the hut. Jaynes arrived on the run. "I could just see his arm when he grabbed for his gun!"

"He grabbed, all right," Sheriff Rudd said. "To keep from falling on a busted leg."

"Oh!" Jaynes stared down. "It looked to me like — "

"Shut up." Rudd yelled at the timber where the two men were holding the horses. "Bring 'em on!" There was a first-aid kit on Melvin's horse.

"Which one is this?" Jaynes asked.

"Sam Castagna." Suspected of seven murders, convicted of one, sentence commuted to life. "Where's Strothers, Sam?"

"Run out on me." With his face against the brown needles Castagna tried to spit explosively. It merely dribbled from his mouth and hung in his black beard. He cursed in Italian, glaring up at Jaynes.

Barker said, "No gun anywhere around the hut. They had two sawed-offs and two .38 pistols, besides the rifle Kaygo swiped at the filling station."

The horses came in at the trot. Pryor circled the swamp and plodded through the grass. He looked at the wounded man. "Castagna, huh? Nice boy who likes to put bombs on car-starters. The other two are still going down the trail, Sheriff."

"Straight to a highway," Rudd said. "Let's patch him up and move on."

"I'm going to eat here," Pryor said, "if you have to leave me. I'm going to beat the blowflies to some of that deer." He began to build a fire.

Melvin and Barker made splints for Castagna's broken leg. They wrapped his hand. He watched them stolidly. When they pulled his leg, he ground his teeth and sweated. Melvin got him a drink of water afterward.

"Thanks." Castagna held the cup in a trembling hand, slopping part of the water down his chin and into the thick black hairs at the base of his neck.

"Where's Strothers and Kaygo, Castagna?" Jaynes asked.

Castagna looked hungrily at the meat Pryor was roasting on a green limb. He lay back on the ground and closed his eyes. There was a depression under his head and it caused his face to tilt straight into the sun. Melvin took off his coat and rolled it under the wounded man's head.

They squatted around the fire, roasting cutlets chopped from the loin with a hand ax, too hungry to bother with a frying pan. Blood from half-raw meat ran down their chins when they chewed.

None of us is far removed from the wolf, Melvin thought; but there is a difference between men like Rudd and Sam Castagna. There has to be. Yet where was the difference between Castagna and Jaynes, who cleaned his rifle before he ate?

Melvin glanced at the gleaming weapon, laid carefully aside on the dry grass. He felt an urge to hurl the rifle far out into the beaver pond.

Sheriff Rudd ground his meat moodily. "I never used to stop when I was on the chase. We stop to gorge ourselves while a desperate man keeps going. The difference is he *has* to get away and we don't *have* to catch him."

"Him? Who do you mean?" Jaynes asked. "Why don't we have to catch him?"

"Oh, hell," Rudd said. "Gimme the salt, Barker."

"I don't understand what — " Jaynes said.

"Before we leave here, Jaynes, you throw into that pond every damn hunting bullet you got," Rudd said. "I'm going to watch you do it."

They all looked at Jaynes. He could not grasp the reason for their hostility. "Shells cost money. I'll use that old coffee can over there and bury them under the lean-to. Next fall I'll be through here hunting."

"Do that then," Rudd said. "Every damn soft-nose you got." But Rudd seemed to find no satisfaction in the trifling victory.

He knew he was only scratching at the surface, Melvin thought.

The sheriff twisted around toward Castagna. "Some deer meat, Sam?"

"Yeah. Yeah, let me try it." Castagna ate greedily, and then he lost everything before they could get him onto a horse.

The green plane was cruising southwest of them. A few minutes later it came over Boston Park, dipping low. It went southwest again, circling six or seven times.

"Uh-huh," Rudd said.

"He must be over the Shewalter Meadows," Jaynes said. "That's all down-timber between here and there."

"Not if you know the way from the sawmill set." Rudd swung up. "Catch Castagna there if he starts to fall."

There were still two sets of man-tracks down the logging road. Just before they reached the sawmill site they found a sawed-off shotgun laid across a log, pointing toward one of the sawdust piles near the creek. Under it an arrow mark scratched in the black soil pointed in the same direction.

"Now that's a cute trick," Jaynes said. He sighted through his 'scope at the sawdust piles, age-brown mounds blending into the wilderness. He was suspicious, but he was confused.

"It reads to me that Strothers wants to quit, and want to be sure we know it," Rudd said.

"Suppose he's still got the pistol? Suppose it's Kaygo?" Jaynes asked.

"Most likely Kaygo is over there where the plane was circling," Melvin said. Kaygo had left the others at the Uncle Sam Mine. The sheriff, at least, was sure of that, and Melvin had accepted it. Still, he did not like the quiet of the sawdust piles, warm and innocent-looking out there by the creek.

Rudd said, "Come on, Melvin. The rest of you stay here. Take Castagna off the horse and let him lay down a while."

"I'd better —" Jaynes said.

"Stay right here," the sheriff said.

Rudd and Melvin leaped the creek and tramped upon the spongy surface of the sawdust piles. In a little hollow of the shredded wood they found their man, asleep.

His blond whiskers were short and curly. The sun had burned his face. His green shirt, washed recently in the stream, was spread near him and now it was dry. His heavy prison shoes were set neatly together near his feet.

"Strothers, all right," Rudd said. "Wake up!"

The man was snoring gently. He jerked a little but he did not rouse until Rudd tossed one of the shoes on his stomach. Strothers opened his eyes and yawned.

"What kept you so long?" he asked.

Cold and deadly, the bulletins had read; he had never killed a man, but he had always entered banks prepared to kill. He had studied law, and later, engineering. It was said that he could have been successful in either. Now he sat on a pile of sawdust in the wilderness, ready to go back to the isolation cells.

"Local yokels, eh? I didn't think those lazy bastards of guards would come this far. Got anything to smoke, Constable?"

"Where's Kaygo?" the sheriff asked.

Strothers yawned again. He felt his feet. "Talk about blisters!" He began to put on his shoes. "Why, Marty left us at a rat hole on the side of a cliff day before yesterday."

"We know that," Rudd said.

"That's why I mentioned it." Strothers reached toward his shirt.

"Hold it!" Melvin picked up the shirt. There was no weight in it, nothing under it. He tossed it to Strothers, who rose and began to put it on.

"Where's the other thirty-eight?" Rudd asked mildly.

"The other? So you got Weyerhauser. Can I have a smoke?"

Melvin lit a cigarette and tossed it to Strothers. The sheriff and his deputy glanced quickly at each other.

"I don't know who's got it," Strothers said. The horses were coming out of the timber.

He saw Castagna. "Did you ask Sam?"

The sheriff's eyes were tight. He spoke easily, "Sam's clean. You look clean. So Kaygo's got it. Why'd you give up, Strothers?"

"Too much of nothing here. No future." Strothers grinned, dragging on his cigarette, watching the horses from the corners of his eyes. The surface was smooth, but there was steel savagery underneath. Castagna was a bully who had graduated to bombs on starters and bundles of dynamite against the bedroom walls of gambling kings; Strothers was everything the long F.B.I. reports said.

"You could have given up with Castagna," Melvin said.

"That two-bit character! I play it alone." Strothers puffed his smoke. "Do I get some chow?"

"Yeah," Rudd said. "Half-done venison."

"Raw will be fine, Constable."

"Walk on over toward the horses," Rudd said. "When I say stop — stop."

"Sure, Constable. Just don't stall. I want to get home as soon as possible. I'm doing some leather work that can't be neglected."

Not the usual bravado of a petty criminal — Strothers was too coldly intelligent for that. He was spreading it on lightly for another purpose. He wouldn't have much luck with Rudd, Melvin knew. Let him find it out.

Strothers limped ahead of them. "When my last blister broke, that was when I decided to hell with it."

"Right there, Strothers," Rudd said, when they were twenty feet from the horses. With the exception of Jaynes, the posse was relaxed. The first heat of the chase had been worn from them, and this third easy victory coming toward them was nothing to cause excitement.

Rudd nodded at Melvin, making a circle with his finger in the air. Melvin walked wide around Strothers and freed his lariat from the saddle.

"The great big Strothers, he comes easy," Castagna said sullenly.

Strothers ignored Castagna; his eyes were on the rope in Melvin's hands. Barker and the others looked at Strothers dully, but Jaynes sensed what they did not. He pushed his 'scope sight down and raised his rifle.

"Never mind!" Rudd said sharply, standing several paces behind Strothers. "Put that rifle down, Jaynes. Drop your pants, Strothers."

Strothers smiled. "Now look, Constable . . . " He was watching the loop in Melvin's hand.

And that was when Rudd stepped in and slammed Strothers to
the ground with the butt of his rifle. Melvin drove in quickly then.
Strothers was enough for the two of them for a while, but they got
his arms tied behind him at last.

The little automatic, flat, fully loaded, was tied with strips of
green cloth from Castagna's pants legs to the inside of Strother's
thigh. Castagna cursed bitterly, clinging to the saddle horn with
his one good hand.

"Why didn't you search him right at first?" Jaynes demanded
angrily.

"It takes more steam out of them to let them go right up to where
it looks like it's going to work," the sheriff said. "Build a fire,
Pryor. We may as well eat again before we split up."

Strothers chewed his meat with good appetite. He had struggled
like a wolf, but that was done now and his intelligence was at work
again. "What tipped it, Constable — the cigarettes?"

"Partly," Rudd said. "You wouldn't have left both packs with
Sam unless you figured to be with him soon. That wasn't too much,
but I knew you would never go back down the river and let them
say Ora L. Strothers was caught asleep and gave up without a fight.
You really were asleep, too — on purpose."

"Sure. I got the nerve for things like that. It made it look real."
Strother's good nature was back, but he was not thinking of his
words. His mind, Melvin knew, was thinking far ahead now, to
another plan, setting himself against walls and locks and ropes and
everything that could be used to restrain a man physically, pitting
his fine mind against all the instruments of the thing called society.

There was a lostness in him that appalled Melvin. Strothers was
a cold wind running from a foggy gorge back in the dawn age of
mankind. The wind could never warm or change or remain confined. Compared to Strothers, Sam Castagna was just a lumbering
animal that knocked weaker animals out of the way.

"You would have taken Castagna with you, if you could have
knocked a couple of us off and got to the horses?" Melvin asked.

"Sure," Strothers said. "We planned it that way."

That was talk to be repeated in the prison yard, to be passed
along the corridors of the cell block. Talk to fit the code. But not

to feed the vanity of Ora L. Strothers, because it was a lie. Let Castagna, lying feverishly on the ground in Melvin's jacket, believe what Strothers said. Castagna had been left behind to build up the illusion that desperate men would surrender without a fight. That he was injured and had to be left was not primary in Strother's mind; it was merely helpful coincidence.

"Which one of us was to've been first?" Melvin asked.

Strothers wiped his lips. "You, I thought. Then I changed my mind." He glanced at Jaynes.

"Yeah," Jaynes said. "I read you like a book. I wish you had tried something, Strothers."

The two men stared at each other. The antagonism that separated them was as wide as the sky.

"I'll bet you're the one-shot Sam," Strothers said. "Did you shoot Joe Weyerhauser, too?"

Jaynes did not answer. Watching him, Melvin thought: He lacks the evil power of Strothers's intelligence, and he lacks the strength of natural good. He doesn't know what he is, and he knows it.

Strothers smiled. "I've taken half a million from the banks and never had to shoot a man. You, Snake Eyes, you're just a punk on the other side because you don't have the guts and brains of men like me. How about it?"

Jaynes leaped up. His wasp voice broke when he cursed Strothers. He gripped his rifle and stood with the butt poised to smash into Strothers's face.

"Whoa there, Jaynes!" Sheriff Rudd said, but it was not he who stopped the rifle. With his legs tied and one arm bound behind his back, Strothers looked at Jaynes and smiled, and Jaynes lowered his rifle and walked away. After a few steps he turned toward the creek and went there, pretending to drink.

Barker and Pryor stared at Strothers. "Don't call *me* any of your names," Barker growled.

Strothers looked at him as he might have glanced at a noisy child; and then he forgot them all. His mind was once more chewing facts and plans, even as his strong teeth chewed meat.

If this man had been led by Marty Kaygo, what kind of man was Kaygo? thought Melvin.

Rudd said, "I'll take everybody in but you and Jaynes, Melvin. Do you feel up to staying on the trail?"

There was no place where a plane could set down to pick up Castagna. Two and a half days out, Melvin estimated. Rudd would need five men to keep an eye on Strothers day and night. They were out of food, too.

"All right," Melvin said.

Jaynes had overheard. He came back from the creek. "I'm staying, too."

Strothers smiled.

"I'll send the green plane over Shewalter Meadows three days from now," Rudd said. "With grub. Now what else will you need?"

"Send me another coat," Melvin said. "Send Jaynes another sleeping bag. We both better have packs, too."

The sheriff nodded. He put Strothers on a horse and tied him there. They lifted Castagna to the saddle again. He was going to suffer plenty before they reached the highway. Castagna looked at Melvin and said thickly, "Thanks for the coat."

Strothers smiled at Melvin from the corner of his eyes. The smile said: Chump!

A hundred yards down the creek a logging road took off to the left, and there went the tracks of Marty Kaygo. Melvin and Jaynes walked into second-growth timber. The sounds of the horses died away. Under his belt Melvin was carrying the pistol he had taken from Strothers.

Jaynes said, "I damn near smashed that Strothers's ugly face for him."

"Uh-huh."

"You can't hit a man tied up like that, not even a pen bird."

"No."

"Of course not," Jaynes said.

The road began to angle to the right, along a ridge.

"This won't take us straight to where the plane spotted Kaygo," Jaynes said. "Let's cut into the timber."

"I'm staying with his tracks. I don't know what that plane was circling over."

The road turned down the ridge again, on the side away from

Shewalter Meadows. Kaygo's tracks were still there, but Jaynes was mightily impatient. "I'm going straight over the ridge," he said.

"Go ahead."

"Where will I meet you then?"

"At the Meadows."

"You sure?" Jaynes asked doubtfully.

"This old road runs into one hell of a swamp before long. I'm betting he went to the Meadows, but I'm going to follow his trail all the way."

They separated. Melvin was glad. He wanted to reduce the chase to the patient unwinding of a trail, to an end that was nothing more than law and duty; and he could not think of it that way so long as Jaynes was with him.

Where the swamp began, Kaygo had turned at once up the ridge. There was something in that which spoke of the man's quality, of an ability to sense the lie of a country. Most city men would have blundered deep into the swamp before deciding to turn.

Jaynes was right about down-timber on the ridge, fire-killed trees that had stood for years before rot took their roots and wind sent them crashing. Melvin went slowly. Kaygo had done the same, and before long Melvin noticed that the man had traveled as a woodsman does, stepping over nothing that could be walked around.

Kaygo would never exhaust himself in blind, disorderly flight. What kind of man was he?

Going down the west side of the ridge, Melvin stopped when a grouse exploded from the ground near a rotting spruce log. He drew the pistol and waited until he saw two others near the log, frozen in their protective coloration. He shot one through the head, and five more flew away.

Now an instrument of the law had broken the law for a second time during this chase; but there were, of course, degrees of breakage. A man like Strothers no doubt could make biting comments on the subject.

Melvin pulled the entrails from the bird and went on, following Kaygo's trail. The man had an eye for terrain, all right. He made few mistakes that cost him time and effort, and that was rare in any man crossing unfamiliar, wooded country.

A woodsman at some time in his life? Melvin went back over

Kaygo's record. Thirty-five years old. Sixteen of those years spent in reformatories and prisons. An interesting talker. Athletic. Generally armed, considered extremely dangerous. Approach with caution. The record fell into the glib pattern of the words under the faces on the bulletin board in Rudd's office.

Gambles heavily. If forced to work, seeks employment as clerk in clothing store . . . There was nothing Melvin could recall to indicate that Kaygo had ever been five miles from pavement.

The sun was getting low and the timber was already gathering coolness in its depths when Melvin came out on a long slope that ran down to the Meadows, two miles away.

Where the sun still lay on a bare spot near a quartz outcrop Melvin stopped, puzzled by what he saw. The mark of the steel buttplate of Kaygo's rifle and the imprint of his shoes, one flat, the other showing no heel print, said that Kaygo had squatted near the ant hill; four cigarette butts crushed into the ground said that he had been here for some time.

Coolness had diminished activity of the ants, but they were still seething in and out of their dome of sand and pine needles; and Kaygo had squatted there for perhaps an hour to watch.

It was Melvin's experience that some perverseness in man causes him to step upon ant hills or to kick them in passing. This one was undisturbed. Kaygo had watched and gone away. Melvin had done the same thing many times.

What if I have and what if he did also? he asked himself. Does that change what I have to do? But as he went on, Melvin kept wondering what Kaygo had thought as he squatted beside the ant hill.

Near dusk Melvin lost the trail where the wide arm of a swamp came up from the drainage basin of the Meadows. But Kaygo was headed that way, Melvin was sure. One gentle turn too far to the left, back there on the long slope, would have sent Kaygo into the ragged canyons near the lower end of the Meadows.

He must have spotted the place from the top of Clover Mountain; but seeing from the heights and finding from a route through timber-choked country are two different things.

Kaygo had a fine sense of distance and direction, though. I can grant him that, Melvin thought, without feeling anything else about him to impede my purpose. The purpose — and Melvin wondered why he had to keep restating it — was to bring Marty Kaygo out, dead or alive.

On the edge of Shewalter Meadows, where the grass stood waist-high to a man all over the flooded ground and the beaver runs that led to the ponds out in the middle, Melvin stopped behind a tree and scanned the open space. There was only half-light now, but that was enough.

Beavers were making ripples in the ponds and trout were leaping for their evening feeding. The Meadows lay in a great dog-leg, and the upper part was cut from Melvin's view by spruce trees and high willows. The best windfalls for sleeping cover were up there, and that was where Jaynes would be, undoubtedly.

Let him stay there tonight alone. Sooner or later Melvin would have to rejoin him, and that would be soon enough. Melvin went back into the timber and cooked his grouse. He ate half of it and laid the rest in the palm of a limb, head-high.

The night came in with a gentle rush. He dozed off on top of his sleeping bag, to awaken chilled and trembling some time later. The night was windless, the ground stony. Melvin built up the fire and warmed himself by it before getting into his sleeping bag.

Dead or alive. The thought would not submerge.

One Kaygo was a vagueness written on a record; Melvin had learned of another Kaygo today. They made a combination that would never give up.

If Melvin had been here just to fish and loaf, to walk through the dappled fall of sunshine in the trees, and — yes, to be caught away from himself while watching the endless workings of an ant hill; to see the sun come and go on quietness; to see the elk thrusting their broad muzzles underwater to eat; to view all the things that are simple and understandable . . . then, he knew, he would be living for a while as man was meant to live.

You are Bill Melvin, a deputy sheriff. He is a man called Kaygo, an escaped murderer.

Dead or alive . . .

He came from dreamless sleep when the log ends of the fire were no longer flaming but drizzling smoke across a bed of coals. He felt the presence near him by the rising of the hackles on his neck, from deep memories forgotten by the human race.

Carefully, not breaking the even tenor of his breathing, he worked one hand up to the pistol on the head shield of the sleeping bag.

The man was squatted by the fire with a rifle across his knees. His hair was curling brown that caught a touch of redness from the glow of embers. The light outlined a sandy beard, held steady on wide cheekbones, and lost itself in the hollows under massive brow arches. The man's trousers were muddy, at least as high as the knees, where the fabric was stained smooth by his position. They might have been any color. But there was no doubt that the shirt was green.

The face by itself was enough.

It was Marty Kaygo.

He was eating what was left of Melvin's grouse.

He turned the carcass in his hands, gnawing, chewing; and all the while his face was set toward the shadows where Melvin lay.

Slowly Melvin worked the pistol along the edge of the ground until, lying on his side, he raised it just a trifle. The front sight was a white bead that lined across the coals to Kaygo's chest. Melvin's thumb pushed the safety down.

Long rifle cartridges, just a spot of lead that could sing over space and kill. Kaygo, the cop-killer. Speak to him, tell him to put up his hands and let his rifle fall. If he swung the rifle to fire, the pistol could sing and kill.

From where came the whisper that fire and food must be shared even with a deadly enemy? From the jungle all around that might pull them both beneath its slime an instant later?

The sabre-tooth and the great reptiles were out there in the night. And men were men together, if only for a moment. The jungle was not gone, merely changed.

Melvin let the pistol rest upon the ground.

Marty Kaygo rose. He was not a tall man. Even in his prison shoes he moved lightly as he stepped to a tree and replaced the carcass of the grouse. He grinned, still looking toward where Melvin lay.

And then he was gone.

Melvin lay a long time before he fell asleep again.

When he rose in the bitter cold of morning, he went at once to the dead fire. There were the tracks. He took the grouse from the limb. One leg was untouched.

Staring out to where the first long-slanting rays of the sun were driving mist from the beaver ponds and wet grass, Melvin held the chilled grouse in his hands.

What's the matter with me?

The truth was, Jaynes was Melvin and Melvin was Jaynes, great developments of the centuries: and Kaygo did not fit where they belonged. But . . .

Melvin shivered.

He went out of the timber into the sunshine, and he sat down to let it warm him while he ate the rest of the grouse. There before him, leading through the gray mud out toward the wickerwork of the beaver dams, were the tracks of Kaygo. He had crossed the boggy ground by night, walking the beaver dams above deep water, returning the same way. It was not an easy feat even in daytime.

I wish I could talk to him, Melvin thought. I wish . . .

The shot was a cracking violation of the wilderness quiet. It came from somewhere around the dog-leg of the Meadows.

Melvin went back to the camp site and got his gear.

Before he turned the dog-leg, he saw Jaynes coming toward him. Jaynes stopped and waited.

"What the hell happened to you, Melvin?" There was blood on Jayne's shirt.

"I followed his trail, just as I said I would. You shoot a deer?"

"Yeah. That's one thing there's plenty of here. Kaygo's around. I saw his tracks in the upper part of the Meadows last night. We'll get him. I know every inch —— "

"Let's get at the deer."

They roasted meat, and then Jaynes was impatient to be off.

"Just hold your steam," said Melvin. "We've got another two days before the plane drops chow, so we're going to start drying some of this meat."

"There's lots of deer."

"We'll dry some of this. We don't know where that plane will drop our supplies, or what they'll be like when we get to them. And you're not going to shoot a deer every day, Jaynes."

They cut the meat in thin strips and laid it on the gray twigs of a fallen tree until the branches were festooned with dangling brown meat. Camp-robber birds were there at once, floating in, snatching.

"How you going to stop that?" Jaynes asked.

"By staying here. I'm going to do some smoking with a willow fire, too. Take a turn around the Meadows. See what you can find out. You know every inch of the land."

"I'll do that." Jaynes took his rifle and strode away.

He was back at noon. "Where'd you camp, Melvin?"

Melvin told him.

"Well, he was there, this morning. He crossed the swamp and went back the same way. He's in the timber on this side somewhere. He's getting smart now about covering his tracks."

"What's he eating?" Melvin asked cleverly.

"I don't know, and I don't care. He slept one night under a wind-fall. Where'd he learn that, Melvin?" Jaynes was worried.

"I think it must come to him naturally. He's probably enjoying more freedom right now than he's had in his whole life."

Jaynes grunted. He eyed the tree that was serving as a drying rack. "Hey! Do you suppose we could pull him in with that?" He looked all around at the fringe of trees. "Say we go down into the timber on the other side and then circle back to that little knob over there . . . About three hundred and twenty-five yards." Jaynes rubbed the oily sheen of his rifle barrel. "One shot, Melvin."

"You think he's hungry enough to try it?"

"He must be."

"The birds will scatter our meat."

"Part of a lousy deer, or one jailbird! What's the matter with you, Melvin?"

The venison was not going to cure before the plane came in and Melvin knew it. He had stalled long enough.

They went a half-mile beside the lower Meadows. On the way Jaynes stepped sidewise to jump into an ant hill and twist his feet; and then he went on, stamping ants loose from his shoes. "He must be hungry enough by now."

They went back through the timber and crept behind a log on

the little hill across the field from their camp. The smoky birds were having a merry time with the meat.

Now Jaynes was patient. His eyes caught every movement across the park, and his position did not seem to strain his muscles. They stayed until the shadows lowered cold upon their backs. It was then that they heard the rifle shot somewhere in the lower Meadows, two miles away.

"He's got his own meat." Melvin laughed.

Jaynes rose. "What's so damn funny about it?"

Melvin had wrapped his undershirt around a venison haunch, but the blowflies had got to it anyway. He brushed the white larva away.

They roasted meat and ate in silence.

Marty Kaygo was still around Shewalter Meadows. They cut his sign the next day, and they found where he had killed the deer. The convict was here, and it seemed that he intended to stay.

Jaynes was infuriated. And he was speechless for a while when they returned to camp that night and found that Kaygo had stolen Melvin's sleeping bag.

"Who are the tenderfeet around here?" Melvin laughed again.

"You don't act like you want to catch him! By God, I do, and I'll stay here all summer to do it, if necessary!"

"To catch him?"

"To kill him! I'm going to gut-shoot him for this little trick!"

"You would have, anyway." There was no humor now in Kaygo's stealing the sleeping bag.

The plane came in on the afternoon of the third day. Clouds were scudding across the peaks and the pilot was in a hurry to beat out a local storm. He banked sharply to look down at the two men standing in the open dryness of the upper Meadows.

He went on east, high above the timber. They saw him fighting a tricky wind. On the next bank he kicked out the box. The parachute became a white cone. Lining out with a tailwind boosting him, the pilot sped away toward Scott.

"If he had any brains he'd've stayed to make sure we got it," Jaynes said. "Typical State employee."

A great wind-front flowing in from the mountains struck them with a chill that spoke of the rain soon to follow. Melvin watched the plane bouncing jerkily in downdrafts above the canyons. "The pilot's all right, Jaynes."

"Look at that thing drift!"

They knew for sure after another few moments that the box would not land in the upper Meadows. Melvin said, "Wouldn't it be something if it lit right at Kaygo's feet?"

"Big fine joke, huh?"

They trotted across the creek and down along the edge of the Big Shewalter to keep the 'chute in sight. They were a long way from it when they saw it splash into the water near the opposite side of the flooded area. An instant later the rain boiled down on them.

"I hope they had sense enough to put the stuff in cans." Jaynes turned up the collar of his jacket.

The ponds were dancing froth now. Through the mist they saw Kaygo run from the timber and wade out after the box.

Jaynes dropped to one knee. He pushed his 'scope down and began to click the sight-adjustment. "Eight hundred yards," he muttered. His rifle bellowed with the thunder on the mountains. "Where'd I hit?"

"I couldn't tell."

The first hard blast of rain was sweeping on. Jaynes fired again, and this time Melvin saw the bullet strike the water to the left of Kaygo, chest-deep now, towing the box to shore with the shroud lines of the chute.

"About five feet to the left," Melvin said.

Kaygo sprawled into the grass when the next shot came.

"That did it," Melvin said.

"No! He ducked."

Kaygo raised up. Skidding the box over wet grass and mud, he reached timber while Jaynes tried two more shots. Over that distance, through wind and rain, Jaynes had performed well — but Kaygo was still free.

Kaygo's boldness was worth applause, but Melvin felt only a bleak apathy. The end had been delayed, that was all.

"Come on!" Jaynes said.

"Across that open swamp? No, thanks. We'll work through the timber."

"He's got our stuff!"

"He's got a rifle, too."

The box had been fastened with wing-nuts, easy to tap loose. The packs Melvin had asked for were gone, and the jacket, and about three fourths of the food, Melvin estimated. The sleeping bag had been unrolled. Rain was filtering through the pines on a manila envelope containing a note.

They peered into the gloom of the wet forest. It was no time to press Kaygo hard, and they both knew it.

While Jaynes raged, Melvin read the note.

"Rudd started in at noon today with big posse. He say not to take any chances. He says there were *two* .22 pistols and a hunting knife taken from the filling station."

"That's a big help!" Jaynes cursed the weather, the pilot, and the stupidity of circumstance.

"I told you on Clover Mountain I was sick of you, Jaynes. Now shut up! You're lucky Kaygo didn't slice your sleeping bag to pieces or throw it into the water."

"I'm fed up with you, too, Melvin! You didn't even try to shoot a while ago. You act like the stinking louse is your brother!"

My brother. The thought plowed through Melvin, leaving a fresh wake. It was not fashionable to speak of men as brothers; you killed your brother, just like anybody else.

They plodded toward camp, carrying the cans of food in their hands. The labels began to soak off. Melvin finished the job on the cans he was holding.

"That's smart," Jaynes said. "Now what's in them?"

"You're right, they're no good to us any more. A hungry man has to know what he's getting." Melvin began to hurl the cans into a beaver pond, until Jaynes pleaded with him.

"Then shut your mouth for a while!" Melvin cried.

They went on to camp through a cold rain that soaked into Melvin's soul.

"Soup!" Jaynes said later, when they sat under a dripping tree before a smoking fire. "Kaygo's back in the timber having hot coffee and canned chicken."

Jaynes could not destroy everything, for he had the unrealized power to give laughter. Melvin began to laugh while Jaynes stared at him angrily. Was it the sound of laughter, as well as the smell of fire, that caused the monsters of the long-ago jungle to raise their heads in fear?

"I said I'd get Kaygo if it took all summer. You sit here and laugh some more, Melvin. *I'll get him!*"

They found the second pack the next morning, empty, hanging on a tree. "He's cached part of the grub somewhere," Jaynes growled. "He couldn't have put it all in one pack. Smart! He did it in the rain, and now we can't backtrack him."

But they could trail him in the fresh dampness. Kaygo had realized that, too; he had gone far south of the Meadows, and on a rocky ridge they lost his trail. The ridge was a great spur that ran down from Spearhead Mountain, bucking through lesser cross-ridges arrogantly. The lower end of it, Melvin knew, was not eight miles from the highway.

"Maybe he's clearing out," Jaynes said. "He read that note about Rudd. He knows he's going to get it. He's headed for the highway now. Somebody else will get him, after all we've done!"

"Pathetic, ain't it?" Melvin looked at Spearhead Mountain. "Maybe he went that way. He likes mountains."

"What do you mean?"

"Nothing you'd understand. He's gone toward Spearhead, Jaynes."

"The highway! I'm going after him, Melvin. If I don't cut his trail by the time I hit Bandbox Creek, I'll come back. Don't sneak off this time and camp by yourself. He could have walked right in on you that night."

"Yes, he could have killed me, I suppose."

Jaynes's eyes narrowed. "Those tracks beside your fire the next morning — one of yours was on top of one of his, Melvin. He sneaked in while you were asleep, didn't he? And you were ashamed to mention it to me! It's a wonder he didn't take your rifle and sleeping bag right from under you. I'll mention that to Rudd when he gets here."

"You do that, Jaynes." Harlan Rudd had shared food and fire with outlaws in the old days, and he was not ashamed to talk about it now that he was sheriff. "Get out of my sight, Jaynes, before I forget I'm a brother to you, too!"

"Brother?" Jaynes gave Melvin a baffled look before he started down the ridge.

There was something Kaygo could not have known about this ridge: It appeared to be the natural route to Spearhead, but higher up it was a jumble of tree-covered cliffs.

Melvin stayed on it only until he found where Kaygo had slipped from his careful walking on rocks and left a mark which he had tried to smooth away. Then Melvin left the ridge and took a round-about, but faster, route toward Spearhead.

He went too rapidly. In midafternoon he saw Kaygo far below him, between two curving buttresses of the mountain. The fugitive was not pushing himself.

While Melvin watched through his glasses, Kaygo removed the stolen pack and lay down in a field of columbines, pillowing his head on the stolen sleeping bag. The wind was cold on Melvin's sweating skin as he hugged his vantage point behind the rocks.

Jaynes might have made a shot from here; he would have tried, although the range was four hundred yards greater than yesterday across the Big Shewalter. Melvin knew his own rifle would do no more than scare Kaygo down the hill.

Like hunting sheep, he thought. You have to wait and try to make them blunder into you.

Kaygo lay there for an hour. He was not asleep. He moved occasionally, but mostly he lay there looking at the sky and clouds.

He was wallowing in freedom; that was it. Damn him! He would not do what fugitives are supposed to do. He insisted on acting like a man enjoying life.

My brother down there, Melvin thought. Yes, and I'll kill him when he comes near enough on the saddle of the mountain.

Kaygo rose at last, but he did not go. He stretched his arms to the sky, as if he would clutch a great section of it. Then he sat down and smoked a cigarette.

The sweat was tight and dry on Melvin. The wind scampered through his clothing. Of course I have to kill him, he told himself. He's found something he loves so much he won't be taken from it any other way.

Kaygo went up at last. Melvin slipped behind the rib of the mountain and climbed steadily. The wind was growing quiet now. There was a sullen heaviness in the air. It would rain again today.

Melvin was far ahead when he took a position among rocks that overlooked the saddle. He could see Kaygo, still in no hurry, coming up the harder way, coming over a red iron dike that had made the notch on Spearhead back when man clutched his club and splashed toward refuge as the clamor broke out in the forest.

It was his job. Society paid him, Melvin reminded himself. Climb faster Marty Kaygo. You will have your chance to go back where you belong, and when you refuse, the job will be done quickly.

The air grew heavily quiet. Melvin blinked when he heard a tiny snap and saw a blue spark run along his rifle barrel. He rubbed his hand against his woolen shirt. His palm crackled with pinpoint sparks and the fibers of the sleeve tried to follow the hand away. He stroked his hair and heard the little noises and felt the hair rising.

All this was not uncommon on the heights in summer when a storm was making, but Melvin had never experienced it before. It gave him a weird sensation.

Kaygo came into the saddle when the air was fully charged. He jumped when blue light ran along his rifle barrel. He was then two hundred yards away from Melvin. He would have to pass much closer. Kaygo stared in wonder at his rifle, and then at the leaden sky.

He held up his hunting knife. Sparks played upon the point. Kaygo laughed. He raised both knife and rifle and watched the electricity come to them.

A little later he discovered steel was not necessary to draw static from the swollen air. Kaygo's fingers, held aloft, drew sparks. He did a dance upon the rocks, shouting his wonder and pleasure. Strange balls of light ran along the iron dike and the air was filled with a sterile odor.

This day on Spearhead Mountain, Marty Kaygo roared with joy.

Melvin had never heard laughter run so cleanly. Laughter from the littered caves above the slime; laughter from the tree-perch safe from walking beasts; laughter challenging the brutes . . .

It did not last. The rain came just after the first whistling surge of wind. The bursting air cleared.

Kaygo trotted easily for shelter, his head lowered against the pelt of ice. He came straight toward the rocks where Melvin lay. There was a clatter somewhere behind Melvin, granite slipping on granite, but he had no time to wonder.

"Kaygo!" he yelled. "Drop it!"

The man threw up his head as he ran and he brought the rifle up, not hesitating.

My brother, Melvin thought. That held him one split second longer, with his finger on the trigger and his sights on Kaygo's chest.

Another rifle roared behind him. Kaygo's legs jerked as he tried to keep running. He went down and his hands reached out for the wet stones. That was all.

Jaynes came limping through the rocks. "I hurt my knee, but I got him, rain and all!"

Melvin could not rise for a moment. He felt frozen to the rock. At last he came up, slowly.

"You were right," Jaynes said. "He took the hard way. After I left you I got to thinking that was what he would do."

They went across the stones to Kaygo. Jaynes turned him over. "Heart. I said I didn't miss running shots, not very often." That was all the interest he had in Marty Kaygo; and now that vanished, too.

Jaynes slipped the pack from the dead man's back. "Steal our chow, would he! Grab your sleeping bag and let's get out of here. Rudd and the others can take care of the chores now. Four for four, Melvin."

"You're counting Strothers?"

"I wish that big-mouth had tried something."

The rain was the coldest that ever fell on Melvin. He unrolled the sleeping bag and covered Kaygo with it, weighting the sides with stones.

Jaynes started to protest, but near the end he helped. "I guess even Kaygo deserves something. He wasn't a bad-looking character at that, was he?"

All this time Melvin had not looked at Jaynes. Now he picked up Jaynes's rifle. Deliberately, Melvin began to smash it against a rock. He splintered the stock and the forestock. He bent the bolt and he battered the 'scope until it was a twisted tube hanging by one mount, and he continued to beat the breech against the rock until the front sight ripped his palm and the impacts numbed his wrists.

He dropped the rifle then and stood breathing hard.

Jaynes had cursed loudly at first, but then he had stopped. The hard glitter was gone from his eyes.

Now, in the voice of a man who lives with splinters in his soul, Jaynes said, "By God, you're going to buy me a new rifle, Melvin. What's the matter with you, anyway?"

Melvin said nothing. Then together they started down the rain-soaked mountain . . .

(From New World Writing)

A CHANGE OF AIR

BY IVAN GOLD

PROLOGUE

*B*OBBIE BEDNER at the age of nineteen during the course of three warm August days and nights lost not her virginity which she had long before misplaced in the back of an automobile but the memory of it, and almost, along with this, the capacity to remember. What she knew when she awoke on the first of the August mornings was that on such a fine sunny morning one had to be completely out of one's head to go to work in a button factory what with a hundred better nicer cleaner things to do, and damn her mother and the button factory, she would go for a long walk out of doors or maybe to a movie. What she knew as well (but not as loudly) as her not going to work was exactly where she was going and why. But what she did not know . . . what she could not possibly know when she got on the bus (which passed one park and two movie houses on its journey along an avenue of New York's lower East Side, but which also stopped almost directly outside the clubroom of the silk-jacketed Werewolves, membership thirty-five, and many friends) was that when she returned home seventy-two hours later, she would do so minus her underwear, the greater part of her emotional stability, her future in the button factory, and eleven pounds.

For the two or three young men of her acquaintance whom she expected to find in the clubroom at this early hour (they living there, being otherwise unhoused and temporarily unemployed) she found in the clubroom, running win, place, and show in a fabulous, all-night, seven-man stud poker game, and consequently filled to overflowing with philanthropy (love for one's fellow man). She walked in boldly, then hesitated, seeing seven card players and three hecklers, ten in all, counted on Tony, Frank, and Fat Andy for the protection she thought she wanted, found them extremely interested in her presence, but averse to any plan of action which did not include their intimates at the card table, who were now poorer (and they richer) by three hundred dollars. Decided finally, persuaded by Frank's embraces and the uniqueness (ten of them — why not the hecklers too — on the same day) of the prospect, communicated her decision by her slightly hysterical laugh, running crazily up the scale and halfway down, and thereby set out to make East Side of New York (and possibly national) history.

For . . . although unrecorded in the Werewolves' minutes, or in any other written source (ignoring the possibility that one or more of the half-dozen or so twelve- to fifteen-year-old young men she devirginized during the three-day period was sentimental enough to keep a diary), it is proved beyond any doubt by an unchallengeable number of oral affirmations that Bobbie Bedner (although expressing some desire to leave about four o'clock of the same afternoon when the situation seemed to be getting out of hand) nevertheless was taken, or rather had, one hundred and sixty times during seventy hours by a total of fifty-three persons (the entire membership of the Werewolves, their younger brothers and friends) of all nationalities and sizes, slept a grand total of seven hours during the three days and nights, consumed a bottle of milk, two of beer, a number of pretzels and a ham sandwich, called her mother on the evening of the first day to assure her that everything was under control and (it was Friday) she was spending the night at a friend's house and did not know exactly when she would be home, and returned home two and one-half days later when one of the Werewolves, preparing to make the trip for the third time, suddenly and concernedly noticed how peaked she was. They put her on a bus at eight o'clock on Monday morning, thoughtfully providing her with carfare, warning her to keep it quiet which they did not have to do since she truly bore them no animosity, and she returned home, eleven pounds less of her, to her mother and to the police who had preceded her by only twenty minutes, and fainted in the doorway.

When she awoke, tight-lipped, in a hospital, heard the doctor proclaim to the police and nurse the girl has suffered an ordeal, been without food and raped many times, laughed her crazy laugh, and had to say you screwy sawbones you it wasn't rape and how many times and laughed the crazy laugh for many minutes at the doctor's guess of thirty the nurse's forty the police's fifty, told them how many times (having kept a careful count), told them laughing crazily it was all her own idea and she might have a go at it again, but worth less than nothing to the forces of law and order in the names and places department.

They sent her away. They had to. Her mother wrung her hands, cursed her God and the memory of her husband. They sent her away for two years. When she returned from Rehabilitation School she had regained the eleven pounds and five additional. There were other, apparently deeper changes.

Franklin Cripple DeTorres, carrying himself well at five foot-seven, absolutely sound of limb and body, derived his middle name, twenty-five cents, and a good part of his reputation as a result of an encounter in (and with) a subway. Always sure of himself, acutely conscious of his heritage — Puerto Rico (for his birth and the year afterward), New York and bravery — never more so than at five A.M. on a liquored Sunday morning, Cripple (Crip to his friends) conjectured aloud on the fate of his foot provided he left it where it was, hanging over the parapet above the tracks, a void soon to be filled by an incoming subway train.

His friends, not realizing the full extent of his courage, liking him and wishing (in good spirits) to create the opportunity to apply to him a large number of defamatory epithets (which they would be in a position to do when he snatched his foot out of danger), offered (one of them did) the sum of twenty-five cents to the soon-to-be-martyred if he left his foot there until and after the train arrived. It was not the money which decided him, but the attitude which prompted its offer. Placing his foot up to the heel (with which he clutched the edge of the parapet for support) over the parapet, Cripple waited. The train came. He did not even flinch, not until the train (with its agonized conductor) hit him, and then he did not flinch but fell down parallel to the tracks, landing on his elbows, the foot which earned him the name the money the reputation seemingly unhurt, and shouted very loudly, unhysterically, but with great conviction, get me to the hospital.

His ten weeks in the hospital he found dull but not unbearable, being able to leaf through the books previously stolen from the bookstore where he stockclerked, being always interested in culture, and favored daily by visits from his friends, the entire membership of the Werewolves, most calling his act of bravery the stupidest thing anyone had ever done, but all admiring, and the six weeks after that when he walked with an ever-lessening limp were just that, six weeks, so he suffered nothing finally except the money he did not make (more than compensated for by the quarter which he had framed and hung in the Werewolves' clubroom threatening death and other penalties to anyone who removed it), and he gained a name which it seemed to outsiders should offend him, until they learned the manner of its origination.

On the day Bobbie Bedner did not go to work, Frank Cripple DeTorres won one hundred and forty dollars. It was the largest longest most expensive poker game ever played in the Werewolf clubroom, it was the most money he had ever won, and although by no means feeling guilty (perhaps even seeing a way to call a halt to the contest before his luck began to change), Cripple, when he saw her walk in, felt that the least he could do for the boys he had taken over was to get them to the slut as long as she happened to be around. He was the first on line, then, as the affair began to mush-room (something he did not foresee but which did not make any difference), thirty-first and again one hundred and sixth. He was sorry to hear (he did not hear, but deduced from her absence) that the girl had been sent to a reformatory.

When the Werewolves disbanded (after a police raid which led to the twelve Werewolves present at the club spending some time at headquarters, and the two of them identified by the badly battered grocery proprietor remaining after the others were allowed to leave) Cripple devoted himself to intellectual pursuits, spending most of his evenings at Gelber's Chess Club on Seventeenth Street. He went usually with Joe Muneco, or met him there. They were the only two young men (except for occasional visits from Joe's friends) in what was otherwise a storm center for the old. Together, these two, they either beat (they played well) or talked down every old man in the place.

A problem to Early Environmentalists (the key to personality lies in the first three or five or nine or eleven years) , *Joseph Muneco* (of whom they had never heard) spent the first three years of his life running around the streets of San Juan, Puerto Rico, the next four-teen years escaping policemen (for playing stickball on New York City streets and mugging usually close-to-penniless passersby) , then, being expelled from three high schools (for non-attendance of classes and smoking marijuana) , finally happening across a novel by Thomas Wolfe, impressed enough to read this author's entire works, discovering James Joyce, and in his twentieth year, and his fourth high school, becoming the editor (and first prize winner in a na-tional short story contest) of his high school literary magazine.

Made many friends in this high school (at home on all intellectual strata) , fell in love with and was loved by the editor of the high school newspaper (a Jewish girl of orthodox parents who were destined to object to their daughter's keeping company with a Gen-tile, and with a Spanish Gentile, and with one who looked so typi-cally and unhealthily Spanish) , went to a city college (his girl and he) , saw the girl every day and on Saturday nights, and devoted the rest of his social time alternately to Cripple (alone or with mutual acquaintances, members of the long-defunct Werewolves) and to his other high school friends (the last high school) , cream of the intel-lectual crop, the boys who read the books, who thought about writ-ing them (as he did — although he only thought) , and who by fairly frequent remarks pertaining to his dual heritage (the literate hoodlum, and variants, with lots of laughter, although he had for a long time now adhered to the straight and narrow path) contributed to the growth of his impassioned unusual campaign of self-justifica-tion.

Impassioned unusual campaign of self-justification . . . not with his girl Anne, with whom he was in love; nor with Cripple and with these friends with whom he fitted in so perfectly that there was no need of it; but with the others . . .

With *Phillip Zand,* literary critic until his junior year at college, thinking now of psychology, seeing it as a back door to the world he didn't live in; a great reader and a great listener to music, and a self-styled neurotic, finding himself replete with wrong things to say (to women), and not enough women to say them to; not pretty, but (not that this mattered) not as unpretty as he thought he was, weakly contemptuous of the others, his close circle of friends, in the only regions where he was qualified to be contemptuous, books and music, finding them in these regions, although reasonably well informed, nevertheless with sufficient (for the purposes of ridicule) misinformation . . .

With *Lee Miller,* a college man, sporadically read in Schopenhauer, Nietzsche, and Philip Wylie, with some Havelock Ellis (being interested in sex); contentious but without a conciliatory delivery (far from it; always unpleasant, not going out of his way to be unpleasant, but being that way because it came easiest), with the result that among his group of friends, he had no friend; cherubic in appearance (and thus with a number of conquests to his credit which Phil Zand — by no means accidentally — was forever hearing about, but still . . .), a lecher at nineteen, being famed (and given no peace) for the most amazing collection of pornographic snapshots and literature perhaps ever assembled, delighting in lending certain parts of his collection to Phil since he knew what he used them for, a good but strange mind; a flair for chess, a match for Joe Muneco, a terrific and serious rivalry building between them, a result of and a further prod to mutual dislike . . .

With *Benjamin Brock,* the only one of them attending a college which it required money to attend, assuming therefore a certain superiority in the quality of his education, never having to mention the felt superiority for them to know that it was there; doubting especially (again tacitly, or if not tacitly, then blatantly in jest) Muneco's claim to higher understanding (Joe having not written since the days of his high school triumphs — Ben writing all the time — two long years ago, unable to take his typewriter out of pawn, and besides, being busy — with his girl and with Cripple —

being happy), Muneco feeling Ben's doubts, and the doubts of the others, knowing the realm of the intellect to be his as well as (if not more than) theirs, but feeling it always necessary to prove it to them, and so . . .

Joseph Muneco's impassioned unusual campaign of self-justification, the utilization of a phenomenal memory, an almost photographic memory, committing to it the equivalent of three large volumes of verse, from Sappho to Cummings, and considerable prose, quoting some part of his repertoire at the least provocation, creating his own provocation, irrelevant (the quoting) to anything occurring or even said in his immediate environment, but illustrating to Phil and to Lee and to Ben and to anyone else around that he, Joseph Muneco, had a sizable portion of the world's literature at his fingertips, had the best that man's mind has yet created stored (with an understanding of it, if anyone pursued the matter) in his memory, that he, Joseph Muneco was, whatever else he might also be, an intellectual.

With this and these in mind, we can begin the story.

The Story

Gelber's Chess Club was partly that. More, it was a place to play cards and a place to stay, on cold winter nights and dull summer ones. In the back of the club, away from the two windows overlooking Seventeenth Street, was a small room with a stove in which Mrs. Gelber made and sold coffee and sandwiches. The long, large room which was the club was divided by common consent into the section for chess players and for card players; there were the few benches in the chess player section for those who wished to sleep, to think, or to read the paper. On the door of the club was a sign reading FOR MEMBERS ONLY and inside the club a sign said MEMBERSHIP DUES, ONE DOLLAR A YEAR. Neither of these mattered. Gelber was friendly, did not need the money, and owned the building. The signs were put up at the insistence of his wife and Gelber neither desired to, nor did he, reinforce them. The club had been on Seventeenth Street for twenty-two years, and although the faces changed, at intervals, the mean age of the members did not. The men at the club — and they were all men aside from Gelber's wife — averaged fifty-five years of age. If not for the presence of Joseph Muneco and Franklin DeTorres, who came often enough to necessitate their inclusion in any mathematical calculations, the average age of the members of Gelber's Chess Club would have been fifty-seven.

Frank DeTorres was talking to Joe Muneco.

"Okay Ace," he said. "Push the pawn. Before the place closes, Ace. I guarantee the safety of the pawn move."

Frank had arrived at 11 o'clock and had played chess with the old men. He won more than he lost and he enjoyed his conversation and the reactions to it. At one o'clock Joe Muneco walked in, earlier than usual for a Saturday night, but his girl had gotten sick and he took her home early, leaving her a block from where she lived in case one of her parents happened to be looking from the window. Meeting her on Saturday nights was no problem since she had a job ushering at concerts in a school auditorium in his neighborhood, and he could meet her afterward, at nine-thirty. On this Saturday night she became ill and he took her home. When he got to the club, he and Frank DeTorres played chess. Muneco was the better of the two but against each other they played carelessly, and games were not won or lost in accord with their ability.

At DeTorres' remark, Joe became angry for the three old men who made up his audience.

"Take it easy, Ace," he said. "Any time you want to play three seconds a move, you let me know, Ace. The pawn move is for the fushas. I give you this." He moved his bishop along its diagonal. One of the old men grunted approval and smiled a toothless smile. Frank addressed him.

"Doesn't he play like a master?" he said. "He is a true Morphy in the way he plays this game. I admire your manipulation of the pieces, Ace," he said to Joe. He looked swiftly at the board and made his move. "Try this one," he said.

Joe guffawed. "Swish, Ace," he said, swooping down upon De-

Torres' unprotected queen, removing it, and upsetting four or five pieces on both sides of the board.

"I didn't see, Ace," Frank said, beginning to smile. Two of the old men laughed. The third yawned noisily and moved toward one of the benches leaning against the wall.

Frank resigned. He began to set up his pieces in preparation for another game. At one-thirty Phil Zand and Lee Miller walked in. They had gone to a movie, had coffee, and come to the chess club looking for Joe Muneco. They knew that he could be found here on Sunday mornings at this time after taking his girl home.

"Watch him!" Joe said agitatedly to Phil, glancing momentarily at Lee, as the two came over and sat down. "You shouldn't have taken him off the leash. He's liable to rape small boys."

"No need," Lee said. "I was refreshed last night. A very sweet young thing I met at a dance. How's Anne?"

The query might have been solicitous, but it was very poorly placed. Suddenly Muneco was no longer amusing or amused.

"She's all right," he said, looking at Lee. "Unless you just killed her by mentioning her name."

Lee laughed. He laughed unpleasantly, the only way he knew how.

"I thought you had signed a non-aggression pact," Phil said.

"Only verbal," Joe said. "It can be busted at any time."

"What's new?" Frank said to Phil.

"I'm glad you asked," Phil said. "My profession. I'm going to be a psychologist."

"That's nice," Frank said. "We are in need of psychologists. But you've got to gain weight if you want to be healthy enough to pursue your studies. You're very thin, in spite of your weight-lifting."

Phil laughed.

" 'I am thy father's spirit,' " Joe said. " 'Doomed for a certain term to walk the night, and for the day confined to fast in fires, till the foul crimes done in my days of nature are burnt and purged away. But that I am forbid,' " he said, " 'to tell the secrets of my prison-house, I could a tale unfold whose lightest word would harrow up thy soul,' checkmate Ace,' he said.

"You're a genius, Muneco," Lee said, sitting in the chair Frank had just vacated. Frank visited Mrs. Gelber for some coffee.

"You didn't like that?" Joe inquired. "Maybe you'd prefer an excerpt from Krafft-Ebing. 'George K., longshoreman, locked in the embraces of Mollie F., housewife suffering from vaginismus, found it difficult to extricate . . . ' "

"No moves back," Lee said, making his first move.

"Make it touch move," Joe said, unsmiling. "Better than that we measure the Galvanic Skin Response. If I catch you thinking about a piece, you got to move it."

"Agreed," Lee said.

Phil laughed: at their seriousness, and at the incongruity which it seemed to him the technical term had in Muneco's mouth.

"What do *you* know about the Galvanic Skin Response?" he said.

"Nothing," Joe said. "Now that you're a psychologist I know nothing about the Galvanic Skin Response. Just as when previously you were a literary critic I knew nothing about literature. And as in consequence of your large record collection, I know nothing about music. If I ever again say anything implying I know anything at all about psychology, may I suffer excruciating pain."

"Okay," Phil laughed. "I'm sorry. You're an intellectual."

Frank returned with his coffee. He knew these two, Lee and Phil, and also Ben, because of their friendship with Joe Muneco. They had graduated from high school with Joe three years ago, and he had continued seeing them, about once a week, since then. They were not particularly interesting, Frank thought, although they were supposed to be bright, and he guessed that this was what Joe saw in them. He could talk to them in Joe's presence, but doubted if he could find anything to say to them under other circumstances. These never arose since he ran into them only when he was with Muneco. Now he returned with the coffee and he saw skinny Phil leaning on the table, his hair mussed, smiling at Muneco, and it struck him what a particularly dull life Phil must lead.

"Hey Phil, you still got it?" he said.

"Got what?"

"Your chastity. Last time I heard, you had still got it."

"Still got it," Phil said, smiling ruefully, but resignedly, as if talking about an amputated arm.

"I can't understand it, Ace," Frank said. "What's the good of going to college if they don't teach you about life? That's why I didn't go to college, because they had no courses in screwing."

"That's right, Ace," Joe mumbled, engrossed in the game.

"You should have gone," Lee said. "You're a great loss to the academic world."

Frank had begun to understand that the things Lee said in jest were no different in tone from the things he said when he was being nasty. It was just the way he talked, everything seeming an insult. He thought for a moment, and decided from the context that Lee was jesting.

"I appreciate this," Frank said.

Frank sat down to kibitz the game, and Phil read the Sunday *Times*. If no one else arrived and even if someone else did, they would spend an hour or two at the chess club, then go downstairs and across the street into the all-night cafeteria (it was too cold in January for the groups to gather in Union Square Park), spend some time there over their coffee, and then go home at four or five o'clock in the morning. They would take Phil, who became tired before anyone else, and who lived the greatest distance (fourteen blocks) from Seventeenth Street, home first, then would walk three blocks uptown to where Lee lived; and finally walk back to the chess club, and three blocks beyond it, to the street on which Frank and Joe lived, in adjoining tenement buildings.

But Ben Brock arrived. Even this wouldn't have made any difference, for Ben Brock often arrived without noticeably disturbing the Saturday night ritual. But Ben Brock arrived with the family car, which meant, if nothing else, that they would all be driven home. It meant however enough more than that on this Saturday night to change the entire texture of the evening.

"Okay," he said, when he saw them around the chess table. "Drop everything. The bus awaits. Let me take you away from all this."

"You park it in the hallway?" Joe said.

"Stop, I can't stand the irony," Ben said. "The car is parked downstairs, three picas from the curb. How many times do I have to tell you, Muneco, I can park a car?"

"Perhaps," Joe said. "As soon as Krafft-Ebing here resigns his lost game."

"Lost game!" Lee said, angrily incredulous. "You talk like a chess player," he said. "But rather than destroy your ego, I agree to a ride in Brock's convertible."

"Anything," Phil said, "for a change of scenery."

Frank sat behind a board, set up the pieces, and beckoned to an old man who sat, half dozing, on a bench. The old man smiled and came toward him.

"Spot me a rook, Kurtz," Frank said.

The old man smiled. "Why not both?" he said. He sat down opposite Frank.

"Hey Crip, you coming?" Joe said to him.

"You college men go for a ride in the car," Frank said. "Driving . . ." (he groped for the cliché) " . . . exerts no appeal on me. I'm gonna teach Kurtz here how to play this game." The others were already outside and down the one landing to the street.

"Okay Ace," Joe said. "Castle early and open up a rook file. I'll see you." He turned and walked toward the door.

"So long Ace," Frank said.

The car was riding north, along First Avenue, toward Forty-second Street.

"Are we going to Times Square?" Phil said.

"If that's what you want," Ben said. "Although I was going to drive you down to Miami. It's time you phony authors and literary critics and psychologists and perverts learned that the East Side of New York is not the center of the world."

"How do you know that?" Joe said.

"Hearsay," Ben said. "But it sounds logical."

"We'll go to Miami next time," Phil yawned. "I've got to wake up early tomorrow."

On the corner of Twenty-sixth Street Ben stopped for a light. Muneco, sitting up front, glanced from the window. "Hey," he said suddenly. Ben, following Joe's eye, saw a figure turn the corner of Twenty-sixth Street and walk out of his range of vision. "Was that Barbara Bedner?" Joe said.

"I don't know," Ben said. "Shall we find out?"

"Who's Barbara Bedner?" Phil said.

"What difference does it make?" Lee said. "It's a girl's name."

The light changed and Ben turned the corner. "I've told you about her," Joe said, peering from the window. The street was dark and he could not be sure. "That's the girl they sent up for the impairment of everybody's morals. The record holder. I didn't know they'd let her out."

"Is it her?" Ben said, slowing down a few yards behind the girl.

"I can't tell," Joe said.

The girl turned off and walked up to a stoop leading to the entrance of a building.

"Well you'd better find out if you're going to find out," Lee said. Joe opened his window.

"Barbara," he called. "Is that Bobbie Bedner?"

The girl turned, startled. It was late at night and she had not heard the car turn the corner. She saw the car but could not see who was inside. The car was a 1950 model, a red convertible. Ben and his father had washed and polished it that same day. It looked like a new car. Bobbie Bedner came, looking very curious, down the stairs and up to the open window.

"Hello," Joe said cheerfully. "I thought it was you. Do you remember me?"

"Yeah," Bobbie said, smiling blankly. "Yeah, I remember you. What's your name?"

Joe grinned. "Joe," he said. "I used to belong to the Werewolves. Remember the Werewolves?"

Bobbie grinned innocently back at him. "Yeah, I remember," she said. "How is everybody? How's Fat Andy?"

"He's fine," Joe said. "He got caught with a stolen car. He won't be around for a while."

"Gee, that's a shame," Bobbie said, meaning it. She laughed. "How's Tony?" she asked.

"I haven't seen him around," Joe said. "I think he's in the army. But where have you been all this while?" he asked her, knowing she would lie, anxious to see how badly. "I haven't seen you for a long time."

Bobbie giggled. "Oh, I been away. I just got back to New York last week."

"You live in this house?" Lee said to her.

For the first time she took notice of the other occupants of the car.

"Yeah," she said, wary, but not unfriendly. Then to Joe: "Who are your friends?"

"Shall I introduce you?" Joe said. She nodded, laughing.

"Bobbie Bedner," Joe said. "This is Brock, the driver and part-owner of the car. This is Miller," and he gestured toward the back of the car, "consultant in pornography, and this is Zand, who is interested in people."

Bobbie laughed, taking her cue from his tone. "What are you doing out so late?" she said. "Just driving around?"

"Yeah," Lee said, anxious to make his presence felt. "How about you?"

"I went to a dance," Bobbie said. "At the Twenty-eighth Street Y."

"Did you have a nice time?" Lee said.

"Not so bad," Bobbie said, laughing.

There was a pause. Ben thought he might as well. She was standing there with her hand resting on the edge of the lowered window.

"Would you like to go for a ride?" he said.

Bobbie laughed uncertainly. "I don't know," she said. "My mother expected me home early, and it's late already."

"So," Joe said, "if it's late already it won't hurt if you come in a little later. Come on," he said persuasively, "we'll go for a ride."

"Where are you going?" the girl asked.

"We don't know," Ben said drily. "That's what makes it so exciting. We might go almost anywhere. Maybe you can help find us a destination."

The girl stood there, her hand on the window. Joe opened the door suddenly and beckoned to her. "Come on," he said. "Any place you say. When you're ready to come back, we'll bring you back."

"It's a nice car," she said.

Joe laughed. He reached out his hand and pulled her one step closer to the car. Then he let go and moved closer to Brock, making room for her. Bobbie Bedner laughed and got into the car.

Ben backed the car to the corner and they were back on First Avenue. He rode to Fourteenth Street and stopped for a light.

"You're looking well," Joe said. "You're looking much better than when I saw you last."

"Yeah," Bobbie said. "I gained a lot of weight."

She had changed. She had gotten into the car, but it wasn't as easy as it once would have been. Joe decided to let DeTorres find out how matters stood with the girl. Although he could have done so, his friends might interpret his efforts as illustrating a lack of sensibility. Or it might give them something to laugh about.

"Drive back to the club," Joe said. "We'll pick up Cripple."

"What club?" Bobbie asked alarmedly. "Who's Cripple?"

"Just a chess club," Joe said soothingly. "You remember Cripple. That's Frank, Frank DeTorres. You remember Frank, don't you?"

"What do you want to see him for?" Bobbie said.

"We don't want to see him," Joe said. "We just thought after all this time, he would be glad to see you. He won't hurt you."

Bobbie laughed. "I know he won't hurt me," she said. "I just thought we were going for a ride."

"We will," Ben said, knowing what was on Muneco's mind. "Just as soon as we pick up Frank."

He turned left on Seventeenth Street, pulled up in front of Gelber's Chess Club, and parked the car.

Frank was happy to have Muneco back and happier still when he saw who was with him. The presence of Bobbie Bedner, he felt sure, would liven up the evening. He thought immediately of his pigeon coop and its steam-heating. When Ben Brock came upstairs, after parking the car, he found Frank and Joe seated near the window, Frank talking earnestly to Bobbie, and Lee and Phil standing some distance away leaning against a chess table. He walked over to these two.

"Set 'em up," he said to Lee. "You can have the white pieces."

"I'll have to beat you in five moves," Lee apologized. "Don Juan is operating, and I don't know how long we'll be here."

"If he's got to operate," Ben said, "you may be here a long time. If this girl is the girl she's cracked up to be she should be on her hands and knees begging for it."

Joe came over.

"How does it look?" Lee said.

"I don't know," Joe said. "Frank is trying to get her to go to his place but she doesn't like pigeon coops."

"Ask her about bar-bell clubs," Phil said. "I've got the key to the club. There won't be anyone up there this time of night."

"I'll keep you posted," Joe said. He walked back to Frank and the girl.

"Your move," Lee said.

Ben looked at him. "I can't understand your hanging around, Miller," he said to him, "in the hope of laying a broad who has already been on intimate terms with everyone in the neighborhood. Haven't you got any standards?"

"Very funny," Lee said. "In this respect I'm like you. When it comes to women, anywhere and anytime."

"Are you looking forward to this prospect?" Ben said to Phil.

"Why not?" Phil said.

"Hell," Ben said, "you've had it so long you might as well save it for your wife. Listen to me," he said earnestly, "and don't throw yourself away on this harlot. Somewhere, there's a sweet, young, innocent girl who has been ordained by heaven to . . . "

"Balls to you," Phil said.

Muneco returned.

" 'The outlook wasn't brilliant for the Mudville nine that day' " Joe began, with every intention of completing the poem.

"Can it," Ben said. "What's the latest?"

"She met a psychiatrist in reform school," Joe said. "He told her the reason she did what she did was her father died when she was six years old and she missed male attention. She agrees with his diagnosis and she's turning over a new leaf."

"You mean all the psychiatrist did was tell her?" Phil asked professionally.

"I don't know," Joe said. "She's been away for two years. Maybe she underwent intensive therapy. Whatever happened, she's metamorphosized."

"So?" Lee said.

"We're going to take her downstairs, try to soften her up," Joe said. "Give me the keys to the car," he said to Ben.

"You going somewhere?" Lee said suspiciously.

"Hey," Muneco laughed, taking the keys from Ben. "You think we'd run out on you, Miller? We can't leave you. This whole party is in Phil's honor. After Phil lays her we're going to nail her over his fireplace for a trophy." He jingled the keys at DeTorres and walked to the door. Frank got up, took the girl by the hand, and followed Muneco. She went without protesting but she did not look happy.

"Does Cripple have a driver's license?" Lee said.

Ben nodded.

"If those guys pull anything," Lee said, "I'm going to make Muneco pay for it."

"You wouldn't tell his mother, would you?" Ben said.

"No," Lee said. "I'll tell his girl. I'll call his girl and let her know how Muneco spends his Saturday nights." He looked toward the window. Phil, following his glance, walked over and looked out.

"The car's still there," Phil said. "Save your money."

"Your move," Ben said.

Lee moved.

"How long we going to wait here?" he said.

"Give them five more minutes," Ben said.

Phil walked over and looked out the window.

"Hey Zand," Ben called to him.

"What?"

"You're basing your life on a lie," Ben said. "You want to become a clinical psychologist. You want to help the maladjusted. Now here is this girl who has been abnormal, at least quantitatively, but has since been returned to normalcy by a practicing psychiatrist. Instead of trying to keep her there you're party to a scheme whose aim is to tear down her defenses and re-sink her in the morass of abnormality."

He looked sternly at Phil; then disgustedly shook his head.

"Look," Phil said. "Better her than me. She's neurotic from too much of it and I'm neurotic from too little. It's her or me. And I've got my career at stake."

"He thinks it's the panacea," Lee sneered. "Once he gets laid, he's solved all his problems. What an idiot."

"Okay," Ben said. "I resign. Let's go downstairs."

They got up and put on their coats. "Hey, Kurtz," Ben called to the old man who had been sitting on a bench watching them. "A lineup. Anybody else, we're charging two-fifty. For you, a buck and a half. How about it?"

The old man coughed up some phlegm and spit it into a handkerchief. He was unimpressed. "If I couldn't do better," he said, standing and stretching himself, "I'd shoot myself."

The three left the club.

Ben looked in at the back window of the car. Joe and Frank were in the front seat with the girl between them. Frank had his arm around the girl and was bending over her. Ben motioned the others to wait. After a while the girl worked an arm free from behind her and pushed Frank's face away. Ben walked to the side of the car and knocked on the window. Muneco opened the door.

"Come on in," he said. "We'll go for a ride."

Lee and Phil got into the back of the car. Ben squeezed into the driver's seat. There were four people in the front of the car. Joe moved over, making room for Ben, at the same time pushing Bobbie closer to Frank. Frank was talking into her ear.

"What's the matter baby? Don't you want to kiss me? Just a little kiss?"

"No-o" the girl said, indicating that she had said it many times before. Frank leaned over her and kissed her. After a great many seconds had passed she pushed his face away.

"I don't know what's happened to the way you kiss," Frank said to her. "It's not like you used to. Who ever heard of a girl kissing with her mouth closed?"

"I don't want to kiss you," Bobbie said primly.

"Two years ago," Frank said, "I wouldn't kiss you. I would screw you. That's more fun, isn't it? What's happened to you in two years?"

"I told you," Bobbie said laughing. Her laugh was heavy, like her voice, and unsteady, but it was not the way she used to laugh. "I don't do that anymore."

"For nobody?"

Bobbie laughed. "I don't know," she said. "But not for you."

"I'm truly sorry to hear that," Frank said. "I guess I'll go home and go to bed. Drive me home, Brock," he said. He leaned over the girl.

Ben made a right turn on Third Avenue and drove to Twentieth Street. He stopped once for a light. On Twentieth a sanitation truck was double parked and he slowed down to squeeze past it. During all this time, Frank, using all his art, was kissing the girl.

"You're home," Ben said.

"Yeah," Frank said. "We're home. Come on," he said to the girl. "We'll go upstairs to the pigeon coop and have a party."

"No," Bobbie said. "I don't like pigeon coops."

"Do you like parties?" Joe said.

"Not that kind," she said, laughing slyly.

"Look," Frank said. "Look what I got for you." He took her hand and pulled it to him, but she wrenched it free.

"I don't want it," she said, annoyed. "Leave me alone."

Ben became slightly annoyed by the proceedings. Not by the proceedings as much as by their lack of success.

"All right Frank, you drew a blank," he said. "We forgive you. If you can't convince this girl, she cannot be convinced. Go to bed." He looked at Bobbie. "I'll drive you home."

"Okay," Frank said. "But I don't know what's happened to this girl. She goes away for a short time and comes back with a whole new system of values. It's something for you college men to figure out."

He got out of the car.

"Don't give up the ship," he said. "A little patience. If this girl is Bobbie Bedner you should lay her before daybreak. I'm going to get some sleep."

The girl laughed as Frank turned his back and walked away. "Don't believe him," she said confidentially. "I don't do any of those things. He's just talking." She directed this primarily at Brock in whom she had mistaken the annoyance with DeTorres' methods for sympathy. Joe smiled. Ben started the car.

"Who's going home first?" he said.

"Home?" The girl was indignant. "I thought we were going for a ride."

"You still want to go for a ride?" Ben said.

"Sure. Let's go to Coney Island."

"No," Joe said to her. "Let's go lift some weights. Phil has the key to his bar-bell club."

The girl laughed. "Ah, die young," she said pleasantly. She recognized that the only serious threat had been Frank, and he was gone. She relaxed now, and looked forward to a good time being chauffeured around.

"You can drive me home," Phil said, seeing the futility of remaining. "I've got to wake up early tomorrow."

"How about you, Miller?" Ben said.

"No hurry," Lee said. "As a matter of fact you can take me home after you drop her off."

The girl laughed. "You ain't gonna miss nothin'," she said.

Joe laughed. "You're a dead pigeon, Miller," he said. "Even this dumb broad reads you like a book. You're shallower than a wading pool."

"That's extremely funny, Muneco," Lee said.

"I'm not a dumb broad," Bobbie said good-naturedly.

"Then what are you a dumb?" Joe said.

"Oh, die young," the girl said.

"Where would you like to go *besides* Coney Island?" Ben said.

"What's the matter with Coney Island?"

"There is nothing open and nobody in Coney Island in January," Ben explained patiently. "So I suggest you suggest something else."

"Let's go where there's excitement," Bobbie said. "Maybe we can see a fight somewhere."

"We have just the thing for you," Joe said. "Take her to Brooklyn," he said to Ben.

"That's right," Ben said. "Brooklyn's a wild town."

"What's so wild about Brooklyn?" the girl said.

"Everything goes positively smash in Brooklyn," Ben said. "There's a fight on every street corner. Trunk murders take place in front of your eyes. Also, there's a little cafeteria right across the bridge where we sometimes sober up after a devil-may-carish Saturday night."

"What's *his* name?" Bobbie said to Joe.

"That's Brock," Joe said. "Author and professional chauffeur. Why, do you like him?"

Bobbie laughed. "He's all right," she said.

"Brock has made a conquest," Lee called from the back of the car.

"I guess you're not interested," Joe said. "Maybe we should drive you home."

"Maybe you should," Lee said. "As a matter of fact, I'm sure you should. I've got a date tomorrow night with this girl I just met. I can use some sleep."

"You poor kid, I'll bet she knocks all hell out of you," Ben said.

Ben turned left, a block before the bridge which led to Brooklyn, and brought the car back to First Avenue. He left Phil on the corner of Third Street, and drove Lee to his home on Sixth Street between First and Second Avenues. He was tired, and got to thinking of the difficulty he would have in finding a parking space.

"Who's next?" he said.

He looked at Bobbie, who was about to protest.

"My old man gets up early in the morning," he lied. "He needs the car to get to work. I've got to bring it back before six o'clock."

"Gee," the girl said. "Your father works on Sundays?"

"Yeah," Ben said. "He's a preacher."

"Gee, that's tough," the girl said.

"Take me home first," Joe said, winking at Ben. "She said she likes you. Don't you like him, Bobbie?"

"Yeah, I like him," Bobbie said. "But I just wanted to drive around."

"You first," Ben said to her. He drove her home.

She got out of the car and turned toward them.

"Well, so long," she said. She laughed suddenly. "I had a very nice time."

"Glad to hear it," Joe said. "We must get together sometime and do the whole thing over again."

Ben leaned over and waved to her. "So long Bobbie," he said.

"Bye-bye Brock," she said. "It was nice meeting you." She walked up the stoop and was gone, into the building.

They sat there for a while, not talking.

"A hundred per cent American girl," Ben said finally. "I'm convinced you had her pegged wrong."

"A hundred and sixty times," Joe said absently, "in three days. That must have been one hell of a psychiatrist."

"He wasn't an East Side boy," Ben said, shaking his head. "He performed a great disservice to an entire neighborhood. He dissolved the last trace of communal endeavor to which we could proudly point."

"Yeah," Joe said, leaning back on the seat, his hands locked behind his head. "Drive around to Seventeenth Street. What we've got to do now is get some coffee."

(From Western Review)

FAREWELL, SWEET LOVE

BY PRISCILLA HEATH

*T*HE GREAT SMACKS of things, bearing down, come all at once sometimes; the whole crazy world swings out and surrounds you — an enormous new country you've got to without knowing it was there. That's what happened to me at Ashe's party, and after, the last time I had with Bo. I've thought about it, and straightened some of it out in my mind; but Ashe's music keeps driving around in my head and I still have the desperate feeling I had then that there's something I can't get hold of but have simply got to fight. I've tried telling Bo about in it letters — it only upsets him. Finally I said I was all right again, not to worry. But I'm not all right. Besides, not knowing when I'll see Bo again keeps snarling me up until sometimes I think I'm half crazy. Meems and I could have talked it through. When we'd be in our beds with the lights out, and distance between, all kinds of monsters got whittled away to bearable size. At least we felt better for trying. But Meems and I won't be talking again, so this is what I've decided. I'll write the whole thing down, all the different ways I felt and what I did, to see if that will help.

It's no use asking why Meems got killed. Some other car could have been just there — but some other car wasn't. Or after the concert Meems might not have noticed her friend; or her friend might have been going on somewhere else so couldn't have offered to drive Ashe and Mimi home. But things happened the way they did. Meems went out of the room that night, her eyes all shiny because Ashe was waiting downstairs, and I never saw her again.

The day of the funeral Ashe was in the hospital still. If they hadn't given him dope he'd have fought his way out, he said, with his one good arm. I think he would have, and gotten there, too, in spite of its being so far. I know it upset *me* more, not being able to go on account of having to play that night, than it would have to see Meems dead. The next day Ashe was back in classes, though, and already saying, whenever he met anyone who'd known Meems pretty well, "Let's have a party." I was shocked — until I remembered I'd told him myself how whenever Meems came back from a lesson that looked like the end, or had practiced for hours without seeming to get ahead, she'd be like a ghost creeping in. After hiding her fiddle away in the closet, without answering whatever I'd said, she'd wander over toward that rug her mother gave me when she came to pack up the things, and just stand. In a while she'd push out her chin. "All right," she'd say, "let's have a party!" — and we'd go for a coke or nibble on something we had in the room. But those "parties" didn't last very long. Pretty soon the fiddle would be out, or sometimes just the music, and Meems would be ready to start all over again. Maybe that's all Ashe was thinking about to begin with, or maybe the music was already working up in his mind. Anyway he kept at us and at us. None of us really wanted to, but we all felt so sorry for Ashe that when he kept on insisting we finally said we would. Then he noticed the sign in the subway about chartering trolleys and talked us into that part of it, too. By the time Bo got word from his draft board, the arrangements couldn't be changed — at least that's what the trolleycar people said. I didn't like it, and said so at first, but as the time got shorter and shorter I was almost glad. Anything, I thought, just anything, to help me get through that terrible last day of Bo's. I didn't know I'd be knocked wide open instead.

First of all, the rain made me late. While it lasted it came down smash, like a *tutti* finale, and my raincoat was lent. I tried doing solfege, because my time in the practice-room was up, but I couldn't. So I stood in the hall fidgeting, remembering for no reason how Meems had liked walnuts, but not calling a cab because I thought the rain would stop. Finally it did and I opened my case again to be sure Ashe's music was really in. I was all right when I started.

Then, on the way, somehow the ribbon fell off that was holding back my hair so that unless I held it with my hand it was all over my shoulders and half across my face as I ran. That's when I first felt queer, as if losing the ribbon had made something else go snap, too, inside, and sent me awash. Already I hadn't enough breath but I ran.

At Paine, I missed the lights. Tires were making a dismal hiss on the streets, they were still so wet, and the rainwater rushing into the sewers was almost as bad. "Meems," I said, "Meems!" — without quite knowing I would — and afterwards got angry watching how the pink and purple pigeons would come fluffling in all stupid and safe and then, as if nothing had happened, poke back. I kept trying to beat the light, cars were coming too fast, I had to wait. By the time I got over, and on a bit, I was running again so hard I all but smacked down a draggled old woman hooing grapeseeds — at least it was grapes she was holding — onto the sidewalk. Then I saw the rainbow; it seemed too bright. And I scowled, I remember, at where the sky, hanging low, looked like a place you could curl up in and be warm but never, never was. When the clock struck I thought I couldn't run any more but our trolley wouldn't stop there long so I had to.

Bo was waiting, of course, his silly head almost into his book. So many people were milling around I had to bounce quite close because he hadn't seen me come. While he let the book slide down into his raincoat pocket he stayed deadpan. Then his mouth pulled tight. "Why, Shelley," he said, "your hair!" — pretending to be shocked and rebukeful.

"It fell in a puddle," I said — I was panting so hard the words came fuzzy — "and it matched." Bo liked that skirt ("a nice contralto shade of corn," he called it) and I'd been hours finding ribbon the same.

"Ah!" Bo said. "A wig!" And he pulled, not hard.

"No, you clown, the *ribbon!*" Every breath still hurt, as if I was dragging sand through my throat, but that wasn't all. I began to get panicky. I'd been wanting to say so much but when I tried I couldn't even remember what it was. So I thought, what's the use? All that water swirling and roaring away so fast in the gutter made it seem, somehow, as if I couldn't ever catch up now, before Bo was gone, with all I needed to say. But I'd gotten there. Bo didn't say anything either. He took my case, with Ashe's music in it, and my hand. From there it wasn't far; we had time just to walk on down. We'd already seen the trolley, and the crowd of them, waiting outside by the kiosk, when Bo said, "Well, are you ready?"

"I guess so," I said. "I wouldn't do it for anyone but Ashe and Meems, though. Not the way I feel right now." I didn't mean that: when you've promised to play, you play. But all at once I felt how empty and futile Ashe's music was. I might not have made such a mess of things later if I'd said that to Bo then. But I was the only one who'd seen that music. Even Ashe hadn't wanted to hear it until the actual time, so to talk it over with Bo, before, and say how bad I thought it was, didn't seem quite fair.

"Anyone but Ashe," Bo said, "and it would give me the pip, too." He squeezed before he let go of my hand.

Of course it was Ashe who saw us first and came out from the others to meet us. He'd found a top hat the way he said he would and had something new, at least different, for his sling. He took my hand and stood looking at me so long I felt like someone's stuffed salmon hung onto the wall. Then he said, "Shelley!" — very low. It was all I could do not to squirm.

"Yes," I said, "me! All here and complete!" I didn't feel that way, though, and by then I *knew* it was more than the ribbon. But I tried. I'd tell Ashe about that puddle, I decided, and make it funny, and maybe it would help if we all laughed. So I started. But Ashe didn't hear; he'd finally let go and was hanging on to Bo instead.

Some of the others had come over and I said "Hi!" all around and as soon as Molly winked I felt better. "That's very swish black he's got for his sling," she said. "Now I wonder — " We didn't need any more; it's a standing joke all over the School how Ashe never buys a thing he wears if he can possibly borrow or beg it. He's not poor, like Bo; that's just the way he is. He'd put up more than his share for the trolley, though, a lot more. We knew he couldn't afford so much but we'd finally stopped trying to talk him down, deciding, behind his back, that Mimi's dying, especially right before his eyes like that, had left him not quite responsible and he had to be humored. It had hit all of us, naturally, pretty hard but even I, though in some ways I'd been closer, knew it must be a thousand times worse for Ashe. I'd never liked Ashe a lot as a person, and had had a struggle to keep quiet about it when Meems fell for him so hard, but you have to say this — he's good. Really good. We all think he'll get there one of these days, with his playing, if his arm gets well. It had better. It would be so terribly too much if besides losing Meems he had to lose that.

Well, we stood there waiting for Ashe, talking a little but not much, and watching people start for our trolley, see the sign or get told it wasn't whatever car they wanted, and go away. I couldn't help thinking how probably everyone standing there with me knew about Bo and me the way we'd all known, without knowing, about Meems and Ashe, and it made me self-conscious — especially when Hooper said what a duck I was to go through with it. I *would* be mad, I said, if no fiddle turned up. Then Inge, in that slow, bad English she likes to affect, dragged out, "Oh, the fiddle will find. You'll see." No, I said, after working us up to it, Ashe would hardly let the whole thing collapse on account of no fiddle. And of course he didn't. What I couldn't ever have dreamed up, myself, even knowing the state he was in, was the thing he'd actually done. Before long our motorman poked out his head and shouted. Somebody yelled, "Break it up, Ashe. Come on!" and the rest of us started along. Then I looked back, and caught Bo's eye, and waited. In the crush by the door I got bumped, I remember, by the book in his pocket and started to ask what it was only just then I had another idea.

"I want to see that sign for myself," I said, and pushed through to where I could. SPECIAL — there it was in big letters, but it made me feel even worse about Meems, somehow, and almost ashamed I'd gone. Also Bo was looking a little stern, I thought, when I got back, as if maybe it *had* been childish of me. I suppose that's how I came to take such a good long look at the trolley. Orange was what it had started out to be but the paint was peeling and, in places, almost black. It made me think of wrecks I'd seen in those auto "graveyards" garages sometimes have. Then I stepped up, and in, and wanted to laugh because the motorman matched. Not orange and peeling, of course, but dingy and grim in the face and sort of ramshackle all over. Since we were "special" you might have thought he'd try to be jolly. Instead he glared and lashed his arms, all the time growling under his breath, trying to hurry us in. At first I thought that was *very* funny. Then the door slapped shut and I got the swift punch you feel at the pit of your stomach when all at once whatever you're about to do seems a dreadful mistake and you know there's no way out. But as soon as the car started things got funny again. A lot of us still weren't as far as the seats, so when the lunge came we nearly fell. No one else was laughing, though, so I stopped as soon as I could.

Bo and I sat down together. They were wicker seats, double ones facing front on each side of the aisle except for the benches front and back that faced in. I was trying to decide where I'd better stand while I played when Bo giggled. "This car's going to fall apart," he said; "it can't help it. Did Ashe put that in the contract, too?"

It really *was* terrific, the rattling and whirring and grinding that trolley made, so I said, "Why, certainly. Didn't he tell you? Didn't you know this was junk already when Noah began building the Ark?"

Most of the others were talking along like Bo and me but as soon as I thought about it I could see that no one was easy; we all kept looking at Ashe. The way he stood up front, his good hand gripping the pole, made me think of a stupidly earnest old print in the Library back home called "Columbus at Sea." In spite of being in love with him Meems would have seen what I meant and I wanted to tell her. Then I thought how crazy, because if she hadn't died poor Ashe wouldn't ever have stood like that there. I suppose we'd been expecting him to take over, set some kind of tone — it was his party, after all — and when all we had of him was his back it was awkward. We weren't sure whether to talk at all, or if we did which way we ought to act. Bo decided for us. All of a sudden, up he pushed, giving out over the racket the trolley was making: "Mesdames, messieurs: at-*ten*-SHUN!" He did "mesdames, messieurs" with flourishes, very French, and ended with a snarl like a drill sergeant's. Bo is so funny anyway, and we were all so tense, that it worked. We giggled, and a few began to clap, and someone yelled, "Rah, Uncle! Rah, Sam! Rah, rah, Uncle Sam!" It seemed all right until I looked at Ashe. He'd let go of the pole and dropped his face into his hand.

"Bo," I said, trying to stop him, but he went right on. "Listen," he said, with everyone straining to hear. "listen, my children — a secret." That's the way he looked, too, as if he really had one to tell. After a few finicking dabs at his raincoat, as if it were the skirt of a gown, he took a lady-like pose with his hand on the seat-back, breathed in deep, and began. Style! In spite of all the stopping and starting on account of the trolley ahead, that's what he gave us — pure style. At first he was chanting falsetto. Then, turning man, he did it all the ways there are — hymn, aria, ballad, blues. I kept looking at Ashe. He didn't move, just stood with his back to us and his face in his hand. It made me uncomfortable but I couldn't decide what I ought to do so, after a while, I stopped looking. Bo didn't seem to notice Ashe at all. Block after block after block he kept singing, all the way to Central Square, and I'd never heard him handle his voice so well. One of the funniest things was the way he mispronounced to make the rhyme:

The secret of the trolley car
Is pah'r, pah'r, pah'r.

That's all there was to what he sang; just that, over and over, but every time his manner changed it seemed new because, each time, you still felt it wasn't Bo but Bo pretending to be someone else.

Until you get used to it the way Bo's head is shaped makes him look ridiculous and he's not much taller than I am. That's part of what makes him so comic. I know that's how he meant to be when he started — all that fuss with the raincoat! — but before he was through he was different. I didn't know what he was, exactly, but I knew "funny" wasn't it at all.

I'd been watching Bo so long that when I finally looked out of the window everything seemed queer. It took me a minute to see what had happened. It wasn't only that we'd gotten to where I didn't recognize shops or street corners, it was getting dark and everyone's lights had gone on but ours. Meeting cars with their headlights on and passing between neons and store-windows and blinking movie signs, there we were — all dim. What is this? I thought. Are we real? Just for an instant I felt my scalp begin to crawl. But then we met a lighted trolley and, as if we'd caught the brightness there our own lights went on. That's the first time I noticed, though it must have happened before, that the ones farthest front had left their seats to stand closer and even Ashe had crept out of his shell. His good hand was in his pocket now. With his chin on his chest he was leaning again the pole, swaying whenever the car did, and seemed to be holding himself up with his eyes. Those big gray eyes of his were fastened on Bo, right about at the ear. I'd never thought of Ashe as mean or vindictive but he made me think, then, of a witch putting a curse on. I tried to tell myself it was all in my mind but I couldn't get over the feeling that, just at that instant, whatever it was coming out of his eyes wanted to see Bo hurt. He was angry with Bo for singing, I decided, and wanted him punished. But all at once I saw blood, and Bo's head crushed in, the way I knew Mimi's had been. I didn't just think it; I saw it — knowing all the time it was something I'd made up myself. Yet I shivered, and once or twice my stomach turned over. Then Bo began a clever off-beat variation and I was all right again — except still weak from all that running. And my hands had gone cold. I began to work them to bring them back, thinking how too bad, in a way, Bo was so good. I was ashamed already of trying to make Ashe out a witch and I felt sorry about his music. After Bo, the very best I could do, would fall pretty flat. He'd find out sometime but I didn't want to be the one to do it to him, and especially not at his party. So I began to hope that Inge was wrong and no fiddle would find. We'd almost come to the Square by then and Bo was working into a fine finale. He got plenty of hand, and then some, when he finished but he didn't do any bowing. Perfectly deadpan he sat down beside me and dropped his hand over mine. It seemed as if I'd never understood before what a long, long time he'd be gone.

Ashe must have been telling the motorman this was the place. Anyway the car stopped and Ashe got out. Hooper and Bo and I went up toward the door. A few of the others tried to put on a mock ovation for Bo, but Bo just grinned and made motions to shush them down. The motorman's watch was out and he'd hunched himself over it, muttering. "He's a ghoul," I whispered, and Bo nodded.

There are three pawnshops, side by side almost, just the way Ashe had said. We watched him go into them all. Bo's singing had certainly loosened things up because each time, when Ashe came out with no fiddle, there'd be window-banging and boos. Ashe must have noticed, but you wouldn't have known. People going by on the sidewalk looked at us, but not Ashe. Pretty soon a trolley waiting behind us began dinging its cross little bell, and the ghoul stood up. His watch was still in his hand but that's not where he was looking. When Ashe, instead of coming straight out from the third place, started back toward one of the ones he'd been into before, the ghoul shoved Hooper and brandished his watch out the door. "Hey there, you! Mister!" He needn't have bothered. Ashe never stopped and the ghoul snarled at Hooper, "Damn fool don't think he can hock that hat, does he?"

"Hardly," Hooper said. We were shopping around for a fiddle and only the best would do. With a snort, and a simply punishing look at Bo, the ghoul flung up his hands. "More o' that? Sufferin' God!" Then he hunched himself over his watch again, muttering.

Hooper touched Bo's chest with one finger. "For committing Art," he said sternly, "they shall strike thee down."

"Oh, shall they?" Bo said.

Someone sang out just then and I looked, and saw Ashe coming with a fiddle case, and knew I was glad. I would have reached for it when he came in except that he seemed to be holding all of us off with his eyes. The trolley started, of course, the first possible instant, but Ashe stayed where he was, hugging that case as if he'd never let go, and the rest of us stayed where *we* were and watched him. There was a cold and yet excited look on his face that no one seemed to dare to interfere with, not even Bo. But I wanted that fiddle myself now; I was all keyed up and ready. Partly to keep myself from snatching it I backed onto one of the benches and went to work on my hands; partly I was beginning to get disgusted with Ashe. But that didn't stop me from wanting to play. I'd practiced and practiced that music, never really feeling a thing, but perhaps I would now, I thought; maybe it's good after all. So I waited, getting more and more impatient and fluttery, until finally Ashe came over with the fiddle and without saying a word, or even smiling, held it out.

I found the case, later, on a seat farther back so someone must have taken it from me. All I really remember is that first I said, "Why, Ashe, it's lovely!" and afterwards saw the mark, a tiny, worked-over scratch I couldn't mistake. "Oh!" I said. "Oh, Ashe!" But Ashe wouldn't look. How or when he'd gotten it I had no idea; I'd seen it go with the other things. But he had, and what did he want me to do? Should I pop out my eyes and say, "What a coincidence, kids!" Should I trickle away in tears? Or hadn't he thought I'd know? Even if I'd been able to guess, it wouldn't have mattered; I hadn't a muscle in me I could have made move. With nothing ahead, on account of being stopped so long, we really rocked. There was even more noise than before. But I heard Bo say, "Try it! try it! See if it works!" — "All right!" I said, "I *will!*" I didn't think how it sounded — as if I was angry with *him.* But I was angry, all right. I could hardly breathe. Ashe hadn't any right to be *that* crazy. When I thought how he'd gone there ahead and planted it, and then, with all those people in the trolley behind wanting to get home to their suppers, how he'd played it out for suspense, I couldn't even try to be sorry for him. And what was he doing now? Just standing, knowing I'd caught him out and yet looking away, not letting me know what to do. Well, I tuned it. Somehow, in spite of that moaning, decrepit old trolley, I did. Bo had set up my stand, with the music, about halfway along the aisle; I expected to find him waiting there to hold it. Instead he'd walked away. I asked Hooper. Someone had to steady it for me and he was the nearest. With Bo gone, and Ashe off by himself loving his misery and gloating over his secret, probably, the way he would if he was listening to records alone in the dark, I almost lost my nerve. But there I was with Mimi's fiddle — I had to do something. "I want this music played the first time," Ashe had told me, "on a moving trolley, at rush hour, on a pawnshop fiddle." I hadn't seen then, and never did until afterwards, what that had to do with Meems, but to humor him I'd said yes, I'd try. All right, I decided as I stood there, I would! I'd let Ashe and everyone else find out how crude his music was and then tell them the fiddle was Mimi's and see what they thought about that. If they had any sense, they'd despise him.

It was pretty much of a mess to look at. With his right hand bandaged and half of the arm in a cast, he'd had to do it all with his left. First of all, there was *SONATA FOR MEEMS* scraggled across the top in his sad attempt at block printing. I looked at that until I couldn't see it, and looked once more at Ashe (he was being Columbus again only this time he hadn't his hat and I couldn't find where he'd laid it), and then I looked back and began. I never hated a person as much as I hated Ashe then. I hated him for what he couldn't help: for being in that innocent car and getting crashed into, and for throwing himself down afterwards on the highway with the bone pushing out of his arm (he'd told and told us about it) beside Meems who wasn't quite dead. And I hated him for what he could have helped, like writing that music, and planning the party just to use us, but mostly for wanting to torture himself by dragging back the fiddle he'd never heard anyone play but Meems. I was hating the trolley-car people, too, for not being wiling to change when we found out this would be Bo's last day because, once the Army swallowed him, he'd never be Bo again — not the same. I even tried to hate Bo for letting me do it when all the time I'd kept insisting to myself that for Mimi's sake, if it would help Ashe any, I would. What it really was, with Bo, was his walking away like that for no reason. Well, all of that kept building and building inside me until every so often, when I'd come to a little, I'd be surprised to find myself still playing. I'd heard that thing so many times already it never occurred to me, mad the way I was, to listen to what I was doing. Violin unaccompanied is difficult anywhere and as much as came through to me, in all that hubbub, just seemed like one more squall and screech of the trolley. It was lucky I *could* toss it off like that, too, without using much more than the top of my mind, because I'd decided in the very beginning that though it would be easier I mustn't do it sitting down. There wouldn't be a chance for the music then, buried under where no one could see, let alone hear. After what Ashe did I was tempted to, anyhow; but I couldn't. I wasn't going to cheat even if Ashe did and besides, if no one could hear, how would they know how bad it was? So the lurches, throwing me back, kept making my legs bump. That jarred me so badly that, each time, I'd bungle or miss. I had to keep snapping my head, too, because I'd forgotten my hair and some fell onto my face and got tickling. Molly came with some pins but couldn't find a way to grip me right and they didn't stay. Near the end the notes got more wobbly and crowded and by then I was trembling so, and so weak, I thought I couldn't keep going. But I did. It serves you right, I began thinking at Ashe, and when I get through I'll tell them. But I didn't.

I hadn't seen him come close but the minute I stopped there he was, trying to grab my hand. It startled me, too, to see his face working out through the stiffness he'd been hiding it with so long. The others stamped and shouted, hugging us both, and Bo pushed in, louder than anyone, saying how terrific the music was and I'd put it across just right. The surprise of it knocked me dumb. Liars! I thought; you absolute fools! — and disentangled myself as soon as I could. I put Mimi's fiddle away and left the case (recognizing that, too!) on top of the music and then, still shaking all over, I folded up my stand myself. When I saw how the others still gushed over Ashe I decided that I, at least, didn't have to play up any longer. The first chance I could make I told Bo I was leaving. "What's the matter?" he wanted to know. He looked so blank and so foolish I laughed in his face. "I just am," I said, "but you go on with the others, Bo. Go ahead." They were planning to end with spaghetti and meatballs somewhere and I could see he didn't want to miss that. But for me, the way I felt then, just thinking about food was almost too much. Of course I still intended to go to the train — some of the others would be there so Bo wouldn't be hard to find — but I didn't tell him that.

Well, Bo gave me a look I couldn't be sure about and went over to Ashe. I was too ashamed, later, to ask what he said but whatever it was must have been pretty final because before the others knew what was up, the car had stopped. Ashe simply hovered. Just at the door, after I'd said a fairly polite good-bye, he held up his hand, the good one, over both of us and said twice, once for each: "God bless you." I looked him straight in the eye. "You clown!" I said,

sent him east, or I got some really good money for playing somewhere, it could easily be years, I kept thinking, before I'd see him
again. But at least we'd have this, and after we'd been munching
our pizza a while I didn't care so much any more whether we agreed
about Ashe's music or not. Then I happened to look and there that
woman still was, going dig, dig, dig with her eyes. I tried to outstare
her. That time I couldn't. The next time she started mumbling
away to her friend. I tried to hear if it was us she was talking about
but, close as their table was, she didn't say a word I could catch. I
did see her hands, though. Some people have a hobby of trying to
keep their fingernails about half an inch too long. Hers were like
that with here and there a patch of red polish. The rest had chipped
off. So far, I hadn't noticed either of the women paying any attention to the boy (he didn't like his pizza) and I was glad to see that
he didn't bother with them. He watched other people and seemed
to be thinking things over by himself. If one of them had been his
mother, sooner or later she'd have wiped off the thread of tomato
hanging down from his chin.

Our second pizza was nearly gone when someone put a nickle in.
The music came lush and sexy, but somehow that's not what I felt.
We'd been late the night before, saying our real goodbyes, and Bo
had had his trunk to pack after that. I hadn't thought, until I looked
at him with that music playing, how terribly, terribly tired he must
be. Then I began to notice his eyes. Almost while I watched they
went dull, and seemed to grow small, as if he weren't with me any
more. Quite suddenly, it seemed, lines like being old had come into
his face and it frightened me: I'd never seen him like that before.
Perhaps, underneath, I knew already how wrong I was because I
remember that right away I began asking myself what I could possibly have said, or done. "What is it, Bo?" I said. "What's the
matter?" But Bo just looked at me a way he never had, very distant
but somehow not cold, and I didn't know what to do. I tried to
think what *he* might be thinking, about his voice, perhaps, and how
hard he'd worked. But as soon as I'd started that, all the things that
could happen seemed to rush in on me at once. I tried to get hold
of myself. Instead, the horrible flash came back, the one I'd had on
the trolley of Bo's queer nice head all crushed and bloody the way

Mimi's had been. I had to do something to stop it, so — "What's that book you've been reading?" I asked him. *"The Idiot,"* Bo said. "It's not bad." For some reason it seemed wrong, and very sad, that he could be reading a book I'd never heard of, and at the same time the name of it struck me funny and I wanted to laugh. "You mean like that woman over there?" I said, trying not to. "No, infant, more like you." What did he mean by that? "Look, Bo," I said, reaching over with my hand, "is it because of the way I acted?" He didn't say anything but he smiled, and I tried to smile back. I didn't know what else there was to do because I still didn't know what the trouble was. So we sat there, not talking, until I felt those eyes again. I turned; I couldn't seem to help it. Instead of looking away she went for our faces, first Bo's and then mine, as if she'd caught us stealing her purse or something, and then sneered down, with a twitch of her rubbery old lip, to where we were holding hands on the table-top. I gave her my back but I wouldn't let go. Bo didn't either. Then the music stopped and the little boy, as if that was what he'd been waiting for, said, "Babs?" — nicely but quite loud. I wanted to see which Babs was but, this time, all I did was hold my breath. I couldn't hear any answer.

"Babs, if you pour — "

"No!"

"But, Babs — " He only sounded eager, not whiny or showoffish at all.

"No, I said. No!" That came through teeth; you could tell.

I shouldn't have, but I turned my head. I was right. Babs was the one who'd gotten herself into such a simmer over Bo and me. She was giving the boy a glare that those buck teeth of hers made look really vicious but he didn't seem frightened; puzzled more. She must have noticed me move because she took her meanness off the boy and began again on me. That made the boy look, too, and without thinking, I smiled. He seemed relieved, as if I'd told him, all right — go ahead, and he tried once more. "If you pour water on a dead squirrel," he said, very determined this time, and very shrill, "will it bring him alive?" It could have been funny but of course it wasn't. Not then; not for me. Besides, that poor lamb was really hoping, as if he had a particular squirrel in mind, and his face got all tight while he waited. Babs waited, too, long enough to fix back her eyes on him. Then she drew up her hand and gave him a slap that knocked his head sideways, twisting his neck. The boy didn't make a sound but his face went so pale the mark on his cheek showed red. I told Bo to stay where he was. That slap was for me and I knew it.

Half kneeling beside the chair I held the side of my face against his middle and reached around behind. I don't know why I did just that but I remembered what made me feel worst was his little legs dangling, not reaching the floor. His fingers dug into my hair and held tight. I felt his breath go out and in, and not come back.

"Oh! So it's you!" As if that woman hadn't watched me arrive! When I stood up she was twitching herself in her greasy gray suit and patting up to feel if her green beret was all right.

"Please, *please!*" I said, while she looked me up and down. "He's only a baby, and I didn't mean — "

She wouldn't let me finish. "Yah!" she said, jerking her horrid old lip once more. "You, with your flopping-down hair! Nasty little — " Instead of saying the word she closed her mouth, as well as she could on account of her teeth, and made the special up-and- down *"Mm — nn!"* you do make, sometimes, when you kiss and feel it begin. So then I knew. She was jealous, that's all, and it got me. Ashe's music, alive at last and just right, came fizzing up in my head and I walked around to where she was and smacked her back every ounce as hard as she'd smacked that boy. It didn't ruffle her a bit so I slapped her again, as hard as I could. She just sat there and leered. I liked seeing the marks come red on *her* face, too!

Bo had me by then and was taking me out, dropping money on our table and picking up our things. She called after me once, something filthy the whole place could hear, but it wasn't that that finally woke me up. Just as we got to the door I heard a small, tight scream, behind us, and simply had to look. It was the boy, just as I'd thought. He was trying to come and Babs was out of her chair dragging him back by his wrist. I could tell from my own wrist how deep her nails dug in but worse than that was how terrified he was. His head hadn't turned with the rest of him yet and his eyes were begging me. Simply begging. I started to go but she struck him again, so hard he almost fell. Whatever I tried I knew she'd only take it out on him afterward, with no one to help him because everyone else in the place looked too stupid to care, so what could I do but go? When the door came shut behind us he hadn't cried out again but I stood still out there on the sidewalk, listening, and couldn't seem to look at Bo.

Bo patted my arm and sniffed. "Let's not ever go back," he said, pretending we were somebody else. "It ain't so nice."

But I couldn't laugh it away like that, and I wouldn't let him. Bit by bit I began to see it — the whole of what I'd done. I lifted up my head, when I could, and smoothed back my hair. By then I was thinking so hard how I'd say it to Ashe, that he was a hero compared to me, I didn't even remember how late it was. "Bo," I said, "Bo! Where will they be? I want to go back to the party."

So we looked at each other and Bo began to smile. I saw then what else I'd nearly done, how close I'd come to really ruining his very last day. I didn't, not quite, because Ashe was at the train and I talked to him there. And Bo said forget it, I'd made things all right.

But Bo has been gone a long time now — seventeen days — and I can't forget. Ashe's face, and Bo's, and that poor baby's eyes keep finding me out. I didn't know I had it in me to do those things, but I've done them, and if you pour water on a dead squirrel will it bring him alive? The answer is no. Whatever you do goes on and on — like the car that killed Meems. I'll be watching myself next time. That doesn't help about now, though. What I *need* to fight is the way things are, but how can you? And yet if you're a person at all you have to do something. Ashe wrote *SONATA FOR MEEMS*. Even Beethoven's face, whenever I happen to pass where his bust sits on the landing, has a look of managed fury that I never used to see. So I practice. I practice so hard I break strings. But I don't know yet where I am, really, because when am I going to see Bo? When *am* I? And even then, even when we're together again — if we are, it isn't as if anything at all could ever be quite the way it was before.

(From Queen's Quarterly)

THE HOUSE ON THE ESPLANADE

BY ANNE HÉBERT

STEPHANIE DE BICHETTE was a curious little creature with frail limbs that seemed badly put together. Only her starched collarette kept her head from falling over on her shoulder; it was too heavy for her long, slender neck. If the head of Stephanie de Bichette looked so heavy, it was because all the pomp of her aristocratic ancestors was symbolized in her coiffure, a high up-swept style, with padded curls arranged in rows on her narrow cranium, an architectural achievement in symmetrical silvery blobs.

Mademoiselle de Bichette had passed, without transition period, without adolescence, from the short frocks of her childhood to this everlasting ash-grey dress, trimmed at neck and wrists with a swirl of lilac braiding. She owned two parasols with carved ivory handles — one lilac and the other ash-grey. When she went out driving in the carriage she chose her parasol according to the weather, and everyone in the little town could tell the weather by the colour of Mademoiselle de Bichette's parasol. The lilac one appeared on days of brilliant sunshine, the ash-grey one whenever it was slightly cloudy. In winter, and when it rained, Stephanie simply never went out at all.

I have spoken at length about her parasols because they were the outward and visible signs of a well-regulated life, a perfect edifice of regularity. Unchanging routine surrounded and supported this innocent old creature. The slightest crack in this extraordinary construction, the least change in this stern programme would have been enough to make Mademoiselle de Bichette seriously ill.

Fortunately, she had never had to change her maid. Geraldine served and cared for her mistress with every evidence of complete respect for tradition. The whole life of Stephanie de Bichette was a tradition, or rather a series of traditions, for apart from the tradition of the well-known parasols and the complicated coiffure, there was the ritual of getting up, of going to bed, of lace-making, of mealtimes, and so on.

Stephanie Hortense Sophie de Bichette lived facing the Esplanade, in a grey stone house dating back to the days of the French occupation. You know the sort of house *that* implies — a tall, narrow edifice with a pointed roof and several rows of high windows, where the ones at the top look no bigger than swallows' nests, a house with two or three large attics that most old maids would have delighted in. But, believe it or not, Mademoiselle de Bichette never climbed up to her attics to sentimentalize over souvenirs, to caress treasured old belongings, or to plan meticulous orgies of housecleaning amid the smell of yellowing paper and musty air that even the best-kept attics seem to possess.

No, she occupied the very heart of the house, scarcely one room on each floor. On the fourth storey, only Geraldine's room remained open, among the rooms of all the former servants. It was part of the family tradition to close off rooms that were no longer used. One after another, bedroom after bedroom had been condemned: the room where the little brothers had died of scarlet fever, when Stephanie was only ten years old; the bedroom of their mother, who had passed away soon after her two children; the room of Irénée, the elder brother who had been killed in an accident, out hunting; the room of the elder sister, Desneiges, who had entered the Ursuline convent; then the bedroom of Monsieur de Bichette, the father, who had succumbed to a long illness; to say nothing of the room belonging to Charles, the only surviving brother, which had been closed ever since his marriage.

The ritual was always the same: once the occupant of the room had departed for the cemetery, the convent or the adventure of matrimony, Geraldine would tidy everything away, carefully leaving each piece of furniture exactly in place; then she would draw the shutters, put dust covers on the armchairs and lock the door for good. No one ever set foot in that room again. One more member of the family was finally disposed of.

Geraldine took a distinct pleasure in this solemn, unvarying rite, just as a gravedigger may take pride in a neat row of graves, with well-kept mounds and smoothly raked grass above them. Sometimes she remembered that one day she would have to close Mademoiselle Stephanie's room, too, and live on for a while, the only living creature among all the dead. She looked forward to that moment, not with horror, but with pleasant anticipation, as a rest and a reward. After so many years of housework in that great house, all its rooms would be fixed at last in order, for all eternity. Mildew and dust could take possession then; Geraldine would have no more cleaning to do then. The rooms of the dead are not "done up."

This was not the calculation of a lazy woman. Geraldine dreamed of the last door closed and the last key turned in the lock just as the harvester dreams of the last sheaf of corn, or the needlewoman of the last stitch in her embroidery. It would be the crowning achievement of her long life, the goal of her destiny.

It was strange that the old servant reckoned two living people among the dead: Mademoiselle Desneiges, the nun, and Monsieur Charles, a married man and the father of a family. They had both left the family roof, that was enough for Geraldine to class them as nonexistent. The heavy door of the cloister had closed forever on one, while Charles, by marrying a common little seamstress from the Lower Town, had so grieved his father that the old house and all it contained had been left to Stephanie. Charles came to see his sister every evening, but Geraldine never spoke a word to him. For her, Stephanie was the whole of the de Bichette family.

On the third floor, all the bedrooms were closed, with the exception of Mademoiselle de Bichette's. On the second, only the small blue boudoir lived on, a life of dimness and disuse. On the first floor, an immense drawing room stretched from front to back, cluttered with furniture of different periods, each piece bristling with fussy, elaborate knickknacks. The ground-floor doors were always open, with high, carved portals to the vestibule, the parlour, the dining room. In the basement was the old-fashioned kitchen, uncomfortable and always damp. Geraldine was the cook as well as the maid-of-all-work, but was never addressed as such.

If her mistress lived by tradition until it became a religion, Geraldine, too had her tradition, the collecting of bright-coloured buttons. Her black skirt and her white apron never changed, but she used her imagination in trimming her blouses. Red buttons sparkled on blue blouses, yellow ones on green, and so on, not to mention buttons in gold and silver and crystal. In the attic, she had discovered great chests of ancient garments which she stripped, shamelessly, of their trimmings. Apart from this innocent craze for buttons, the big woman with the ruddy complexion made no objection to touring the wine cellar every evening before going to bed, as the last of her duties, conscientiously and even devotedly performed. But where she excelled, was in the observance of tradition where her mistress was concerned.

Every morning, at seven o'clock in summer and eight in winter, she climbed the three flights of stairs and knocked at the bedroom door . . . Two taps, two firm, decided taps, no more, no less. This was the signal for the ceremonial to begin.

Geraldine opened the bed curtains, then the window curtains and finally the shutters. Her aging mistress preferred to sleep in complete darkness, requiring several thicknesses of material and polished wood between herself and the wicked witchcraft of the night. She was afraid of the first rays of sunlight as well, not knowing what to do about them, since they might easily wake you long before the proper time for getting up.

Then Geraldine would return to the passage to fetch a kind of wagon equipped with everything Stephanie might need for the first few hours of the day. Two white pills in a glass of water, coffee and toast, toothbrush and toothpowder, a copper bathtub, white towels, white, starched underwear. Also a feather duster, a broom, a dustpan . . . all that she used for tidying up the room. This wagon was as wide as a single bed, four feet wide, with three shelves. Geraldine had made it herself out of old packing cases.

When Stephanie's breakfast was finished, the maid would bathe, dress and powder her mistress, then do her hair. Stephanie allowed her to do everything, silent, inert, trusting. After that, there was sometimes a moment of painful indecision, an anguished knot in the brain of Mademoiselle de Bichette, when Geraldine leaned over to look out of the window, examining the sky and frowning as she declared:

"I really don't know what sort of weather we're going to have today."

Then the old lady would stare at her maid with such forlorn eyes that Geraldine would say, hurriedly:

"It's going to rain. You're not going to be able to go out this morning. I'll let the coachman know."

Stephanie would grow calm again after that, but she would not be entirely herself until Geraldine had settled her carefully in the blue drawing room, on her high-backed chair of finely carved wood, near the window, her half-finished lace on her knee and her crochet hook in her hand. Only then would the idea take firm root in her brain:

"It's going to rain. I can't go out . . . All I have to do is to handle this hook and this thread as my mother taught me to do when I was seven years old . . . If it had been a fine day, it would have been different, I would have gone out in the carriage. There are only two realities in the world . . . only two realities I can rely on . . . and close my eyes, deep inside them: the reality of going out in the carriage, the reality of making my lace . . . How lost and strange I am when Geraldine cannot tell what the weather is going to do, and I am left in suspense with no solid ground beneath my feet . . . It just *wracks* my brain! Oh! Not to have to think about it, to let myself be carried away by one or the other of these my only two sure and certain realities going out for a drive or sitting here, making my lace . . . "

Even if the day turned out fine in the end, Geraldine never said so. It would have been too much of a shock for her mistress. Imagine what confusion in such a patterned existence if someone had suddenly announced a change, after she had firmly established herself for the day in the reality of lace-making, and dared to tell her she had taken the wrong road? She could never again have believed in any reality at all.

Since her childhood, Mademoiselle de Bichette had been making lace doilies of different sizes, which Geraldine used in many different ways. These doilies flowed from her fingers at the steady rate of four per week, small pieces of white lace that resembled each other like peas in a pod. They were everywhere in the house — five or six on the piano, seven or eight on all the tables, as many as ten on every arm chair, one or two on all the smaller chairs. Every knickknack rested on a piece of delicate openwork, so that the furniture all seemed powdered with snowflakes, enlarged as if under a microscope.

In winter, and in summer, on the days when Geraldine had decided the weather was not fit for going out, Mademoiselle de Bichette would crochet all the morning, in her blue boudoir, sitting up so straight and still that she scarcely seemed real, her feet resting on a stool covered by something that was strangely like the work the old lady held in her hands.

At five minutes to twelve, Geraldine would announce:

"Mademoiselle Stephanie's luncheon is served."

At the mention of her name, the old lady would rise at once; the ritual phrase had touched a switch somewhere within her, so that without effort, without thinking, wtihout even understanding, she would put herself slowly and ceremoniously in motion, descend the staircase and take her place at the table.

If Stephanie did go out, she invariably returned home at a quarter to twelve, so she had ample time to receive the announcement that luncheon was served with the necessary calm.

The outings of Mademoiselle de Bichette were governed by just as incredible a routine. She came out on the sidewalk with tiny steps, her frail little body bending under the weight of that enormous pile of scaffolded curls. Geraldine helped her mistress into the carriage, the coachman whipped up his horse, and the victoria started on its slow, quiet drive, invariably the same, through the streets of the little town. The horse knew the road by heart, so the coachman seized the opportunity for a short nap, his cap pulled down over his eyes, his legs stretched out, his hands folded on his stomach. He always waked up in time, as if by magic, when the drive came to an end, crying out and stretching himself, with a jolly air of surprise:

"Well, well, Mamzelle, here we are back again!"

Just as if the old fellow, when he went to sleep as the drive started, had not been quite sure he would come back when he awoke, or if his return would be to the country of the living!

Mademoiselle de Bichette would disappear into the house, on Geraldine's arm; the coachman would unharness the horse and put the carriage away; and it was all over. With regret, the townsfolk watched the disintegration of this strange conveyance, like a ghostly apparition cutting through the clear morning light . . . the ancient nag, pulling an antique carriage, with a sleepy coachman and a tiny figure like a mummy, swathed in ash-grey and lilac.

After luncheon, Geraldine would lead her mistress into the long drawing room on the first floor, where, without ever laying her crochet aside, Stephanie would receive a few callers, and the maid would serve dandelion wine and madeleines.

The old lady never left her chair, forcing herself to hold her head high, though her neck felt as if it were breaking under the weight of her monumental coiffure. Sometimes, this constant, painful effort was betrayed by a twitch of the lips, the only change of expression that callers could ever distinguish upon that small, powdered face. Then Stephanie would ask: "How is Madame your mother?" in a voice so white and colourless that it might have come from one of the closed rooms, where, according to the gossips of the town, some of the original inhabitants still lived on.

This phrase of Stephanie's had to do for greeting, for farewell, for conversation; indeed, it had to do for everything, for the wine was sour and the madeleines stale and hard as stones. The callers were all so aged and unsteady that the most utter stranger would have had the tact never to ask that preposterous question, but Mademoiselle de Bichette knew no other formula, and in any case, she attached no importance whatever to the words she was saying. If she finished a lace doily while her callers were present, she simply let it fall at her feet, like a pebble into a pool, and began another identical piece of lace. The visiting ladies never stayed very long, and Stephanie seemed to notice their departure as little as she did their presence.

At a quarter past six, Geraldine would announce that Monsieur Charles was waiting below. The programme of the day was ticking on like the mechanism of a good Swiss watch, and the invisible wheels of Mademoiselle de Bichette responded perfectly, warning the limbs of this strange little creature that they must immediately convey her to the ground floor.

Her brother would kiss her brow and smile, rubbing his stubby-fingered hands together and remarking:

"Um-phm! It feels good in the house."

Then he would hang his overcoat up on a hall stand, while Geraldine followed his every movement with her look of triumphant disdain. With her arms crossed upon her swelling chest, she doubtless thought she looked like the statue of the Commendatore, bound on revenge. She would cast a glance of scorn on the threadbare coat, as if to say:

"Well, what did you expect? Monsieur Charles *would* get married to a chit of a girl from the Lower Town, so naturally, his father cut him off, and I locked up his room as if he were dead. If Mademoiselle Stephanie wants him here every evening, it's her own business, but *I'm* going to let him know that I'm *glad* he was thrown out, if I *am* only the servant. I know he's poor, and that's his punishment for disobeying his father. He comes here because there isn't enough to eat at home. So he gobbles up our dinners and carries away on his nasty skin a bit of the warmth from our fires . . . The good-for-nothing!"

If it were true that Charles had only one decent meal a day, it was astonishing that he was not at all thin. He was even fat, very fat, flabby and yellow-complexioned, with a bold head and a shiny face, colourless lips and almost colourless eyes. Geraldine said he had eyes like a codfish and his clothes always smelt of stale grease. Apart from that, she could not forgive a de Bichette for forgetting his table manners.

"To think that his slut of a wife has made him lose all he ever learned in decent society . . . You wouldn't believe it possible," she would grumble to herself.

As dinnertime drew near, Charles became more and more noisily jolly. He never stopped rubbing his hands together; he got up, sat down, got up again, went from window to door and back a dozen times, while Stephanie's eyes ignored him. Then the brother and sister took their places, one at each end of the long table in the dining room. There was no gas chandelier in this room, so it seemed even longer and darker, lit only by two tall candles in silver candlesticks. The corners of the room disappeared into the dimness, and the shadows of the brother and sister danced like black flames on the curiously carved oak panelling of the walls.

Every evening, the atmosphere of this dining room seemed more impressive to Charles. Perhaps he felt unseen forms hiding in the darkness, invisible spectators of this singular repast; perhaps he feared to find the ghosts that haunted the bedrooms above, to see them take their places at the huge dining table, where an old creature presided, small as a cat, white as the table linen, who seemed already to be living in the uneasy world of phantoms.

As soon as Stephanie's brother had swallowed a few mouthfuls of soup, his good humour fell away, lifeless, utterly destroyed. When he entered the house, the smell of cooking would stimulate him, would intoxicate him with its marvellous promise, but now that the promise was kept, the man became gloomy again. Through his own bitter thoughts, he stared at the lace cloth, the heavy silverware, the fine china, and at this sister of his, who was still alive, in spite of her look of belonging to some other world. What mysterious thread was keeping Stephanie here on earth? To look at her, you would have thought the slightest breath might carry her away, yet there she was, still alive.

Geraldine came and went around the table and her sharp eyes seemed to plumb the very depths of the man's thoughts. The brother sat there, knowing himself watched and understood, telling himself, in his embarrassment, that his sister would have joined her ancestors long ago had it not been for this fiendish servant, who by some diabolical process had contrived to keep the dying thing alive in her father's mansion, simply in order to enjoy as long as possible the spectacle of his own failure. In what dread "No Man's Land" of the spirit had the old witch made a pact with Monsieur de Bichette — and with Satan himself? Geraldine had inherited all the father's anger against his son, and faithful to that anger as if to a sacred promise, she was constantly reminding Charles of the curse that lay heavy upon him. At that moment, he raised his head, resenting the eyes he felt fixed upon his every movement, but Geraldine was no longer there, Charles could hear the tinkle of her keys, in the passage between the staircase and the kitchen. He shuddered, for he knew very well which keys she carried at her waist. No cupboard, no inhabited room possessed a key. It chilled his heart strangely to know that the key of his room was there, along with those of the rooms of the dead. It scared him. Then he took hold of himself again and muttered:

"This damned house! . . . Enough to drive a man crazy to sit here night after night with two cracked old fools of women ... The wine must have gone to my head."

But Stephanie had just got up from the table, and Charles followed her as usual.

The evening began like all the rest. Stephanie took up her lace again, while her brother walked to and fro in the long drawing room, his hands behind his back.

And so, night after night, in complete silence, without a single work exchanged between brother and sister, the time passed until the old clock chimed ten. Then Charles, having laid up a store of warmth for the night, kissed his sister's brow, slipped on his overcoat, and with his hands in his pockets, made for Ireland Street, walking slowly along, like an idle fellow accustomed to musing as he walked.

The man followed his shadow as it flickered on the walls. The same thoughts were turning and twisting in his brain; he was used to them, as a man gets used to animals he tends every day. He knew them too well to be surprised by them; he had stopped looking at them straight in the face; they passed to and fro behind his pale eyes without ever changing his passive stare.

As he came near his own home, Charles thought of his wife. He was going back to her, in no hurry, but with a certain feeling of security, as if to a piece of property he knew belonged to him.

Suddenly, he noticed that he was nearly there. Two low houses, identical twins in misery and poverty, stood waiting for him, their tumbledown grey "stoops" jutting out to meet the sidewalk. He rented rooms on the second floor of one of these houses.

He climbed the stairs, lit a candle and went into the bedroom. A hoarse, veiled voice, a well-known voice, that could still charm him in spite of himself, said wearily:

"That you, Charles?"

He set the candle on the night table. The woman shaded her eyes with her hand. He sat down on the foot of the bed.

"How's your sister?"

"Just the same."

This question, this reply, as on every other night, fell heavily into a dull silence. Beneath the words was stirring in the shadows the real meaning, unexpressed:

"Do you think your sister will last much longer?"

" 'Fraid so . . . She's still hanging on . . . "

At that moment, in the house on the Esplanade, Stephanie de Bichette was crossing her tiny cold hands on her breast and abandoning to the great empty gulf of night the small emptiness that was herself, ridiculous as an old fashion plate and dry as a pressed fig.

And Geraldine lay awake, dreaming that death had closed the last door in the old house.

(From Accent)

CHAR ON RAVEN'S BENCH

BY FRANK HOLWERDA

IT MUST HAVE BEEN an exceedingly informal inquest. The Marshall led six coldly disinterested men up the canyon as far as Raven's Bench and then up the draw to where the charred remains of the cabin lay black in a bed of surrounding brown moss. Solemnly they pronounced Harbin a suicide, and the fact that the cabin too was destroyed, showed how determined the man was to leave. The tightly twisted wire around his neck, with the other end over the center rafter not completely burned, was really what did it and the fire was just to make sure.

That was the way to do it around here, the six said to each other and nodded sagely. Don't make a pest of yourself; if that's what you have to do, do it — but make sure. Remember Burke? Burke had done something like that too when he wired the eight sticks of powder to his head, set a short fuse and then jumped into that 312-foot mine shaft. "Had these eight sticks tucked under a wire around his head — they were stickin' straight up, like candles on a cake!" Dynamite, of course, always blew down, so nobody bothered to go lower himself into the shaft to see if Burke made it or not.

Burke made it all right, and so did Harbin. The six went back to town and their daily grinds with pick and shovel, pen and paper, towel and glass, lock and key, mortar and pestle, pasteboards.

The six nodded. All of us nodded too and some sagely. Harbin was gone and couldn't answer questions. But how'd he done that now? Had he slipped the wire around his neck first and then set fire

to the place, or had he started the fire first and then got out the
wire, twisted it around his neck and made the other end fast over
that rafter? It was hard to tell. When the Marshal removed what
was left of Harbin and the rains had beaten the ashes down and the
ravens had worked it over and the wolverines nosed it thoroughly,
there was no point in anyone else's stirring the embers. Just like
when that dynamite went off and Burke only halfway down the shaft.

So everyone minded his own business and if you didn't want to do
that, you could move on, Bub. So you never talked about where you
came from or why you'd come from there; and the name you used
was your own affair; and you read an old magazine in the bunkhouse, hearing the wind moan across the tundra; and you went to
bed and got up and ate breakfast and held your face blank and once
in awhile said "Pass the high-grade" when you wanted it for your
coffee or "Pass the low-grade" when you wanted it for your oatmeal.
And if there was dessert, you might say, "Pass the long-johns." They
were coated with maple frosting.

You knew what your work was and you went out and did it and
they paid you for it and you took the money and saved your checks
till you went to town alone and when you came back you worked
again and said little.

That is, no one said much except John. When he wasn't stoking
his huge frame at the long table, and when he'd reached the point
where he was full to the front teeth of all the things that bothered
him, he'd say a few words. And when John said a few words, everyone knew he'd said a few words. He couldn't speak like other men.
His chest was too big and full of sound wind and his vocal cords
thick as hemp rope. John was so big he looked short. He could
stand flat-footed and place the palm of his hand on anything eight
feet in the air, but his legs were short. His face was brick-red from
exposure to the cold and wind, and from the pressure inside of him.
When John finally said his few words, they echoed back from the
ridges and the walls of the canyons, and everyone including Buck
the Foreman who might be a mile away heard them; and the foxes
stopped on the snow in their dainty tracks and looked over their
furry shoulders.

We'd walk the three miles back to camp from the ancient creek bed where the drill rigs were set up, in the dead of night while the next shift took over where we'd left off. And we'd feel like ghouls walking across the road over the tailing piles, silent and tired and cold in the arctic night. On those bone-chilling walks when it was too cold to smoke and the squeak of your shoepacks on the snow sounded like high C on a violin, John liked to say a few bitter words. He'd hold the sides of his old grey stocking cap and thrust his head up into it, cup his ears in the palms of his leather choppers and then, in silent fury, rewind the toilet paper around his neck and pull his collar over it. Then he'd rear back and scream his defiance at the power lines that crossed the road at one of the bends. He'd stand there with his big red mouth steaming like a hot geyser, obscenities coming out like vomit — faster and faster and out of control. He'd scream and bellow and the ridges would throw the roaring echo and we'd pause there and wait and all look away. And the wires would just hum like stone-frozen death and whine and loop over the cross arms of the pole where the sign read: "Keep off — 33,000 volts."

And sometimes when we'd turn that sharp bend and walk in a dark huddle past the snow- and ice-covered pond lined with stiffened willows, the ice would boom out like splintering thunder and a high-pitched whine would shriek down the valley like the shell of a monster gun. And John would thunder back, *"Hellooooo Addamsssss!"* A sudden chill struck us then that wasn't in the frost of the night. And, for the thousandth time, John would tell us how Addams was going to push the snow off the pond with the big bull-dozer so they could cut the ice out with the steam points and float the gold dredge in. And how they told him the ice was twelve feet thick but it was only twelve inches that spring, and how he cracked through a rotten spot and went down like a plummet — a hundred and sixty feet of inky-black icewater — and rested on the bottom; and the dredge hooked the tractor out later but Addams stayed on the bottom forever with his pockets full of iron wrenches. It was "Dredge Basin 232" on the company charts but we called it "Addams Pond," and that was fair, wasn't it?

It was strange that winter about the feud between John and the juice in those power lines. He could work himself into an almost incontrollable fury over it. The answer could have been that it made

a little man with a switch lever the working equal of John himself.
You didn't need the stone-age strength of John to push a button.
You might mention strong men to John. Then he always spoke a few
words about his brother Elffy. How they worked in a coal mine once,
he and his strong brother, robbing pillars. The powder charge set
off a fire at the entrance to the room in which Elffy was robbing
pillars, so they'd walled it up with cement and pumped soft, flowing
mud into the room and kept the fire from spreading, in fact, put it
out after a year and a half. That was how Elffy made it.

"Couldn't you help him get out, John?"

"I didn't wass dere wit him at de time!"

But if he had been he'd've clawed his way to him and out together.
John would have burst through at the top of the mountain if that
had been the only way.

So, during an early thaw that spring and still a month or so before
the Marshal found Harbin's char, John reached up to draw down the
slack-lever on his drill rig. There was slush on the ground and John
braced himself and buried his feet in it. He'd forgotten about the
old familiar short in that rig and when he took hold of the lever, the
waiting, surging force of a whole battery of generators a hundred
miles away ran through his salty frame to earth in the slush and held
him there quivering and rattling the lever. That was how John
made it. His leather mitten was charred and brittle and curled-up-
dry as he was laid out on the work bench in the pump house. The
wind came up strong again that night and the snow with it, and the
false spring was over for awhile, and John lay there alone and frozen
solid. He was like a fallen statue, lips framed to say a few words.
The feud was settled.

But even then, if John had wanted to do in Harbin, he'd've yanked
his head off and thrown it against a tamarack and let the wolves
carry it off, worry and gnaw it in one of those dens under the Bench.
We knew that . . .

But no one said a word about it, least of all Silent Sam. Silent
Sam, also known as Dirty Sam, who changed his long handles only
in the fall — late fall — and whose tin-pants glistened with the accumulated grime of years. Sam said nothing about it because that was
the nature of Sam and also because Sam wasn't there that spring to

say anything about it. He'd spent the winter in his lonely cabin somewhere on the ridges, trapping ermine in his woodpile and martens in box traps he made to resemble in minutest detail a picture he'd once seen of the manger in which Christ was born. Sam didn't show up that spring, nor ever thereafter. He may have slipped through a hole in the ice somewhere, or frozen on the trail, or stumbled into a snow-covered shaft. He may have made it the cold way and Sam hated the cold. He must have hated the cold even in the summertime. He built fires to guard against it. In his lonely cabin where he spent his winters, he had three stoves with glory-holes and one open fireplace and he kept them all roaring. No matter where we went or what we did, Sam built the fire to boil the water or melt the snow for coffee. Even when it rained and the moss oozed water like a wet sponge, Sam knew where to reach under the lip of an overhanging ledge for dry leaves or dead roots, or peel the bark from a birch and make it explode as though soaked in oil. Sam wasn't around when the Marshal came back from the cabin where Harbin'd tried to pass the winter but couldn't stand the lonely, wind-whipped darkness.

But if Sam had known, he wouldn't have told, no matter where he was, not Sam. Even if he wasn't thawing out and getting soft on a sand bar somewhere.

There were the others too, tight-lipped. There was Charlie, who said his name was Smith, but it'd been that twelve years ago and he'd changed it twelve times since. Charlie sometimes split his bottle with Harbin. There were Big Red, whose name was Morgan now, and Bill "Spruce" and all the others — dulled, silent. Brooders.

There was old, stoop-shouldered, runny-nosed Louey. But when Louey opened his mouth now, when he wasn't at the long, narrow table, he only babbled. It was getting worse with him, and the lucidity which he once must have had was slipping fast, and Louey was on his way to making it — perhaps the soft, easy way. Louey forgot things. Louey was an old dreamer. But he still clacked his fuchsine gums about the girl-beaver he once knew back on the creeks. She'd sit there in the middle of the creek alongside the dam she'd built all night and watch Louey tear it down so the water could flow on down to the dredge pond and the dredge could float and send its endless chain of buckets down to scratch and gouge the bedrock and scoop up the flour-gold. She'd sit there and cry, and Louey could hear her snuffle as he worked and the water drained from behind the logs she'd peeled and plastered down. And the next day Louey'd be back tearing it down again and after a while she'd change her tactics and try other wiles of her sex on him, combing her hair attractively when she saw him coming, and smoothing her long guard-whiskers back along her cheeks and rolling her eyes maidenly. So said Louey. Louey the Fox's Friend, who hung all the camp's stale doughnuts on the tips of the short spruce trees — this for the shy ones; but who could call his old pot-partners to him with the rustle of a paper sack. They came to him from all points, circling him, licking their chops and, in excited anticipation, suddenly feeling a mass urge to urinate, the vixens squatting brazenly just beyond the reach of his hand, the dogs stiff-legged against the willows. To Louey it was seemly. He might do that himself right then — either way.

Harbin killed those foxes. It was easy. Blew their pointed, sharp-eared heads to gobbets and bone chips with No. 8 shot; skinned them out and left their carcasses freeze to blue-black flint that rang to the hammering of the ravens' beaks. Harbin did that the winter before he himself turned into a substance that was black but not flint-hard.

Through the spring and summer Louey was ineffably sad. His simple dream of pet foxes roaming the ridges and barking their greeting to him disappeared into the misty corners of his disturbed mind. His body too, after more than forty years of brutal swinking, was becoming gaunt and withered and his elbow-pads hung loose. So, if he knew that Harbin'd done it, that knowledge stayed behind the tangled drapes in his mind and his skinny arms along his sides. It took Harbin a week to drink off what the pelts brought and to return to camp, bleary-eyed and sullen.

And then one morning Louey left for town. His eyes sparkled and the scrubbed skin of his face shone with the laundry soap not thoroughly rinsed. In his hip pocket he carried the carefully folded checks which he had accumulated during the period of a year or more. He returned four times. Once for his cap which he had forgotten; once for a bag-lunch which he had prepared and secreted a week before; once because he had started out in the wrong direction.

When he returned the fourth time, night had fallen and he was hollow-eyed and fevered with fatigue. But his trip had been successful. His new gloves fitted him well and the woolen socks would sure be warm, wouldn't they? And he'd met a very kind man who had promised to hold his checks for him until such time as he would have further need. The man had even asked him to write his name on the backs of the checks so that he would be sure to remember the name and not confuse it with someone else's.

At breakfast the next morning, someone broke the silence and said, "Pass the low-grade."

It could have been the sound of the words or it could have been just the sound. Louey didn't say. But he suddenly came to. He pushed his plate away, placed his elbows on the table, sighed and asked, "Does anyone here know of a small mine that an old man can work all by himself?" Everyone kept on eating. "Not a big one, understand. No. Just a small one. Just a one-man mine."

No one looked up but the low-grade started from both ends of the long table. Louey coughed lightly then and went outside. Harbin did not return for more than a month.

Louey babbled on through the summer about his girl-beavers and foxes and one-man mines. There seemed to be another thread that sometimes worked its way to the front. Louey would tug at it, dropping the papery lids over his old eyes and holding his brow. But the thread would slip from his grasp and drop back again — back into the snarled skeins.

Then, when the days shortened and the morning sun saw rime on the edge of the creeks, a run-off ditch cracked its bank and had to be sandbagged. It was cold, wet, muscle-tearing work, filling the sacks with sand, handling them, tying them, carrying them, stuffing them in a holding pattern into the break. You hated to spend the money you earned for such work. What could you buy?

That was the day, though — it was all there for anyone to see. The story was there. It was as plain as though a crier had stood there with his back to that clump of white, dusty-trunked birches and called the turns. First of all there was Sam, silently tending his beautiful blaze, keeping the sand from freezing into unwieldly chunks that would not slip into the sacks. It was a clean fire he had that day, clean and fiercely hot. The wood was dry and seasoned, and Sam tended it well, poking the embers with a rod and sending the glowing sparks upward into the cold, clean air. Sometimes he'd warm his hands over it, rubbing them slowly together or standing tensely to one side watching with his eyes aglitter.

Then there was Harbin carrying the sacks from where the necks were wire-tied, to the break in the ditch, dumping them down with a grunted oath and shouldering his way back for another. Harbin liked to shoulder his way. He hunted out narrow walks so that he might jar people, and sometimes things, in passing. And on that day he hunted hard. Harbin in the prime of life, shuffling along with eyes downcast and shoulder cocked.

Buck the Foreman stood to one side.

There was Louey wiping his nose on his sleeve, his hip pockets bristling with the ends of the wire ties. Louey tied the bags after they were shoveled full. He'd slip one of the wire loops over the hook on the end of his bag binder, sniff, wipe his nose, take a deep breath and pull the lever which twisted the wire and sank it into the gathered ends at the neck of the sack. Then he would rest from this exertion and wait for the next bag to be filled with sand.

There was John lifting up the bags for Louey to tie and passing them to Harbin and the others who carried them off to the break. John hugging the heavy sacks like a grizzly holding a hog, swaying slightly as though on a ship in swells and handing the sacks over with one boomlike arm. He didn't say his few words that day, but his eyes were open wide and clear with a light that shone from behind them.

There is the picture then. Old Louey with his tired eyes watching Harbin, squinting now and then at Harbin shuffling off with his loaded sack. Old eyes in an old body, trying desperately and failing miserably to pierce a misty veil. Sudden fleeting light and, as sudden, sooty darkness. Louey tried that day — tried hard, and John watched him trying. And if John saw the creases pull smooth on Louey's face and then return in the space of a heartbeat, perhaps he took it for something else.

Silent Sam stood and watched and tended his fire. He watched John hug the bags and hold them and he watched old Louey tie off their necks and he watched Harbin act the insufferable swine and he watched Buck the Foreman watch them all. And no one said a word — not even the crier with his back to the birches — because it wasn't necessary, was it?

Now it is some weeks later. It is the afternoon of the same day that Harbin happened to meet old Louey in the bunkhouse hallway, shouldered him and then, in a fit of lushy rage, slapped him down; gave him flat open-hands to the jowls that hung Louey's jaw slack, glazed his eyes and hunkered him into a corner, whimpering. Louey sits and stares vacantly, his stinging cheek goes numb, the film in his mind clears and it is as though two loose wire ends there are jarred together and the current flows. The current flows backward as current will do — impelled by a head-ringing slap. Louey is back in his youthful prime. *He is tall and lean and unstooped. He enters the stale-smelling flat and hears the high, whining voice, and his ear-drums shrivel. "They got'im for fair this time, Louey!" she says and hics. Louey tries to make some reply but cannot. Suddenly the thought that this is the woman once entwined with every dream of his life, overwhelms him and he presses his temples. She goes on, "I beat 'im enough, but it din't help. You shoulda done it too — he's yours s'much as mine!" Louey sees the table sprinkled with cheese-parings, an empty bottle on its side. "He'll git thirty years fer it," the voice goes on gleefully. "Come right in, they did, an' hauls 'im out from under 'is bed by the heels." The lights begin to dim for Louey then and he fumbles for the switch . . .* The moment is mercifully short — a spark's lifetime; the ends of the wires glow and burn out. Louey sniffs and rubs his cheek.

It is still the afternoon of that same day and Harbin would have sold his foul black soul for a drink. Now watch! There go the three of them. John in the lead with a bottle of bait bulging his pocket, his eyes strangely lighted; Harbin reels along behind him, eyes glued to John's pocket, lower lip flabby, feet shuffling, heedless of the powdery snow; Louey brings up the rear, following in the track left by Harbin. Louey is warmly dressed this cold late afternoon. Someone has drawn paw-like, wool-lined leather mitts over his new dress gloves. Someone has tucked a warm tissue muffler around his scrawny neck and wound strips of burlap around his ankles to keep out the

.snow. His face is freshly bathed and his cheeks glow pink. Louey clacks and gabbles at the tiny white birds that flit through the stunted spruce. He is breathing open-mouthed, his nose running as usual.

They stop in the lee of the pen stock. Behind its heavy, rough-planked quarter the air is calm. John takes the bottle from his pocket, uncorks it and hands it to Harbin. Harbin drinks long and noisily and clutches the bottle tightly. John steps behind him, picks up the cached gunny sack and hands it to Louey. Louey grins blunt-wittedly, takes the sack and draws out the tie binder. By the time Harbin sees what Louey holds in his hand and wonders about it, John has him from behind. John holds Harbin like a girder-limbed brown bear, reared up, white spittle spraying from the corners of his mouth. It is John who insists on using the gunny sack. "Pull it overrr hees headt, Louey!" he says. Louey slips it over as Harbin strains and flails with his feet. Now Louey fumbles with the wire loop and finally gets an extra long one adjusted. He slips it over the sack on Harbin's head, feels for the neck and pulls the lever. Harbin stiffens, gives a mighty lurch and loses control of his sphincter muscles. Slowly John releases him and lets him sink to the ground, his hands and feet twitching and perking. Louey looks back over the trail, sees the snowbirds and goes off in childish pursuit.

The deed is done. John makes several attempts to pick up the body, drops it and waits a moment longer. And now we see him ploughing through the drifts in the Canyon, his grisly burden under one arm. Up the Canyon he beats his way, past Raven's Bench and up the draw. And look! Who is that to the side and just behind him? Like the wraith of a rusty-coated fox he follows, quietly parting the snow-laden willows, silent, intent and fingering his matches.

John hangs the corpse and quickly heads back to camp and Sam pushes open the door of the ownerless cabin. Sam does his part well and the flames lick heavenward, clean and hot, the smoke smelling slightly acrid.

Much later, the following spring, when the willows still up to their knees in ice have popped their catkins, after the six men have had their solemn say and the Marshal's chore is done, Buck the Foreman discovers that the sack binder is missing. He buys a new one with his own money. He does this of his own accord and without the knowledge of anyone else. He does it the day after he cleans out what Harbin has left behind. This is not unusual work for Buck the Foreman. He has cleaned up after the dead before.

Buck sorts out the things that are left and makes a neat pile of what may have value to possible heirs or to the Law, burns the rest. He burns the old pawn tickets, the union cards, the birth certificate. Buck is not the Foreman because he is a dullard or because the glare on the snow has scathed his vision. He scuffs the maple handle of the sack binder, rubs off the newness and hangs it on the proper hook in the tool shed.

(From the Sewanee Review)

GERTRUDE AND SIDNEY

BY RANDALL JARRELL

*T*HOUGH Gertrude's grammar, syntax, and punctuation were perfectly orthodox, though her style made everything sound as if it had been dictated to her by the spirit of Geometry, she was admired by the most experimental of writers, men who, since high school, had never used a comma, except perhaps to put one after every word of a book of poems. But she was (and they felt this, even if they couldn't say it) as excessive as they: her excess was moral, spiritual, and cut far deeper into life than anything they had managed themselves. Grammar and capital letters are conventions, the last twigs on the tree of life; it was the roots that Gertrude sawed patiently away at. So even the farthest-flung picket of Experimentalism (poor *verlorne Feldwacht!*) loved Gertrude's work, and forgave it its hysterical blindness toward him and his for the sake of its vision of the rest of reality. With them and Gertrude it was a case not of deep calling to deep but of chaos calling to chaos: they were all members of the Sons and Daughters of Old Night, a lodge as strange, in its way, as Florian Slappey's Sons and Daughters of I Will Arise, another lodge of which one used to read.

Gertrude pointed at the world and said, her voice clear and loud: "You see! you see!" But you didn't, she didn't: as you looked along that stretched shaking finger you didn't see, you saw through. Her vision was too penetrating. She showed that anything, anything at all, is not what it seems; and if anything is not anything, it is nothing. How Gertrude did like Swift! His work, that is: in his life, she felt, he was always fooling around with his friends, gossiping, trying to help the Irish, making up proverbs and jokes and riddles, writing letters in baby-talk to that silly woman. In his work only one thing puzzled her: why had Swift liked the Houyhnhnms? Whenever she thought of *Gulliver's Travels* she felt a faint impulse to sweep the last piece off the board, to write an article exposing the Houyhnhnms.

Gertrude could have taken the Houyhnhnms for granted; to anything except a bust of Cato, they expose themselves. But Gertrude hated for anything to be latent or tacit or implicit: if there was an inexpressible secret to the world — or one unexpressed because taken for granted by everybody — she would express it or die. So her books analyzed (besides the sun, the moon, the starry heavens, and the moral order) the dew on the cobweb and the iridescence of Titania's wings; and they did not murder to dissect, but dissected to murder. The blush on the cheek of Innocence is really — one learned this from Gertrude — a monomolecular film of giant levorotatory protein molecules, and the bonds that join them are the bonds of self-interest. She said to the Universe that she accepted it, for analysis.

Of any thousand pigs, or cats, or white rats, there are some who eat their litters and some, a good many more, who do not. Gertrude understood the first, the others she did not understand; she explained everything in terms of the first. They would all have behaved like the first except for — this, that, the other. She saw the worst: it was, indeed, her only principle of explanation. Consequently she seemed to most people a writer of extraordinary penetration — she appealed to the Original La Rochefoucauld in everybody. People looked up to her just as they look up to all those who know why everything is as it is: because of munitions makers, the Elders of Zion, agents of the Kremlin, Oedipus complexes, the class struggle, Adamic sin, *something;* these men can explain everything, and we cannot. People who were affectionate, cheerful, and brave — and human too, all too human — felt in their veins the piercing joy of Understanding, of pure disinterested insight, as they read Gertrude's demonstration that they did everything because of greed, lust, and middle-class hypocrisy. She told them that they were very bad and, because they were fairly stupid, they believed her.

It is partly our own fault — the fault of a great many of us, at least — that writers like Gertrude come into being and stay there: the baby does nothing but cry because, each time he cries, we go upstairs with a bottle, and bounce him on a tender knee. Gertrude was not, alas, a good woman; Gertrude had a style in which you couldn't tell the truth if you tried — and when, except when it was a shameful one, had Gertrude ever tried? But how many of her readers cared? Most of them went on admiring her in the tones of butchers from Gopher Prairie admiring the Murderer of Düsseldorf; they could not mention that style without using the vocabulary of a salesman of kitchen knives. If Gertrude had written another *Remembrance of Things Past,* they would only have murmured disappointedly that it wasn't the old Gertrude. They wanted her to tell them the worst about themselves, and after they had met her they whispered to one another the worst about *her.*

But as a writer Gertrude had one fault more radical than all the rest: she did not know — or rather, did not believe — what it was like to be a human being. She was one, intermittently, but while she wasn't she did not remember what it had felt like to be one; and her worse self distrusted her better too thoroughly to give it much share, ever, in what she said or wrote. If she was superior to most people in her courage and independence, in her intelligence, in her reckless wit, in her extraordinary powers of observation, in her almost eidetic memory, she was inferior to them in most human qualities; she had not yet arrived even at that elementary forbearance upon which human society is based. Most of the time Gertrude was not an ordinary human being but an extraordinary human animal. Her hand was against every man's and every man's was against hers; she had not signed the human contract when the rest of us signed it. She was, like the man in the poem, "free, free!" — free to do anything she pleased; and of all freedoms this is the most terrible.

She was free to destroy Sidney too, if she wanted to; she just, just — just didn't want to ...

Sidney kept Gertrude alive: without him she would have gone on functioning drearily, striking at anything that came in reach, but she would hardly have *lived;* yet Sidney, and the part of Gertrude that lived because of Sidney, never got into Gertrude's books at all

— she would have been ashamed and embarrassed to see them there. Gertrude, unlike many writers, really did have a private life, one she never wrote a word about.

So because of all this — of all this, and so much more — even the best of Gertrude's books were habitat groups in a Museum of Natural History: topography, correct; meteorological information, correct; condition of skins, good; mounting of horns, correct . . . Inside there were old newspapers, papier-mâché, clockwork. And yet, *mirabile dictu!* the animals moved, a little stiffly, and gave the calls of their species, a little thinly — was it not a world?

It was a fairly popular world, even. Gertrude's readers did not understand things, and were injured by them; now for a few hours they injured and understood — and understanding was somehow the most satisfactory injury of all. They did for a while all that fear and pity and ordinary human feeling kept them from doing ordinarily, and they were grateful for it: if Gertrude had had sweep and sex (her method was microscopic, her sex statistical) she might have been considered a Great American Novelist. As it was, she was always called "the most brilliant of our younger novelists." *Brilliant!* People had called Gertrude brilliant before she could talk; she had been called brilliant so much that, five seconds after you said it, she couldn't remember whether you had said that or *hello.* It seemed to Gertrude that she had been writing for several centuries: weren't people *ever* going to stop calling her a younger novelist? But enough raw woman survived in her for her to be pleased in spite of herself with the word *younger.*

The world was the arsenal Gertrude used against the world. She felt about anything: If it's not a weapon what am *I* doing with it? and it turned out to be a weapon. She knew that people must be, at bottom, like herself, and this was enough to justify — to make imperative — any measures she could take against them. And if everybody had been, at bottom, what Gertrude thought she was, she would have been right to behave as she behaved, though it would have been better simply to curse God and die.

If you were one of the ordinary lumps of dough, sacks of flour, that made up the human landscape of her world, you were safe from her; but if you moved or spoke, were for some reason, from the beginning, extraordinary, she slapped you in the face, pointed out to people the marks of her fingers on your flesh, and characterized your response in terms so cruel and funny that people laughed at you and were ashamed of themselves for laughing. If you rejected Gertrude it was because of the slap, if you accepted her it was in spite of it; she had arranged things so that she could never be rejected for herself alone.

If you didn't hit Gertrude she thought you were afraid of her. To her generosity, tenderness, good-humored indifference were unaccountable except as fear or caution, and she herself was willing to know neither fear nor caution: she stripped off all her armor for the fray, her pale eyes blazing, her lips grey with sea-spume — or was it foam? She was willing to go herself, if the rest of things went with her.

It seems to us so hard to be even fairly good — for either it is hard, or else when it is easy we do not think we are being good — that we cannot help feeling that the bad are as much happier than we as they are worse. If the bus companies could have sold conducted tours of Gertrude's head, it would have done more for ethical feeling than all the moralists since Kant.

One day Gertrude met Derek out walking with one of the Afghans. She said hello to him in a friendly though rather lifeless voice — after all, he was in the book. He didn't say anything. "Out walking with Yang?" Gertrude asked.

After a minute he answered gravely, tightening his hold on the dog's collar: "He's not Yang, he's Yin. Yang is a *bad* dog."

This was what Gertrude didn't like about children: they didn't act like grown-ups. She couldn't understand why they didn't act more like grown-ups — a little more like, anyway; it seemed to her almost affectation on their part. Sometimes when we see a poor fat old woman in the bus, we think incredulously: "Was *she* ever a child?" In the same way Gertrude looked at Derek and thought: Was *I* ever like that? She could not believe it.

She had not had as much childhood as most people, and could remember almost none of what she had had. It was queer that she couldn't: she remembered everything else. Her books had all the details of childish existence that they needed, of course — accurate foreign details that she got, taw by aggie, from other people's rememberings; but children not only bored her, she felt that she was right to be bored by them. The double standard that people employ for children and grown-ups seemed to her a grotesquely disproportionate one.

Derek said, "I went to John's."

Gertrude said, "Oh, you did?"

Derek said, "Yes, I did. He told me I could. He's thirteen. He showed me all his turtles."

What can you *talk* to children about, Gertrude thought despairingly; but she said, looking as interested as she could: "And his snakes too?"

"Fern said they would hurt me. Huh, snakes won't hurt me. I have lots of snakes."

"You do? Where do you keep them?"

"In bed at night. Sometimes they wake me up." He started to say something, and stopped. Then he said, in an unexpectedly grown-up voice: "That Fern!" He laughed, and told Gertrude rather confidingly, "She showed me the hole she buried her doll in."

"Buried it?"

"The one Santa Claus bringed her. She took its clothes off, and she broke its arm, and its legs, and its head, and she buried it under the tree where the turtles all are."

"Why did she do that?"

"She was mad, she didn't want a doll. She wanted Santa Claus to bring her a baby with real wax in its ears." Gertrude had enjoyed this section, and filed away that *real wax*; but then Derek said, almost without pause: "I met your husband at the bank."

"Oh, you did?" said Gertrude, brightening at the mention of Sidney.

Derek said, "He let me blot his check. He's a nice man, I believe."

Gertrude had the feeling that would have been expressed, a generation ago, as *Bless his little heart!* Derek went on: "Were you married to Sidney when Sidney was a little boy?"

"Oh no, little boys don't get married."

"*I* think they do," Derek said. Yin was pulling at him, trying to get on with their walk; Derek gave him a tremendous yank, so that they both almost fell down; then they stood there waiting for her to say something. There was a silence: Derek did not say anything and Gertrude, for once, could think of nothing to say; the mention of Sidney seemed centuries away. Yin sat down.

"What grade are you in this year?" Gertrude said at last.

"I don't go to school, I just go to kindergarten," Derek answered. Then he said, looking at her in an odd way, so that he rather squinted: "You look like my mother." He didn't say, "You look like Pamela," as Gertrude would have expected him to; he said, "You look like my mother."

Gertrude hated to be compared to anybody; anybody would have hated to be compared to Pamela Robbins. She said, "I don't think so really, do you? She's got black hair and mine's quite fair."

"Yes, that's right," Derek said, but he didn't look convinced. He pulled Yin up and said, "Well, goodbye, Mrs. Bacon."

"Goodbye, Derek," said Gertrude. She walked away feeling almost miserable, she didn't know why. It had been a depressing conversation.

Gertrude didn't eat much, and Sidney had accustomed himself to not eating much. There were many things that she couldn't eat and more that she wouldn't eat: all her childhood aversions had persisted, and she joined to them the unwomanly but thinly feminine trait of being able to get along on crackers, a sucked lemon, and the last lettuce-leaf in the back of the vegetable-drawer of the refrigerator. *What women eat when they live alone!* a doctor has said — and that is what Sidney ate. Gertrude, as she would say, hated being held down by housework: she floated over the apartment like a balloon, and a few dust-motes from it sailed up past her in the sunlight.

She especially disliked most Southern foods; she said in her rough way, "Grits! I'd as soon eat boiled grubworms as grits," but then her face paled at the thought of the grubworms, and she wished she had spoken like a lady. Mashed potatoes, oatmeal, boiled or poached eggs, almost all soft bland foods were repulsive to her. The foods that she liked were clear green independent standoffish foods: she belonged in our Age of Salads. There was something faintly nauseating to her about the thought of chewing — or, worse still, of eating something so soft that it didn't need to be chewed. She loved sweet things, though. She and Sidney bought a box of candy every week, at one of those candy-shops where you can make up your own box: they would divide the box in half, and each seriously select his own kinds and amounts. "You mean you're not going to get any *black walnuts?*" Sidney would say in astonishment; and Gertrude would answer, "Black walnuts; I'm sick of black walnuts. I got five of them last week — don't you remember, I got so tired of them I traded you the last one for one of your mince-meats."

Her psychoanalyst had told Gertrude that finding so many foods nauseating was "part of her whole pattern of rejection." Admiring as he was, it had not taken him many months to become another part of the pattern. Gertrude was ingenious at finding some way of rejecting — of dismissing as beneath any conceivable consideration — anything or anybody. One fabulist, a black, smiling, Irish creature who said that Gertrude's books were "a Barmecide feast given by a fireworks company," was fond of telling people (Gertrude felt that he did nothing else; Gertrude felt that people *talked about her all the time*) the plot of a play he was writing, a play of which Gertrude was to be the heroine. The play had many characters at the beginning but as Gertrude told each what was wrong with him, and broke with him in the sort of scene of which an actress-manager dreams (the audience whispered, *What a moralist!* — they had seen nothing like her since Savonarola), the cast got smaller and smaller: toward the end only Gertrude was left, and she told herself, sternly, smiling her nasty, jerky, imploring smile, all that was wrong with her, and then broke with herself forever — her hand, flung out toward the darkness of the wings, was that of an Etruscan Fate.

People responded to this story in different ways. Some of them had read something like it in a book; some of them had heard someone say something like it; one of them said, "Why, it's simply Haydn's *Farewell Symphony*"; quite a lot of them — these were the ones with bad memories, I suppose — laughed and let it go at that. The story's wit lay in its exaggeration, all of them would have said.

But the story was not exaggerated. Until Gertrude had found Sidney the story had been exactly true; if anything happened to Sidney, the story would again be exactly true.

Some nights Gertrude would lie patiently waiting to go to sleep, thinking of anything and everything, shifting her limbs to another position, patiently, till she would remember what, she had read, someone had cried out upon the scaffold: *O God, if there is a God, save my soul, if I have a soul!* Instead of these two things there were herself and the people in the world: she thought of herself, of them, of what they had done to her, of what she had done to them, of what they say and feel and *are* — and it was unbearable beyond belief, worse, surely, than any nightmare. She had never had a nightmare; this was her nightmare. She looked at the world, and *saw,* and cried out, her voice rising at the end of the sentence into falsetto: "Why, it wouldn't fool a *child!*" And why say so? — she had known as long as she could remember; God knows that *she* was used to knowing!

Her thoughts went on in their accustomed round. They had worn for themselves a rut, a ditch, a canyon, too deep for them ever to climb out of; so deep that it was hard for Gertrude to distinguish, far down in the darkness below, their dark shining — and sometimes she would have to say, as you say when you recite to yourself, in the darkness, a poem you know too well: "Where am I now?" Then for an instant even habit was no help, as she identified her anger — or was it anguish? — was, for the instant, her anguish. Sometimes she would move her arms and legs and bump them against Sidney, and his slow, stupid, sleepy *Wha, wha is it, Gertrude?* was good and dear to her as she said that she was sorry, she must have been dreaming. (Not even Sidney knew that Gertrude did not dream.) But sometimes in bed beside her sleeping, her perpetually sleeping husband, she felt herself shaking so that, faintly, with a little steely sound, the springs of the bed shook: she said to herself, in wondering agony, *Why am I so angry?* She was *right* to be so angry; and yet, why was she so angry?

One day, as I went by Gertrude's office, there was a fat, dark, pretty girl in ski-trousers standing outside the door. She started away, came back, started away, came back, twice in thirty seconds; Gertrude wasn't there for their conference, she said, and she absolutely had to get her story in because it was a week late already, and she couldn't be at her conference next week because she was going to be at Dartmouth that day, and this was the last day of the week that Gertrude had conferences on, and she *couldn't* get her story in *three* weeks late. "I ought to have it in so she can read it over the weekend," she said. "That's when she reads our stories. She reads awfully fast. Sometimes when she's reading one of my stories — she just glances them over again so they'll be fresh in her mind — she reads a page at a look. She says that when she gets all worked up to a big bunch of our stories, and has to waste herself on only three or four, she feels like the Blatant Beast." She laughed; so did I. Something came up from the clear dark depths of her untroubled eyes, a thought, a memory, something, and she exclaimed, looking rather as you do when you meet the postman blocks from home, and he may have a letter for you: "Who's the Blatant Beast?"

"Something in a long poem that none of *you*'ll ever have to read," I said, smiling at her. She said in astonished pleasure, "Do you know, that's *exactly* what Miss Johnson said to me when I asked her. But what is it really?"

"Oh, a dragon all full of pamphlets — he's the Pope, too. He's in the *Faerie Queene*."

I couldn't make up my mind whether or not the name meant anything to her, but my sentence certainly did; she exclaimed more pleased than before: "That's an extraordinary coincidence. You know, that's — well, anyway, in some ways, that's *very* like my story." When she said *my story*, she glanced down at it; it came in a pretty blue cardboard folder. She looked at it in hope, and said: "I'm *sure* it's the best story I've ever written. I hope she thinks so. You never can tell with her, though."

"What's your story about?" I asked.

"It's about a bug that turns into a man."

"Really?" I said. "That sounds very unusual."

"Oh, it *is*. It's — it's influenced by Kafka," she said, looking down shyly. Then she said, "You don't remember meeting me, but I've met you — I met you last year at the tea for the juniors. My name's Sylvia Moomaw."

I said that I remembered meeting her very well, but that I hadn't remembered her name. (This wasn't so: I had remembered her name but had forgotten her.) She said. "Ever since I can remember I've wanted to be a writer when I grew up. Did you when you were young?"

"No," I said, "I wanted to be a physicist." She laughed, thinking that I was joking. She was a sort of student familiar enough to me, a soft, gentle, officious, trudging sort, as good as dough; I said in vague amity, "Just give me your story and I'll give it to Gertrude on my way home — I go right by her place."

She asked, astonished at my rashness: "Do you think I ought? She says a writer's home is her castle."

"It's all right," I said. "She won't mind."

She was pleased, but still doubtful. "Do you know her *that* well?" she asked.

"I've known her quite a long time. Is her class fun for you?"

"Fun?" she said. "It's just out of this world! I've never *had* a teacher like her — not the least bit like her."

We talked a moment longer and parted; but she came back after a few steps and said, "You can read it if you want to."

I said that I'd like to very much. I read it as I walked along to Gertrude's. There was a part where the man said, "Could I have ever *really* been a bug?" Waves and waves of the queerest most mixed-up feelings went over me; I would have cried out from their depths, *Alas, poor Moomaw!* except that . . . except that this would not have done justice to the facts of the case. She had adjusted herself — as she would have said — to Gertrude, to Kafka, exactly as if each had been Sylvia Moomaw; and I had not yet entirely adjusted myself to her — *Alas, poor you!* she could have said to me.

I shivered: it was not as if she had been walking over my grave, exactly, but more as if . . . I felt that a Moomaw was walking through my ruins, and looking their date up in her guidebook.

After I had rung the doorbell and after Gertrude had come to the door, we looked at each other and saw that we were not exactly ourselves. She looked tired and distracted and irritable. I held the story out to her wordlessly, and she said after a glance: "That dope!"

I said, "Once upon a time there was a princess who lay down on seven mattresses, and slept like a baby all night through, and when she woke up in the morning she said, 'I dreamed there was something under my mattress,' and they looked and there was a horse."

Gertrude said, "Do you want me just to give your story a grade, or shall I go over it with you and tell you what's wrong with the point of view? Yeah, she has that effect on me sometimes. But you don't give her enough credit: *she* knew there was something under the mattress."

I said helplessly, "Yes, it's like that proverb of Dr. Rosenbaum's: 'The goose said to her daughter, *You are a perfect goose.*' It'd be so much easier if she were worse. There isn't a — a mean bone in her body."

"Or any other sort," Gertrude said, snorting. She recited in a hard firm voice: "Blessed are the poor in spirit, for they shall inherit the earth . . . Over my dead body they will. Come on in."

"You're working."

"Come on in anyway. I don't feel like working. I haven't got three sentences done all morning."

She looked haggard and jumpy, and the apartment was in remarkably bad shape — for once it didn't look bare but cluttered. The sofa was covered with magazines, most of them *Partisan Review*. "I was looking up something I was sure was in *Partisan*," Gertrude said, "but I can't find it there or anywhere else." She pushed some magazines away to make herself a place to sit, and a pile of them fell on the floor; she made a cross, impatient, helpless noise, like a child who's been hurrying so much that he's lost his temper, and burst out: "I just can't concentrate today." Then she said, dropping her voice: "I suppose we'd better not talk so loud — Sidney's asleep."

"Sidney's here?"

"Yes, he couldn't go to work. He's been sick ever since Tuesday. Maybe he's awake now — I'll look in and see. You'll be a distraction for him. He doesn't feel like reading."

She opened the door of the bedroom, very softly for her, and peeped in at Sidney. "No, he's still asleep," she said. Her face softened, as your face softens when you look at a cat and her kittens, in a box in a closet. "Look at him," she said.

He lay there in unhappy sleep. He had two pillows propping up his head; the noise of the cars in the street or of Gertrude's typewriter must have bothered him, for he had put another pillow over his head, a tremendous ochre one from the living room. A wan segment of his face showed from under it, like a mouse lying under a loaf of bread. I felt sorry for Sidney. The devil, come to drag Sidney's soul off to hell, would have felt sorry for Sidney. His body was curled into a miserable (yet somehow homey) mound, and his pajama'd arm was clutched around — no, it wasn't clutched around anything, and yet it looked so much as if it were that you could almost tell what the thing was: it was either a teddy bear or a cloth duck, and I stared hard at it, trying to make it out — but it was no use. "He feels pretty bad," said Gertrude. "He said to me, 'Gertrude, I feel so bad.' "

I said, "Poor thing! What is it that's wrong with him, do you know?"

"Something he ate, he thinks." My thought were mostly a mother's thoughts, as I looked at him, but I couldn't help thinking at *this:* "I'll bet it was." The things Sidney must have eaten!

Gertrude went on: "And he has a cold, of course — a bad one. We think he's generally run down. He's been forgetting to take his vitamins — well, to tell the truth, I forgot to get any more when the last bottle ran out. I've just got too much on my mind — the books, and all these students, and I do most of the shopping, here. Sidney does it all at home. Life is more difficult out here, that's all there is to it. You just *have* to live in New York if you want your life to be convenient."

A voice from the bedroom said feebly, "Who's that, Gertrude?" Gertrude told him, and he was feebly glad to have me there, and asked me, feebly, to come in. I talked to him for a little, but it was hard for him to pay attention to what we were saying; he nodded as amiably as ever, though, and said yes as politely as ever — but oh, so feebly. Finally he said with weak hope: "Gertrude, may I have some lemonade?"

"You can if you'll take it hot without any sugar."

"That's just not lemonade," Sidney said disappointedly.

"Oh, all right," Gertrude said to him. Her voice wasn't grudging,

really, but gracious, and she said to me in an undertone, as she
squeezed the lemon: "The least I can do is give him some lemonade.
There's so little you can do for someone when he's sick . . . "

I said, "Yes, they live in a different world. I think the Scythians,
instead of deciding everything once drunk and once sober, should
have done it once well and once ill."

Gertrude wasn't listening, and said mechanically: "The Persians.
I'd a lot rather be sick myself. It's so easy when *I'm* sick." She went
on absently, "I don't worry about myself when I'm sick."

It was so: she was the best of patients. I remembered getting to
hear her say to Sidney when *she* was sick, "It simply hurts, Sidney,
and there's no use your making a fuss about it. No, I don't want
anything to eat, and I've already had two aspirins, and if I can't
sleep I'll read. You can play the radio if you don't turn it up too
loud — just shut the door and let me alone and I'll be all right in
the morning." Not even sickness could make an ordinary human
being out of Gertrude: she was indomitable.

Not even sickness — but Sidney's sickness seemed to be a different
affair. I said, "Gertrude, after I've left why don't you take a nap
yourself? Maybe you can get something written after you wake up."

"I'm going to," Gertrude said. "I'm *exhausted.*" She took the
lemonade in to Sidney, and Sidney sat up halfway in bed, and drank
it in weak gulps and, when it was gone, said in a troubled voice:
"I feel bad, being such a nuisance for Gertrude; she's hardly got
anything done since I've been sick."

"Don't you worry, Sidney," said Gertrude. "I could do *this* book
with both hands tied behind my back."

Sidney was well in a week. But Gertrude took longer to recover
from his illness. One night of that week she got up to go to the bathroom, drank some water out of the faucet — her mouth tasted bad,
and the water had the sweet, pure, insipid taste of water drunk at
such a time — and as she straightened up she saw herself in the
mirror over the wash-basin. It was still only half past two; her head
ached, her red eyes stung with sleeplessness, and as she looked uncomprehendingly into what seemed to her worthless, her own face,
she had a queer fraction of thought: two thoughts going on at the

same time, one over the other. What would I do if something happened to Sidney? was the top thought, and appeared infinitesimally sooner, and the thought under it was: How long will Sidney go on being Sidney?

Gertrude was afraid of nothing. She said to the world: "If you can do without me I can do without you" — she wanted, almost, to get rid of it so as to prove that she could do without it. But could she say, "If Sidney can do without me I can do without Sidney"? There in the middle of the night, rubbing her hurting eyes, staring into the scrambled flaccid face that had not yet even made itself into Gertrude, she felt an abject physiological certainty that she could not. Without the sweet, pure, insipid taste of Sidney in her mouth she would — she didn't know what she would do.

She had trusted Sidney entirely because Sidney needed her entirely: how could Sidney possibly get along without *her*? But now that she saw she could not possibly get along without Sidney, her trust was shaken. When Sidney found out that she was in his power — if he found out, her heart substituted hastily — what would he do? How could you trust *anyone* with such power?

It didn't occur to Gertrude that she had had such power for a long time, and that Sidney had trusted her and had been right to trust her. All power corrupts, and absolute power corrupts absolutely, Gertrude was fond of quoting — though she, of course, quoted it correctly and said *tends to corrupt*. (And she always said *to paint the lily:* she knew that this was a commonplace phrase and that the memory of mankind had transfigured it, and she was contemptuous of people who said *to paint the lily* — just as she was contemptuous, in a different way, of people who said *to gild the lily* — but she couldn't bear to have anyone think that she didn't know which one it really was. She didn't care how you misjudged her, as long as you knew that she *knew*.)

In the world there were people who were bad to her and people who were good to her, people she was bad to and people she — and Sidney. Sidney was what Gertrude could be good to. From the black steel of Gertrude's armored side there opened a kind of door, and from it a hand emerged and held out to Sidney a glass of lemonade — cold, and with sugar in it, even if it was bad for him — and the

hand, seriously and with interest, watched Sidney drink the lemonade. Then the door closed; but still, it had been open for that long:
for that long there had been nothing between the world and Gertrude but a hand holding a glass of lemonade.

It always surprised Gertrude that people, ordinary people, could
take themselves seriously; surely even they must see how ridiculous
they were! But as she watched Sidney drink the lemonade she did
not see how ridiculous he was, but watched seriously and with interest, taking him on his own terms.

Gertrude knew that she herself was a very exceptional person,
a person ordinary in no sense of the word. Yet this did not help
her to think that Sidney would continue to need her, continue to
love her. I heard her say once, in vexed impatient wonder: "People
just aren't *lovable*." Love — or affection, or tenderness, or good-
humored acceptance — seemed to her a precarious state arduously
maintained; if Sidney had come home from work some evening and
had said to her, "I'm not interested in you any more, Gertrude,"
she would have thought this a disastrous but perfectly reasonable,
perfectly predictable thing for him to say — he would simply have
come to his senses.

She thought about Sidney; she thought for some time about how
difficult it must be for Sidney, being Sidney — *keeping on* being
Sidney! The complaints he didn't make! the retorts he didn't utter!
All the admiration he gave instead of getting, all the triumphs he
walked in chains at the tail of, barefoot, without even a slave to
whisper in his ear what he had never had the opportunity to forget:
Remember that you too are mortal! She realized for the first time
how hard things were for Sidney, as she for the first time put herself
in Sidney's place. She put herself into it as she would have put
herself into the skin of a cinnamon bear, and as she walked along
being Sidney she could have been recognized — as Gertrude, that is
— at an astronomical distance.

She went slowly, with soft thoughtful steps, back into the bedroom; as she started to get into bed Sidney stirred, with a little
whimpering sigh, and she looked down at where he was, in the
darkness, and said to herself, No, I might wake him. She went out
and closed the door. She got the last two blankets from the linen

closet — I wish we had more *blankets,* she thought — and, feeling absurd, went to the sofa with them, made a cozy bed for herself, and lay down in it: but not, alas, to sleep.

How much Sidney had to put up with! She thought about it for a while, putting herself in Sidney's place; but she wasn't used to doing this, and got tired of thinking the same thing over and over . . . But luckily, Sidney wasn't clever, so people interested him. She herself could have said, "People just aren't *interesting.*" She hadn't for many years even expected them to be. She *knew* what people are like, had known for so long that it was almost as if she had always known, and yet she still couldn't reconcile herself to the knowledge. If she had been allowed to pick one word for what people are, it would have been: *irritating.*

Once John Whittaker had told me the plot of his favorite science-fiction story. It was a rather sad, nostalgic story about a man of the future, one who is retiring from his position, an important one, at the age of a thousand. I said, "Did they think he was so old he was about to die, or what?" John answered, "Oh no. But they can't use them in jobs any more after they're a thousand: they get too irritable."

Sometimes when I was with Gertrude I would think of this story: she was a thousand years older than other people. Yet irritability is, as I remembered from biology, one of the primary properties of protoplasm. Gertrude was as protoplasmic as they come. She didn't suffer fools gladly; and as she looked around at this fools' purgatory in which we live, a rational malice at everything, an impatient dismissal of everything would overcome her, and soothe a little as they overcame — she was like a magic sword that is content only as it comes shining from the scabbard.

She dismissed the world generally, but writers, competitors, people who mattered, particularly — death or a bad book was a joy to her, and the world's swift forgetfulness best of all. She thought often: Well, that does for him. If she had learned that not seven but six cities had competed for the honor of being Homer's birthplace, it would have given her a little thrill of pleasure.

Lying there on the sofa under the blankets, she kept walking aimlessly around and around in the maze of herself, suffering sometimes, triumphing sometimes, sometimes only walking, and at about the time she could see dawn over the walls her steps slowed and she fell asleep. But she knew about Sidney and herself, now; and until the newness of her knowledge had worn off, things were harder than usual for Gertrude. And harder, alas, for Sidney. She felt that she must not at any price let Sidney see what she had seen — just mustn't give him a *chance* of seeing; how glad she was that Sidney wasn't smarter! Some of her usual absentminded good humor toward him disappeared, though only for a few weeks. Sometimes when she had some slight cause for vexation, and sometimes when she had none, she spoke to him more severely than she had spoken to him for a long time: she *had* to, it was for his own good, if he only knew. Sidney would look at her uncomprehendingly and try to figure out what he had done, and when he couldn't, he knew that he didn't know because he did not understand things as well as Gertrude, but that she knew. One evening this response was so plain on Sidney's face that Gertrude's heart failed her, and she said, "Oh no, I didn't mean that, Sidney. I — I don't know what could have come over me."

He smiled at her in gratitude — the dark day had turned fair — and said that she'd been working on the book so hard that week, all that new part about Mrs. Whittaker, and she was tired. "That's a *wonderful* part about her and her little girl — what's her little girl's name really?"

Gertrude said, looking at him gratefully: "Fern." Her whole heart was in that *Fern;* as she stared at Sidney she repeated, without knowing that she had done so: "Fern." After a moment she heard the sound, the sound made her think of the name, and the name made her think of the world. Brought back to it from whatever place she had been, she thought of it — and from the midst of her own accustomed, exasperated, despairing thought, the oldest and deepest of her being, she said, dropping her head on Sidney's shoulder. "Oh, Sidney, people are such *dopes!*"

How beautiful the school was as, in glade and in grove, it lay there in the level light of evening! as beautiful, more composed and eternal, than later in the diminishment of moonlight; all things seemed steady there beneath the sun. In those moments, in all the moments of those spring days, it justified everything that Gertrude Johnson had said of it. She had said it — read it, rather — to a predominantly scientific Committee on Aims (her Chorus of Elder Sociologists of Thebes, she used to call them) to which she was unfortunately and unwillingly attached.

Gertrude believed that people hoarded and fed and slept and knew not her; it was her strongest belief, and she took all the measures that she could to strengthen it. As she began to read, the Sociologists looked narrowly at her enthusiasm for Benton, moving their necks in their collars — it was one of the only signs of liking she had ever shown. But when she had finished they looked at her with friendly dazzled eyes, thinking *Why, that's beautiful;* it sounded to them like Veblen or the Bible. Gertrude had read them a passage that began by calling Benton a home of lost causes. But it went on to say that the causes were not lost: "No, we are all seekers still! yet seekers often make mistakes, and I wish mine to redound to my own discredit only, and not to touch Benton. [She paused.] Beautiful spot! so young, so lovely, so unravaged by the fierce intellectual life of our century, so serene!

'There are our *junge Mädchen* all at play!'

And yet, steeped in truths as she lies, spreading her gardens to the moonlight, and whispering from her towers the first enchantments of the Future Age, who will deny that Benton, by her ineffable charm, keeps calling us nearer to the true goal of all of us, to the ideal, to perfection — to beauty, in a word, which is only truth seen from the other side? — nearer, perhaps, than all the science of M.I.T. . . . Adorable Benton! — " It went on so, with a few necessary judicious alterations, to the end.

When she finished Gertrude said apologetically that out of its context it might seem a little abrupt or — or too lyric and old-fashioned; but they did not feel that this was so. They had not known that Gertrude was so good a writer; and they felt better, too, about Gertrude's soul.

In the moment that Jerrold congratulated her upon "the eleva-

tion, the almost Victorian eloquence of her style"; in that moment,
as in many more — though not in so many as she could have wished
— the pain under Gertrude's right breast, just beneath two of the
lower ribs (though sometimes it was higher, sometimes lower), was
gone . . . or if it was still there, she had for the time forgotten it.
It was a pain almost like the stitch in the side that runners get,
and was faintly nauseating in the same way: a knotting or fluttering
or gnawing of muscles, or the memory or anticipation of this, that
was always there: Gertrude's flesh catching its breath. Or rather, it
was an idea that Gertrude's body had had, and could not get rid
of; it was the fixed idea of her flesh. Sometimes it was bad, sometimes it almost was good, but good or bad, like weather, it was there.

Gertrude had been afraid of it when it first came, and had gone
to her doctor with questions about ulcers and cancer and tuber-
culosis: there was nothing; and from then on Gertrude did not mind
it, hardly remembering it when it was gone, would pay no attention
to it when it was barely there — she could endure anything, feel
safe with anything, that was "merely functional." She did not mind
it because she understood it: it was part of the price of being Gertrude.

Did not mind it, medically speaking, intellectually speaking; yet
sometimes as she lay awake in the darkness, without any world there
to distract her from herself, the stitch in her side grew and grew until
it seemed to her bigger than the world, a sea of boredom and nausea
upon whose swells she and the earth floated in vexed, unending,
senseless misery. It did not seem possible to her that she had ever
been without it, and to be without it seemed to her happiness; and
when she shifted herself or wadded her pillow against it so that it
grew smaller, she seemed to herself to have two hearts, one on the
left and one on the right; and the last, her real heart, was a heart
of pain.

She lay there in the darkness. If Gertrude hit out at the world
when she and it were together, it got its own back from her when
they were apart: it had taken its own back, that is. Nothing nice
had ever happened to Gertrude in bed. There applied to her, in a
much more general sense, the words in which the Bible tells the
story of David and Abishag:

"Now King David was old and stricken in years; and they covered him with cloths, but he gat no heat. Wherefore his servants said unto him, Let there be sought for my lord the king a young virgin: and let her stand before the king, and let her cherish him, and let her lie in thy bosom, that my lord the king may get heat. So they sought for a fair damsel throughout all the coasts of Israel, and found Abishag the Shunammite, and brought her to the king. And the damsel was very fair, and cherished the king, and ministered to him: but the king knew her not."

The world was very fair, and cherished Gertrude, and ministered to her: but she knew it not. She lay there beside that homely negligible extension of herself, that fifth limb, Sidney Bacon, and cried to the men and women of her world, those *divinités du Styx:* "Far be it from me to implore your cruel pity." She went on to say — so to speak, so to speak — that she died unmoved; and that, dead or alive, she was Gertrude Johnson still. . . . This formula was first used by Medea, but Gertrude repeated it with as much relevance and grace.

And the next morning, lying back in the bathtub watching her husband, that Constant Reader, shave, she said to herself in the dreamy voluptuous spirituality of being in hot water up to her head: "My destiny is accomplished and I die content." How often she made such quotations as these, said or felt or was them! For just as many Americans want art to be Life, so this American novelist wanted life to be Art, not seeing that many of the values — though not, perhaps, the final ones — of life and art are irreconcilable; so that her life looked coldly into the mirror that it held up to itself, and saw that it was full of quotations, of data and analysis and epigrams, of naked and shameful truths, of *facts:* it saw that it was a novel by Gertrude Johnson.

(From The Saturday Evening Post)

NO WAY DOWN

BY ALMET JENKS

(On the third expedition to conquer Mount Everest — the first three were all English — that of 1924, two climbers, George H. Leigh Mallory and Andrew Irvine, making the final assault, were briefly seen at a point some 800 feet below the summit. It was then afternoon, but they were still climbing. This story, with changes in time, topography and in the persons and incidents concerned, is fiction, based on several accounts by members of that expedition.)

*T*HE LAST and highest camp was Camp VII. This was to be pitched at 27,300 feet (about), some 1700 below the summit. We had started from Camp VI at eight o'clock that morning — Norman Joyce, Holmes Canning and I, with the three picked porters. We were out of our tents — Joyce, Canning and I — at five A.M., but once again it had proved impossible to get an early start — the way one could, for instance, climbing in the Alps. Vitality was low indeed at these tremendous altitudes, and the business of getting out of your two sleeping bags, putting on your boots, rousing the porters, making them cook and eat, then eating our own distasteful breakfast — the only thing that appealed that high on the mountain was something to drink — all this was sheer torture. Getting the porters on their feet was the worst. Camp VI was at 25,500, and the porters had little heart for going higher. They were all sick, or said they were sick, and the best one, Nemsang, was lame. Norman Joyce, who, of all the expedition, spoke their language best, talked to them for a good hour, and finally, three hours after we got up, the party

started. We were not using oxygen. We had been living at Camp
V at 23,000, officially known as the "acclimatization camp," for more
than two weeks, with several visits to higher altitudes, and we meant
to reach the summit without using gas. When I say "we," I mean
Norman Joyce and Holmes Canning alone; they were the assault
troops; I was in support.

You may ask here why I, the youngest member of the expedition,
was allowed to go along with Joyce and Canning to the last camp.
Ordinarily, it would have been just the two of them up here, the
porters having been sent down the afternoon before. You might
think that I was being rewarded for having done something note-
worthy on the mountain. Of course, that was true all the way, so
far as Norman Joyce and Holmes Canning were concerned: they
had been ordained from the beginning for the final attempt on the
summit. Norman Joyce had been on two preceding expeditions and
had been turned back each time; on the first by the threat of an
early monsoon, on the next by the tragic death of the porters. Loving, and, at the same time, perhaps hating the great mountain — the
way one might feel about a stubborn and wholly honorable opponent — he could not leave the enemy alone. Norman Joyce, when
he wasn't climbing mountains, was a writer and a poet, and I first
met him when he came to school to lecture, with pictures, on the
first expedition of all. Owing to him, I did a little climbing in the
Swiss Alps on two summer vacations, and that had something to do
with my being a member of the expedition. He was thirty-four
years old.

As for Holmes Canning, he was in his late twenties, five or six years
older than I, and already had a great reputation as a mountaineer.
He had, too, what is known as independent means, for he wasn't,
evidently, engaged in any business or profession. This expedition
was my last big adventure before settling down to the usual hum-
drum existence, but Holmes Canning, who didn't have to work
for a living, could go on till he got too old and stiff for the mountains, and then he could take up something like — well, growing
roses — and the reason I say that is because of Mrs. Canning, who,
evidently, was a great gardener. Just before we took off on the expedition, Holmes Canning invited me for a week end in the country,

and it was there I first met Mrs. Canning; there were also two quite small kids, both girls, as I remember.

The Cannings talked very little about mountain climbing, but I knew he had done many of the big Alpine peaks and some of the great rock climbs of the Dolomites, and that Mrs. Canning had been along on several. She was not only very beautiful but also, though rather quiet, tremendously friendly right away, and always laughing about things.

For instance, I said something of the purposes of the expedition — the flora and fauna, geological specimens, atmospheric data, and so on — and she laughed and said, "The only reason why Norman Joyce and Holmes and you" — and being bracketed with them was flattering to me of course — "and all the rest of you are going is to get to the top of the mountain. Especially Mr. Joyce," she said, turning serious suddenly. Then she went on, amused again, "So don't bring up that nonsense about 'scientific purposes.' It reminds me of what someone said about some honorary order — the Order of the Garter, wasn't it? — 'no damned merit about it.' Something like that."

We all laughed, knowing she spoke the truth, more or less. I saw her again, the day she came from the country to see some of the expedition off, and I managed to be with her for about an hour while we waited at the airport, but, though she was terribly kind and friendly, it was really only Holmes Canning she was interested in, and I thought he must be feeling very low at leaving her. I was glad when the plane was ready for us. If I had seen any more of her, it would have been a serious thing for me.

But I did not explain why I was with Norman Joyce and Holmes Canning on the climb to the last camp, the jumping-off place for the final assault. One thing, being the youngest, I had, perhaps only for that reason, come through in the best physical condition so far. The climbers — I call them that to distinguish them from the native porters, though the distinction is invidious except when we reached the very high altitudes and most of the porters began to fade — the climbers had all suffered the usual afflictions; diarrhea, two cases of snow blindness, sore throats and racking coughs, and all the rest. But I, except for loss of weight — some fifteen pounds, I suppose — had been lucky. For that reason I was picked to go along with Joyce and Canning, up to the last camp. There was certainly no honor in it for me — no damned merit, as Mrs. Canning would have pointed out. I was simply in support; we called it that. To do the chores after the porters had been at last sent down; be cook and bottle washer, and to wait there at Camp VII during the fateful day. And when they returned, from victory or, once more, defeat, to go to meet them with vacuum flasks of hot drinks, and then to try to get us all down to a lower camp, if possible, that same night. There was another reason, I should add in fairness, why I was chosen as support: I was the smallest of the climbers, and what with the loss of weight, I would fit, in a pinch — literally — into the little tent meant to sleep only two. Well, yes, you might call it a small honor, in a way.

As I have said, we started from Camp VI at eight that morning. Besides worrying about the porters, how much higher we could get them to go, there was also the threat of the monsoon. We were late for the final assault, and we all knew it must be tomorrow, and that would be all, this time. And never again, probably, for Norman Joyce. One didn't get to go on an expedition like this every other year or so, and by the time the next one was organized, he might well be too old. On the mountains — his kind of mountain, the really rugged ones — you get old, as in the prize ring, fast.

The bitter, terrible cross wind from the west was blowing again that morning, and we were slow along the rock face of the northwest wall. There was one quite bad, unforeseen traverse where we had trouble getting the porters, with their loads, which were light now, across; coming down, without loads and with Nemsang, a good man even though lame, on the rope, they would be all right. I know I was glad to have Holmes Canning ahead and the rope from him, and the rope back from me to Norman Joyce. They were among the best in the world, and between them, even on that sheer wall of rock and ice, you were safe as a church, but I remember thinking then I wouldn't want to cross that place alone.

Two hours and then the ascent steepened, and now the way was straight up over slabby rocks and occasional patches of snow, not quite steep enough to use one's hands, but affording a quick drop, in case of a slip, into the abyss and onto the glacier, 3000 feet below. We were well over 26,000 now, and as we continued to go higher, the agony of breathing grew worse. Holmes Canning, who was still leading, established a kind of rhythm of climbing, which the rest of the party was soon following: twenty steps, rest a minute; twenty steps, rest a minute; twenty steps.

The porters, who could have done better, since they never had the trouble breathing we did, were entirely agreeable to this terribly slow rate, and, as morning passed all too swiftly into afternoon, we knew they would not go much higher. We passed several places bare of snow, where, with the necessary, inevitable platform building, the little tent could be pitched, and at each place the porters lingered and had to be urged on. For every yard made good today would be so much gained tomorrow.

We had planned, as I have said, to place Camp VII at about 27,300, but we soon realized we would never make that. And with afternoon upon us, there came over me a terrible depression. And I wondered if Norman Joyce and Holmes Canning, knowing that the porters were failing at every step and that we could not push them very much farther, felt the same black despair that came so readily to me at these great altitudes. I hoped not; they had been picked to make the final attempt; they, therefore, had so much more to lose.

About four o'clock in the afternoon we stopped to rest on a tiny ledge, a shelf, cut, as if by a giant stone cutter, into the great wall of the northwest face. I looked up and saw above us an even steeper slope of rock and ice, and I knew then the porters would go no higher.

This narrow ledge on which we rested afforded some lee from the wind, which was now blowing even more strongly from the northwest, and the rock floor could, with the addition of loose stones, be made into a platform large enough to accommodate the tent. The decision was forced on us by the collapse of the porters; here, not farther on up, was the proper site for Camp VII, and here we would stay. When the platform was built, the little tent pitched and weighted with rocks, the scanty rations stowed, we let the porters go. I have never seen people so glad to leave any place.

You would think that after that day's climb and after the evening chores, the awful labor of melting snow for cooking, and cooking a meal and filling the vacuum flasks for the morning at that extreme altitude, we might have been blessed with the deep dreamless sleep of near exhaustion. Right after the tasteless meal we climbed into our two sleeping bags apiece, jammed together in the little tent with all our clothes on; only our boots removed and two pairs of dry socks pulled on. But at these altitudes, when the cold was very great, many of the climbers found it impossible to get any real sleep. I lay there wondering whether the tent guys and stone weights would serve to hold our tent there on the mountain wall or suddenly, without warning, a more terrible gust of wind would carry it away. I knew, as we all knew, what that would mean; no one could hope to survive a night in the open, up where we were. I wondered what my companions, who, I could sense, were also wide awake, were thinking. About tomorrow, I supposed, and what would be decided then. For them it would be like a night before battle — and then I told myself I was making too much of a drama of all this, because tomorrow would not be, as in war, actually a matter of life or wound or death. Tomorrow our assault party would either reach the summit in time to return here before nightfall or, seeing that it could not safely be done, would once again turn back. Now, strangely, at that moment — he might have known what I was thinking — Holmes Canning spoke out of the dark. "If you keep on with this sort of thing, Jonathan, don't you ever take it too seriously."

I didn't say anything for a moment. The words were addressed to me, but I had the feeling that he hoped Norman Joyce would answer. At last I said, "That sounds as if you'd be retiring after this one."

"He'll have the right to," Norman Joyce said, quiet, firm, absolutely confident. Confident, I mean, about their getting to the top the next day. I was amazed and, for some reason, afraid; never before, from the day the expedition set out, had anyone taken success for granted; too many good men had failed. It seemed to me that Norman Joyce was really needling the enemy. After a silence, he added, "No more worlds to conquer."

"No more worlds," Holmes Canning said, making light of it,

"but plenty of mountains. I assure you, Jonathan, it's all in the way of sport. Don't ever make your world a mountain."

No one spoke for a space. In the dark, lying there close by Norman Joyce's side — I was between them — I could not see his face, but in my mind I could see it, without the sunglasses, sparsely bearded — nothing like Holmes Canning's great golden beard — staring up at the tent wall, through the wall, up toward the great final pyramid of the mountain. His face would have — as it had that time when he lectured at school — a dedicated look; like one of the earlier, holier saints. That's the way I thought of Norman Joyce, as if he were a presence of some kind. . . . But what was it Holmes Canning had said? "Don't ever make your world a mountain." I wasn't sure — but Norman Joyce was sure.

"Do you think, Holmes," he asked in his quiet, gentleman's voice, "that I've made this mountain my world? I've been told that people have said so."

"I think it's a danger we're all prone to," Holmes Canning answered, taking evasive action. "I think we should face the possibility of being beaten again, Norman. Yes, again. I know . . . We should have done better today — do I sound like a defeatist?"

"Did you," Norman Joyce said suddenly, "land on Red or Blue or Yellow Beach having in mind the possibility of returning to the boats?"

"That's just it!" the other exclaimed. "No, of course not. But that was a war. Surely — "

"This mountain," Norman Joyce broke in, "is like the enemy on the beach: to be conquered!" And then, even he, who took this thing so seriously, must have smiled at this pronouncement, for he added, more reasonably, and humorously, "To be licked, that is."

"At any cost?" the other asked.

Norman Joyce didn't answer, and there was a silence for several moments. And then his friend began to speak, and it was rather like a speech — I mean a public speech, but of the kind you so rarely hear: quiet, clear, absolutely reasonable — no flourishes, no deep chest notes, no damned oratory.

"I don't suppose," said Holmes Canning, "that the men who crawled up that beach thought of anything except to keep edging on. Get to the airstrip — the first objective — or get thrown back into the sea. But that was a war, and quite a different thing from climbing mountains, as you know."

"Do I know?" Norman Joyce asked quietly. "I was unfit," he said. I thought so much of him — it seemed an unnecessarily brutal way of putting it. He had volunteered for all the services and had been turned down by all — a heart murmur, something like that. Think of all the mountains he had climbed — the mountain he was climbing!

So he compared climbing his mountain to storming an enemy beach. Land and hold the beach, seize the airstrip — that is, get to the mountain's top — at any cost. There was an analogy, all right, but, Holmes Canning argued — we were past all thought of sleep now — they were not really the same. In war, one had no thought for anything except the mission to be accomplished; one was always ready and willing to give one's life to that end. But in climbing mountains it was very wrong to go that far; one did not, one should not, heedlessly throw his life away in an effort to reach the summit.

"In a book I greatly admire," he said at last, "it says someplace — I can't quote it exactly — 'Climbers making an attempt on the final peak must be prepared to turn back, however close to the summit, in good time to be sure of a return to camp before night.'" He paused. "Wasn't that the way you put it, Norman, more or less?"

"I'm afraid I did," Norman Joyce said, and he sounded almost as if he were sorry he had written it. They were silent then, the way older people stop talking — sometimes! — to give a younger person a chance to speak, and I felt it was up to me. But all I could think of to say was that there was a true analogy between war and mountain climbing that Holmes Canning had not mentioned, which was that any member of a climbing party would most certainly risk his life to go to the rescue of another — would even give his life to save the life of a friend, just as in war men had, with only the fraction of a second to decide, thrown themselves on live grenades — to me, the ultimate in heroism. But I knew this would sound callow and awkward after Holmes Canning's speech, so all I said was that I thought we should try to get some sleep.

When the luminous dial of my watch finally said five o'clock I spoke to them, as arranged, but they were awake too. None of us

wanted anything to eat. The flasks had been filled with coffee the
night before, we had no porters to bother about, but even so, everything — the mere act of pulling boots on, I remember — took an
interminable time at that great altitude. Norman Joyce and Holmes
Canning did not get away till almost six-thirty.

They roped up for the rock-and-ice wall just above our ledge; beyond that the ascent appeared to present no particular difficulties
until they should come to what was generally known as the last
"step." This was a jagged cut in the ridge leading to the base of the
final pyramid, and, so far as we could judge, presented a steep rock
climb — it would be that way! — to what was believed to be an
easy slope up the face of the pyramid to the summit. Fairly easy, it
looked, but this was not to speak of the lack of oxygen, the icy, terrible cold, made more intense, more bitter, by the fierce northwest
wind, the shortness of daylight in view of the slow, exhausting pace
imposed, and, worst of all, perhaps, the psychology of man in the
face of what many believed to be the impossible, the unconquerable
mountain.

So I wished them the best of luck, saying, "See you on the top!"
meaning that I would see them from far down below if the day was
clear, and then the sun showed over the piddling peaks to the east,
and I saw it was going to be clear, and I had great hopes for them.
I watched them for several minutes, roped together and using their
axes now and then, up the rock-and-ice wall, and then I couldn't
bear to watch that slow, heartbreaking pace any longer, and I told
myself that if I went back into the tent for a while, they would go
much faster, and when I came out again, they would be much farther
up. The pot would be boiling.

I made myself stay in the tent for two good hours, and on the dot
I crawled out — into a gray world of mist! It was hard to believe.
Two hours before, as the sun struck our tent, the sky had been a
clear, brilliant blue — I should be able to see them, I thought then,
almost all the way to the summit. Where had this blinding bank of
mist come from? It was, in a way, like being at sea on a bright
sunny day when suddenly, rolling in with appalling speed comes the
feared, the hated fog.

I waited there, in the now more bitter cold, for the cloud to pass and show me how much farther up they had gone. But the cloud or mist did not pass; it swirled and clung over the entire upper half of the mountain, and all the time the terrible northwest wind blew. I stood there, staring upward, the way one does at sea, standing in the bow of a boat, trying to pierce with one's eyes the gray curtain of the fog.

I began to see things — figures on skis, figures glissading on the slopes, crevasses opening up. I grew bitterly cold, there was nothing to be done here, so I went back into the tent. Every few minutes I lifted the flap and looked out. No change. No change.

At noon I melted snow and made myself soup. I still had no appetite for solid food. But I was thirsty almost all the time. You might think that waiting there alone, with nothing to do, nothing I could do, except look out every minute or so, almost like clockwork, into the swirling mist — you might think that the hours would seem endless. But I was with them all the time, and time passed with frightening speed. You see, I knew very well that because of our poor showing yesterday, they had a much longer climb today than had been counted on when their plans were made. And now, when they must be approaching the final pyramid, I was with them, and I was praying for time, more time, so that they might get there and then get back before night fell. I tell you, for me the hours went by like minutes.

And then, a little after two o'clock, a queer thing happened. For no reason I can explain, I suddenly felt forsaken and terribly alone on that ledge, in that never-ending gray fog and — yes, very much afraid. I had been afraid before on the mountain, on other mountains, but never had I felt this hollow, sickening fear. Of what, I couldn't say. There was nothing for me to be afraid of, no danger, except possibly that one bad traverse on the descent to Camp VI and then the three of us would be roped together —

I crawled out of the tent and struggled to my feet on the rocky ledge. I looked up; I stood there, staring up toward the summit. And then — and it was like some tremendously dramatic thing on the stage, so beautiful, so awesome that it made your heart almost burst — the cloud above me split asunder and revealed the great ridge rising from the west wall, the final pyramid, and the summit itself. And in that moment of time, I saw against a patch of snow — on rock I should never have seen them — just below the last step, a small black dot, and, behind this one, a little lower down, another. Moving . . . slowly — oh, so slowly! And then the black dot in the lead stopped, the black dot in the rear joined it, and to me they seemed as one. Thus they remained for a little while, and I thought, *It is afternoon, it is too late; now they are deciding, this is the farthest point; now they will turn back* — and then the one separated itself from the other, and both began to move again, and I saw, in horror, and I could not believe — I could not believe — they were moving on up toward the last step. And then the great cloud of mist closed down and hid them from me.

When Norman Joyce, who was leading, stopped to rest this time, Holmes Canning did not stop, too, but, taking up on the rope, closed the short distance that separated them. They stood together, heads down, ice axes planted in the little patch of snow, leaning against the wind as the gray mist suddenly cleared, gasping at the thin, dry, subzero air. By their watches they both knew it was a little after two in the afternoon.

"Time to try back, I'm afraid," Holmes Canning said, his voice harsh, cracked.

"Back?" the other whispered, staring.

Holmes Canning could not see, through the dark glasses they both wore, his friend's eyes, and he wondered what look was in them, and suddenly his heart came up into his throat.

"I'm going on," Norman Joyce said.

"It can't be done." Holmes Canning's voice broke; now he had no hope at all. He spoke the dread word they both understood so well: "Benighted."

Norman Joyce unstuck his ice ax and faced the sheer rock wall of the last step. Holmes Canning stood there a moment, turning the slack of rope in his gloved hands. And what should he do? He thought, despairingly, of driving his ice ax deep into the snow, belaying the rope and holding his friend there by force. But of course that wouldn't do. He thought, *If you are trying to rescue a drowning man, and he, in panic, grabs you round the neck and threatens to drag you under with him, you knock him out with a blow to the chin and swim him, limp, unconscious, to shore.* But that, which might work in the sea, was no good on the mountain.

Norman Joyce, as if suddenly remembering something, turned round again, quickly unroped himself, and dropped the coil on the snow between them. He leaned close to his friend.

"You go back, Holmes. I've got to go on."

Holmes Canning stood there a moment. He himself had certain obligations. There were, after all, such things as a wife, children — little children — to be considered, but in that moment of decision these did not, for some reason, loom large. He saw that Norman Joyce had started to climb again. Could he, Holmes Canning, turn back now and let him go on alone? Holmes Canning untied the rope from round his waist and let it fall in the snow. It would mean climbing the last steep step unroped. What difference did it make, one way or the other? He pulled his ax free and, glancing up toward the final pyramid, followed his friend.

Something like that is what some people believe happened up there. But I do not believe it. They had a chance. It could be done. I have worked it all out by the tables. Climbing without oxygen on the last thousand feet, they might make three hundred feet of altitude an hour, perhaps more on the final fairly-easy-looking slope — estimates have gone as high as five hundred feet an hour. That would bring them to the summit not long after four o'clock — time enough to return to Camp VII before dark. Sure, they had a chance. Not a very good one, perhaps, but what else would men like Norman Joyce and Holmes Canning do, with the summit within their grasp and a sporting chance of getting back.

I spent that night, of course, at Camp VII. And I spent the next night there in the same swirling mist, waiting for them, although I knew all along it was hopeless. The next morning I started down, leaving the tent and their gear and sleeping bags and the rations — the way one puts out food for a ghost. The descent, by-passing Camp VI to V, was easy, except for that bad traverse, which, on the way up, I thought I should not want to take on without a good man on each end of the rope. Well, the good men were not there now, and would not be again. I took that traverse in my stride, so to speak, and halfway across I got crying, and I would not have cared much if I had come off the mountain and gone plummeting down to the glacier. I kept thinking then, as I've always thought since, I hoped I would have done what Norman Joyce and Holmes Canning chose to do — to go on . . .

And when, one day recently, on my commuters' seven-forty in the morning, bucketing safely along at the low, the shameful level of the sea to the office in the city, I opened the morning paper to read that the summit of the great mountain had finally been reached, I was glad, of course, and I have no wish to belittle that tremendous achievement, but always I shall hope that two other good men got there first.

(From The Yale Review)

THE LATTER END

BY GEORGE LOVERIDGE

*W*HEN old Wilbur Cartwright's wife died, he had nobody left in the world but his son, and he went to live with him.

The son, John Cartwright, occupied a six-room, mortgaged bungalow, with his wife, Louisa, and their four-year-old son, David.

The old man proposed to sell his own place, which was also mortgaged, and pay off $5000 of the mortgage on John's, in return for a home for the rest of his life. "I prob'ly won't live long anyway," he said. He was seventy-six, and the death of his wife had struck him hard.

John and Louisa talked it over between themselves. It wasn't that they didn't like the old man or didn't want to help him or didn't need the $5000; John, indeed, was unusually fond of his father, and Louisa liked him, too. But such an arrangement, as they knew, doesn't always work well, in spite of good will and affection on both sides. There was no doubt that Grampa ought to sell his house, but whether it would be better for him to take a room in a lodging house or in a home for the aged or come to live with them, John and Louisa didn't know. Suppose he should have a long illness? Perhaps it was the prospect of reducing their mortgage that decided them, though they never discussed the mortgage as though it were significant; they hardly spoke of it at all, for it seemed a factor unworthy to be considered in the circumstances. Perhaps, as they said to one another and believed, it was the welfare of the old man that weighed most.

At any rate, he moved in. They had three bedrooms. John and

Louisa used one, Davy another, and the old man the third. They wanted Grampa to sell all his furniture, because they already had enough, but he said damn if he would sell the bed he and his wife had slept in for so many years, and he kept a dresser and an easy chair, too. They let him put the chair in his bedroom, but they made him store the rest in the cellar, where he was also permitted to keep his carpenter's tools. Grampa had not been a carpenter — he had been a furniture salesman in a department store — but he had liked carpentry all his life.

The household seemed to absorb Grampa without trouble. When he wasn't outdoors, he kept to his own room most of the time, and he didn't intrude when John and Louisa had company. He would have a drink and say a few sociable words, then withdraw to his room and close the door, and either read or go to bed. He was neat. He didn't eat much. He didn't complain about anything.

Best of all, he was good with Davy, his grandson. He played with him, told him stories, took him for walks, and was always on hand to look after him and the house when John and Louisa wanted to go out.

Matters went along this way for a year or so; then there began to be a little friction, though nothing serious. Grampa was an old man and John and Louisa were in their thirties, that was all; there was bound to be a difference in points of view, habits, manners. Grampa thought Louisa coddled Davy, Louisa thought Grampa didn't get his hair cut often enough, John thought his father's political opinions were stupid, and so on. They never drew blood, but there was a change. Finally, Grampa persuaded John and Louisa to let him build a room for himself in the cellar. He bought some plywood and two-by-fours and made a sound and pleasant room. Once more he slept in his own bed, and he brought his easy chair downstairs and set up the dresser. He had a small radio, his pipes, a few books, and a picture or two that he had kept. He was content. John and Louisa liked it better, too, though they were a bit ashamed at first to have their friends know that Grampa had moved into the cellar. They said that Grampa had insisted on it. Between themselves, they agreed that Grampa was failing. He had to have his glasses changed; he sat more; arthritis got into his fingers.

His great interest in life nowadays was Davy. He played marbles with him, spun tops, made kites, read stories. Two or three times a week they went to a park about half a mile distant. If there was wind, they flew kites; if not, they looked at the animals in cages and fed the ducks.

It was in the park that they met another grandfather and his grandson. The old man's name was James Sheffield and his grandson's Malcolm Sheffield. The boys were of an age. They played together, running and wrestling in the leaves, throwing acorns, taking turns holding the string of the kite, while the grandfathers sat close at hand on a bench and smoked and talked.

In the first week they were acquainted, they discovered that they had something in common besides being grandfathers. Mr. Sheffield's son, Duncan, was the boss of Mr. Cartwright's son. They worked in a manufacturing plant. Duncan Sheffield was superintendent and John Cartwright was a machinist; the younger man had already shown inventive ability that was valuable to the company, and there was little doubt that he would rise to a good position, perhaps be superintendent himself some day, or get an important job in another plant.

After the two grandfathers had met, Duncan Sheffield seemed more friendly to John Cartwright. He stopped one morning, while making a round of the factory, and said to John, "I hear your father and mine have quite a time of it at the park, with the kids."

"Yes," John said, "I guess they do."

The superintendent smiled and went on.

Telling his wife at night, John said, "I was surprised. He hardly ever speaks to anybody. He's all right, but he never speaks to anybody."

"He doesn't need to be stuck-up because he's the superintendent," she said.

"He's not stuck-up," he said. "He's just not the kind that has much to do with anybody except about business. He can't afford to, I suppose. He's the boss."

"Even so."

"Well, maybe Grampa has made a useful friend for us."

"Maybe he has," she replied, nodding. "Little things like that, you never know what they may lead to."

Soon afterwards, Grampa and Davy came home later than usual

one afternoon. "We were over to Sheffields'," Grampa said.

"Who was there?" Louisa asked.

"Nobody. Just the old man and me and the kids. Quite a place. They must have money."

"Well, he makes a lot," John said. "Where is it?"

"About half a mile the other side of the park, over in Westwood. Lots of big places there. They got twelve rooms. A brick house. Real nice."

He went on, old-time furniture salesman that he was, to describe the furniture, and Louisa said, "When John's superintendent, we'll have a place like that."

"It won't be tomorrow," her husband said.

Yet he was pleased by the increasing strength of this link between his family and the Sheffields; he hoped Grampa wouldn't make a nuisance of himself. He looked at his father affectionately and with a certain sadness. The old man was showing his age. He was stooping. The hand grasping the pipe trembled, and the arthritic fingers fumbled. It occurred to John that it was a long time now since the old man had worked with his tools.

About a year after the two grandfathers had met, Grampa Sheffield took sick of pleurisy and lay abed in the brick house, where Grampa Cartwright visited him, and then in a hospital, where Grampa Cartwright again faithfully kept him company until, despite everything that specialists could do, Grampa Sheffield died. Grampa Cartwright was one of the bearers, and John and his wife sent flowers.

Then, a couple of times a week, Grampa Cartwright and Davy went to the Sheffields' and took Malcolm to the park. He could have gone with the maid, but he preferred going with Grampa Cartwright. He invited Grampa Cartwright and Davy to his birthday party when he was six. Many times, now, the superintendent had stopped at the machinist's bench for a word or two about their children and about Grampa Cartwright. John said to his wife, "The boss isn't a bad guy, not when you get to know him. He sure thinks a lot of Pa. Well, what harm can that do? Hey?"

One night, about eight o'clock, Mr. Sheffield telephoned to John and said, "I'm in a hole. My wife and I had arranged to go out tonight, and now, at the last minute, we haven't anybody to stay with Malcolm. Two or three unforeseen things came up. What I want to know is whether your father could come over and stay with the boy. I don't like to impose on him. . . ."

"I'm sure he'd be glad to," John said. "If you'll wait just a minute, I'll ask him, Mr. Sheffield."

He hurried down cellar and asked his father. "Sure," he said. "Sure I'll go." He put on his hat and coat, and John drove him over to the Sheffields'.

It was early in the morning when John heard an automobile stop in front of the house and his father quietly come in and go to his room.

The old man didn't get up for breakfast, but in the evening he told John how the night before he had sat and watched television after Malcolm went to sleep.

"And I had beer and cheese out of the icebox," he said. "Lived high. Good cigar. Mr. Sheffield said to take all I wanted. I suppose he didn't want to offer to pay me, so he said take some cigars. I took a couple. Didn't want to overdo it."

He smoked one of his cigars after supper. "Here," he said to his son. "You have the other one."

"Thanks," John said. He lighted it. "Bet those cost fifty cents apiece. Maybe more. I hope you have to go over again, Pa."

It was two days afterwards that Mr. Sheffield summoned John into his office, closed the door, and said, "John, I've got something to ask you. I hope you won't be offended and your father won't be. It's this: my wife has lost a diamond ring worth close to a thousand dollars. She's ready to swear she had it night before last. She thinks she left it on her dresser. But maybe she left it somewhere else. Or maybe she didn't have it at all. I don't know. The only thing we're sure of is that it's gone. I don't like to tell the insurance company or the police until I check everything I can think of. My wife's looked all over the house. She's asked the maid and Malcolm. We thought she might have left it on a table downstairs, or on the mantel — she's been careless like that before — and your father might have happened to see it. You don't mind me asking you?"

"Not at all," John said, though he was uncomfortable. They

looked each other in the eye, neither quite certain what the other was thinking. Then Mr. Sheffield smiled and said, "Well, don't worry about it. Just ask your father, if you will, John. What I expect is that Mrs. Sheffield will suddenly remember where she left it. You know how women are."

John nodded and said yes, he did, and smiled and went out.

All day long while he was working, he thought about the ring. His hands and a part of his mind were occupied with tools and metal, but another part of his mind was pondering and questioning. Did Mr. Sheffield's words mean only what they seemed to mean, or had they another significance? Did Mr. Sheffield intend to accuse his father of stealing the ring? Or John himself? After all, he had gone into the house with his father, and even upstairs, to say good-night to Malcolm. How certain was Mrs. Sheffield that she remembered the last time she had seen the ring? Had something happened — had she carelessly dropped it where it couldn't be recovered, or even pawned it, or given it away, or been swindled out of it — that she didn't want her husband to know about? What about the maid? And the cook? What business had people to own jewelry as valuable as that anyway? It served them right to lose it. If they had insurance, they didn't have to worry. Maybe some thief had slipped into the house and taken the ring. A delivery-man might have done it. A thousand dollars was a lot of money. Even with inflation, it was a lot of money.

Well, what if it is? he said to himself. It's not your headache. Maybe by now she's found it. They have more rings, anyway.

When he reached home at night, he didn't say anything to his father at once, because it occurred to him that his wife might be upset. She'd think, perhaps, that Mr. Sheffield would be down on him unless the ring were found, and his job and their future might be endangered, and things like that; she was easily disturbed. He waited until after supper, when Davy was in bed and his wife had gone to the drugstore. Then he said to his father, in a joking way, "Pa, you didn't see a thousand-dollar diamond ring lying around at Sheffields', did you?"

His father took his pipe out of his mouth, his hand trembling a bit, as it did nowadays, and said, "Diamond ring? Why, no. Where would I see a diamond ring?"

"I don't know. Mr. Sheffield asked me to ask you." He told his father what Mr. Sheffield had said. "Serves them right," he concluded. "They ought to take care of things like that."

"Some people got more money than brains," his father said. He went on smoking. "Prob'ly turn up somewhere." He had been reading a magazine, and he took it up again, but he seemed unable to find his place; he went from page to page, his arthritic fingers separating the pages with difficulty.

There was something about the old man's attitude and fumbling, something about the way he had said "Diamond ring?" and had for an instant dropped his glance, that troubled his son. Was he, on this basis, to suspect his father? He was astounded that such a thought should even occur to him. But immediately another possibility arose: that Malcolm, the Sheffields' little boy, had had something to do with the disappearance of the ring and Grampa knew and was protecting him. John stared at his father's head, as though he were trying to penetrate the mysteries inside, to compel a plain answer.

Of all the damn things, he said to himself. Who would think some little thing like this could get you so stirred up? But, after all, a thousand-dollar ring was no little thing. All from Grampa being a baby sitter, he went on in his thoughts. Trying to help somebody out. You get in more trouble in this world trying to help somebody out than being a stinker to them.

When his wife returned, he did not mention the matter to her, nor, he noticed, did his father. John said, "I'm going down cellar a little while. I got something to do." He left his wife and father in the living room and went to the cellar, where he put a stick of wood in the vise on his father's workbench and began to plane shavings off it, just to do something.

Now suppose, he thought, they don't find it and they tell the insurance company and the insurance company tells the police and then they begin to question everybody. They question me, because I was there, and they question Pa. And suppose he does know something about it and they get it out of him, even though he maybe didn't do anything wrong. Maybe they might even search this house. Suppose they found it here.

He paused, drawing a long shaving out of the plane, and shook his head. Now use some sense, he said to himself. Use some sense. Why would it be here? How could it possibly be here?

But, as he went on planing, he went on thinking; he couldn't help it, worrying and supposing. From far back in his childhood, a Bible story drifted into his thoughts, the one about Joseph putting the valuable cup into the sack of grain that his brother Benjamin was going to take home from the land of Egypt. Now, suppose the Sheffields, for some reason, had planted the diamond ring in one of his father's pockets? Why would they do that? He didn't know, but life was full of strange events, and the actions of men and women were often curious. They might have a reason; it might have something to do with insurance, though he didn't take them to be that kind of people. Or perhaps Malcolm had been playing with the ring and had slipped it into Grampa's pocket for a joke. Maybe Grampa had found it there and didn't know how to return it. Or perhaps it was there and he didn't know it. But, more than likely, neither Grampa nor Malcolm had had anything to do with the ring.

It's stupid to be thinking all these things, he thought. You're just worrying yourself for nothing. Things were better before Grampa ever got acquainted with the Sheffields. Who'd think it'd lead to something like this? Well, there you are.

He had planed the stick down to the jaws of the vise. Now he put the plane away and swept up the shavings. He removed the stick from the vise and broke the stick across his knee, tossing the pieces into a box with other scraps of wood. He could hear the radio upstairs. Grampa and Louisa were listening to a melodrama.

John went quietly into his father's room. There was a steel wardrobe in one corner, near the foot of the bed, and he opened it with a silent hand. Two coats were hanging on the bar. Feeling in the pockets, John encountered a pipe, a handkerchief, two glass marbles, probably Davy's, and a jackknife. He closed the wardrobe and, ashamed, felt under his father's pillow. Nothing was there. He poked around with his finger in a flat glass dish on the dresser containing cuff links, a tie clasp, common pins, two or three pennies, a key, a book of matches, and the stub of a pencil. Looking at himself in the mirror over the dresser, he tried to read the thoughts behind his own eyes, but he couldn't. The urgent rhythm of a commercial radio announcement came to him through the floor of the living room. He heard a chair move. But nobody came downstairs.

Instead of searching the dresser drawers from the top down, he knelt and began at the bottom. Under some shirts and underwear lay a candy box. When he gently shook it, something rattled. He removed the cover. The box was more than half full of pins set with cheap artificial stones. They looked like the kind of pins one sees on the counters of five- and ten-cent stores, and they were still affixed to small white cards. He turned them out onto the bedspread. Among them he noticed a pearl earring, not at all valuable, that Louisa had missed a month ago — at least, he thought it was that earring — and a cuff link of his own; he didn't often wear cuff links and hadn't missed it. When he spread out the small carded pins, there was a ring, too, under one of the cards. It was a woman's diamond ring, and the diamond seemed to be genuine. He held it to the light. Inside, there were three initials, *R.B.S.*, the *S* for Sheffield, without any doubt; he didn't know Mrs. Sheffield's first name.

Now that he had found the ring, he know that he had felt certain of finding it, as though he were playing a childhood game. Everything but the ring he returned to the box, and the box he returned to the drawer. Putting out the light, he left his father's room and sat on a sawhorse in the cellar.

He felt neither ashamed of the old man nor angry with him, but he was frightened. He sat quite still, looking at the concrete floor, his hands gripping the sawhorse. It was evident from the pins that the value of them meant nothing to his father; it must be the mere glitter, and the same with the ring. He would never have bought them. He must have picked them up, really stolen them, while he was wandering through the the stores. John had heard of this failing. Kleptomania. Was that the word? He couldn't remember any more about it. The old man must be getting a little hazy in the head. How strange that he should take this turn, for all his life he had been notably strict, prompt to pay his bills, respected by all his customers.

It was bad enough that he should grow old and feeble and a little touched, but the matter of the ring, and the probability that he would be detected some day at his innocent shoplifting were worse. John grimaced. He certainly couldn't give the ring back and say his father had taken it. The Sheffields probably wouldn't believe it was just an amiable failing, and, even if they did, they weren't likely to be any more pleased about it.

And where would that leave me? he said to himself. What could I expect in the shop after that? Even if he didn't fire me right out, he'd find some way to get rid of me. Anyway, am I going to tell him my father's a thief, even if he doesn't mean anything by it?

But if the Sheffields didn't recover the ring, they'd go to the police, or the insurance people would go, and the police, as a matter of course, would question his father. Ten to one they'd get it out of him. Then there'd be hell to pay.

He couldn't return the ring anonymously, either. Mr. Sheffield would certainly suspect him, after having talked to him about it. He would never be able to look Mr. Sheffield in the eye again. For that matter, he wouldn't anyway, regardless of what he decided to do.

Why had his father had to act like this? He had worked hard all his life, provided a good home, was nice with kids, didn't make a nuisance of himself, helped to pay the mortgage, and was as good an old gentleman as anybody could want, and yet he went around to five-and-tens slyly collecting junk jewelry. Now where was the sense in that? Why did he have to do that? And if he had to, why couldn't he stick to five-and-tens? Why did people have to get old anyway?

While he was in the midst of these reflections, half exasperated and half melancholy, his father came down the stairs.

"Exclusive tonight, ain't you?" he said. "What you been doing down here all this time?"

"Nothing. I can't stand those programs."

"Well, I wouldn't drive a man out of his own living room. I . . . "

"You didn't, Pa. I had something to think about."

"What? Something at the shop?"

"In a way." He glanced at his father, but the old man didn't seem to suspect anything. He scratched his head with the stem of his pipe and said, "Well, it'll come out all right. How to get a job done?"

"Yes."

"Well, sleep on it. That's what I always did." He nodded, opened the door of his room, said, "Good night," and closed the door.

When John went upstairs, his wife was listening to another mystery on the radio. "You were down there a long time," she said.

"Not so long," he said.

Already she was back with the mystery. He took up the evening paper and pretended to read. What would she think if she knew? How was this going to affect her and Davy? It might ruin the lives of all of them, a little thing like this, some tiny, mysterious screw coming loose in the old man's head.

That night, he lay awake a long time, with Louisa sleeping beside him. He thought of Davy sleeping in the next room and the old man sleeping in the cellar. I was Davy's age once, he thought, and Pa was my age, and I do a lot of things for Davy, and Pa did a lot for me, but I hardly remember now, and I suppose Davy won't remember, either. You get wound up in just trying to get a living and you forget everything. Maybe it's because you know you can't pay back anyway. Things just go on and it's too much bother and . . . The complexity of life, of merely trying to live, overwhelmed him and pinned him down and suffocated him, as though a mountain had fallen on him. He gave up, lying there like one stunned and helpless.

Gradually a different mood came upon him. He was thinking of his childhood. He saw, for some reason, his father making him a wooden whistle, cutting a branch off a poplar tree, making a notch and a lip on it and twisting off the bark; even the tone of the whistle, shrill and surprising, recurred to him. Then he was building a snowman with his father. He rolled a ball of snow bigger than himself, and he went into the cellar for pieces of coal to serve as eyes, mouth, nose, and buttons. This scene gave way to one in the cellar of their home, when they were making a cage for rabbits. It was a long time since he had remembered his rabbits. He had won two of them, a white one and a brown one. They had got out of the cage one day and a dog had killed them. He had seen it; it was the first time he had seen an animal die, and it made him sick. He suffered nightmares afterwards. Then he forgot all about it, and why he remembered it now he could not say. His mind remained passive.

There occurred in it the thought that his father, an old man, had once been a child and had had a father who had been a child; and this thought was both beautiful and discouraging to him. He did not know why and he did not have the energy to try to find out. He lay like one entranced, and presently fell asleep.

In the morning, when he went to work, he still had not made up his mind what to do, except that it would have to be something to keep the old man's name clear. It surprised him that Louisa did not notice how worried he was; she was going to give a bridge party in the afternoon, and no doubt her mind was busy with arrangements. She had set up a certain pleasant pattern of life; that was the way with women. As though from long distance, he contemplated his life and hers, the pleasant pattern of it, into which his father had begun to weave a new, mysterious, and sinister figure. The old man was standing in the yard lighting his pipe when John drove away. They waved to each other.

At his bench, John could not work. The tools with which he was accustomed to perform skillful feats rebelled. No matter what he did, he could not release his mind from the thought that Mr. Sheffield was expecting a report from him on their conversation of the day before; and he saw again that his father was almost certain to be found out.

Abruptly putting down his tools, he walked through the shop, among the clattering machines, to Mr. Sheffield's office. He was admitted.

"Yes?" Mr. Sheffield said, smiling.

"Is that the ring?" John asked, taking it from his pocket and handing it to Mr. Sheffield.

Mr. Sheffield glanced at him in astonishment. Then he examined the ring, looking inside at the initials. "Yes, it is," he said.

"I took it from your house when I was there the other night," John said, not flinching. "I saw it on a table and I picked it up. I don't know why."

They looked at each other for some seconds, perhaps twenty or thirty, though it seemed much longer. Then, Mr. Sheffield made a slight gesture with his hand, dismissing him. John returned to his bench.

His thoughts were in disorder. Why had he said that? He'd certainly be discharged. He might as well pack his tools. Probably he'd be arrested. There was some pay coming to him. What was he going to tell Louisa? She wouldn't understand what he had done. He didn't understand it himself. He had been a fool. But what else was there to do? What must Mr. Sheffield be thinking? John began to make up a story to tell Louisa, about quarreling with Mr. Sheffield over some work. But of course, that wouldn't do if he were arrested. If he had to look for work somewhere else, he wouldn't even have a recommendation. Mr. Sheffield might make it impossible for him to work anywhere, even if he didn't have him arrested.

The thumping and whirring of the machines forced him back into the routine. He took up his tools. He might as well be doing something till he found out what was going to happen. There was nothing he could change. He couldn't unsay what he had said or undo what his father had done.

He worked all day unmolested. Perhaps Mr. Sheffield wanted to have him arrested at home, where it wouldn't disrupt the work in the shop. He passed an uneasy night. Next day, he went to work again, not knowing what else to do.

On payday, there would, at least, be a notice in the envelope. But there wasn't.

A week, a month went by. Twice Mr. Sheffield came into the shop to speak to him about work. He spoke briefly, gravely, but without disdain or anger.

In four months, he promoted John. Perhaps he believed what John had said but forgave him in view of his record. Whether or not he suspected the truth, John never knew.

The other matter, too, took care of itself. The old man's fingers became more and more subject to what seemed to be arthritis, until he couldn't pick up anything even if he wanted to. John or Louisa filled his pipe and lighted it, and fed him. When Louisa was sick for a couple of weeks, the old man had to be sent to a nursing home. A few months later, he died there. He was eighty.

John went fishing one day. Alone in the boat, he emptied the candy box of cheap pins into deep water. All day he sat without catching anything, not caring, thinking of years ago when he was a boy and the old man used to take him fishing on that same lake.

(From The New Yorker)

THE GAME

BY FRANCES GRAY PATTON

*N*OW, if we had religion — " Lillian Duncan began. Thought-fully, as though removing the wrapping from an idea, she lifted the cozy off her blue-and-white teapot. (She had culti-vated a fussy perfectionism about tea; although she hot-watered it and milked and sugared it from silver jugs, she brewed it in stoneware — and she hoped her guest understood this, instead of supposing her silver tea set incomplete.) "I mean if we *really* did, you know — " she began again. "Shall we have a little rum in this cup, Maria? In weather like this, one needs a liquor stronger than tea to bathe one's veins in the knowledge of spring." She flushed, because the way she was talking — flying off at a tangent from a solemn subject, and using those "one"s and that tortured literary allusion — sounded to her like lines from a play and certainly wasn't at all the way she was accustomed to talk. At least, she hadn't talked so for a long time until this afternoon, when she had chanced upon Maria Hopwood at a hosiery counter in Hutzler's and had been caught up again in the pattern of an old girlhood intimacy.

"Dear me, yes" Maria said. Her tone, lightly imitative of Lillian's, showed her to be aware that the other woman's airiness was studied and in the nature of a lark. (That had always been the comfortable charm of Maria's company, Lillian reflected; in it you were safe and free. You could assume any whimsical attitude that struck your fancy, or indulge in that hyperbole of the moment that is the leaven of conversation, without the danger of being held to account later.) "Remember, Lil, when we were kids and first heard of rum in tea? We couldn't find any rum in Tryon's Neck, of course, but Woody was an acolyte, so he sneaked us some sacramental wine."

"Darling Woody! What a card he was!" Lillian exclaimed, allowing her voice to be as stagy as it would, "When I picture him in holy orders —"

"He's still a darling and still a card," Maria said dryly of Woody, who was her husband. "But that wine in that tea! We drank it in the bathroom with the door locked. Woody had his in Papa's shaving mug, and you and I used toothbrush glasses. The tap water was rusty and not very hot, and the whole thing tasted like an infusion of rotten grape leaves. We felt so wordly and so witty and so sick!"

"Well, my Newburyport won't do as much for our wit as those vine leaves of the past," Lillian said. "It can't, because it's legal."

"Oh, I don't think our *wit* needs a thing," Maria said. "I think we're being brilliant as Jupiter and all his moons. Every time you open your mouth, you release an epigram." She tucked herself deeper into the corner of the sofa. "But those wintry veins you mentioned could use a dram."

Lillian smiled at her old friend, who was settled, at home as a cat, with her feet tucked up under her on the Chippendale sofa. True, Maria had taken her shoes off — they sat side by side on the carpet, looking as *dégagé* as their owner — but even so, no one else, to Lillian's knowledge, had presumed to put foot, shod or unshod, upon that sofa. She wondered if Maria had an inkling of what the damask of the upholstery would fetch by the yard (if, indeed, such material were any longer obtainable), or of the fact that its age, which had faded it to a subtle shade of green, like weathered copper, had increased rather than diminished its value. But she did not resent Maria's feet; the odd and moving thing — the thing that reassured Lillian about her own unshrunken capacity for friendship — was that she considered her fine sofa honored by their presence.

The green damask, though lovely, wasn't a flattering background for Maria. Against it, her pale complexion had a wan cast, and her brown hair, going gray in a shadowy way, had no lustre. Maria was a slight-built woman, beginning to be angular, who had lost more prettiness than is usual, these days, at thirty-seven. (Persons wishing to speak pleasantly of her said that she had character in her face, or that her bones were good.) But, curiously enough, the falling away of beauty had left Maria a look of youngness — a clarity of brow and features — that she mightn't otherwise have had. She appeared distinctly younger than Lillian, who was within a month of her age and who, in the obvious things like figure, hair, and skin, had yielded little to the passage of time. Lillian perceived this without rancor and with tenderness.

She rose. "I keep a bottle of rum in the bookshelf," she said. "I do it for old times' sake, because I always admired your father's keeping his flask of peach brandy in *his*."

"Behind *Tristam Shandy*," said Maria.

"Mine's behind Lord Byron," Lillian said. "I'll never forget Judge Ballou downing his digestive, neat, before Sunday dinner. And your mother used to purse her mouth at your little brothers and say, 'Tch, tch! Poor Papa has to take his horrid medicine!'"

Lillian crossed to the bookshelves that filled one entire wall of the small, square, high-ceilinged room. As she did, she experienced, for perhaps the thousandth time, a faintly intoxicated pleasure in the colors of the old Aubusson carpet — the various blues and roses and turquoises, soft and miraculously fresh — and a familiar satisfaction in all the furnishings of the room. That satisfaction was nearly as poignant as passion; it was like the stabs of feeling that had shaken her years before when she gazed down upon her sleeping child, serene and perfect in infancy. For everything around her — absolutely everything — was perfect. The sofa, of course, and the rug, and the lamps; the ormolu clock on the mantel, the Hepplewhite tables, and the Sheraton desk; the carved rosewood chair with the velvet-covered medallion back she had been sitting in, and even the overstuffed armchairs (for there was something vulgar about a sitting room that contained nothing but showpieces) — every last thing was the best of its kind. The calm landscape over the fireplace and the pencil sketch of a nude girl in an awkward posture over the desk were authentic Corot and Degas. The books on the shelves, as well as those that lay scattered about with old letters stuck in them as if to mark a place, were good books in content and binding; most of them were brown, because brown was the color Lillian favored for books and because it blended with the mellowed walnut panelling of the walls. Yes, Lillian was proud of her possessions and of the way she had assembled them. But what made her *love* them was that they were expensive. They had cost her so much money.

Lillian Duncan was married to a generous man of means and position, and while she relished the by-products of this connection — the consequence and security and material comfort — she thought them trivial beside the sheer fact of wealth itself. Just as the imaginations of some people expand to music, of others to chess, and of still others — among them her husband — to black beef cattle in a pale-green field, so her imagination did to money. To Lillian the value of money was intrinsic and its beauty palpable to the senses. She was particularly fond of it in paper that had grown soft and wrinkled with much exchange. When an old bill came her way, she was likely to caress it with her fingertips, as one might stroke down the feathers of a frightened bird, thinking, Oh, my pet, you have lit at last in the hand of your nest! Then she would lay it in the shallow secret drawer of her desk. When the drawer was stuffed full, and not before, she spent its contents. And when she had swapped her hoard for some precious object — suffering, in the transaction, as though flesh were being torn from her body — she felt obliged to project toward her new acquisition part of the emotion she'd lavished upon what she had relinquished for its sake.

As Lillian removed the volume of poems from the shelf and seized the squat bottle it had concealed, she wished she might disclose to Maria the true romance of her life. Heaven knew she had already been open to the point of rashness with Maria. She had told her what had happened (with none of the humiliating details glossed over, either) between herself and Bill Ferebee, the man to whom she'd been engaged before she left for Baltimore. She had told her how, later, she'd caught Harold Duncan, and what she thought of his mother's intellect, and how, a good deal of the time, he bored her to the limit of her endurance. She had even told her about the mess young Sally had got into at school. And yet she hadn't been able to look straight at her friend, dropping all reserve, and say, quite simply, "Maria, I'm rich." That fact, as honorable as it was exquisite, she could attempt to convey only by indirection.

Lillian's attempt had been valiant. She had begun it by referring to her pretty town house — two centuries old and famous for its bal-

anced proportions — as a "little old *pied-à-terre"* where she and
Harold "camped" when business or society compelled them to
desert their farm in Green Spring Valley. She had added, in a pious,
wifely tone, that she thought every man ought to live on a farm —
it kept his blood pressure down — and didn't Maria agree? And
Maria, evidently imagining a resemblance between the Duncan's
gentleman's estate and the run-down, cotton-bled farm a few miles
inland from Tryon's Neck, North Carolina, that her own mother,
Mrs. Ballou, had inherited and kept out of respect for a piece of
ancestral land and regard for the Negro tenants who managed to
scratch a living from its impoverished soil — Maria then, had said
she reckoned so, if a man's taste ran to the rustic, but that the country could get abysmally dull, and it was nice to have a retreat in
town. Next, Lillian had pinned her hopes upon the effect of
Brooks, her butler. Surely Maria, seeing him — a lean, gray-haired
mulatto with the chiselled features and aloof presence of a Roman
senator — couldn't fail to be somewhat awed. Awe, however, was
not in Maria's nature. Letting Brooks take her damp coat, she had
made to him the sort of pleasant remark about the weather that
manners down in Tryon's Neck would have required one to make
to the Ballous' old "Uncle" Admire or any other elderly servant.
Lillian had made one more try. Before tea was ready she had led
Maria into the dining room to show her Sally's portrait. "An Au-
gustus John," she had murmured. But Maria either hadn't caught
the name or hadn't cared. She had stood in silence before the like-
ness of the yellow-haired girl in the pink hunting coat, observing
the arrogant lines of the young body, the stubborn, imperious mouth,
and the eyes whose carefully opaque expression could not quite
disguise the look of the startled fawn. Then she had said, "Who
was the poet who wrote about 'beauty like a tightened bow'?" And
Lillian, grateful for the flattering question, because it released in
her a rush of sympathy for her daughter, had found herself relating
the unhappy tale of Sally's disgrace.

The child had been whisked off to Coventry, socially speaking,
she informed Maria, and was now up in Pennsylvania at one of
those wholesome coeducational Quaker academies. For two years
previously, she had been a pupil at Green Valley Country Day
(really the most desirable girls' school in Maryland; people fought

and bled to get their daughters on its list!), but she had been requested to withdraw, on account of a letter she wrote to one of its
few male instructors. The letter had been incredible. In it, Sally
had declared her hopeless passion for the teacher and announced
her plan to seek peace in a nunnery.

"And it wasn't as if he'd been the riding master!" Lillian cried.
"The little man taught her English Literature!"

"At fifteen, anything enchants," Maria said. "Poetry as well as
horseflesh."

"It was infinitely disagreeable. We had to take her to a psychiarist, and I hate to imagine the questions he must have asked her,"
Lillian said. She added crossly, "And what Sally may have told
him about *me!*"

"What did he say about her?"

Lillian laughed. Somehow, now that she'd spoken of the sad
fiasco and it hadn't shocked Maria, she saw its humorous aspect.
"He said she was quite normal. She wasn't even oversexed," Lillian
replied. "He said she'd just fallen in love!"

"Well, at least now you know she *can*. They say some people
can't," Maria said. She touched Lillian's arm. "It's easy, though,
for me to be objective. In your place I'd have been frantic."

At that point, comforted, Lillian had almost let good taste go
hang and told Maria in unequivocal words what she yearned to
make certain she knew. No, not in my place, Maria, she'd been
tempted to explain. In my place there is something to keep calamity at a certain remove. You see, *I have plenty of money.*

Of course, she hadn't actually said it. She had ushered Maria
into the sitting room and given her tea from the Sheffield tray that
had been brought in presently by the lofty Brooks. ("Isn't that
silver waiter too heavy for the old boy?" Maria had said after the
butler left them.) In this particular room, Lillian was persuaded,
with its elegant simplicity that came so much dearer than ornateness, the delightful truth would seep into Maria's consciousness.

But more than an hour had passed and Lillian had observed no
sign of seepage. There Maria sat, as easy and oblivious as if she
were down in Tryon's Neck in the shabby, artless, anomalous room
that the Ballous had always gatherd in and had called the "the
library." She dug her stockinged heels into the sofa. She glanced at

the Corot as coolly and politely as she might have glanced at a landscape executed by somebody's untalented grandmother. She doubtless believed (if she considered the matter at all) that Lillian's teapot was made of domestic clay and had been purchased for three-ninety-eight at a department store.

Lillian and Maria and Maria's husband had been children together in Tryon's Neck, an old town on an arm of one of the sounds that stretch all along the coast of North Carolina. Tryon's Neck was a town that the world had moved away from and that families, it would seem, continued to dwell in from habit alone. There was no stir of change, or desire for change, in its quiet air, and its business section was only a cluster of dingy shops, a movie theatre, and a café called the Busy Bee. But the town had its charms. Its few large houses had widow's walks on their roofs and, over their doorways, great fanlights, which were chinked in places and stopped up with paper to prevent the ingress of bats but were very graceful in design all the same. It had an eighteenth-century church with a cock, commemorative of poor Saint Peter's moment of moral panic, on the steeple; its main street, called Captain's Lane, was paved with cobblestones, and its trees were everywhere, softening with perpetual shade even the dreadful papier-mâché lobster in the window of the Busy Bee. The trees, live oaks and sweet bays, all listed to leeward; their leafy crowns were shaved flat by the wind off the water, and morning and evening the oblique beams of the low sun laid a trim of gold lacquer on them, so that they looked like trees in the middle distance of an Italian painting.

The two girls and the Hopwood boy had grown up in houses on the same block. Maria had lived in the middle house, which had the finest widow's walk in town. Woody had lived in a house that was haunted and neglected and decayed, and would obviously be condemned before it was much older. Lillian, orphaned in infancy, had lived with her great-aunt, Miss Imogene Archer, in the house with the most elaborate fanlight. Miss Imogene had been kind but harassed by a fear of germs — she had refused, for instance, to touch money or to permit her niece to touch it unless it was in coin and had been boiled in a kettle for twenty minutes — and Woody's stepmother had been a peevish woman, so Lillian and Woody had escaped, whenever they could, into the bosom of the Ballou family. They and Maria Ballou had been inseparable. The three had shared their innermost thoughts and had woven an esoteric pattern of make-believe, which they called "the game." When they were alone together, they liked to pretend to be grown up and to be meeting again, after a long separation, in some exotic spot like an oasis in the Sahara Desert or a hostel in the Alps, and they entertained one another for hours with recitals of the adventures incident to their imaginary pasts. The game did not quite end with the end of childhood. After the players were in their teens — even after they'd been off to boarding school — they were likely to drop back, without warning, into fantasy. "This," Woody might say, drawing Judge Ballou's ivory paper knife from its tooled-leather sheath, "is the dagger my Spanish dancing girl wore in her garter." The girls would take their cue from him and speak of their personal triumphs in the Russian ballet, their careers as spies for the diplomatic corps, or the visions they'd seen in the opium dens of Peking. They laughed at themselves, but the game gave their lives a sort of continuity that kept them from being afraid of the future. And then — quite suddenly, it seemed — reality had reared its invulnerable head.

Mrs. Ballou had fallen victim to a lingering illness, which absorbed her daughter's attention. Woody, having decided to become a gentleman of the cloth, had departed for a seminary in Tennessee. Lillian, emotionally entangled with Bill Ferebee, who had treated her badly, had wished to die.

Lillian hadn't died, of course, but her aunt had, leaving her the house and a thousand dollars in a savings account. The house had been heavily mortgaged; Lillian had let it go without a whimper. She had withdrawn the money from the bank, and with the bills, unboiled, in her pocketbook, she had set out for Baltimore, where she had some prosperous cousins who would be obliged by common decency to offer a show of protection to a young and lonely kinswoman. "I am burning my bridges!" she had said to Maria, suiting action to the boast by flinging a snapshot of Bill Ferebee into the fire. "I am going to seek my fortune!" And shortly thereafter, at the table of one of the Baltimore cousins, she had taken the fancy of Harold Duncan, and her fortune had been found.

At first, Lillian and Maria had maintained a desultory correspondence, but it soon languished. Maria, distressed by her mother's discomfort and eventual death, had not been inspired to compose entertaining letters, and later, when she married Woody and had babies, she had been too busy. To Lillian, moving in a new and buoyant element, the life she had left seemed as remote as the beach and the timid baskers on it seem to a bather floating on the swells beyond the breakers. Then, this afternoon, she had found Maria Hopwood, and the whole scene of her youth, complete with its sounds and sights and the texture of its prevailing mood, had emerged from the recesses of her mind. Nothing was changed. The light lay on the trees, the gulls mewed in the harbor, and her old feeling for her friend was exactly the same.

Lillian had recognized Maria instantly. She'd had no reason to think that Maria was anywhere near Baltimore, she hadn't seen her for seventeen years, and Maria's apppearance was sadly altered — the delicate, mobile brilliance suggestive of prisms depending from a lamp was gone from her face — and yet Lillian had known her! It was her heart that had recognized Maria, Lillian felt. That thought had warmed her, for of late, in bleak, pinched moments, she had wondered if her comprehensions were more than surface-deep.

Lillian had been shopping, for no good reason, drifting from store to store as a method of passing idle time on a mild, bright day in May, when the weather changed without warning. A cold rain, spearheaded by a thunderstorm, had blown into town on a gusty east wind, and she had ducked into Hutzler's to wait out the violence. Once inside, Lillian, who was not above the practice of petty economics, had been attracted to a counter where nylon stockings were "on special" at eighty-seven cents a pair, and before the woman standing beside her spoke or turned her head, Lillian had known who she was.

"Maria," Lillian had said.

"Lil," Maria had responded.

Neither had exclaimed. It had seemed very natural to be standing there together.

Maria, Lillian learned, had been in town for a week and was leaving at ten that evening. Her eldest child, a boy of thirteen, had undergone an operation at the Hopkins. It had been an anxious business, Maria had said, a bone tumor on the kneecap, but the tumor had been benign and removable and Judge ("He's named John, but everybody calls him Judge because he's the image of Papa") would not even limp.

"Why didn't you call me?" Lillian had asked reproachfully.

"I forgot," Maria had replied with disarming frankness. "I was so scared about Judge that I forgot you existed." She had gone on to say that she'd found a room with a semi-private bath in a tourist home near the hospital. She'd scarcely stirred from it except to visit her son and consult with surgeons, but that day one of the internes ("a boy from North Carolina") had had a half day off and had driven Judge, whose leg was in a walking-cast, to Washington to visit the Smithsonian. "So I have time off, too," she finished. "My, you look smart, Lil! Just the same, only svelter — more urbane."

Suddenly, Lillian had regretted being caught hovering over bargain stockings. "My car's parked in the garage here; let's get it and go home for some tea," she'd suggested. "Harold and I live in the country most of the time, but we do keep this little old *pied-à-terre* in town."

The car was a British import, finished in black. Maria, settling herself against its tan leather cushions, inquired innocently. "What make of automobile is this, Lil? An old Hudson?"

"It's a little Jaguar," Lillian said.

"Oh," Maria murmured. "I never heard of that kind."

"And it doesn't look in the least like a Hudson, old or new," Lillian said, torn between exasperation and amusement. "You can't tell one car from another and never could. It's like being tone-deaf."

"I know. It infuriates Judge," Maria said affably. A few minutes later, as they drove up Charles Street through the still dripping and grumbling elements, she clapped her hands. "Lil, this is uncanny," she said. "This is like the game. You know, the farewell ritual we went through when we had to stop for supper. We'd join hands and chant, 'When shall we three meet again, in thunder, lightning, or in rain?' "

"Why, yes," Lillian said. "Yes, it is."

"Remember the last time we were together in a real storm?" Maria asked. "We were trolling for rock — you and Woody and me — and

Uncle *Ad*mire was along because Papa wouldn't let us take the boat beyond the Point without him. Remember?"

"Vaguely," Lillian said.

"That was the summer Woody was an atheist," Maria reminded her. "We were out in the open sound when the squall sprang out of nowhere. Lightning came straight down like a twisted rope of fire and — "

"How could I ever forget!" Lillian cried. "Woody stood up in the boat and shook his fist at the sky and said, 'O God — if there is a God — strike this boat!'"

"And the way old *Ad*mire knelt down in the bow and commenced praying!" Maria put in. "'O sweet Jesus, don't listen to him! He ain't nothin' but a po' damn fool! Don't listen to him, Lord! Listen to *me!*'"

"I was terrified," Lillian said, "but I never laughed so hard in my life."

"And afterwards *Ad*mire apologized to Woody for having called him a bad name," Maria said, "and you told him he'd used admirable restraint."

"He had, too," Lillian said. "How is *Ad*mire now?"

"Dead," said Maria. "He died last winter, in his little house in the yard — gently, from plain old age. I nursed him by day and Woody by night, and just before the end he thought he saw Mamma playing on a golden harp."

"Perhaps he did," Lillian said. "Who knows?"

"Perhaps, but even in Heaven I don't believe Mamma could pick out a tune," said Maria. She sighed. "There's been a lot of passing away since you left. Mamma and Papa, of course, and old Mr. Merriman, and Bill Ferebee — he had cirrhosis. Your Auntie's house is a funeral parlor now and there's a huge electric clock where the fanlight was. Woody sets his watch by it and calls it Old Mortality."

"Tell me, does the town look the same in general?" Lillian asked. "Is the rooster still on the steeple?"

"Oh, yes," Maria said. "And the state Society for the Preservation of Antiquities has restored the church. Scraped the paint off the floor and laid red carpet in the aisle and taken out those awful memorial windows. Remember the one with the lamb that looked like a tomcat?"

Lillian giggled. "And the boot?"

Maria looked puzzled. "What boot?"

"You know the boot!" Lillian insisted. "The rubber wading boot that hung right over Captain's Lane to weight the telephone wire so it wouldn't flap in the wind."

"It's gone," Maria told her. "It's been gone so long I'd forgotten it. The Lane is paved with asphalt now, and the trees for two blocks each way from the center of the business section have been cut down."

"The trees!" Lillian cried.

"Bill Ferebee had them cut when he was mayor," Maria said. "He claimed a town couldn't have progress without a white way, and couldn't have a white way with trees. He was always an ass, rest his soul."

"What did I see in him, dead or alive?" Lillian asked rhetorically as she drew to the curb in front of her house. Young Bill Ferebee's reckless, handsome face, with the indefinably bruised look that had both repelled and drawn her, passed across her mind's eye. She waited to feel a fleeting pain leap in the arteries at her wrists, but the pain didn't come.

"He was a good dancer when he was sober," Maria said absently. "Is this your little brick house, Lil? It's cute."

So they had gone in. Over their tea they had rattled on — reminiscing, philosophizing, gossiping of weddings and deaths and scandals in North Carolina. The curtains were drawn, a log burned in the fireplace with the tawny marble facing, and the snug room seemed immune to harshness and chill. But Lillian knew it was the quality of Maria's society, more than material comfort, that held the world at bay. Maria's perceptions were acute, her irony was delicate, and she had a sense of comedy so irrepressible that even when her tales were pathetic, it flitted through them, the way a stray sunbird, coming through the crack of a closed blind, dances upon a wall in a house of mourning.

"It's difficult to imagine being grown up in Tryon's Neck," Lillian said. "What do you *do* there?"

"We talk," Maria said. She looked reflectively down into her cup. "We've remained at the Neck somewhat longer than we intended," she continued. She had an air of detachment, as if she were discussing the affairs of chance acquaintances. "Mr. Merriman was gathered to his fathers shortly after Woody was ordained, and Woody succeeded him in order to oblige the bishop — nobody else would. Besides, I had the house, and it seemed rather touching for Woody to begin his priesthood in the church where he'd been christened. But we didn't consider it permanent."

Lillian nodded. She tried and failed to imagine the Hopwoods in another town.

"Three years ago, Woody missed a plum," Maria said. "A flourishing parish in a suburb of Richmond made overtures to him. But just then Woody preached a sermon about sin."

"Why not? That's an ancient and honorable custom of ministers," Lillian said. "Don't they know about the Devil in Virginia?"

"Well, Woody approached the subject from an original angle," Maria said. "You see, it was this way. The fishing community at Larkin's Pass, over on the banks, is really a part of our parish. Those people can't attend our services regularly — Woody goes to them at intervals and baptizes babies and sees that such courting couples as ought to get married have the matter called to their attention — but now and then they all get in boats and come to Tryon's Neck."

"I remember the bankers," Lillian said. "They said 'hoy toide' and had ruddy faces and blue eyes and a wonderful dash in their bearing. Especially the men. The women shrivelled early. But I never saw them in church."

"Mr. Merriman made them feel gauche," Maria said. "He was such a ladylike man." She went on then to describe, with sympathy and many anecdotal embellishments, which weren't true digressions, because they deepened the meaning of her story, the nature of life on the outer banks. She explained how the fortunes of the fisherfolk were mortgaged to fuel-oil companies and at the mercy of winds and tides; how when the fish didn't run the children at Larkin's Pass went hungry, and how when they ran too well the market was glutted and the whole catch ("mountains of mackerel and blues and big red snappers") had to be dumped back into the sea, and how on rare occasions ("As in life and love," she said) everything ran smooth — the nets were heavy, the market was right, and the men returned to their homes with money in their pockets.

"Ah!" Lillian sighed.

"But success goes fast to a fisherman's head," Maria said. "The men strut across the sand like lords of creation, and they say the things that go on in the dunes on a night after a big catch — the roistering and drinking and carrying-on with pretty girls — are very improper indeed! And, of course, when the liquor's all drunk up at last, and the girls get coy again, and the wives are outraged, the men's tempers turn sour and they begin to fight among themselves. As soon as enough heads are broken, remorse sets in. The following Sunday, the flotilla comes to Tryon's Neck."

"They must love Woody," Lillian said.

"Woody loves them," said Maria. "And you know his temperament — he can't stand to see anyone discouraged. So that morning when he watched them trooping up the aisle — the women all tight-lipped and sort of shooing the children away from their fathers, and the men in their stiff, dark Sunday suits, with their arms in slings or with court plaster on their faces, and looking so hangdog and woebegone — his impulse was to revive their pride. He told them to quit moping and to magnify the Lord like the 'whales that move in the waters.' (We always sing that canticle when the fishermen come.) He said that Christians must bear their sense of sin with grace and fortitude, and that remorse was worse than sin, anyhow, because it mortified the spirit." She paused. "Naturally, he phrased it better than that. It was a charming sermon."

"Did the sinners understand it?"

"Perfectly. They're very shrewd and sensitive," Maria said. "But there was a journalist in our midst. He'd come to do a story on the restoration of the church and instead he did one on Woody. His feature article appeared in several of the leading state papers. It was headed, 'Man Bites Dog in Tryon's Neck As Parson Comes Out for Sin' " She shrugged. "We heard no more from Richmond."

"Oh dear," said Lillian.

"We'd have missed blue water and the rooster," Maria said. She held out her cup. "Is there a drop left in the pot?" Her composure was so unruffled that Lillian couldn't decide whether her story was meant to be sad or funny.

"Plenty," Lillian said. Then, since she hadn't wished to change the current of conversation so abruptly as to suggest either pity or indifference, she had introduced her fragmentary observation upon the possession of religious faith and had let that trail off, to be lost, she hoped, in chatter about bottled spirits. Now she returned to her chair. She poured the tea, lacing it stoutly with rum.

Maria tasted hers. "This is better than our bathroom brew," she said. "You spoke of religion?"

"I did," Lillian admitted, sorry she had. "I was going to say — " She hesitated. What was she going to say, now or ever, upon that abstruse subject? "I mean if we really had it," she began lamely, "the way *Ad*mire did when he saw dear Mrs. Ballou with her harp. The way the penitent fishermen did when they rowed across the sound to Woody — "

"They came in motor launches," said Maria.

"But they came," Lillian said, starting to enjoy herself. "If we had that faith, how simple life would be! I think I had it once, back in my youth, but I laid it down and forgot where. Careless of me."

"It was easy to mislay," Maria said. "There were all those bright boys who wrote for the *Carolina Magazine* and told us how sophisticated disillusionment was. Even Woody that summer — "

"It wasn't an intellectual revolt with me," Lillian said. "I just lost it." She waved her hand. "As lightly as I lost my — "

"If you intend to say what I think, don't," Maria warned her. "It would be a lie. You were far from light about *that*. You're beginning to play the game."

"Why shouldn't I?"

"The rules are too intricate for us," Maria said. "As we grow older, we grow less astute at distinguishing between fact and fiction."

"We've been playing at something, off and on, all afternoon," said Lillian.

"Attitudes. Harmless even to adults," Maria said. "But to return to our enthralling topic — Woody's in a turmoil. He's not convinced he's consecrated. He says he may switch to banking."

"He'd be dandy in a bank," Lillian said. "He'd never refuse a loan."

Maria laughed, but on a note of constraint, and Lillian was sorry she had spoken flippantly of Woody. After all, Maria could hardly be expected to view him with objectivity; as his wife, she must find it offensive to hear him treated, however affectionately, as a figure of fun.

Lillian lifted the bottle of Newburyport. "Guess why I chose Byron's works to hide this behind?" she said, picking her way back to safe ground. "Because of two lines in *Don Juan* —

> *There's nought, no doubt, so much the spirit calms*
> *As rum and true religion . . ."*

"The shipwreck canto," Maria said promptly. "Woody read some of *Don Juan* aloud to us, and Mamma was mad. Remember?"

"She objected to the passage where a maiden was compared to a poultice," Lillian said. "She told us that if we understood the reference — which she was sure we didn't — we'd see that it wasn't a polite thing for a boy to read to girls."

"And now that I have daughters, I quite agree with Mamma," said Maria.

"With Sally in mind, I'm against all poetry in mixed company," Lillian said.

"And we are shipwrecked, I suppose, like all humanity," Maria said gaily. "But under such happy auspices! Getting slightly oiled and bewailing our want of true religion!"

"At least there's plenty of rum," Lillian said. "Let me — "

"No more, thanks."

Maria stretched, untucked her legs, and stuck her feet into her shoes. She rose. "I must go. Judge will be back and my packing's yet to do."

"Stay a little longer," Lillian begged her. "There's so much we haven't settled." And she thought that she could not allow Maria to leave without telling her everything. There was no taint of snobbery in her desire, she insisted to herself. It was not that she wished rumors of her opulence to be bruited about Tryon's Neck.

It was only that between her and Maria — the alter ego of her youth — nothing would do but candor.

"It's been wonderful, Lil. It's been as if we'd never been separated — like picking up a conversation just where we'd left it off," Maria said. "But time and tide, you know!"

"I have an early engagement — a silly cocktail party before a dinner — or I'd run you down myself," Lillian said. "Brooks will call a cab."

Maria parted the brocade window curtains and peered out. "No. The rain's stopped," she said. "I'll walk a ways and then take a bus." She hushed Lillian's protests. "I find it refreshing to walk in a city. And don't bother Brooks. I saw where he put my coat."

"I'll get it," Lillian said, stepping into the hall.

She brought the wrap, a full blue corduroy garment with a schoolgirlish hood attached, and held it for Maria.

"This coat belongs to my Ellen," Maria said. "She won't be twelve till June and she's as tall as I am."

"Children grow. Time passes," Lillian said vaguely, for the sake of saying something.

"We mustn't let so much time pass before we resume *this* conversation," Maria said. "Come down home soon and I'll show you all the changes and all the things that never will change, Lord help them!" She spread out her hands, palms up, in an inclusive gesture. "Ah, Lil! Your perfectly charming room!"

"You do like it?" said Lillian.

"It reminds me of our old library," Maria said. "That's a room of the past now, you know. We rent the west wing out to teachers. Of course, this is more elegant than ours ever pretended to be, but it's so unfixy, and then you *use* your good things, like Mamma did hers. I have a silver tablespoon — an heirloom — that's lopsided from her stirring custard with it."

"I knew that spoon," Lillian said.

"But even Mamma wouldn't have made a casual cup of tea in a Straffordshire salt-glazed pot!" Maria continued, gazing down at the tea set. Almost reverently she touched the lid of the pot with her finger. "You ought to keep this under glass, Lil. It's a museum piece."

Happiness burned behind Lillian's breastbone. Its warmth rose into her throat and cheeks, increasing until she thought it must surely burst her skin. "Maria, dear Maria!" she cried. "How can I bear to lose you again? Listen. I'll renege on both my parties. I'll — "

Maria said no. She was taking the nice interne out to dinner and afterward he was driving her and her son to the train. It was arranged.

"Are you positive you don't want a cab?" Lillian asked. "Is there nothing I can do for you?"

"Well — " said Maria. She looked, with a speculative air, about the room. Her glance rested upon the Degas sketch, upon the ormolu clock, and upon a small compote of Waterford glass, and then it returned to the teapot. She lifted her head and smiled at Lillian. Her smile was engaging, unembarrassed, and slightly amused. "Can you let me have a hundred dollars?" said Maria.

Lillian caught her breath. She could feel her features stiffening into a mask, to cover her astonishment. "Why — why *yes!*" she cried. She spun on her heels and fairly hurled herself across the room to the desk.

Maria laughed. "I'm not in that big a hurry," she said. "Take your time."

But time for deliberation was precisely what Lillian dared not take. Only haste and heat would serve her now. She pressed a panel of the desk. The concealed drawer slid open. In it lay the neat stacks of green money that she had saved and stroked so lovingly. Often, on wakeful nights, she had counted those bills in her mind, as some insomniacs count sheep. Often she had anticipated the torments of parting with them, almost hating the object (perhaps a Sheraton caddy-and-blender or a portrait of herself before she faded) that would someday tear them from her.

"How will you have it, Maria?" Lillian asked. "Twenties? Tens?"

"It doesn't signify," said Maria.

Lillian selected three twenties, three tens, and two fives. "Wouldn't you like a bit more?" she said, marveling at the control in her own voice. "A hundred and fifty? Two hundred?"

"No, thank you," Maria said, as calmly as if she were declining a second slice of cake. "A hundred is what I need."

Lillian closed the drawer. She returned to Maria. "Here you are, then," she said.

Maria took the money and thrust it, bunched, into her purse. "Now I can breathe again," she said. "By the way, I have no notion when I can pay it back."

"You must never try to," Lillian said. "And don't insult me with gratitude, either."

"I won't," Maria promised. "I may not even write you. You know how stupid my letters are."

The two women walked together to the front door. They embraced briefly, letting their cheeks touch. Then Maria was gone.

Lillian came back into the sitting room. The atmosphere of the room had a curiously hollow feeling, as if it still held, barely below the threshold of audibility, the echo of voices and laughter. Naturally, I'm glad I gave it to her, Lillian told herself fiercely. She imagined Maria as she must look now, walking down a city street in the opalescent twilight with that loose, unsuitable coat blowing in the wind. ("I can breathe again," Maria had said.) She thought of the boy with his leg in a cast and of Woody, pure in heart and absurd and marked for unsuccess. Of course I'm glad!

But a hundred dollars, honesty compelled her to add. *A hundred dollars and nothing to show for it. Not even a tax-deduction slip.* She gasped. Was she a monster? *Nothing to show for it!* And was an old friendship nothing? Lillian shook her head. That wasn't for show and she hadn't bought it. She'd had that already, free.

She moved to the table and poured a small amount of rum into her empty cup. "To true religion," she murmured tentatively, hoping to recapture the heady mood she had so lately enjoyed. But the words sounded inane and pretentious and even impious. She dashed the contents of the cup into the fire. The log hissed and spurted blue flames, like a Christmas pudding.

Lillian sat down on the sofa where Maria had sat with her feet up. She trembled, because she felt disassociated in an ignoble way, from life, because her private, self-contained worlds had collided, like planets run amok, and had not merged but had done each other injury, and because she had nothing perfectly pure and beautiful left to love. From now on, whenever she saw children playing games of the imagination and was reminded of Maria, she would wince for the money that was gone. And whenever she held money in her hand, sighing over its bloom, she would think how even the past was not inviolate, how the air and light of Tryon's Neck were contaminated — and had always been contaminated — by the mundane troubles of ordinary human existence. Then she remembered that the trees in the heart of the town had been destroyed, and she began to weep.

After a while, Brooks entered the room. If he had been *Ad*mire he would have said, "Oh, Missy! Tell me where yo' mis'ry's at!" But Brooks knew his place. He appeared to notice nothing strange in Lillian's distress. Noiselessly, he put the cups, with the other tea things, on the tray, and took the tray in his hands.

"Be careful of the teapot, Brooks," Lillian said. "It's irreplaceable."

"Yes, madam," Brooks said, in a tone so correct and uninflected that it verged upon contempt. "I know." He went out, leaving her alone.

(From Harper's Magazine)

THE RED MOUNTAIN

BY ROBERT PAYNE

FOR THREE YEARS Anselme Sainteny had been in charge of the Tham-vaung tin mines in northern Annam. When he awoke in the morning he could see from the wide window the whole extent of his territory from the red honeycombed mountain in the north to the winding green sluggish river, where the small paddle-steamer rested against the jetty, and everything in between belonged to him. The dispensary belonged to him, and so did the palm-leafed hospital, and so did the railway which came across the plain, bringing the payloads into the smelting sheds, and beyond the smelting sheds lay the powerhouse and the bright yellow smoke-stack which kept coughing out plumes of yellow smoke. The company stores, the coolie-lines where the Chinese miners lived and the other coolie-lines where the Annamite clerks lived, all these were his, or rather they belonged to the company with its headquarters in Paris; but it was the red mountain with its faint scorings, its yellow-ish outcroppings, the little caves dotted all over the surface and reached by wooden ladders, which delighted him most. At night the huge conical mountain with the forest crowding at its foot was the darkest indigo unless the moon shone directly upon it, and then it was pure silver. And at dawn it was always a mysterious rose-red, seeming to float upon the earth.

That morning, Sainteny woke up in excellent humor. The Annamite woman sprawled over the bed was smiling drowsily in her sleep. She was small and very beautiful, and her fat pigtails lay over her breasts, rising and falling rhythmically. She was so animal-like in her dark grace, so much like a small ripe fruit lying against the white sheets, he had no heart to disturb her. He simply gazed at her, bending low over the bed, breathing gently the smell that arose from her, a smell compounded of chocolate and curdled milk and frangipani flowers. Once she murmured, "Anselme," in her sleep, and this pleased him so much that he made a little involuntary gesture over her, a kind of hovering benediction with his long, lean hands, which fluttered for a moment over her sleeping face, but afterward, afraid that the shadow he had thrown would disturb her, he walked out on tiptoes to the bathroom, saying to himself over and over again: My God, why do I love her so much? She is completely admirable.

In the bathroom, with the cold water plunging into the marble basin, he wanted to announce at the top of his lungs that the world was wonderful and especially created for him that morning. Streams of yellow sunlight flooded through the bathroom window. He could see the tops of the waving palms and the small silky threads of white mist hovering over the blood-red mountain, and already there was the familiar noise of throbbing machinery, the screech of the tip-cars on the rusted railway, and the horrible tubercular coughing of the engines in the powerhouse, but somehow the coughing sound, which usually annoyed him, was pleasant this morning. The water glistened against marble tiles. He could hear the cook busily preparing breakfast. A brightly colored bird was swinging dizzily on a branch just outside the window. "It's quite impossible that there should ever be a better day," Sainteny murmured, and then he hopped out of his bath, threw a towel round his waist, and went into the bedroom. She was still lying there, exactly as he had left her. "My God, you're unbelievable," he said aloud, and then hurried back to the bathroom. All the time he was shaving he was humming stupid, happy little tunes to himself.

He breakfasted alone. There, in the small dining room heaped with the flowers which Néné gathered on the sides of the mountain, among the silverware imported from Paris, the wineglasses gleaming in rows, and the flower vases painted in strange Annamite patterns. As he dipped his *brioche* in the *café au lait*, Sainteny went over the plans for the day. He would walk over to the sorting sheds, go over some accounts with the Chinese overseer, Wang Dieh, make his usual morning inspection of the hospital, and then he would ride down to the river and take an *apéritif* with *le capitaine* Jerome on the old paddle steamer which took the tin ore down river and brought up his supplies. The rest of the day was his own. Perhaps he would sleep during the afternoon, for it promised to be a hot day, or he would read the five-weeks-old copies of *Le Temps,* or if there was time he would row over to the village of Tham-vaung and have the usual monthly talk with the headman.

Dressed in a tweed coat, a blue shirt open at the neck, and jodhpurs, Sainteny strode towards the mines, absurdly pleased with himself. He was nearly forty, long and square-faced, and like many Normans he had reddish hair and thick pepper-colored eyebrows. He did not look like a Frenchman. In his manner there was something of a Scot, and in his younger days he was often called *l'Ecossais,* and when he addressed one of the Annamites he would always bend slightly, and there would be an amused sympathetic look on the strong face. All round the tin mines lay the forest. It did not frighten him. He liked to think of himself as an embattled conquistador: here for a few years he would hammer out a victory against the corroding elements which demanded their fee of pain and labor and life and death.

"Well, how is everything?" he shouted to Dubonnet, his young assistant, who was standing outside the sorting sheds with a solar topee two sizes too large for him. "My God, man, didn't I tell you the sun won't harm you. It's an absurd confession of weakness to wear the damned thing."

Dubonnet smiled weakly. He never argued with Sainteny, but he did not remove the solar topee.

"Have you heard of the accident?" Dubonnet asked.

"What accident?"

"There was a cave-in in one of the tunnels. Some of the Chinese were trapped. They're just bringing them in."

"You mean it all happened this morning?"

"That's right. Half an hour ago — on the first shift. I've just come down from there."

The sweat was streaming down Dubonnet's face, and his eyes,

though hidden in shadow, looked frightened. He looked absurdly young, almost a boy, and simply because he was young, Sainteny could not prevent himself from bending slightly and putting on a sympathetic air and addressing him in the same tones as he would address the Chinese overseer or the Chinese doctor.

"You shouldn't worry so much, *mon cher*," Sainteny said. "The Chinese can stand anything."

"I think two of them will die," Dubonnet went on. "They were terribly mangled."

Sainteny put a hand on Dubonnet's shoulder.

"A tin mine is like a war, you understand. We must expect wounds sometimes. It is the price we pay for — "

He did not go on. Quite suddenly he realized that young Dubonnet was suffering from a real grief and a real shock.

"You were there?"

Dubonnet nodded.

"Then, my dear fellow, permit me to suggest you take the morning off and have a stiff glass of whiskey."

Afterward, when Sainteny continued his tour, he realized that he had hopelessly failed to console young Dubonnet. The raw wound, concealed beneath the solar topee, was now festering. Whenever there was a cave-in, alarm bells were automatically set ringing. It occurred to Sainteny that he had not heard the alarm bells because the wind was coming from the northwest. Still, there had been accidents before. After seeing Wang Dieh, he would make his way to the hospital and see what could be done for the Chinese.

As Sainteny walked through the plant, he observed that the colors of the place were especially bright this morning. It was some trick of the light perhaps: more likely it was his own contentment, the blood racing in his veins, the extraordinary joy he had felt ever since he woke up. He told himself that the Chinese were always getting into accidents, because they were always taking risks and cutting corners, and laughed at the safety regulations. They gambled and smoked opium and ran after the Annamite women, and this was troublesome, because the headman of the village was now complaining that a woman had been abducted, and had even sent a description of the woman, asking for her immediate release and the punishment of the abductors. Somewhere, he believed, perhaps in the edge of the forest or in one of the disused caves of the mine, the Chinese kept three or four Annamite women prisoners. There was something slovenly about the Chinese workers, their bodies calloused by knuckles of falling rock, their eyes inflamed by powder-blasts. And though they were slovenly and at the same time hard-working, he could not help liking them.

"*Bonjour, Monsieur Sainteny.*"

He turned to see the almond eyes of Wang Dieh gazing up at him. Wang Dieh was a spruce little man with a wrinkled, pock-marked face and the manners of a clerk, but the most remarkable thing about him was the almond eyes. Few Chinese have eyes like that. They were soft and warm, and there was a wonderful curve to the eyelids. Wang Dieh knew he had good eyes. All his intelligence, all his sensitivity were expressed through the eyes.

"It has been a bad accident," Wang Dieh said. "It is my understanding that three men have been hurt painfully."

Sainteny nodded gravely.

"Three men hurt painfully and four others less painfully," Wang Dieh went on, with a wry apologetic little smile. It was not that he found anything amusing in the accident: it was simply that he always smiled whenever accidents occurred because he could never understand them, never console himself with them, never reconcile himself to the jagged wounds and bruised flesh.

"Where are they?"

"In the hospital."

"Then I'll go there at once," Sainteny said quickly, and he was surprised when Wang Dieh tugged at his arm. There was a look of terrible fear on Wang Dieh's face.

"You don't want me to go?"

"No, it is not good to go. It doesn't help, Monsieur Sainteny."

Sainteny gripped him by the bone-thin arms. Wang Dieh's voice had risen into a thin high-pitched scream.

"Yes, I understand what you are suffering, but it's no use raising your voice. You ought to go riding, Wang Dieh. Do something about those muscles of yours — tone yourself up. You take things too seriously." He went on, speaking softly in French, overcome by a relentless fit of tenderness for the pock-marked little man who worked so industriously. "The important thing is never to give way to the emotions, you understand. In this climate it's dangerous to give way to the emotions. I've kept myself fit, haven't I? And why? Because I exercise my body. I ride. I have women. I am always active. And you? You are always working, or smoking opium."

"Only a little opium." Wang Dieh smiled sheepishly.

"We won't go into that now," Sainteny replied. "But you don't need it. It lowers the vitality. Opium is the religion of the people — well, of your people."

They exchanged smiles. The color was coming back to Wang Dieh's face. Sainteny put one hand heavily on Wang Dieh's shoulder, and then led him in the direction of the hospital sheds.

"You know what I have done about safety regulations," Sainteny said. "Well, you know they are all my children — I do the best I can for them, and now we'll see what can be done for them in the hospital."

Slowly, immersed in their thoughts, they walked toward the palm-leafed hospital shed. Even there you could hear the pounding of the engines in the smelting factory, the rumble of the paydirt coming down the line, the distant echo of the picks in the caves. There were tiles on the floor of the hospital, and all the walls were whitewashed. There was the heavy smell of iodiform and lime, and the place was unusually quiet. In the beds beneath the gray mosquito curtains the patients lay listless, some like cocoons in their bandages, others with faces streaked with Mercurochrome, others gaunt and sickly with skins turning blue as a thrush's egg. In starched white cotton dresses and white stockings the Annamite nurses hovered down the lane between the beds. The Chinese doctor from the Shantung Medical College, peering through thick spectacles which made his eyes resemble enormous pebbles, came out of the small operating theater to greet them, but Sainteny was not looking at the doctor. He was looking at the boy who lay outstretched on a bed near the operating room: something in the boy's hopeless eyes, so dark, so sunken, so deep, drew Sainteny to him. His chest and shoulders were wrapped in thick bandages, and already the bandages, the gauze, and the cottonwool were stained rust-red with blood. The boy recognized Sainteny, smiled, made an effort to rise, and then fell back heavily on the bed.

"Opium," the boy said, his mouth a little cave.

"You want opium?" Sainteny asked, bending down.

The boy's eyes clouded over. He was evidently in great pain. The doctor was making signs: signs which could mean only that the boy was not expected to live.

"Tell her to come here," the boy murmured. "Tell her to come now."

"You want the nurse?"

"No, not the nurse."

"Who do you want?" Sainteny went on, stroking the boy's forehead, now running with sweat. "If there is anything you want, I'll bring it to you."

"I want the girl," the boy said.

"Which girl?"

There was no answer. Wang Dieh was standing near, and so was the Chinese doctor. They were all listening to Sainteny's conversation with the wounded boy. Like many healthy men, Sainteny could be extremely tender with people when they were hurt. He smiled at the boy and then bent down to listen to his whispers. He did not know Chinese well, only enough to pass the time of day with the workmen when they were coming off shift. He was popular with them, and he could understand elementary phrases, and prided himself on being able to say the few words that pleased them, but all he could understand from the boy was that there was a girl somewhere in one of the caves. It was what he had suspected. He was about to pull himself to his full height when he observed through the window two coolies lifting a dead Chinese into a wooden coffin. He could observe this only with great difficulty, for the window was painted over on the outside, but some of the white paint had flaked away. By shifting his position a little, Sainteny was able to observe one of the coolies, then the dead Chinese, then the other coolie.

"I can't make out what the boy is saying," he said to the doctor, his voice shaky. "If he wants opium, I suppose it won't do any harm to give it to him."

"He will be dead in an hour," the doctor said.

Sainteny walked blindly out of the hospital, and all the time he was thinking of the boy who would be dead in an hour. The boy could not have been more than seventeen, and he had come over the frontier only recently — you could tell that because there were no blue scars on his face. He had delicately boned hands, high cheekbones, a small but determined chin, and his face was a soft warm brown. You had to admit to yourself that he was an unusually handsome specimen of his race. Thinking of his own virile body, untouched by any rockfall, Sainteny said: "They ought to be more careful — oh Jesus, they ought to be more careful," and then he decided to make his way to the old rusting paddle steamer. He would talk to Jerome. They would drink and laugh for a while, and they would put all their worries behind them.

Walking down the long avenue of palms Sainteny felt the hot wind against his cheeks. Some brown and turbaned Annamite women passed him, and as he always did he bowed reverently. "They like these little attentions," he told himself, smiling. "It gets known in the village. They know, too, how much I admire them."

Climbing the gangplank he saw the Annamite sailors pretending to be busy cleaning the brass. They were stripped down to their drawers. As he walked across the deck they eyed him surreptitiously, and he was sure they were whispering about him. A black trickle of smoke crawled listlessly from the flaking funnel. He shouted out to Jerome, and there was a great answering shout. The cabin door was flung open.

"I can't tell you how glad I am to see you," Sainteny said, when he was sitting comfortably opposite Jerome.

Jerome was a rather ugly man, with high cheekbones, hollow temples, and pale watery eyes. He was heavily built, and he had a short heavy neck: the back of the neck was wrinkled reminding Sainteny of an elephant's hide. Yet there was something extraordinarily pleasant in the man's wide-mouthed smile. He spent most of the day reading interminable French novels with yellow backs to them; the cabin was piled high with these novels. As usual, the room was in disorder, there were bottles everywhere, the smell of stale tobacco hung on the air, and the navigating charts had slipped to the floor. Propped on a small pile of novels was a photograph of Jerome's wife taken when she was seventeen: she looked deeply religious, and there were mysterious lights in her dark, deep-set eyes. She had died long ago, but Jerome often entered into long silent conversations with the photograph in the gilt frame.

Sainteny breathed deeply and watched Jerome pouring out the red wine.

"I'm pushing off tomorrow," Jerome remarked, "and I don't mind telling you I will be glad to go. This damned place gets on my nerves."

He said this very cheerfully, lifting his glass so high that the rim of it touched the low ceiling.

"You like the towns, and I like the villages," Sainteny said. "We agree to differ, eh? I wouldn't mind going down the river with you sometime, though."

"Why don't you come this time?"

"I wouldn't impose on you."

"Nonsense, Anselme, there's room enough for you. I could turn my chief engineer out of his bunk, or I could bed you down in my cabin. You ought to get away sometimes."

Sainteny stared reflectively at the ceiling. In another year he would receive eight months leave: no use in taking leave now. If he went with Jerome, it would be at least twelve days before he could return to the mines, and Dubonnet was too young, too inexperienced to run the place.

"No," he said slowly, and it occurred to him that there was nothing more restful than a river boat, even an old paddle steamer nearly falling to pieces. Here on the edge of shore no wind stirred, there was no rustle of falling leaves, no high-pitched voices of Chinese, no dulled explosions from the cliff face: only the lapping of the river against the ship's sides, and somewhere the Annamite women talking together as they washed clothes along the shore.

"Is it Néné?" Jerome asked, holding his head to one side. "You don't want to leave her, eh? Well, that's understandable. But I could make room for Néné, too, if you wanted to come."

"It's no use, Jerome," Sainteny said at last, smiling and shaking his head. "There's young Dubonnet to think about. There was an accident this morning — two or three Chinese hurt in a powder blast — the usual thing — but Dubonnet took it to heart. He is a young man with the proper sympathies, an excellent boy, I'm fond of him, but he doesn't know the beginning of a tin miner's life. If you're going downriver tomorrow, why don't you come and have dinner with me tonight? I'll get Néné to prepare something charming, and she'll be delighted to have company."

Jerome looked across the table with a strangely mocking expression. "I couldn't do it," he said. "You know how it is on the last night, when we are battening down the hatches. I've got to be here."

"To prevent thieving — ?" Sainteny asked, though he knew that the question was absurd.

"That, and other things."

"What sort of things?"

"The worst of them is opium. I'm not going to take the risk of the river police coming on the boat and finding unlicensed opium hidden away in the engine room."

"It's always opium," Sainteny smiled. "Wang Dieh admitted to me this morning that he smokes the stuff, and there was a Chinese boy lying on the hospital bed. He asked for opium, and then went rambling on about a girl. You know, they've got girls hidden away in the caves."

Jerome nodded. He had known this for a long time, much longer than Sainteny had known it. Sainteny amused him. He was so fresh, so virile, but half the things that happened in the mine passed unnoticed by him.

"I didn't know you knew," Sainteny admitted.

"I know an awful number of things I shouldn't know," Jerome said, laughing. "I know what your nickname is."

"Well, what is it?"

"I'm afraid I can't tell you," Jerome said reddening. "You have one nickname from the Annamites, and another from the Chinese. I'll say this. They're very good at inventing nicknames."

"So you knew about the Annamite women in the caves?" Sainteny said, anxious to change the subject, although he was in good humor and he was not in the least annoyed by Jerome's talk of nicknames. "That's one thing I have against them — taking women to their caves. They know I've forbidden it. They keep the women there, never let them out, they are no more than slaves — those women. I do my best for the Chinese. No one can tell me I do not treat them as though they were my children, and still they do things like that. I've had another letter from the headman — another woman abducted. If we are not careful, we shall find open war between the Annamites and the Chinese."

"It might happen."

"You seem to take it very cheerfully — "

At this, Jerome burst out laughing, reached for the bottle, poured some more wine, and remarked casually: "I won't have to face the music. I'm leaving tomorrow morning."

"Then you think it will happen soon?"

"What will happen?"

"You don't have to be evasive. I mean, trouble between the Annamites and the Chinese."

"Oh, it might happen at any time."

Sainteny was no longer sure whether to take this conversation seriously. There was a half-mocking, happy look on Jerome's face. It occurred to him that Jerome was enjoying himself.

"I'm deadly serious," Sainteny said.

"So am I."

"Then you really think there will be trouble?"

"There's trouble already, Anselme. That accident this morning. Doesn't it occur to you that the Annamites might have caused it. The Chinese are very careful when they blast. They've learned their lesson. The Annamites, for all I know, may have caused a premature explosion — "

"Oh, nonsense."

"I am only suggesting it."

"You are really allowing your imagination to get ahead of you, *mon cher capitaine*. There are of course some malcontents, but on the whole you can see that they get on well together. The Annamites don't harbor grudges. I suppose the abduction of the women — I believe there are three or four women, not more, in the caves — I suppose it's serious enough, but they wouldn't kill each other over it. I am their friend — I treat the Chinese and the Annamites equally."

"Because you are their friend doesn't alter the fact that they are at each other's throats, Anselme."

Sainteny wanted to change the subject. It was hot and airless in the small cabin. Jerome was smiling and brushing the ends of his mustache with an upright movement of his hands, and the bottles were in disorder, and already they had drunk five or six glasses of wine. He heard his own voice dying away in the little room where no air ever stirred, no wind ever blew. Well, it was absurd to think about. The Chinese and Annamites had brought it upon themselves. Had he not given them a hospital, medicine, facilities beyond any they possessed before? He had fought to give them higher salaries. They worshipped him, or at least they pretended to worship him. When his eight years were over, he would be able to look back approvingly on his own conduct among them, for had he not brought civilization to the remote tin mine on the edge of the jungle?

"When you go down, there's a favor I'd like to ask of you," Sainteny heard himself saying. "Please inquire about some nuns."

"Some nuns?" Jerome asked, in an astonishingly loud voice.

"Yes — French nuns. It would help a great deal if we had some nuns working in the hospital. It would help to elevate the morals of the workmen."

"I've no doubt," the captain said, not without a touch of sarcasm.

"Then you don't believe me?" he asked.

"I don't believe or disbelieve. If you think a couple of nuns would work a miracle — "

"Then what do you suggest?"

"Bring some Chinese girls. Buy them from Shanghai — you won't get them in Saigon except under false pretenses. Announce in the Shanghai newspapers that the girls are expected to live high up on the cliff face for a period of two or three years. Everything they could dream of will be given them. The Chinese workers will buy them every kind of expensive perfume, every kind of clothing they could desire. Their food will be especially prepared for them. They will be swaddled and looked after as though they were princesses, but not once during the period they are here must they leave the cliff face. The others are loaded with jewels, and though they never see the sun, I assure you they are perfectly content."

"Then you have seen them?"

"Yes, I've seen them," the captain said, and there was a long silence.

Shortly afterward, Sainteny made some excuse to leave the paddle boat.

As he came down the gangplank he felt hot and angry. It was nearly midday, the sun very high and white, and all the earth breathless before him. The heat came out of the sun like a sword, and the palm trees were stiff and silent in the heat, and so was the red honeycombed mountain, but he could no longer distinguish in the brightness the entrances to the caves. He thought for a moment of going to the village on the other side of the river. He would have a quiet talk with the headman. He would explain what was being done. He would take the old headman into his confidence. After all, you could not deny that the slender and turbaned Annamites had cause for complaint. It piqued him that *le capitaine* Jerome knew more about the affair than he had suspected, and perhaps there was something to be said for Jerome's suggestion, but it would need a considerable outlay in money and headquarters in Paris could hardly be expected to approve. The vultures were still circling overhead, throwing their lazy blue shadows on the earth, and the slow creaking train, filled with reddish ore, was coming down the mountain.

That afternoon Sainteny summoned Wang Dieh to his office.

"I'm told there are four women in the mountain," he said quietly.

He was determined not to put Wang Dieh in a position where he would take offense.

"Let's speak about it man to man. We are faced with difficulties. It has been suggested to me that the explosion this morning may have been caused by our beloved friends, the Annamites. What do you think?"

"Yes, Monsieur Sainteny, I am listening."

"Please be reasonable. Please try to understand the position I am in. You are all brothers and sons to me. You must give up the women."

"Yes, Monsieur Sainteny."

"I am glad you are so reasonable, Wang Dieh. I've always trusted you, haven't I? You must believe me that I am not thinking about this in terms of morality — simply in terms of the greatest benefit for the Chinese workers."

"You ask us to surrender the women, is that right? Previously you have asked us to give up opium. No, Monsieur Sainteny, we cannot give these things up. After work there is nothing for us — only work and heat. No women. No opium. You want to take all these away. Why should we live?"

Feeling discouraged, Sainteny returned to his house on the edge of the clearing. For the first time he was beginning to hate the tin mines. Néné was waiting for him, wearing a flowered skirt slit to the thighs. She smiled sleepily, kissed him, showed him the flowers she had gathered on the mountain, and busied herself putting them into the painted pots, until the room smelled like a gravemound piled with wreathes. All evening he pondered the problem. In Indochina the light falls quickly, and soon the last tip-cart had disappeared into the red corrugated shed and the last puff of yellow smoke had been coughed out of the powerhouse chimney. He saw the paddle-boat lying dark and silent at the end of the jetty, and beyond the plowed fields on the opposite shore blue smoke arose to meet the moonlight. The palm leaves waved tranquilly, the silver bellies of the leaves assuming the whole color of the moon. The air was oppressively humid, and as usual at night there came from the forest a heavy exhalation like a warm and evil-smelling breath. Néné was smiling. She was accustomed to this weather: it did not disturb her to hear the sounds of the forest animals, a sound which grew louder and fiercer as the night progressed.

"Are you all right?" she smiled, putting her soft brown hands on his forehead.

"Yes, quite all right."

"You look preoccupied, Anselme — "

"Of course. Business worries — don't disturb your pretty head about them."

All through dinner she would cast little sidelong glances at him. After dinner he listened to Radio-Saigon, drank Cointreau, and rested for a while with her head on his lap. Her hair was scented and oiled. When he squeezed one of the plaits, it was like squeezing a fruit. He drank some more Cointreau, inserting his tongue in the small glass until the last golden drops were absorbed, and then went to bed. Néné followed him, but he kept to his side of the bed.

He could not sleep. The moon shone brilliantly outside, and to make matters worse a huge palm leaf kept scraping against the window, and sometimes, when he was about to doze off, he heard the faint scream of the animals in the forest. Now, more vividly than during the day, he saw the blood-soaked body of the Chinese being lifted into the coffin, and he saw the boy lying on the hospital bed. He tried to dismiss them from his mind, but they would not go. He tried to tell himself that they were only something in a ledger, a cost account canceled because it served no useful purpose, something to be mentioned casually in a report sent to the Boulevard Haussmann — "Three Chinese workmen were unfortunately killed in an explosion."

Néné was smiling calmly in her sleep, but her calm smile did nothing to reassure him. He wanted to say: "You understand. I love you. Have patience. I am faced with insoluble problems." How still everything was! How beautiful the moonlight! I mustn't give way to my emotions, he told himself, and he gazed out of the window to see whether any clouds were forming, but there was no change in the sky — only the dark blue sky with the silver stars, a sky sodden with humidity, raining down a perpetual ceremony of heat even in the middle of the night. When the pillow was sodden with sweat, he got up and fetched another: and though there was comfort in its coolness, he knew there was no lasting comfort. He was filled now with a profound sense of pity, not for himself or even for the dead Chinese boys, and certainly he had no pity for the Annamite women high up in their cave: it was pity for all the poor devils who live out their lives on the shores of the river and below the red mountain, a vast pity which knew no end.

It's no use, he told himself. I can't go up to the cave and remove the women, they wouldn't let me, and yet if the women are not removed, the Annamites will desert the mine, or cause more explosions, or slit all our throats. You see, there is nothing I can do. I can't write to Paris and say: "The Chinese have abducted some women and put them in the caves. They have everything they want — brocades, silks, jewels, cushions, everything. It's a strange mountain. It's full of ghosts. If we are not careful, murder will come out of one of the caves."

In the stupor of weariness he had the illusion that phosphorescent lights were streaming out of Néné's eyes. The moonlight was still blinding. He dozed for a little while, and then woke up sharply, but it was only the wind, a faint breath of wind, and outside the air was still warm and the stars were growing larger, as they always did before dawn.

When the dawn came at last, he staggered to the bathroom. When he cut himself shaving, he found himself remembering every detail of what he had seen in the hospital: the rust-red bandages, the two coolies lifting the Chinese into the coffin. When he had dressed, he went out of the house, thinking he would see Jerome. They would take breakfast together, they would talk about Paris. In the bluish light of dawn, watery and swollen, he found himself going down to the river, but the paddle-steamer had already left, leaving a gaping hole. He wanted to shout after it: "Come back, Jerome. Please don't desert me now when I need your advice." Along the shore a few palms were waving listlessly, and for some reason the villagers on the other side of the river were beating drums. He watched them in the wavering heat haze as they formed into a procession, waving pink and purple banners. It was some religious ceremony, and very faintly across the river he could hear the chanting voice of a priest.

(From Harper's Bazaar)

THE MANGO TREE

BY ROSANNE SMITH ROBINSON

*W*HEN her father's taxi drove up in front of the house Nora was hanging by her knees from the lowest branch of the rubber tree and her short blond hair, sun-bleached almost white along the part, barely grazed the round disk of black earth that had been scuffed in the matted grass. Nora grasped the branch with both hands, flipped backward to the ground and raced to the sidewalk.

Her father paid off the taxi and then turned and looked down at her. He was wearing a blue suit and he looked very pink and white and a fringe of stiff sandy hair was growing on his upper lip. Nora took her hand down from her mouth where it had somehow strayed, and smiled. The sandy-haired man smiled back. His face looked the way hers felt when she smiled.

"I must have made a mistake," he said gravely. "I used to have a little girl who lived right in this house, but she wasn't so tall as you are."

His knees bent and then his face was level with hers. "You know," he said, "most girls are a lot older than you before they get a chance to kiss a man with a mustache." He held his hands out to her and Nora moved into his arms.

"I like mustaches," she said and gave him a hard kiss that mashed her nose against his. She didn't feel the mustache at all.

"My goodness," her father said. He was rubbing his nose. Then he straightened up and carried Nora, her legs twined about his waist, up the path to the front porch that was wrapped like a cocoon with jasmine and wild white rose vines. Nora held her arms tightly around his neck. He smelled wonderfully, like clean laundry just taken in out of the sun, and he had hair growing out of his ears. It would be so warm and drowsy to go to sleep like this.

And then he put her down on the steps and said, "I'll just get my bag." Nora opened the porch door and screamed, "Edie, he's here. He's here, Edie." He was back with his bag when Edie streamed out on the porch in a dress and apron so white and starched that she seemed to gleam almost phosphorescently in the cool gloom of the porch.

"Well, Edie," Nora's father said. He put his bag down and took her hand in both of his. "It's wonderful to see you. How are Buddy and Sylvia?"

"The same, Mr. Townsend," Edie said. "The same and a little more."

"Edie won sixty dollars at Belita," Nora said, jumping up and down on one leg. "She's got it wrapped in tissue paper in the top of her sock. It's all one-dollar bills. Isn't it, Edie?"

"Try keeping something from that child," Edie said. She drew her hand away and finally found a place for it under her apron. "We missed you," she said simply.

"I know, Edie, I know," Mr. Townsend said.

"Miz Townsend be back before supper," Edie said, her eyes on Mr. Townsend's shantung tie. "I got your room all ready."

"Where's Margaret?" Mr. Townsend asked.

"She's scared," Nora said. "She's gone to Mrs. Hodak's to watch television."

"I can go get her," Edie said. "I'll get her back here. Don't want to meet her own father. I never . . . "

"Never mind, Edie," Mr. Townsend said. "She is a young lady almost. We'd better let her come on her own steam. Thank you anyway."

"It's no good them not seeing you more," Edie said. "You call me if you want anything. I'm in the kitchen." She reached over and hauled his bag from the floor.

"Never mind that, Edie," Mr. Townsend said, making a move to stop her.

"Never mind no never mind," Edie said and left them smiling at each other in the gloom.

"Well, now," her father said. He settled himself in a rattan chair and lighted a cigarette. "Now tell me everything and how it is that you're getting so beautiful."

Nora flushed and pulled her arms behind her back. "I'm not beautiful," she said, watching him closely.

"I think you are," he said.

"Mother says I look like an alley cat in everything she puts on me."

"I'm sure she doesn't mean it. Tell me what you do all day so that when I think about you I'll be able to close my eyes and see what you're doing."

"Oh," Nora said, "I just fool around."

"What do you fool around with," her father asked pleasantly.

"Oh, just play around and stuff."

They sat silently for a moment and then Nora launched into speech. "I'm not allowed to go out between twelve and four. It's too hot, mother says. But sometimes if she asks me I go over to Mrs. Hodak's and watch her television. She's very old and she hasn't washed her hair for three years. I wish we had a television set. Dana says he's going to get one."

"Dana?" her father said. He could make one eyebrow go higher than the other. "Oh, yes. Mr. Miller. He rents the garage apartment."

"He gives me a quarter when I polish the orange tree," Nora said, squirming back in her seat. The edge of the chair started to bite into the back of her legs and she squirmed forward again.

"How do you polish an orange tree?" he asked.

"You know," Nora said. "You wipe off the leaves and then they look real shiny and green. When it rains they get all splotched again and I go out and wipe them off. It's not a very big tree. Dana stole it one night from an old grove somewhere. Mother held the flashlight for him. I saw them from the window when they got home."

"Really," her father said and turned his face from her toward the doorway that led into the house shuttered dark against the tropical sun. Her mother's voice came gliding in to them like the petal of a flower moving on a slow current. Nora followed her father through the doorway. Light filtering through a pale apricot shade met them suddenly from the half-light of the living room, and her mother stood there looking as if she had been magically created in that moment that the switch had been turned. Her lips were pulled together ever so slightly in a way she had when she was waiting for a pause in which to speak and Nora could see the brown speckles in her hazel eyes.

"My God, Clarence," she said. "You look like a bloody British captain." She released her lips into a smile that lifted only one corner of her mouth.

Clarence moved toward her quickly. She met him with the open palm of her hand brought up against his chest. "I'm afraid," she said in her curious lilting voice that sounded strange and evocative on the ear even after a few hours' separation from her, "that you will have to content yourself with the most discreet of wifely salutations until you do something about *that*." She offered her cheek to her husband, and then walked over and seated herself on the long low couch, her legs stretched out on the cushion next to her.

Clarence Townsend seated himself in a chair across the room and Nora stood in the shadow beside him. "I hope, Leah," he said, "that my visit hasn't inconvenienced you. It seemed a shame not to see the girls and there were some things I thought we ought to settle one way or another. This arrangement is ridiculous."

"Naturally," Leah said. "I'm afraid you'll find Margaret in rather a difficult phase. She's decided to be a nun, you know. Most restful after the Bergman period, I assure you. Nora, run over to poor Mrs. Hodak's and fetch Margaret and don't pound your way out. Walk. She should have been a boy, you know. I thought you'd want to dine with the girls since you will be here two days. We can talk later. Run along, Nora. He'll still be here when you get back."

Nora felt her father's hand caressing on her arm as she turned to go. She walked out through the porch quietly, and shut the door and then stood for a moment. She heard her mother's voice, "Of course, it's Nora I'm really worried about. I'm not sure I shouldn't have someone see her . . ."

Nora cleared the porch steps with a leap that landed her on her heels. Her heart felt swollen twice its size. Leah would tell him now. She would tell him about Jimmy and Mac. She should have known it was wicked. She knew it now. They asked if she wanted to look and she did want to look. She was running toward Mrs. Hodak's now and her heart was splitting the way it had the moment after her mother had come through the garage door and her eyes had narrowed to slits. She had slapped Jimmy and Mac on their bare bottoms and then turned and said through her teeth, "You little slut. Go to your room and stay there." She had stayed in her room until yesterday when the call had come from her father. And now Leah was telling him. She was telling him all about it. She must get back as fast as she could to stop them talking.

She reached Mrs. Hodak's door, rattled the screen door and yelled in, "Margaret, mother wants you to come home. Right now." She wheeled and ran back. She stood for a moment on the porch, trembling, sweat running down the inside of her arms and legs. Then she crept into the room, staying out of the light so Leah would not see her crimson face, and stood once more next to her father's chair.

"They've completely changed the ninth hole," her mother was saying. Nora relaxed and let the blood pounding in her ears drown out all the other sound.

Margaret arrived in a moment, stiff-legged and glowering. With her long arms hanging at her side and and her feet turned slightly inward, she stood like a sulky baboon in the middle of the room. She bobbed her head and said, "How do you do, Mr. Townsend."

Leah laughed, her hands on the side of her face, and Clarence Townsend stood up and offering his hand to his oldest daughter said, "Hello, my dear." Margaret held out her hand as though she were offering him a knife across the table and he shook it briefly but gravely. And then Edie came in to say that dinner was on the table and she bore Nora away to the bathroom to wash her hands and face. . . .

She slipped into her chair in time to hear Margaret say, "That's where Dana sits."

"Yes," Leah said, spooning French dressing over her avocado, "he's been taking most of his meals with us. There's no decent restaurant for miles around here, and I must say the children have become most fond of him. I think Margaret really has a crush on him."

"I loathe him," Margaret said.

"I see," Mr. Townsend said, reaching for another roll, "that Edie's cooking has in no way deteriorated."

Nora was peering over the rim of her iced-tea glass at her father when the doorbell rang. She jumped slightly and a thin trickle of cold tea ran down her chin and dripped on her plate.

"Margaret," Leah said, "would you please answer the door and tell whoever it is that we are having our dinner."

Margaret held on to her fork. "Why can't Edie go," she said in an uncloistered tone.

"Young lady," Leah said tranquilly without looking up, "answer the door."

Margaret walked from the room, knees locked like a robot, her mouth clamped with rage. They heard her hiss, "Beat it, you little jerk. We're eating and she's not supposed to play with you any more and you know why."

Nora saw her father's eyebrow go up and he looked questioningly toward the other end of the table. Leah looked as though she were eating alone in a great room by candlelight. Margaret came stomping back and started to sit down. As Nora watched she disappeared on the other side of the table. In her stiff-kneed rage she had knocked her own chair out from under her, but the look on her face as she had gone down had shown clearly that she believed and would go on believing for the rest of her life that Nora had somehow contrived to kick the chair out from under her if by no other process than the sheer maliciousness of thought and wish.

It was too much for Nora. She broke into a long excruciatingly painful wail of laughter. She laughed and laughed until her laughter had moved beyond the range of sound. She recovered slightly and then caught a glimpse of her sister's face and began laughing again. She simply gave up to it and laughed and laughed as though she were being tickled by a thousand Lilliputians. During an involuntary pause for breath she heard her mother say, "I put up with her all year. You can take care of her this once."

And then she was in her father's arms being carried into the living room. His face had a look of bemused amusement, and this set Nora off again. He carried her upstairs to her room and Edie took over and helped her to the bathroom where she was quite sick. She fell asleep to the sound of insects pinging against the screens at the windows of her room and the faraway counterpoint of her parents' voices.

She was up and outside long before anyone else was awake and before Edie arrived to make breakfast. She had taken the Oz book she was reading out with her and she looked for a suitable place in which to read it. Finally she tilted the rain barrel and let the little water that was in it slosh out on the ground and then moved it under the branch of the great mango tree that grew in the back yard beside the garage and its upstairs apartment. Standing on the rain barrel she balanced the book on the branch that grew out from the trunk almost horizontally and then carefully swung herself up into the tree. She settled herself and started reading about the wicked gnomes planning war against the beautiful Glinda. But it was hard not to keep drifting away from the print. The tree, heavy now with the pale yellow fruit speckled like some great bird's eggs, seemed to have a movement of its own. It almost groaned with ripeness and the waxen yellow freckled globes of fruit seemed to have been tied to a tree too small for their swollen weight. She hated their greasy juiciness and the slightly turpentine taste they left in the mouth. She stopped trying to read when she heard Dana starting to cough, as he did every morning because of his sinus trouble, and the sound of the water tap running in his bathroom.

She skinned down from the mango tree and was standing down at the bottom of the steps when he finally came down.

"Hi dumpling," he said, his curly hair glistening with water. "Your old man get here all right?" He was whispering.

"Yes," Nora said and her eye caught the glisten of spinning silver from the coin he had tossed in the air. The coin landed tilted in the grass. "But I haven't . . . "

"That's all right, dumpling," he whispered. "Payment in advance." He winked at her and stepped over the sill into the garage. In a moment she heard his car back out of the garage. Usually he waited and had breakfast with them.

Clarence Townsend came outside shortly after Edie arrived, and Nora ran for her beebee gun and showed him she could shoot a kitchen match against the screen and light it. They took turns shooting the gun, watching the matches flare into light as they hit the screen and fall, some still burning, to the ground.

After breakfast, Edie packed a picnic lunch and Nora and Margaret and their father drove off to the beach. Leah stayed behind.

"I simply cannot stand the sun for that length of time," she said, sitting over her coffee in a gray chiffon negligee.

"Then why do you persist in living down here," her husband said.

She sugared her coffee and said, looking up at him, "I find living here has innumerable other conveniences."

"Leah," he said moving toward her, "I . . . "

"Not now if you don't mind," she said. "And keep an eye on your small darling. Particularly if there are small boys around. I shouldn't be at all surprised if she were nubile."

For Nora the day was ecstasy. This, she knew, is the way I shall feel when I am a grown-up. Margaret pinched her only a few times and allowed herself to be drawn into a conversation with her father about her school and where she would like to go when she finished Junior High. They stopped for frozen custard and sang all the way home.

Dana's car was parked in front of the house. They went in the back door, leaving the picnic basket in the kitchen. Dana put his drink down and stood up when her mother introduced him. Her father held up his hand, in which he holding a towel and his sunglasses, in apology.

"You'll excuse me while I change," he said and walked upstairs.

Dana winked at Nora and Margaret.

"Go upstairs and change, girls," Leah said, "and then go outside or occupy yourselves until dinner. Your father and Dana and I are going out someplace where we can talk."

Dressed in clean denims and a white shirt, Nora went outside and sat on the cool grass. She could hear the voices in the living room but not what they were saying. Her skin began to feel prickly from the long day in the tropical sun and she pulled the shirttail out from her jeans and unbuttoned the shirt to ease its weight across her burnt shoulders. Jimmy was coming along the sidewalk, his short cropped blond head stuck out from his shoulders as he stepped gingerly with his bare feet on the sidewalk still hot from the torrid sun. He hopped off the sidewalk onto the grass in front of her.

"You're a snake," he said.

"I'm not," Nora said.

"Well, your mother is," he said, screwing his face into a sneer. "She's a mean snake. She called my mother up."

Nora stood up and tugged at her pants which were too tight for her.

"She better never come round my mother," Jimmy said. "My mother'll tell her a thing or two. My mother says *she* should talk."

"Oh, shut up," Nora said.

"You shut up yourself," Jimmy said, giving her a shove.

Nora shoved back and Jimmy grabbed her and tripped her with his leg. They rolled over and over on the grass punching and pulling at each other. Neither heard the screen porch door slam.

"God damn it, Nora, stop that," her mother said from the top of the steps, "before I turn the hose on you like a couple of dogs." Nora sat back panting in the grass. Her mother came down the steps, leaving Dana and her father standing behind her. She turned, one hand on her hip and said to Clarence, "Now you see what I mean."

Jimmy scuttled like a crab off the grass and ran away down the sidewalk. Her mother reached Nora in one step and slapped her across the face. "Button your shirt," she said.

Tears welled in Nora's eyes from the sting of the slap. She saw a blurred vision of her father as he stepped down and grabbed her mother's wrist.

"Leave her alone," he said. "You're a grown woman. You don't need to use a child for camouflage." Her mother pulled her arm from him and walked down the path to Dana's car and got in and slammed the door. Nora turned and ran. She ran down the alleys and through side yards and across streets until she could run no more. Then she turned and walked slowly back toward her house. The sky was wild with orange and purple when she reached home and the fireflies had begun to wink like diamonds in the caves of the gnomes.

Edie was waiting for her in the kitchen. Neither spoke. Edie waited while she ate her supper and then went with her and helped her undress for bed, easing the shirt from her burnt shoulders.

"I'm downstairs," Edie finally said. "Good night."

In the morning he was gone. The bed was made. She remembered that she had awakened briefly when her father had come in and sat on her bed. He had smoothed the hair from her forehead and kissed her on the cheek. She had wanted to awake fully and throw her arms around him but she had thought how he must hate me and glided back into sleep.

There was a note and a package on her bed.

Dearest Nora,

I must leave sooner than I expected. Your mother will explain to you. I shall see you again at Christmas. I know you are a good girl and I love you very much.

Daddy

Nora put the note back in the envelope and stuffed it under the mattress before she opened the package. It was a limp flat package and inside was a handkerchief with a border of lace two inches wide. A card inside said, "For my beautiful daughter Nora."

Nora did not weep. She got up and dressed. She put the handkerchief inside her shirt and went down the steps with her usual tread and outside. She found the beebee gun in the garage and went back in the house for a handful of matches which she put in her shirt pocket. The rain barrel was still upside down under the mango tree. Resting the butt of the gun against the barrel with the barrel balanced against the trunk of the tree, she climbed up on the branch and then reached down for the gun.

With the gun in one hand she climbed up in the tree gaudy with fruit until she was level with the screen windows of Dana's garage apartment. She could not see into the room from the brightness outside. She loaded the gun with a kitchen match and then sat waiting. There was no breeze but the great heavy fruit seemed to sway slightly on its stem from sheer force of weight. The cold green leaves hung motionless.

She waited for what she knew was coming — the voice that might well be the voice of this mango tree. Her eyes closed, the curious lilting voice, languid and muffled, came as though from the crown of the tree. Opening her eyes, moistening her lips, Nora raised the gun and fired.

(From The New Yorker)

IN THE FRENCH STYLE

BY IRWIN SHAW

*B*EDDOES got in from Egypt in the middle of the morning. He went to his hotel and shook hands with the concierge and told him that the trip was fine but that Egyptians were impossible. From the concierge he found that the city was crowded, as usual, and that the price of the room had gone up once more, as usual.

"The tourist season now lasts twelve months a year," the concierge said, giving Beddoes his key. "Nobody stays home any more. It is exhausting."

Beddoes went upstairs and told the porter to put his typewriter in the closet, because he didn't want to see it for a while. He opened the window and looked out with pleasure at the Seine flowing past. Then he took a bath and put on fresh clothes and gave Christina's number over the telephone to the woman at the switchboard. The woman at the switchboard had an insulting habit of repeating numbers in English, and Beddoes noticed, with a smile, that that had not changed. There was the familiar hysteria on the wires as the woman on the switchboard got Christina's number. The telephone in Christina's hotel was down the hall from her room, and Beddoes had to spell the name slowly — Mlle. "T" for Théodore, "A" for André, "T" for Théodore, "E" for Edouard — before the man on the other end understood and went to tell Christina an American gentleman demanded her on the telephone.

Beddoes heard Christina's footsteps coming down the hall toward the telephone and he thought he could tell from the sound that she was wearing wearing high heels.

"Hello," Christina said. There was a sudden crackle on the wire as Christina spoke, but even so Beddoes could recognize the breathless, excited tone of her voice. Christina answered the phone as though she expected each call to be an invitation to a party.

"Hi, Chris," Beddoes said.

"Who's this?"

"The voice of Egypt," said Beddoes.

"Walter!" Christina said happily. "When did you get in?"

"This minute," Beddoes said, lying by an hour to please her. "Are you wearing high heels?"

"What?"

"You're wearing high heels, aren't you?"

"Wait a minute while I look," Christina said. Then, after a pause, "Did you turn psychic in Cairo?"

Beddoes chuckled. "Semi-Oriental fakery," he said. "I brought back a supply. Where're we going for lunch?"

"Walter!" Christina said. "I'm in despair."

"You have a date."

"Yes. When are you going to learn to cable?"

"That's O.K.," Beddoes said carelessly. He made a point of never sounding disappointed. He had a feeling that if he asked Christina to break the date she would, but he also made a point of never pleading for anything. "We'll make it later."

"How about a drink this afternoon?"

"We can start with that," Beddoes said. "Five?"

"Make it five-thirty," Christina said.

"Where're you going to be?" Beddoes asked, minutely annoyed at the postponement.

"Near the Etoile," Christina said.

"Alexandre's?"

"Fine," Christina said. "Will you be on time for once?"

"Be more polite," Beddoes said, "the first day the man comes to town."

"*A tout à l'heure,*" Christina said.

"What did you say, ma'am?"

"All the kids are speaking French this year." Christina laughed. "Isn't it nice to have you back in town."

There was a click as she hung up. Beddoes put the phone down slowly and went to the window. He stared at the river, thinking that this was the first time in a long while that Christina hadn't come over immediately when he arrived in Paris. The river appeared cold and the trees were bare and the sky looked as though it had been gray for months. But with all that, the city looked promising. Even the sunless, snowless winter weather couldn't prevent Paris from looking promising.

He had lunch with a man from the A.P. who had just come back from America. The man from the A.P. said that things were in unholy shape in America and that even if you ate in drugstores it cost you at least a dollar and half for lunch and Beddoes ought to be damned glad he wasn't there.

Beddoes got to the café a little late, but Christina hadn't arrived. He sat on the glass-enclosed terrace, next to the huge window, feeling it cold from the winter afternoon against his sleeve. The terrace was crowded with women drinking tea and men reading the evening newspapers. Outside, under the trees, a little parade was forming, the veterans of some World War I unit, huddling, middle-aged, and chilled in their overcoats, with their flags and decorations, preparing to walk behind an Army band up to the Arch and put a wreath on the tomb in memory of comrades who had fallen in battles that no one any longer remembered. The French, Beddoes thought sourly, because Christina was late and the afternoon had failed its promise, are always finding occasions to block traffic. They have an endless supply of dead to celebrate.

He ordered a beer, because he had drunk too much at lunch. He had also eaten too much, in the first wave of gluttony after Egyptian food. His stomach felt uncomfortable, and he was suddenly very tired from all the miles he had travelled in the past twenty-four hours. After the age of thirty-five, he thought, in evening melancholy, no matter how swift the plane, how calm the air, how soft the cushion, the bones record the miles inexorably. He had turned thirty-five three months before and he had begun to reflect uneasily upon age. He stared at his face in mirrors, noticing wrinkles under his eyes and gray in his beard when he shaved. He remembered hearing that aging ballplayers shaved two and three times a day to keep managers and sportswriters from seeing the tell-tale flecks in beard stubble. Maybe, he thought, career men in the foreign service ought to do the same thing. Seventy minus thirty-five leaves thirty-five, he thought. It was an equation that came ominously to mind, especially late in the afternoon, more and more often after the midway anniversary. He stared out through the cold glass at the shuffling veterans, ranked shabbily behind their flags, their breath, mingled with cigarette smoke, rising in little clouds above their heads. He wished they'd start marching and get away from there. "Veteran" was a word that suddenly fell on his ear with an unpleasant sound.

He also wished that Christina would arrive. It wasn't like her to be late. She was one of those rare girls who always got to places on the appointed hour. Irrelevantly, he remembered that she also dressed with great speed and took only a minute or two to comb her hair. She had blond hair, cut in the short Parisian manner, which left the back of her neck bare. Beddoes thought about the back of Christina's neck and felt better.

They would give themselves a gay evening, he thought. One should not permit himself to feel tired or old in Paris. If the feeling gets chronic, he told himself, I'll move away for good.

He thought about the evening ahead of him. They'd wander around to a couple of bars, avoiding their friends and not drinking too much, and go to a *bistro* in the markets where there were thick steaks and heavy red wine, and after that maybe they'd go to the night club where there was a queer, original puppet show and three young men who sang funny songs that, unlike so many night-club songs, really did turn out to be funny. When you came out into the street after their act you were charmed and amused and you had the sense that this was the way a man should feel in Paris at two o'clock in the morning.

The night before he left for Cairo, he had taken Christina there. The prospect of going back on this first night home gave him an unexplained but pleasant feeling of satisfactory design. Christina had looked very pretty, the prettiest girl in the room full of handsome women, he'd thought, and he had even danced, for the first time in months. The music was supplied by a pianist and a man who got quivering, rich sounds from an electric guitar, and they played those popular French songs that always made you feel how sweet was love in the city, how full of sorrow and tempered regret.

The music had made Christina a little mooney, he remembered, which was strange for her, and she had held his hand during the show, and kissed him when the lights went out between numbers. Her eyes had filled with tears for a moment and she had said, "What am I going to do without you for two months?" when he spoke of his departure the next morning. He had felt, a little warily, because he was affected, too, that it was lucky he was leaving, if she was moving into that phase. That was the pre-yearning-for-marriage phase, and you had to be on guard against it, especially late at night, in Paris, in darkened rooms where pianists and electric guitars played songs about dead leaves and dead lovers who were separated by wars.

Beddoes had been married once, and he felt, for the time being, that that was enough. Wives had a tendency to produce children, and sulk and take to drink or other men when their husbands were called away to the other side of the earth for three or four months at a time on jobs.

He had been a little surprised at Christina. Yearning was not in her line. He had known her, although until recently not very well, almost from the time she arrived from the States four years before. She did some modelling for photographers and was pretty enough to have done very well at it, except that, as she said, she felt too silly making the fashionable languorous, sexy grimaces that were demanded of her. She knew how to type and take dictation and she found odd jobs with American businessmen who had work for a month or two at a time in Paris. She had picked up French immediately, and drove a car, and from time to time she got curious little jobs as a companion for old American ladies who wanted to tour through the château country or into Switzerland. She never seemed to need any sleep (even now she was only about twenty-six) and she would stay up all night with anybody and she went to all the parties and had had, to Beddoes' knowledge, affairs with two friends of his — a free-lance photographer and an Air Transport Command pilot who had been killed in a crash outside

Frankfurt. You could telephone her at any hour of the day or night without making her angry and you could introduce her into any group and be pleased with the way she behaved. She always knew which *bistro* was having a rage at the moment and who was singing at which night club and which new painter was worth seeing and who was in town and who was going to arrive next week and which little hotels outside Paris were pleasant for lunch or a weekend. She obviously didn't have much money, but she dressed charmingly, French enough to amuse her French friends and not so French that she made Americans feel she was trying to pretend she was European. All in all, while she was not a girl of whom your grandmother was likely to approve, she was, as Beddoes had once told her, an ornament to the wandering and troubled years of the second half of the twentieth century.

The veterans started to move off, the banners flapping a little in the dusk as the small parade turned past the airline office and up the Champs-Elysées. Beddoes watched them, thinking vaguely of other parades, other banners. Then he saw Christina striding diagonally across the street, swift and sure of herself in the traffic. She could live in Europe the rest of her life, Beddoes thought, smiling as he watched her, and all she'd have to do would be to walk ten steps and everybody would know she had been born on the other side of the ocean.

He stood when she opened the door into the terrace. She was hatless, and Beddoes noticed that her hair was much darker than he remembered and she was wearing it longer. He kissed her on both cheeks as she came up to the table. "Welcome," he said. "In the French style."

She hugged him momentarily. "Well, now," she said, "here's the man again."

She sat down, opening her coat, and smiled across the table at him. Her cheeks were flushed from the cold and her eyes were shining and she looked glitteringly young.

"The spirit of Paris," Beddoes said, touching her hand on the table. "American division. What'll it be to drink?"

"Tea, please. I'm so glad to see you."

"Tea?" Beddoes made a face. "Anything wrong?"

"No." Christina shook her head. "I just want tea."

"That's a hell of a drink to welcome a traveller home on," Beddoes said.

"With lemon, please," Christina said.

Beddoes shrugged, and ordered one tea from the waiter.

"How was Egypt?" Christina asked.

"Was I in Egypt?" Beddoes stared at Christina, enjoying her face.

"That's what it said in the papers."

"Oh, yes," Beddoes said. "A new world struggling to be born," he said, his voice deep and expert. "Too late for feudalism, too early for democracy . . . "

Christina made a face. "Lovely phrases for the State Department archives," she said. "I mean over a drink how is Egypt."

"Sunny and sad," Beddoes said. "After two weeks in Cairo you feel sorry for everybody. How is Paris?"

"Too late for democracy," Christina said, "too early for feudalism."

Beddoes grinned and leaned across the little table and kissed her gently. "I mean over a kiss," he said, "how is Paris?"

"The same," Christina said. She hesitated. "Almost the same."

"Who's around?"

"The group," Christina said carelessly. "The usual happy exiles. Charles, Boris, Anne, Teddy . . . "

Teddy was the free-lance photographer. "You see much of him?" Beddoes asked, very lightly.

"Uh?" Christina smiled, just a little, at him.

"Merely checking." Beddoes grinned.

"No, I haven't," Christina said. "His Greek's in town."

"Still the Greek?"

"Still the Greek," Christina said.

The waiter came and placed the tea in front of her. She poured it into the cup and squeezed the lemon. She had long, competent fingers, and Beddoes noticed that she no longer used bright nail polish.

"Your hair," he said. "What happened?"

Christina touched her hair absently. "Oh," she said. "You noticed?"

"Where're the blondes of yesteryear?"

"I decided to go natural." Christina stirred her tea. "See what that was like for a change. Like it?"

"I haven't decided yet. It's longer, too."

"Uh-huh. For the winter. The back of my neck was cold. People say it makes me look younger."

"They're absolutely right," Beddoes said. "You now look exactly eleven."

Christina smiled and lifted her cup to him. "To those who return," she said.

"I don't accept toasts in tea," Beddoes said.

"You're a finicky, liquor-loving man," Christina said, and placidly sipped at her tea.

"Now," Beddoes said, "the evening. I thought we might skip our dear friends and go to that place in the markets for dinner, because I'm dying for a steak, and after that —" He stopped. "What's the matter? Can't we have dinner together?"

"It's not that, exactly." Christina kept her head down and stirred her tea slowly. "I have a date —"

"Cancel him," Beddoes said promptly. "Cancel the swine."

"I can't really." Christina looked soberly up at him. "He's coming to meet me here any minute now."

"Oh." Beddoes nodded. "That makes it different, doesn't it."

"Yes."

"Can't we shake him?"

"No," Christina said. "We can't shake him."

"The man doesn't live who can't be shaken," said Beddoes. "Old friend, you say, who just arrived from the horrors of the desert, just escaped dysentery and religious wars by the skin of his teeth, needs soothing, you say, and tender attention for his shattered nerves, et cetera."

Christina was smiling, but shaking her head. "Sorry," she said. "It can't be done."

"Want me to do it?" Beddoes said. "Man to man. See here, old fellow, we're all grown-up, civilized human beings — That sort of thing?"

"No," Christina said.

"Why not?" Beddoes asked, conscious that he was breaking a long-standing and until now jealously adhered-to rule about not pleading for anything. "Why can't we?"

"Because I don't want to," Christina said.

"Oh," said Beddoes. "The wind is in that direction."

"Variably," Christina said softly, "in that direction. We could all have dinner together. The three of us. He's a very nice man. You'd like him."

"I never like any man the first night I'm in Paris," Beddoes said.

They sat in silence for a moment while Beddoes remembered all the times that Christina had said over the phone, "O.K., it's sinful, but I'll brush him. Meet you at eight." It was hard to believe, sitting across from her, noticing that there was no obvious change in the way she looked at him, in the way she touched his hand, that she wouldn't say it in the next minute or so.

"Two months is a long time, isn't it?" Beddoes said. "In Paris?"

"No," Christina said. "It's not a long time. In Paris or anywhere else."

"Hello, Christina." It was a tall, rather heavyset young man, smiling and blond, who was standing, holding a hat, next to the table. "I found the place all right." He leaned over and kissed her forehead.

Beddoes stood up.

"Jack," Christina said, "this is Walter Beddoes. John Haislip. Dr. Haislip."

The two men shook hands.

"He's a surgeon," Christina said as Haislip gave his hat and coat to the attendant and sat down beside her. "He nearly had his picture in *Life* last year for something he did with kidneys. In thirty years he's going to be enormously famous."

Haislip chuckled. He was a big, placid, self-confident-looking man, with the air of an athlete, who was probably older than he looked. And just with one glance Beddoes could tell how the man felt about Christina. Haislip wasn't hiding anything in that department.

"What'll you drink, Doctor?" Beddoes asked.

"Lemonade, please."

"*Un citron pressé*," Beddoes said to the waiter. He peered curiously at Christina, but she was keeping her face straight.

"Jack doesn't drink," Christina said. "He says it isn't fair for people who make a living out of cutting other people up."

"When I retire," Haislip said cheerfully, "I'm going to soak it up and let my hands shake like leaves in the wind." He turned to Beddoes. You could tell that it took a conscious wrench for him to stop looking at Christina. "Did you have a good time in Egypt?" he asked.

"Oh," Beddoes said, surprised. "You know about my being in Egypt?"

"Christina's told me all about you," Haislip said.

"I swore a solemn oath that I was going to forget Egypt for a month once I got here," Beddoes said.

Haislip chuckled. He had a low, unforced laugh and his face was friendly and unself-conscious. "I know how you feel," he said. "The same way I feel about the hospital sometimes."

"Where is the hospital?" Beddoes asked.

"Seattle," Christina said quickly.

"How long have you been here?" Beddoes saw Christina glance at him obliquely as he spoke.

"Three weeks," said Haislip. He turned back toward Christina, as though he could find comfort in no other position. "The changes that can take place in three weeks. My Lord!" He patted Christina's arm and chuckled again. "One more week and back to the hospital."

"You here for fun or for business?" Beddoes asked, falling help-lessly into the pattern of conversation of all Americans who meet each other abroad for the first time.

"A little of both," Haislip said. "There was a conference of sur-geons I was asked to attend, and I moseyed around a few hospitals on the side."

"What do you think of French medicine now you've had a chance to see some of it?" Beddoes asked, the investigator within operating automatically.

"Well" — Haislip managed to look away from Christina for a moment — "they function differently from us over here. Intuitively. They don't have the equipment we have, or the money for research, and they have to make up for it with insight and intuition." He grinned. "If you're feeling poorly, Mr. Beddoes," he said, "don't hesitate to put yourself in their hands. You'll do just as well here as anyplace else."

"I feel all right," Beddoes said, then felt that it had been an idiotic thing to say. The conversation was beginning to make him uncomfortable, not because of anything that had been said but because of the way the man kept looking, so openly and confessingly and completely, at Christina. There was a little pause and Beddoes had the feeling that unless he jumped in, they would sit in silence forever. "Do any sightseeing?" he asked lamely.

"Not as much as I'd like," Haislip said. "Just around Paris. I'd've loved to go down south this time of the year. That place Christina keeps talking about. St. Paul de Vence. I guess that's about as different from Seattle as a man could wish for and still get running water and Christian nourishment. You've been there, haven't you, Mr. Beddoes?"

"Yes," Beddoes said.

"Christina told me," said Haislip. "Oh, thank you," he said to the waiter who put the lemonade down in front of him.

Beddoes stared at Christina. They had spent a week together there early in the autumn. He wondered what, exactly, she had told the Doctor.

"We'll make it the next trip," Haislip said.

"Oh," said Beddoes, noting the "we" and wondering whom it included. "You planning to come over again soon?"

"In three years." Haislip carefully extracted the ice from his lemonade and put it on the saucer. "I figure I can get away for six weeks in the summer every three years. People don't get so sick in the summertime." He stood up. "Pardon me," he said, "but I have to make a couple of telephone calls."

"Downstairs and to the right," Christina said. "The woman'll put the calls through for you. She speaks English."

Haislip laughed. "Christina doesn't trust my French," he said. "She says it's the only recognizable Puget Sound accent that has ever been imposed upon the language." He started away from the table, then stopped. "I sincerely hope you'll be able to join us for dinner, Mr. Beddoes."

"Well," Beddoes said, "I made a tentative promise I'd meet some people. But I'll see what I can do."

"Good." Haislip touched Christina's shoulder lightly, as though for some obscure reassurance, and walked away between the tables.

Beddoes watched him, thinking unpleasantly, Well, one thing, I'm better-looking, anyway. Then he turned to Christina. She was stirring the tea leaves at the bottom of her cup absently with her spoon. "That's why the hair is long and natural," Beddoes said. "Isn't it?"

"That's why." Christina kept stirring the tea leaves.

"And the nail polish."

"And the nail polish."

"And the tea."

"And the tea."

"What did you tell him about St. Paul de Vence?"

"Everything."

"Look up from that damned cup."

Slowly Christina put down the spoon and raised her head. Her eyes were glistening, but not enough to make anything of it, and her mouth was set, as with an effort.

"What do you mean by everything?" Beddoes demanded.

"Everything."

"Why?"

"Because I don't have to hide anything from him."

"How long have you known him?"

"You heard," Christina said. "Three weeks. A friend of mine in New York asked him to look me up."

"What are you going to do with him?"

Christina looked directly into his eyes. "I'm going to marry him next week and I'm going back to Seattle with him."

"And you'll come back here in three years from now for six weeks in the summertime, because people don't get so sick in the summertime," Beddoes said.

"Exactly."

"And that's O.K.?"

"Yes."

"You said that too defiantly," Beddoes said.

"Don't be clever with me," Christina said harshly. "I'm through with all that."

"Waiter!" Beddoes called. "Bring me a whiskey, please." He

said it in English, because for the moment he had forgotten where he was. "And you," he said to Christina. "For the love of God, have a drink."

"Another tea," Christina said.

"Yes, madame," said the waiter, and went off.

"Will you answer some questions?" Beddoes asked.

"Yes."

"Do I rate straight answers?"

"Yes."

Beddoes took a deep breath and looked through the window. A man in a raincoat was walking past, reading a newspaper and shaking his head.

"All right," Beddoes said. "What's so great about him?"

"What can I be expected to say to that?" Christina asked. "He's a gentle, good, useful man. And now what do you know?"

"What else?"

"And he loves me." She said it in a low voice. In all the time they'd been together, Beddoes hadn't heard her use the word before. "He loves me," Christina repeated flatly.

"I saw," said Beddoes. "Immoderately."

"Immoderately," Christina said.

"Now let me ask another question," Beddoes said. "Would you like to get up from this table and go off with me tonight?"

Christina pushed her cup away, turning it thoughtfully. "Yes," she said.

"But you won't," said Beddoes.

"No."

"Why not?"

"Let's talk about something else," said Christina. "Where're you going on your next trip? Kenya? Bonn? Tokyo?"

"Why not?"

"Because I'm tired of people like you," Christina said clearly. "I'm tired of correspondents and pilots and promising junior statesmen. I'm tired of all the brilliant young men who are constantly going someplace to report a revolution or negotiate a treaty or die in a war. I'm tired of airports and I'm tired of seeing people off. I'm tired of not being allowed to cry until the plane gets off the ground. I'm tired of being so damned prompt. I'm tired of answering the telephone. I'm tired of all the spoiled, hung-over international darlings. I'm tired of sitting down to dinner with people I used to love and being polite to their Greeks. I'm tired of being handed around the group. I'm tired of being more in love with people than they are with me. That answer your question?"

"More or less," Beddoes said. He was surprised that no one at any of the other tables seemed to be paying any special attention to them.

"When you left for Egypt," Christina went on, her voice level, "I decided. I leaned against that wire fence watching them refuelling all those monstrous planes, with the lights on, and I dried the tears and I decided. The next time, it was going to be someone who would be shattered when *I* took off."

"And you found him."

"I found him," Christina said flatly. "And I'm not going to shatter him."

Beddoes put out his hands and took hers. They lay limp in his grasp. "Chris . . . " he said. She was looking out the window. She sat there, outlined against the shining dusk beyond the plate glass, scrubbed and youthful and implacable, making him remember, confusedly, the first time he had met her, and all the best girls he had ever known, and what she had looked like next to him in the early-morning autumnal sunlight that streamed, only three months before, into the hotel room in the south, which overlooked the brown minor Alps and the distant sea. Holding her hands, with the familiar touch of the girlish fingers against his, he felt that if he could get her to turn her head everything would be different.

"Chris . . . " he whispered.

But she didn't turn her head. "Write me in Seattle," she said, staring out the window, which was streaked with moisture and in which the lights from within the café and the lights from the restaurant across the street were reflected and magnified and distorted.

Beddoes let her hands go. She didn't bother to move them. They lay before her, with their pale nail polish glistening dully, on the stained wood table. Beddoes stood up. "I'd better go." It was difficult to talk, and his voice sounded strange to him inside his head, and he thought, God, I'm getting senile, I'm tempted to cry in restaurants. "I don't want to wait for the check," he said. "Tell your friend I'm sorry I couldn't join you for dinner and that I apologize for leaving him with the check."

"That's all right," Christina said evenly. "He'll be happy to pay."

Beddoes leaned over and kissed her, first on one cheek, then on the other. "Goodbye," he said, thinking he was smiling. "In the French style."

He got his coat quickly and went out. He went past the airline office to the great boulevard and turned the corner, where the veterans had marched a half hour before. He walked blindly toward the Arch, where the laurel leaves of the wreath were already glistening in the evening mist before the tomb and the flame.

He knew that it was a bad night to be alone and that he ought to go in somewhere and telephone and ask someone to have dinner with him. He passed two or three places with telephones, and although he hesitated before each one, he didn't go in. Because there was no one in the whole city he wanted to see that night.

(From The New Yorker)

THE SHORN LAMB

BY JEAN STAFFORD

*O*H, *THERE's* no whitewashing the incident. The child's hair is a sight, and it will be many moons, I can tell you, before I'll forgive Hugh Talmadge. But listen to me. The worst of it is that this baby of five has gone into a decline like a grown woman — like you or me, dear, at our most hysterical. Sudden fits of tears for no apparent reason and then simply hours of brooding. She won't eat, she probably doesn't sleep. I can't stand it if she's turning mental."

The child, Hannah, sitting hidden on the attic steps, listened as her mother talked on the telephone to Aunt Louise. The door to the bedroom, across the hall, was half open, and through the crack of the door at the foot of the attic steps Hannah saw that in the course of the night her parents had disarrayed the pale-green blanket cover and now, half off the bed, drooping and askew, it looked like a great crumpled new leaf, pulled back here and there to show the rosy blankets underneath. In the bedroom it is spring, thought Hannah, and outdoors it is snowing on the Christmas trees; that is a riddle.

Her mother lay in the center of the big bed, which was as soft and fat as the gelded white Persian cat who dozed at her side, his scornful head erect, as if he were arrested not so much by sleep as by a coma of boredom and disgust. A little earlier, before he struck this pose, he had sniffed and disdained the bowl of cream on his mistress's breakfast tray, and when she had tried to cajole him into drinking it, he had coolly thrashed his tail at her. In the darkness of her enclosure, Hannah yearned, imagining herself in the privileged cat's place beside her mother, watching the mellowing, pillowing, billowing snow as it whorled down to meet the high tips of the pine trees that bordered the frozen formal garden. If she were Nephew, the cat, she would burrow into the silky depths of the bed up to her eyes and rejoice that she was not outside like a winter bird coming to peck at suet and snowy crumbs at the feeding station.

It was ugly and ungenerous here where she was, on the narrow, splintery stairs, and up in the attic a mouse or a rat scampered on lightly clicking claws between the trunks; some hibernating bees buzzed peevishly in their insomnia. Stingy and lonesome like old people, the shut-ins worried their grievances stealthily. And Hannah, spying and eavesdropping (a sin and she knew it), felt the ends of her cropped hair and ran a forefinger over her freshly combed boy's cut — the subject of her mother's conversation. Something like sleep touched her eyeballs, though this was early morning and she had not been awake longer than an hour. But it was tears, not drowsiness, that came. They fell without any help from her; her cheeks did not rise up as they usually did when she cried, to squeeze themselves into puckers like old apples, her mouth did not open in a rent of woe, no part of her body was affected at all except the eyes themselves, from which streamed down these mothering runnels.

"Why did he do it?" Her mother's question into the telephone was an impatient scream. "Why do men do half the things they do? Why does Arthur treat you in public as if you were an enlisted man? I swear I'll someday kill your rear admiral for you. Why does Eliot brag to Frances that he's unfaithful? Because they're sadists, every last one of them. I am very anti-man today."

"What is antiman?" whispered Hannah.

The stools on either side of the fireplace in the den were ottomans, and sometimes Hannah and her mother sat on them in the late afternoon, with a low table between them on which were set a Chinese pot of verbena tisane, two cups, and a plate of candied orange rind. At the thought of her mother's golden hair in the firelight, and the smell of her perfume in the intimate warmth, and the sound of her voice saying, "Isn't this gay, Miss Baby?" the tears came faster, for in her heavy heart Hannah felt certain that now her hair was cut off, her mother would never want to sit so close to her again. Unable to see through the narrow opening of the door any longer, she leaned her face against the wall and felt her full tears moistening the beaverboard as she listened to her mother's recital of Saturday's catastrophe.

"On the face of it, the facts are innocent enough, Louise. He took her to town on Saturday to buy her a pair of shoes, having decided for his own reasons that I have no respect for my children's feet — the shoes he got are too odious, but that's another story. Then when he brought her back, here she was, cropped, looking like a rag doll. He said she'd begged to have it done. Of course she'd done nothing of the kind. To put the most charitable construction on the whole affair, I *could* say that when he went into the barbershop to have his own hair cut, he'd had a seizure of amnesia and thought he had Andy with him, or Johnny or Hughie, and decided to kill two birds with one stone. And then afterward he was afraid of what I'd say and so cooked up this canard — and more than likely bribed her to bear him out. The way men will weasel out of their missteps! It isn't moral. It shocks me."

He did *not* think I was Andy or Johnny or Hughie, Hannah said to herself. In the barbershop at her father's club there had been no one but grown men and a fat stuffed skunk that stood in front of the mirror between two bottles of bay rum, its leathery nose pointed upward as if it were trying to see the underside of its chin in the looking glass. Through a steaming towel, her father had muttered, "Just do as I say, Homer, cut it off," and the barber, a lean man with a worried look on his red face, flinched, then shrugged his shoulders and began to snip off Hannah's heavy curls, frowning with disapproval and remarking once under his breath that women, even though they were five years old, were strictly forbidden on these premises. On the drive home, her peeled head had felt cold and wet, and she had not liked the smell that gauzily hovered around her, growing more cloying as the heater in the car warmed up. At a red light, her father had turned to her and, patting her on the knee, had said, "You look as cute as a button, young fellow." He had not seemed to hear her when she said, "I do not. I'm not a young fellow," nor had he noticed when she moved over against the door, as far away from him as she could get, hating him bitterly and hating her nakedness. Presently, he'd turned on the radio to a news broadcast and disputed out loud with the commentator. Hannah, left all alone, had stared out the window at the wolfish winter. In one snow-flattened field she saw tall flames arising from a huge wire trash basket, making the rest of the world look even colder and whiter and more unkind. Her father scowled, giving the radio what for, swearing at the slippery roads — carrying on an absent-minded tantrum all by himself. Once, halted by a woman driver whose engine was stalled, he'd said, "Serves her right. She ought to be home at this time of day tending to business." As they turned in their own drive, he said a lie: "That was a fine idea of yours to have your hair cut off." She had never said any such thing; all she had said, when they were having lunch in a brown, cloudy restaurant, was that she would rather go to the barbershop with him than wait at Grandma's. But she had not contradicted him, for he did not countenance contradiction from his children. "I'm an old-fashioned man," he announced every morning to his three sons and his two daughters. "I am the autocrat of this breakfast table." And though he said it with a wink and a chuckle, it was clear that he meant business. Johnny, who was intellectual, had told the other children that an autocrat was a person like Hitler, and he had added sarcastically, "That sure is something to brag about, I must say."

The voice speaking into the phone took on a new tone, and Hannah, noticing this, looked out through the crack again. "What? Oh, please don't change the subject, pet, I really want your help. It isn't a trifle, it's terribly important, I really think it is the *final* effrontery . . . All right, then, if you promise that we can come back to it." With her free hand, Hannah's mother lightly stroked the cat, who did not heed, and she lay back among her many pillows, listening to her sister but letting her eyes rove the room as if she were planning changes in its decoration. "Yes, I did hear it but I can't remember where," she said inattentively. Then, smiling in the pleasure of gossip, forgetting herself for a moment, she went on, "Perhaps I heard it from Peggy the night she came to dinner with that frightful new man of hers. That's it — it was from *him* I heard it, and automatically discounted it for no other reason than that I took an instantaneous dislike to him. If he is typical of his department, the C.I.A. must be nothing more nor less than the Gestapo."

Hannah's head began to ache and she rolled it slowly, looking up the steep, ladderlike steps into the shadowy attic. She was bored now that the talk was not of her, and she only half heard her mother's agile voice rising, descending, laughing quickly, pleading, "Oh, no! It's not *pos*sible!" and she sucked her fingers, one by one. Her tears had stopped and she missed them as she might have missed something she had lost. Like her hair, like all her golden princess curls that the barber had gazed at sadly as they lay dead and ruined on the tiled floor.

Now that Hannah's hair was short, her days were long: it was a million hours between breakfast and lunch, and before, it had been no time at all, because her mother, still lying in her oceanic bed, had every morning made Hannah's curls, taking her time, telling anyone who telephoned that she would call back, that just now she was busy "playing with this angel's hair."

Today was Wednesday, and Hannah had lived four lifetimes since Saturday afternoon. Sunday had been endless, even though her brother and her sister had been as exciting as ever, with their jokes and contests and their acrobatics and their game of cops-and-robbers that had set the servants wild. But even in their mad preoccupation it had been evident that the sight of Hannah embarrassed them. "The baby looks like a skinned cat," said Andy, and Hughie said, "It was a dopey thing to do. The poor little old baby looks like a mushroom." The parents did nothing to stop this talk, for all day long they were fighting behind the closed door of the den, not even coming out for meals, their voices growing slower and more sibilant as they drank more. "I hate them," Johnny had said in the middle of the long, musty afternoon, when the cops were spent and the robbers were sick of water-pistol fights. "When they get stinking, I hate them," said Johnny. "I bet a thousand dollars he had had a couple when he had them cut the baby's hair." Janie shouted, "Oh, that baby, baby, baby, baby! Is that goofy baby the only pebble on the beach? Why do they have to mess up Sunday fighting over her? I'm going crazy!" And she ran around in a circle like a dog, pulling at her hair with both hands.

On Monday morning, when Hannah's father took the older children off to Marion Country Day School on his way to the city, she had nearly cried herself sick, feeling that this Monday the pain of their desertion was more than she could bear. She would not let go of Janie's hand, and she cried, "You'll be sorry if you come back and find I'm dead!" Janie, who was ten and hot-blooded — she took after Daddy, who had Huguenot blood — had slapped Hannah's hand and said, "The nerve of some people's children!" Hannah had stood under the porte-cochere, shivering in her wrapper and slippers, until the car went out the driveway between the tulip trees; she had waved and called, "Goodbye, dearest Janie and Johnny and Andy and Hughie!" Only Johnny had looked back; he rolled down the window and leaned out and called, "Ta-ta, half pint." They were all too old and busy to pay much attention to her, though often they brought her presents from school — a jaw-breaker or a necklace made of paper clips. The four older children were a year apart, starting with John, who was thirteen, and ending with Janie, and when family photographs were taken, they were sometimes lined up according to height; these were called "stair-step portraits," and while Hannah, of course, was included, she was so much smaller than Janie that she spoiled the design, and one time Uncle Harry, looking at a picture taken on Palm Sunday when all five children were sternly holding their palms like spears, had said, pointing to Hannah, "Is that the runt of the litter or is it a toy breed?" Andy, who was Uncle Harry's pet, said, "We just keep it around the house for its hair. It's made of spun gold, you know, and very invaluable." This evidently was something the barber had not known, for he had swept the curls into a dustpan and thrown them into a chute marked "Waste." She wondered how long they would keep her now that her sole existence was gone.

In the other days, after Daddy and the children left and the maids began their panicky, silent cleaning, flinging open all the windows to chill the house to its heart, Hannah would run upstairs to the big bedroom to sit on the foot of the bosomy bed and wait while her mother drank her third cup of coffee and did the crossword puzzle in the *Tribune*. When she was stuck for a definition, she would put down her pencil and thoughtfully twist the diamond ring on her finger; if it caught the sun, Hannah would close her eyes and try to retain the flashing swords of green and purple, just as she unconsciously tried to seal forever in her memory the smell of the strong Italian coffee coming in a thin black stream out of the silver pot. Hannah remembered one day when her mother said to the cat, "What is that wretched four-letter word that means 'allowance for waste,' Nephew? We had it just the other day." Finally, when the puzzle was done and Edna had taken away the tray, she stretched out her arms to Hannah, who scrambled into her embrace, and she said, "I suppose you want your tawny tresses curled," and held her at arm's length and gazed at her hair with disbelieving eyes. "Bring us the brush, baby." All the while she brushed, then combed, then made long, old-fashioned sausage curls, turning and molding them on her index finger, she talked lightly and secretly about the dreams she had had and Christmas plans and what went on inside Nephew's head and why it was that she respected but could not bear Andy's violin teacher. She included Hannah, as if she were thirty years old, asking for her opinion or her corroboration of something. "Do you agree with me that Nephew is the very soul of Egypt? Or do you think there are Chinese overtones in his style?" After telling a dream (her dreams were full of voyages; one time she sailed into Oslo in Noah's ark and another time she went on the *Queen Mary* to Southampton in her night clothes without either luggage or a passport), she said, "What on earth do you suppose that means, Hannah? My id doesn't seem to know where it is at." Bewitching, indecipherable, she always dulcified this hour with her smoky, loving voice and her loving fingers that sometimes could not resist meandering over Hannah's head, ruining a curl by cleavage through it as she exclaimed, "Dear Lord, I never saw such stuff as this!" Actually, her own hair was the same vivacious color and the same gentle texture as Hannah's, and sometimes her hands would leave the child's head and go to her own, to stroke it lovingly.

Lately now, for this last month, when the afternoons were snug and short and the lamps were turned on early and the hearth fires smelled of nuts, there had been another hour as well when Hannah and her hair had been the center of attraction. Every day at half past two, she and her mother drove in the toylike English car over to Mr. Robinson Fowler's house, three miles away, on the top of a bald and beautiful hill from which it was possible, on a clear day, to see the beaches of Long Island. In a big, dirty studio, jammed with plaster casts and tin cans full of turpentine and stacked-up canvases and nameless metal odds and ends, Mr. Fowler, a large, quiet man who mumbled when he talked, was painting a life-size portrait of Hannah and her mother. Her mother, wearing a full skirt of scarlet felt and a starched white Gibson-girl shirt and a black ribbon in her hair, sat on a purple Victorian sofa, and Hannah, in a blue velvet jacket trimmed with black frogs and a paler-blue accordion-pleated skirt, stood leaning against her knee. In the picture, these colors were all different, all smudgy and gray, and the point of this, said Mr. Fowler, was to accent the lambencies of the hair. Before they took their pose, all the morning's careful curls were combed out, for Mr. Fowler wanted to paint Hannah's hair, he murmured in his closed mouth, "in a state of nature." Occasionally, he emerged from behind his easel and came across to them with his shambling, easygoing, friendly gait, to push back a lock of hair that had fallen over Hannah's forehead, and the touch of his fingers, huge as they were, was as light as her mother's.

Hannah liked the heat of the studio, and the smell of the tea perpetually brewing on an electric grill, and the sight of the enormous world of hills and trees and farms and rivers through the enormous windows, and she liked the quiet, which was broken only once or twice in the course of the hour's sitting by an exchange of a casual question and answer between Mr. Fowler and her mother, half the time about her hair. "It must never be cut," said the painter one day. "Not a single strand of it." After the sitting was over and Hannah and her mother had changed back into their regular clothes, Mr. Fowler drew the burlap curtains at the windows and turned on the soft lamps. Then he and her mother sat back in two scuffed leather armchairs drinking whiskey and talking in a leisurely way, as if all the rest of the time in the world were theirs to enjoy in this relaxed geniality. Hannah did not listen to them. With her cup of mild, lemony tea, she sat on a high stool before a blackboard at the opposite end of the room and drew spiderwebs with a nubbin of pink chalk. Mr. Fowler and her mother never raised their voices or threw things at each other or stormed out of the room, banging doors, and Hannah was sorry when it was time to go home where that kind of thing went on all the time, horrifying the housemaids, who never stayed longer than two months at the most, although the cook, who had a vicious tongue herself, had been with them ever since Johnny could remember.

The picture, when it was finished, was going to hang in the drawing room over an heirloom lowboy, where now there hung a pair of crossed épées, used by Hannah's father and his adversary in a jaunty, bloody *Studentenmensur* at Freiburg the year he went abroad to learn German. The lilac scar from the duel was a half moon on his round right cheek.

Now the picture would never be finished, since Hannah's corn-tassel hair was gone, and the sunny hour at the start of the day and the teatime one at the end were gone with it.

Hannah, sitting on the attic stairs, began to cry again as she thought of the closed circle of her days. Even her sister's and her brothers' return from school was not the fun it had been before; her haircut had become a household issue over which all of them squabbled, taking sides belligerently. Janie and Andy maintained it did not matter; all right, they said, what if the baby did look silly? After all, she didn't go to school and nobody saw her. Johnny and Hughie and the cook and the maids said that it did matter, and Johnny, the spokesman for that camp, railed at his father behind his back and called him a dastard. But all the same, no one paid any attention to Hannah; when they spoke of "the baby," they might have been speaking of the car or a piece of furniture; one would never have known that she was in the room, for even when they looked directly at her, their eyes seemed to take in something other than Hannah. She felt that she was already shrinking and fading, that all her rights of being seen and listened to and caressed were ebbing away. Chilled and exposed as she was, she was becoming, nonetheless, invisible.

The tears came less fast now, and she heard her mother say, "How can I *help* looking at it closely? I shall eventually have to go to an analyst, as you perfectly well know, if I am to continue this marriage until the children are reasonably grown. But in the meantime, until I get my doctor, who can I talk to but you? I wouldn't talk to you if you weren't my sister, because I don't think you're discreet at all." Sad, in her covert, Hannah saw that her mother was now sitting up straight against the headboard and was smoking a cigarette in long, meditative puffs; the smoke befogged her frowning forehead.

"Forget it, darling," she continued. "I know you are a tomb of silence. Look, do let me spill the beans and get it over with. It will put me into a swivet, I daresay, and I'll have to have a drink in my bath, but the way I feel, after these nights I've had, that's in the cards anyhow . . . Oh, Christ, Louise, don't preach to me!"

Briefly, she put down the telephone and dragged Nephew to her side. Then she resumed, "Excuse me. I was adjusting my cat. Now, dear, right now, you can forget my 'charitable construction' because, of course, that's rot. At this juncture, neither one of us does anything by accident. I cannot believe that criminals are any more ingenious than wives and husbands when their marriages are turning sour. Do you remember how fiendish the Irelands were?

"Well, the night before the haircutting, we had a row that lasted until four, starting with Rob and going on from him to all the other men I know — he thinks it's bad form (and that's exactly how he puts it) that I still speak fondly of old beaux. He suspects me of the direst things with that poor pansy the decorators sent out to do the carpets on the stairs, and he's got it firmly rooted in his mind that Rob and I are in the middle of a red-hot affair. He doesn't know the meaning of friendship. He's got a sand dune for a soul. He suggested loathsomely that Rob and I were using Hannah as a blind — oh, his implications were too cynical to repeat.

"All this went on and on until I said that I would leave him. You know *that* old blind alley where any feint is useless because when five children are involved, one's hands are tied. Unless one can be proved mad. If only I could be! I would give my eyes to be sent away for a while to some insane asylum like that one Elizabeth loved so.

"It was hideous — the whole battle. We were so squalid with drink. We drink prodigiously these days. The ice ran out and we didn't even take time to go get more, so we drank whiskey and tap water as if we were in a cheap hotel, and I kept thinking, How demeaning this is. But I couldn't stop. This was the worst quarrel we've ever had — by far the most fundamental. The things we said! We could have killed each other. In the morning, not even our hangovers could bring us together. And let me tell you, they were shattering. If I hadn't known it was a hangover, I would have sent for an ambulance without thinking twice. Hugh sidled around like a wounded land crab and swore he had fractured his skull. Fortunately, the children, all except the baby, had been asked to the Fosters' to skate, so at least we didn't have to put up appearances — we do that less and less as it is. But finally we began to pull ourselves together about noon with Bloody Marys, and when he proposed that he take Hannah into town and buy her lunch and some shoes, I almost forgave him everything, I was so delighted to have the house to myself. I would not rise to that bait about my neglecting the welfare of my children's feet. All I could think of was just being alone.

"I should have known. I think I might have sensed what was up if I hadn't been so sick, because as they were about to leave, the baby asked why I hadn't curled her hair and Hugh said, 'You leave that to me today.' Now, looking back on it, I can see that he rolled his eyes in that baleful, planning way of his and licked one corner of his mouth. But even if I had noticed, I still would never have dreamed he would be so vile.

"It goes without saying that we have been at swords' points ever since, and it doesn't help matters to see the child so woebegone, wearing this look of 'What did I do to deserve this?' How can one explain it away as an accident to a child when one perfectly knows that accident is not involved? Her misery makes me feel guilty. I am as shy of her as if I had been an accessory. I can't console her without spilling all the beans about Hugh. Besides, you can't say to a child, 'Darling, you are only a symbol. It was really *my* beautiful hair that was cut off, not yours.' . . .

"Rob *crushed?* Oh, for God's sake, no, not crushed — that's not Rob's style. He's outraged. His reaction, as a matter of fact, annoys me terribly, for he takes the whole thing as a personal affront and says that if Hugh had wanted to make an issue of my afternoons in his studio, he should have challenged him to a duel with the Freiburg swords. His theory, you see, is that Hugh has been smoldering at the thought of these testimonials of his manliness being replaced by the portrait. Rob claims that Hugh hates art — as of course he does — and that it is the artist in him, Rob, not the potential rival, that he is attacking. Needless to say, this gives him a heaven-sent opportunity to berate me for living in the camp of the enemy. He was horrid on Monday. He called me an opportunist and a brood mare. It depresses me that Rob, who is so intuitive about most things, can't see that *I* am the victim, that *my* values have been impugned. Today I hate all men.

"What am I going to do? What *can* I do? I'm taking her this afternoon to Angelo to see what he can salvage out of the scraps that are left. I'll get her a new doll — one with short hair. That's all I can do now. The picture will never be finished, so the duelling swords will stay where they are. And I will stay where I am — Oh, there's no end! Why on earth does one have children?"

For a minute or two her mother was silent, leaning back with her eyes closed, listening to Aunt Louise. Hannah no longer envied the cat curled into her mother's arm; she hated his smug white face and she hated her mother's sorrowful smile. Hot and desolate and half suffocated, she wished she were one of the angry bees. If she were a bee, she would fly through the crack of the attic door and sting Nephew and her mother and her father and Janie and Andy and Mr. Fowler. "Zzzzzzz," buzzed the child to herself.

After the telephone conversation was over and her mother had got up and gone to run her bath, Hannah let herself silently out the door into the hall and went downstairs to the kitchen. The cook was dicing onions, weeping. "There's my baby," she said as Hannah came to stand beside her, "my very own baby." She put down her knife and wiped her hands and her eyes on her apron and scooped Hannah up in a bear hug.

"I love you, Mattie," said Hannah.

The cook's teary face looked surprised and she put the child down and said, "Run along now, kiddikins — Mattie's got work to do."

Hannah went into the den and kneeled on the window seat to watch the snow settling deeply on the branches of the trees. "I love you, snow," she said. It fell like sleep.

(From Woman's Day)

THE PALE GREEN FISHES

BY KRESSMANN TAYLOR

IT WAS full summer when Charles Corey came home from a week's selling trip, on a scented, burnished afternoon of goldenrod and gentle airs that was very pleasant to walk in, after the cindered heat of local trains, the icy air-conditioning of hotel lobbies and barrooms. When he reached his house and came down the graveled pathway from the gate, he saw his wife at work, and his younger son with her, amid the greenery of the side garden with its masses of rosy phlox and crimson hibiscus, the river gleaming darkly in long glints and streaks through the shadowy willow trees beyond their heads. He noted that she had chosen to work in the flowers, and not in the vegtable garden (where he would have preferred to find her), but his mind made the reflection without animosity. He even had a pleasant sense of forgiving her for a minor neglect of duty, because this was his day of return, and these weekly home-comings were always fraught for him with an almost moist-eyed tenderness (he felt the glow of it within himself now), a desire to enwrap, to embrace this little family circle that he ruled, that he had made, to close them to himself, to shut out the world. As the gravel grated under his shoes he watched his wife, still busily working, still unaware of him, and the sight of her compact, golden body in the sunlight, her short, rather heavy thighs and freckled shoulders emerging from the faded calico-red shorts and halter she wore, sent a sharp sting of possessive satisfaction through him.

The boy saw him first and broke away from his work, leaping toward the man with his awkward nine-year-old gait, and flung himself convulsively at his father's knees.

Charles Corey held his son off, a bit impatiently. "All right, all right, you little son of a gun. Give me a chance to kiss your mother first, will you?"

He handed the boy his heavy briefcase, and the youngster turned and went loping ahead of him, his right shoulder sagging importantly with the weight. Mary Corey stood up and wiped the hair back from her forehead with her bare arm. Her look changed from serenity to a slow pleasure of welcome, a brightness that touched all the lines of her body and quickened her small fragile face to vividness. She came towards him, moving quickly, a garden trowel in her hand.

"Don't get that damned thing on my clothes," he said and reached down for her mouth, kissing her slowly, his lips moist and probing, while she lay against him happily, and the boy, Richard, watched them absorbedly, his young eyes showing his contentment at having them together like this.

Now it would begin, the boy knew, that fine first day, and he was full of eagerness as they began to walk to the house, his father holding his mother to his side in an embrace, while she held the garden trowel away from them with her free hand.

And, as always, his father went first to pull the shades down, for he liked the rooms dark and cool in summer. His mother always kept windows and blinds open, letting the sun play in little flickering hot lights over the dark woodwork, underlighting the warm glow of the Turkey-red curtains, the late afternoon sun throwing its ruddy spangles, its languid beams through the deepness of the room. But when his father pulled the blinds down close there was a still, bloody darkness, a stale hush of air, as if the house had closed inexorably around them in a hot, binding silence and red-brown dusk, and they could never, never get out.

But it was in that strange ruddy twilight that everything began. His mother would bring in two glasses of beer with foam piling on the top as if it were going to spill over, and tiny bright bubbles that kept climbing up and up the glass. The liquid looked a rich brown color, although Richard knew that in the light it would be golden. And sure enough, after his father had taken a deep drink, so deep that you could see how it satisfied him, and wiped the edges of his mustache with folded handkerchief, his voice began to rise to that fine tone of importance, and he began to tell them everything, bringing the unknown world of busy cities and bustling crowds, the strange places, the men with the wonderful names, that his father knew, into their own house, into the red-brown hush with them. And his mother sat smiling and smiling with pleasure, and now and then sipped carefully at her beer, tentatively, testing it, as if it were something bitter that she discovered anew each time, but that still pleased her with its taste. And his father talked.

His father knew all about everything. His mother did not know so very much. She was always asking herself questions. She couldn't understand why some leaves, like the willows, grew so long and thin, while others were finger-edged and flat. She was always tasting, sniffing, feeling things with her hands — bark and little stones and fur and the smooth of dishes. If you watched you could catch her at it, and she would grow a little shy and embarrassed; but the boy could see very well why she was obliged to do it. He himself could not get enough of the cool resistance of the river water when he ran his hands through it, or of the springy separate blades of the grass against his bare toes. His mother was not quite adult. She was always testing the world in her slow, pleased way. She was always wondering at it. But his father knew it. His father knew, surely, all about everything.

It was wonderful to hear him talking now, his voice so exultant and alive, and his mother marveling at him. The boy's heart glowed with joy for this fineness, with his mother sitting beside him, both of them receiving, silent and intent, this drinking in of marvels that the rich voice gave them. Even the men with the important names had to stop, to listen, to recognize the wonder of his father.

His father crossed his knees and lighted a cigar, and the tip glowed rosy and round in the dimness and depth of the room, while the sweet strong scent smote their nostrils.

"I gave it to him absolutely straight," he said, his voice throbbing with masculine exultancy. "I told him, 'Look here, J. F., do you want me to lay it on the line for you?' And then I gave it to him. I gave it to him straight from the shoulder. And he couldn't say a word. He knew I had him. My God, Mary, I wish you could have seen the big blusterer's face."

The boy knew that "J. F." was president of his father's company, and he could see the whole scene as his father painted it, this "J. F." with a white face, cowed and waiting, while his father stood proudly over him and "laid it on the line." The very words were wonderful, and the boy marveled as he was bidden at the pride, the handsomeness, the splendid sureness of his father. A proudness shone from the man, from the taut, cream-colored fabric of his summer suit buttoned around his heavy girth, from the thick curl of hair that flowed back in assurance from his high, forward-sloping forehead. Richard's face flushed and he looked at his mother. But her eyes had suddenly lost their happiness, although her mouth still smiled loosely. She was going to say something. She was going to spoil it all. He hated her.

But his mother did not speak, and his father went on talking, and gradually the warmth came back into the boy, while, surreptitiously, he watched his mother's face begin to brighten, to receive his father again.

"The war situation . . . " his father was saying, and a moment later, "credit situation . . . " and the words "war situation, credit situation," as he spoke them had a distant thunder in them, an ominous hugeness. The hugeness and dark roar of them swelled and began to occupy, and lurk in, the far corners of the room; for this rosy darkness was a wonderful thing, and if the boy gave himself to it, lost himself in it, he could evoke jinn in its distant corners. Now he made out a spiral there, something heavy and dark that moved and curled and waited, over there where the dining-room door should be; something unquiet that kept changing its shape in the same way the great masses of summer clouds, which looked so still until you really watched them, billowed and frayed and changed. You could discover a monstrous head, and before your eyes had even caught it the long fangs threaded away into vapor and the shape writhed and became the crude, stretching body of an animal. His father's words sounded on his outer ear: " . . . they're covering it up. I got it absolutely straight from Jim Regan, down in Washington." And the deep, portentous tone of the words intensified for the boy the menace, the overwhelming swirl of darkness and thunder and danger in the corner there.

The thin trail of cigar smoke that floated in a brownish plane above their heads rolled almost imperceptibly, in the still air, closer and closer to the end of the room, closer to the edge of that dangerous coiling dusk. The boy watched in fascinated tremorousness until the first tentacles of smoke touched and entered the gloom, and he was no longer listening but was absorbed, rapt, half afraid and half excited, on the near side of those brown and thickening shadows that sucked in and ate the faint smoke.

Always this menace lurked behind the pleasant every-day world; everywhere there were these dark and shapeless powers that reached silently out of corners, out of shadows, out of night, searching for him, shaking him, luring him almost against his will, closer and closer to the edge of fear, of dark and nebulous chaos. The waiting evil spread its brown smoke-tentacles in the hot and silent darkness, and dreading it, desiring it, all his senses tuned to the thin danger of it, he began to float like smoke, was drawn, moved closer, was sucked nearer, nearer . . .

Silence in the room broke him out of his absorption, and he saw his mother's eyes fastened on him in troubled warning. He said, "Yes, sir," quickly, automatically, aware, with a pang, that his father had spoken to him, but unable to hear the words, which had touched only his outer ear and floated now somewhere in his mind like an echo, but just out of reach. He tried to meet his father's eyes boldly.

"Dreaming again," his father said contemptuously, and he answered:

"Yes, sir. I'm sorry," very quickly.

"I asked how you were doing in school," the man's voice told him.

"Oh — all right," he said. "All right, I think."

"You think?" his father demanded coldly. "Don't you know?"

"Yes, sir," he said. "I'm doing all right."

His throat was immediately full of a choking closeness, and he felt sick as if he were going to throw up. Because his father's face had grown hard and punishing, and the fineness of the day was all broken, and it was he, Richard, who had done it. He watched, despairingly, his father turn the hard look on his mother and begin to say:

"Give the boy time enough alone with you and you'll make a woman of him yet. That's what you'd like, isn't it?" in a bitter, scathing tone of voice.

Then Richard saw that his mother was going to save them. Her face did not grow hushed, turned inward, flinching, as it usually did when his father spoke to her like that. Her eyes remained merry, and she pursed her lips in a pretty pout and laughed, and his father's face grew red and pleased, and he pulled mother close against him and covered her lips with a slow long-held kiss. Only, his mother no longer relaxed in the embrace, as in the garden. She held her mouth up to the kiss, but her shoulders were curled and tight, and her hands were two small fists at her sides instead of spreading out happily on his father's back. She had saved them but she was ashamed; she was suffering for it. But the boy, clinging wildly to the remnants of the magical day — still safe, still going on — was too relieved to care.

They had dinner on the screened porch that looked out over the river, the three of them. His older brother, Gordon, was spending two weeks at Scout camp, and his father had not yet mentioned him. There was cold watermelon, and Richard was very careful not to spit the seeds, glancing hopefully at his father from time to time to see whether he observed how well his young son was eating. But his father was not caring, yet, how they behaved. All that would come tomorrow. He was still full of exuberance and talk, and when they had finished eating he leaned back and sighed, and then called Mother over and made her sit down on his knees, and caught her arms in his hands and bent his head a little, and said suddenly in a low voice, half impelling, half pleading, "You do believe in me, don't you, Mary?" And his mother's head lifted quickly and her face lightened, and she put up one hand and touched his hair. Then his hands gripped her arms tightly and he pressed his head down against her bosom and said, "Please believe in me. Please love me."

And his mother murmured in a sort of singing tone, only shyly, "All right," and her face was very lovely and she was smiling.

His father lifted his head and ran his hands over Mother's shoulders and up into her hair, and he said to her, "You have a little brown mole on your neck, just under your left ear," and they both laughed, and his mother was very happy again. And up the river the sun was going down in a red haze behind the mountain, and all their faces were flushed with its pink reflection, and on the table the plates lay in a shining triangle, full of rosy pools of watermelon juice, and the smell of coolness came up to them from the river, and everything was wonderful.

The morning light came white and thin, with a low mist screening the river and the feeling of heat already strong in the day. The boy slid hurriedly out of bed, hearing noises from downstairs, a clinking of dishes, the closing of the icebox door, and voices in the kitchen. The fragrance of toasting bread came floating up the stairs, and the hot, iron smell of the frying pan.

In the shower stall he stood flat against the side and turned the handles on carefully — because the water usually came either too hot or too cold at first — and then edged his body into the pelting spray. He was never really dirty because he was in and out of the river so much. A stripe of white skin stretched around his loins in bright contrast to his brown legs and brown belly. He remembered that his mother had said he was painted in three sections, now that he lived all day in his swimming trunks. Without curiosity he tested, by means of soap and shower brush, the indelibility of the hue on his thighs: the browning was an inexplicable gift from the sun, a summer-change in himself. It pleased him but at the same time it baffled him that the elements could so work on him, could reach down from the far spaces around the sun and mark him thus, without his will. He lifted his head and thrust it under the full force of the shower, letting the water wash through his hair and dribble pleasantly over his face and his closed eyes.

Dressed, and with the front of his hair carefully combed where he could see it in the mirror, he made for the stairs; and before he remembered, he took a kangaroo leap down the three steps to the landing, his stiff Sunday shoes banging against the bare wood, jolting him and sending a tremor up his legs to his knees. The voices in the kitchen stopped. Then his mother's voice called quickly, a shade too lightly:

"Try to come down a little more quietly, Riccy."

But his father's voice cut across her sentence, stern and peremptory. "Dick! Do you hear me?"

"Yes sir," the boy answered, standing still on the landing, waiting and holding his breath for what he knew was coming.

"Turn around where you are." His father's voice was cold and contained. "Go back up the stairs, and then walk down them. Are you able to understand what that means? I said *walk*. Do you think you can do it?"

"Yes, sir," he called miserably, and tiptoed to the top again, where he turned and, half resentful, began a cautious descent, slowly, with bent knees, and apprehensively because his leather heels made a clopping sound on each step.

He crossed the kitchen to the breakfast table and stood very stiffly before his father, whose proud and coolly offended eyes looked him slowly up and down. "Good morning, sir."

His father made an impatient noise. "May I ask whether this is your usual way of coming down the stairs to breakfast?" His face was set and heavy. There was always this foreboding morning heaviness about his father.

"No, sir."

His father leaned back in his chair and his elbows moved the red-checkered breakfast cloth on the table, so that the silver clinked together. "During the week, while I am not here, you come down the stairs quietly, without this unholy clatter and racket?"

"Yes, sir," he said unhappily, his throat closing rebelliously, because lots of times he did walk down.

"I see. You mean that the only time you go crashing and battering your way around this house like some kind of mountain goat is when *I* am home? You do it for my benefit? Is that what you mean?"

"No, sir. I mean — " He stopped, cornered. His father's eyes were cold and demanding, forcing him to answer when he would not.

"Go on. What do you mean?"

"I'm sorry. I forgot."

The corners of his father's mouth moved slightly, and there was just a trace in them of a cool, self-satisfied smile. Now his face grew less harsh, more conciliatory, a father talking things over reasonably and honestly with his son.

"Tell me, now, isn't it true that sometimes, during the week when I am not here, you go jumping down the stairs?"

Richard relaxed his guard. "Sometimes."

"All right." The man's eyes suddenly glinted. "I thought we'd get at it eventually. So sometimes you go crashing around, beating up the house, when I am away. Is that right?" The voice was laden with justice, so much in the right, so strong.

"Yes, sir."

His father's face grew icy cold. "And what does your mother say when you start tearing the place down? Be honest, now. Just exactly what does she say?"

The boy's whole mind was in struggle. He had sensed that this was coming, but he never knew how to avoid it. "She tells me not to."

"Oh, she tells you not to, does she? I wonder — just how does she go about telling you not to? What does she say? Come on, speak up."

The boy wanted frantically to run and hide his head against his mother. But he had to stand there. He could not think what to say.

His father's voice grew steely. "What's the matter with you? Can't you answer a simple question?"

"Please, Charles," his mother said very low, from where she stood by the stove, all the brightness drained from her face.

"Keep out of this," his father said fiercely, without turning his head. "This is between the boy and me. We'll see if he can give an honest answer to a simple question. Now tell me," he said stonily to the boy, weighting every word with authority, "just what your mother says to you when you jump. Does she scold you?'

"Sometimes," the boy cried, seizing on the desperate truth, giving up under the overpowering pressure of his father's fierceness. But it was terrible. It was just what he should not have said.

"Sometimes!" his father exclaimed triumphantly. "I thought so. And that means that most of the time she lets you go crashing and bulling your way around here without interfering, without even trying to stop you. Isn't that so? Isn't it?"

"Sometimes she stops me," the boy cried. He began to weep.

The man turned a blazing, injured face towards his wife. "Do you see what you're doing to the boy?" he demanded. "Look at him. Absolutely undisciplined, making a wreck out of the few sticks I manage to scrape together to cover our heads with. How can I afford to keep a decent place for us to live in when you don't care anything about it? You'd let the whole place go to pieces, wouldn't you?"

His mother's eyes were hot with anger in her pale face. Her lips moved. "That's not fair," she said tightly, almost inaudibly.

"What's that?" his father cried sharply.

His mother turned with a little gasp of fury, and saw Richard shrinking there between them. The anger slowly drained from her face and she gave a quick little toss of the head as if to free herself of something. "I do believe in a certain amount of discipline, Charles," she said firmly, and then, before his father could answer, she came swiftly to the table with a coffee cup and a blue platter on which ham curled pinkly and the shining eggs sent up a steam from their yellow centers. "Come on and eat, you two, before everything gets cold," she said.

Richard could see that the danger was not yet over. Something dark hung and balanced in the air, about his father. The big man took an impatient gulp of coffee, set the cup down hard, and then turned back to it, lifted it again and drank more slowly. "Not bad coffee, for a change," he said, and Mother gave a quick little laugh designed to make things better, and his father turned his eyes on her, not pleased, but no longer angry, ready to wait, and then he picked up his knife and fork and began to eat rapidly, chewing heavily and enjoying it.

Richard eased himself into his chair and began to eat. Sunlight had started to stream thinly through the outside mists and to filter through the window curtains, a pallid white sunlight on the bright red cloth and the blue breakfast crockery. Everything in the house tingled and waited, as it always did when his father came home. Richard felt a curious hollowness in the region of his stomach, but it was not altogether the emptiness of hunger; it was partly discomfort from the scene just ended, and partly a stirring apprehension and excitement for what the day would bring. There was something about his father that made things happen: the weekends were always crowded with the imminence of catastrophic event. It was like floating in the air over a bright valley crossed by threatening and erratic thunderstorms: his father kept them all moving through the hours with a high, sure vigor; but you never knew when you would unwittingly come too close to the edge of boiling cloud and find yourself shaken, lightning-struck, with thunder growling through the sky.

The long deliberateness of Sunday breakfast protracted itself almost unbearably. They ate silently except for the light ting-ing of knives and forks against the plates (his father did not encourage conversation at table), waiting for his father to announce the program for the day. Only, today everything was queer. It was because Gordon was not there and the family arrangement was all lopsided. His father could have spoken to Gordon and the strain would have eased. They were close together, Gordon and his father. But this Sunday morning his father was all alone, reaching for the extra ham and eggs, eating ponderously, his displeasure deliberately suspended over them. If Gordon had been there his father might have ended the trouble by making a joke about it, and Gordon would have laughed and his father would have been satisfied. But now the strain was still there, and time kept drawing out and everything was still queer.

Then his father did an extraordinary thing. He laid down his knife and fork, wiped his mouth carefully with his napkin, and turned to Richard a face that seemed to have forgotten all his indignation. "Well, son," he said, "how about you giving me a hand today, when we get back from church? I've got to fix that broken ladder, and I want to put a new spring on the screen door. Do you think you can handle a hammer without beating your thumbs to pieces?"

"Sure," Richard said excitedly, grinning. "I mean 'Yes, sir.' "

"Well, we'll give it a try," his father said, smiling. "Maybe it's about time for you to start living in a man's world."

When they got up from the table he clapped his hand on Richard's shoulder companionably and walked with him out onto the porch, but Richard noticed that he hadn't spoken to Mother, nor looked at her yet, and it gave him a sort of empty feeling inside, in spite of the excitement of having his father notice him, because usually when things were bad they were left together, and that way they could rather encourage each other and not mind it so much.

Today his mother behaved very well in church, not turning her head once to look at the stained-glass window that she liked, where the light came blazing through, red as satin, but keeping her eyes steadily on the minister, her face all peaceful and cool. Richard looked at her once to see whether she was suffering, but she was not. She was not happy, either; she was just herself. And that was all right, and Richard, too, was able to behave very well, hardly wriggling at all, so that his father had to nudge him only twice. His father sang very loudly on the hymns, "Wash me, and I shall be whiter than snow," and "Rock of Ages, cleft for me," as he did when things were going well, and Richard did not have to pay much attention to the sermon because there was a picture of a woman and a baby on the front of his Sunday School leaflet — Mary, the mother of Jesus — and he loved her face. There was a deep shadow of sorrow in her eyes, only she seemed to have gotten used to it so that it didn't interfere with her gladness over her baby, and in a way she reminded him of his mother and he glanced sidewise to make sure. It was true, they were much the same, both so quiet and sweet and knowing that they would be hurt; and a rush of love for his mother welled up and filled his heart and trembled in his bones.

Walking home from church his father spoke to his mother for the first time and said he would like cherry pie for dinner, and his mother was glad to make it, and they all strolled slowly through the edge of town, down their own road, where the dusty goldenrod was hot in the sunlight and they could feel the burning of the pavement through their shoe soles, and his father took off his coat and carried it, and rumbled snatches of the hymns in his bass voice, all the way to the door of the house.

It was the middle of the day, hot and torpid, a time that stretched and stayed, with sunlight blazing on the bare wooden walls inside the little workshop behind the house, and nothing alive that wanted to move — except his father, who was busy with a plane, making thin strips and curls of shavings peel off the piece of board that would be the new ladder rung, his father and the flies, which liked the heat and droned in endless circles and occasional downsweeps in the glare above their heads. His father showed him, very man-to-man, that this was a good sound piece of wood, the grain running lengthwise and no knots to spoil its strength, and he drank the knowledge in, sensing that this was his father's secret of power, that there were things to be learned and known, useful things that would come in handy and that you could tell someone else and show to everyone that you were a man who knew how to do things right.

Richard held the ladder firm while his father took the brace and bit and bored out the pegs that had held the broken rung. There were two nail holes in the side of the ladder and his father frowned at them.

"Where did these come from? Did you do this?"

"No, sir," Richard told him, glad that for once he wasn't guilty. "Mother tried to mend it."

"Oh," his father said, and he darkened for a moment; then he clapped his hand on Richard's knee and let out a low laugh. "Well," he said, "she's only a woman; you can't expect her to have good sense."

He was treating Richard exactly as if he were Gordon, sharing his knowledge with him, teaching him, starting to laugh with him; and this about his mother was a joke that his father and Gordon often made between themselves. Now his father was waiting for a response from him, and the moment drew out a little too long, and Richard knew a fleeting panic that he might fail his father and lose this new closeness; only, it hurt him to joke about his mother, because this jest always made her head lift a little and her face grow still and contained; so, whereas Gordon would have laughed out loud, very jolly, now Richard managed only, and just in time, to smile. But his father saw it and was satisfied.

They put the new rung in the vise, and his father held it in place while Richard brought the jaws tight, twirling the stout metal bar. His father had placed a thin strip of smooth wood on either side of the rung, to prevent the jaws of the vise from biting into the newly planed surface.

"There's always a right and a wrong way of doing anything," his father said proudly, with finality. A sentence to be remembered, a piece of knowledge, a part of his father's sureness — with the man's heavy voice giving it the final authority. But there was something perverse in Richard, something inside his mind that lightly mocked him as he tried to memorize for all time, for a new security: *There's always a right and a wrong way* . . . Suppose, the lightly mocking voice queried, suppose there are more than two ways? What if there are millions and millions — trillions and trillions? Wouldn't you get all mixed up? Only that was never true of his father. His father's sureness was a power so strong that everything moved aside for it. How did you learn to be so sure? Did you learn like this, one thing at a time, remembering forever which of two ways was right and which was wrong? But how did you get to the end? How did you know which two ways to start with?

Gordon grasped these matters instinctively. Gordon was like his father. It was a deep-seated despair in Richard that he could not see his way into his father's world, that he kept wandering through the richness of the earth in uncertainty, never quite finding his bearings. How was he to learn? How was he to know how to be so sure and final in judgment, in the midst of the kaleidoscopic profusion of things, when the surety itself was an alien place and whenever he tried to reach it the mocking questions raised their heads and he had to ask them? Only, it would never do to ask his father. "Of all the fool questions!" his father would say. That was certain. Richard knew that much. He had always looked like a fool to his father. Only today was amazingly different, with his father taking him in and teaching him, and he tried again to learn: *There's always a right and a wrong way of doing things.* But the words didn't come home to him. It was like trying to memorize a piece in school that didn't make sense. You began to repeat the words, but after you had said them a few times they weren't words any more — the meaning went out of them. He began to roll them on his tongue: *wrong way, rong way, rongway* — a soft gong sound that was pleasant, a lovely noise in his throat, but it didn't mean anything at all.

Sweat from the close heat of the little shop stood on Richard's forehead in tiny beads, and a drop of it gathered and ran damply down his nose. It was splendid to be here with his father like this,

but it lasted so long. He wished they would stop work and go swimming. He and his mother always went in the river at this hot time
of the day, before they ate, but his father would think the suggestion
outrageous, with work to be done, so he kept quiet and just thought
about it. It would be wonderful to be hanging on to the edge of the
big float, anchored well out from the shore, and to dip down under
the water where the float's shadow made an expanse of deep green
beneath the surface. The float was much too wide to swim across
under; he was afraid he couldn't hold his breath that long, although
he often tantalized himself by thinking of doing it; but it was exciting just to duck himself under the edge where the water was dark-
bright, and to feel the heavy wood between himself and the sky.
This was the first summer he had learned to do more than dog-
paddle in the water, although his crawl was still too quick and
choppy and he couldn't keep it up for very long. Every day, it was
wonderful, with his mother, to leave the sun-drenched lawn, to hurry
down the stairs between the slithering willows that grew in tall
clumps beside the riverbank, to take off their shoes on the pebbles,
and then to feel the sweet cold shock of the water as they waded in.
The water was milky-green and a little brackish with the long up-
wash of tidewater from the ocean fifteen miles away; and after they
had waded out arm-pit deep — feeling their way slowly over the
slippery, rounded stones — if they stood still for a minute, the pale
green fishes would come up to them and nibble at their legs.

He remembered how it had frightened him the first time it had
happened — the strong rubbery nibble on his thigh. He had
screamed to his mother for help, and clung to her hand when she
had swum to him. He was not an unusually timid boy, but he had
been young, only seven, and the attack had been so unexpected.
Richard smiled now to think of what a cowardy custard he had been.
But he remembered very clearly what had come next: how they had
put their faces under water and how, after the first blur, they had
stared through the distorted glassy water-world; feeling even now
the enclosing touch of the cool water around his head, and reliving
the watery vision of the fishes, not too far away, suspended, hardly
moving — the flat, silver-green sides and the blunt snouts, the transparent quivering fins, and the single unwinking eye observing them

without emotion — the round, the glassy, the unlidded eye.

"They were investigating us," his mother told him when they stood with their heads in the sunlight again, "to see whether we were good to eat."

"They're mean. They bit me," the boy insisted.

"No, that's not true," his mother said. "Meanness has nothing to do with it. They did bite you, but it wasn't much of a bite, when you come to think of it. We are something new in the water, and they had to find out what we are. They might have eaten us if they could, but our bodies are too big and alive and solid for them.

"What do they eat?"

"Oh, small fishes, water worms. They'll snap at very odd things, bright bits of metal in the water, and they'll eat dead things."

"Would they eat us if we were dead?"

"Yes, I imagine they would. Dead bodies grow soft underwater; they're no use anymore. The fishes help to clean things up. The only thing for you to remember — " his mother's face grew intent as it did when she spoke seriously to him — "is that they don't do it from meanness, biting at anything, dead or alive. It's just the way they are. And it's very important to learn how things are. Not the way you're afraid they are, or wish they were. Not either one. How they *are*. You have to discover that the world isn't thinking about you, not lurking, lying in wait to harm you, although lots of people, when they're young, think that and are afraid it's so. And it isn't waiting, trying to please you, either. There are lots of things in the world that will bite you."

"Ants," he cried, from immediate experience.

"And bees, and snakes and spiders and fishes — lots of things. But the thing you have to learn," she said, very earnest, "is that they don't do it from choice, not from wishing to hurt. It's from a singleness of direction, a sort of simplicity of nature in them. There they are. They are what they are. They go their way and sometimes it collides with your way, and they may hurt you. But not from meanness, not from desire. It's only people who are able to hurt from choice." Her face grew quiet from thinking. "And when people reach a singleness of direction, it seems to be a singleness that either wants to hurt or never to hurt — one or the other. The time will come when you have to choose . . . But that's too much for you," she cried, suddenly seeing him, so young. "The thing you have to remember is to meet things as they are, not to lie to yourself about them, not to fool yourself — not ever."

She suddenly smiled at him, very merry, and then, since he was too small to swim so far, she told him to hang on to the inflated inner-tube that he used to buoy himself over deep water, and she towed him out to the float, the vast heavy raft that swung up- or down-river against its moorings, with the tide, a soggy wooden island, gray with long weathering and green with salt-rust around the bolts; and they crawled up on its coarse, splintery surface, the old wood so water-logged that it floated half awash as they lay on it, watching the stretching water and soaking up the sun. . . .

"Hold the gluepot," his father ordered him, and he came back abruptly to the sweltering shop, to the drone of flies and the scent of wood shavings. "Take it up in a cloth. Don't burn your hands. That's right. Now see if you can hold it steady and not slop any of it."

Richard wrapped the pot in a thick rag and held it close to his father, concentrating on steadiness; and his nostrils were full of the acrid, nauseating odor of hot glue, as his father dipped a thin stick into the brown mass; and he held the pot very hard and very upright, and even when the glue adhered to the stick and tried to pull against him, he did not let it tilt.

Dinner was on the porch again because of the heat, and it was late because Mother had stopped to bake the pie, and consequently his father was displeased with her. There was roast beef, brown and crusty on the outside, but ruddy and oozing juice in the middle when the knife sliced into it, and there was lots of gravy for the mashed potatoes; and pretty soon, eating began to ease his father's annoyance, as it always did; and the first thing they knew his father began to talk, to talk about Richard — to boast about him.

"The little son of a gun did all right," he said. "He's not such a fool as he looks when he runs wild. He held that gluepot steady as a rock, and it was heavy, and hot."

It was intoxicating — it was too heady — the sudden elevation to an approbation he had never tasted before. Richard began to puff up inside. He wanted to swagger. He wanted to shout. And all the time, his father's eyes were on his face with that keen glint of approval.

"Damned if he isn't going to be a chip off the old block," his father said, laughing, pleased at what he saw in him. "Give him time. He's a comer, this kid of mine."

Richard could hardly hold himself in. He felt terribly strong and fine. He felt six feet tall. He wanted to gloat, the way his father did. There was something in him that his father liked, after all — liked and was proud of. He felt full of a fierce vigor, as if he could do anything. He burned with vainglory, the admiration in his father's face making leap and tug within him the prancing horses of his pride. Give him time: he'd learn to "lay it on the line," too. He'd show everybody.

When the cherry pie came on, his father tasted it judiciously. "A little too sweet for my taste," he said decidedly. "I like my cherry pie good and sharp, with a real tang to it. I don't think she quite hit it on this one. What do you say, son?" He turned to Richard, grinning at him, welcoming his opinion, welding the two of them together, the pride and force in the man laying hold upon the boy, raising him to a terrible stature, claiming him with the strong tie of their shared masculinity. The unfamiliar swollen headiness in the boy suddenly burst its bounds and he broke out in laughter, drunk with power and position.

"Well," he said, "she's only a woman; you can't expect her to have good sense."

His father guffawed with pleasure and reached around the table corner to slap him on the knee. And Richard looked up, straight into his mother's eyes, very wide and dark and startled, looking at him. Just for an instant her face was stricken and her mouth flinched, before she caught herself and her lips formed a small, strained smile. Then she made a gesture he'd seen in her before, when his father taunted her: she tossed her head up like a young animal, like a pony, the way she did when she came up out of the water, shaking her hair back to free her head from the underwater tightness — to free herself of pain. Then she smiled brightly at

Richard, not forgiving him, not reproaching him — having recovered herself now — just liking him and seeing how it was with
him.

But it was to Richard as if he had struck her. There she was, her
face brave and bright — all alone now, betrayed in her love for him.
If she had turned on him in anger, rising in honorable wrath to
punish him, he would have welcomed it. He was all hollow inside,
with his own terrible words ringing in his ears. And yet she only
tossed her head in that high way of hers and smiled at him. He
flung his napkin down, and mumbling "Please excuse me," bolted
from the table.

"Hey," his father called after him, "don't you want your pie?"

"No thanks," he managed to get out. "I'm full." And he ran
desperately down the steps from the porch and down across the lawn,
his feet clumping monotonously, like weighted things, pounding out
upon the grassy earth the leaden beat of his anguish.

He was sitting on a dark, twisted root at the riverbank, gazing
outward, a slender web of trailing willow branches enshrouding
him, spreading a transparent veil of green and silver leafage between him and the bright, aching sky. And within him the gloomy,
terrifying coils of darkness swirled — not creeping upon him from
without, as his mind had always foreboded, but rising like brown
and evil fumes from within himself, choking and sweeping down
around his burdened heart. Oh, not from outside, whispering from
corners, the brown horror threatened, but rising from within, the
engulfing, sickly miasma of evil possibility — of evil done. The
taste of revulsion at the easy power he had grasped and abused was
brassy on his tongue. His dark deed was not to be evaded, the thing
he had done boiling like a cloud within him, cutting him off forever from sunlight and pleasant hours, from all future happiness.
He ached to go back and live the last hour over again, to change it,
to wipe it out; but there it hung, implacable, achieved, not to be
undone — the unendurable, the guilty, the irretrievable act lying
between him and his life.

He seemed to have been sitting there for hours, the sickness dark
and heavy within him, the flush of shame curling in his flesh. And
nothing changed, there was no escape, it would not go away. And

he began to hate them, pulling him between them the way they did, his bitterness turning in its desperate unrelief, into resentment, into blame — beginning now to want to hurt them, to injure, to punish them, and to flee, then, far away — to escape, to stop feeling, to stop being anything — not to be anything at all . . .

Then his father would be shocked and, for once in his life, ashamed, because it was really all his father's fault and his father would know it and would have to pay for it. The reason he had done what he had done, really, was to please his father. His father had intended him to do it. And his father would have to face what he had done, then; and he would groan, and even cry. And his mother would see, then, that he hadn't meant to; she would know how much he had loved her, because he hadn't been able to stand it. He stared over the water, his resolution growing stern and frightening within him; and there, far out, floated the moored raft, gray, sodden, half awash, and very wide — its wet surface twinkling under a thin pall of cloudy sunlight.

He took off his shoes and socks on the pebbles, then let his Sunday trousers slip down around his ankles, and slid out of his shirt. He folded the discarded clothing carefully, ritualistically, and laid the neat little pile on the willow root.

The river was cold after the hot air, and the ripples slid tingling over his body like reminders of all the summers he had known, as he dog-paddled outward, his muscles knotted and his breathing harsh and rapid. It surprised him that he reached the float so quickly, but everything was tight and dreamlike, and went too fast. He grasped the ancient, hairy wood with his hands, and took three deep breaths as he did when he was going to surface-dive, and then he pushed himself down and went under.

The water under the raft was deep green and crystal clear, not fogged and thickened as it was where light lay on the surface. He swam a few strokes strongly through it, towards the darkness. Dark slippery weeds hung from the underside of the raft and tickled his back, and once his shoulders bumped against the old wood above him. He reached what must have been about the center of the raft and put a hand up, suspending himself for a moment in this strange underworld. His resolution was still strong and bitter within him, but the knives of anguish had ceased to cut into his heart with their keen edges; his heart held only a deep, recessive hurt, like a bruise. He tried to think about drowning, but his eyes kept seeing the water, bright as glass, and every moving shadow around him, and he couldn't think of anything.

A school of tiny minnows skittered past, turning and wheeling away from him, and then he saw the big ones, not swimming, just materializing out of their own element — the two large fishes, their flashing scales a pallid green in the underwater light, not moving, suspended but alive, seeing him there with their unblinking crystal-rimmed eyes. For the flick of an instant it occurred to him that they were hanging there waiting for his body to grow dead and soft and ready to be eaten, but the thought did not disturb him, and faded instantly. There they were, the beautiful shapes, so firm and shining and cold; and instantaneously all time fled away from him, and with it the silliness of anger and of being hurt and of shame. There they hung, almost close enough to touch — the bright fishes, with their little speckles and streaks and feathery fin lines and the clear bubblelike eyes from which their lives looked out at him; and swiftly, not with the deliberateness with which things move in time, but with the swiftness of thought, the waters swelled out and grew big, grew into all the waters he had ever known or dreamed of, all the waters since time began, all black resounding oceans tasting of brine that reached out their long-threading fingers to him here in this brackish tidewash, and all sweet streaming rivers and great foaming falls, and small flat stagnant pools, green with scum and insect-haunted. And through them all forever, undisturbed, unchanged, vanishing and reappearing, moved the pale cold fishes, equable, unhurried, hungry, alive — forever themselves and undecipherable — forever, from the first touch of life in the first waters.

The two cool metallic shapes that hung before him now moved slightly, and he saw again how alive they were; and now, mysteriously, long streams of joy like cool green beams streamed out of them to him and out of him to them and lighted all the waters, and he was shaken with the wonder and the irreplaceable richness so that he could have cried out, and just as he knew he must shut his eyes to blot out for an instant the strain of beauty and unendurable bliss, the fishes suddenly flicked sideways, both as one, and shimmered briefly against the darkness and were gone, leaving him wild and shaking, still suspended there in the liquid greenness, and all the terrible glory of the world and its vast waters was strong and sweet in his mouth. Then, because a vigorous and ennobling laughter filled him, he let out an expulsive blurt of breath and knew there was no air to draw in again, and he was half-way under the raft and his lungs were aching and his chest was pinched by an enormous hand.

He moved then, motivated not by fear but only by a furious endurance, and began stroking toward the light. He would hold his breath one more stroke, and then one more, while the little bubbles oozed relentlessly out between his lips and his ribs caved and his head pounded and his throat was wracked with strain, and he could not endure it, and made one stroke more, one stroke more . . . And there was air in his lungs, so harsh it seared them, and the weathered gray wood of the raft edge rasped against his cheek.

He hung there while a long time passed, one arm clinging to the soggy old timbers, his straitened lungs still gasping and filling with the moist river air. He looked across the shining plate of the river to the silver willows, tranquil and undisturbed, and there on the beach he saw his mother in her faded red bathing suit, come down to join him. And even from out here he could see that her attitude, the set of her body, was not as he had dreaded and pictured her, not touched by tragedy and awaiting expiation, not darkened and bent by grief; nor was there disappointment or schooled courage in her easy movement. She was just quietly there, in the hot smoky afternoon — wading in now and reaching down to touch the cool of the river water with both hands.

(From Fantastic)

THE THIRD GUEST

BY B. TRAVEN

*M*ACARIO, the village woodchopper, had one overwhelming
desire which he had nourished for fifteen years.

It was not riches he wanted, nor a well-built house instead
of that ramshackle old hut in which he lived with his wife and his
eleven children who wore rags and were always hungry. What he
craved more than anything in this world — what he might have
traded his very soul for — was to have a roast turkey all for himself
combined with the opportunity to eat it in peace, deep in the woods
unseen by his ever-hungry children, and entirely alone.

His stomach never fully satisfied, he would leave home before sunrise every morning in the year, weekday and Sunday alike, rain or
shine. He would disappear into the woods and by nightfall bring
back a load of chopped wood carried on his back.

That load, meaning a full day's job, would sell for one bit, sometimes even less than that. During the rainy season, though, when
competition was slow, he would get as much as two bits now and
then for his load of fuel.

Two bits meant a fortune to his wife, who looked even more
starved than her husband, and who was known in the village as the
Woman with the Sad Eyes.

Arriving home after sunset, Marcario would throw off his pack
with a heavy groan, stagger into his hut and drop with an audible
bump upon a low crudely made chair brought to the equally crude
table by one of the children.

There he would spread both his arms upon the table and say

with a tired voice: "Oh, Mother, I am tired and hungry, what have
we for supper?"

"Black beans, green chile, tortillas, salt and lemon tea," his
wife would answer.

It was always the same menu with no variation whatever. Knowing the answer long before he was home, he merely asked so as to
say something and, by so doing, prevent his children from believing
him merely a dumb animal.

When supper was set before him in earthen vessels, he would be
profoundly asleep. His wife would shake him: "Father, supper's on
the table."

"We thank our good Lord for what he allows us poor sinners,"
he would pray, and immediately start eating.

Yet hardly would he swallow a few mouthfuls of beans when
he would note the eyes of his children resting on his face and hands,
watching him that he might not eat too much so that they might
get a little second helping since the first had been so very small. He
would cease eating and drink only the tea, brewed of *zacate de
limon,* sweetened with a little chunk of *piloncillo.*

Having emptied the earthen pot he would, with the back of his
hand wipe his mouth, moan pitifully, and in a prayerful voice
say: "Oh, dear Lord in heaven, if only once in all my dreary life I
could have a roast turkey all for myself, I would then die happily
and rest in peace until called for the final reckoning, Amen."

Frequently he would not say that much, yet he would never fail
to say at least: "Oh, good Lord if only once I could have a roast
turkey all for myself."

His children had heard that lamentation so often that none of
them paid attention to it any longer, considering it their father's
particular way of saying Grace after supper.

He might just as well have prayed that he would like to be given
one thousand doubloons, for there was not the faintest likelihood
that he would ever come into the possession of roast chicken, let
alone a heavy roast turkey whose meat no child of his had ever
tasted.

His wife, the most faithful and most abnegating companion a man
could wish for, had every reason to consider him a very good man.

He never beat her; he worked as hard as any man could. On Saturday nights only he would take a three-centavo's worth nip of mezcal, and no matter how little money she had, she would never fail to buy him that squeeze of a drink. She would buy it at the general store because he would get less than half the size for the same money if he bought the drink in the village tavern.

Realizing how good a husband he was, how hard he worked to keep the family going, how much he, in his own way, loved her and the children, the wife began saving up any penny she could spare of the little money she earned doing odd jobs for other villagers who were slightly better off than she was.

Having thus saved penny by penny for three long years, which had seemed to her an eternity, she at last could lay her hands on the heaviest turkey brought to the market.

Almost exploding with joy and happiness, she took it home while the children were not in. She hid the fowl so that none would see it. Not a word she said when her husband came home that night, tired, worn-out and hungry as always, and as usual praying to heaven for his roast turkey.

The children were sent to bed early. She feared not that her husband might see what she was about, for he had already fallen asleep at the table and, as always, half an hour later he would drowsily rise and drag himself to his cot upon which he would drop as if clubbed down.

If there ever was prepared a carefully selected turkey with a true feeling of happiness and profound joy guiding the hands and the taste of a cook, this one certainly was. The wife worked all through the night to get the turkey ready before sunrise.

Macario got up for his day's work and sat down at the table for his lean breakfast. He never bothered saying *Good Morning* and was not used to hearing it said by his wife or anybody in the house.

If something was amiss on the table or if he could not find his machete or the ropes which he needed for tying up the chopped wood, he would mumble something, hardly opening his lips. As his utterings were few and these few always limited to what was absolutely necessary, his wife would understand him without ever making a mistake.

Now he rose, ready to leave.

He came out, and while standing for a few seconds by the door of his shack looking at the misty gray of the coming day, his wife placed herself before him as though in his way. For a brief moment he gazed at her, slightly bewildered because of that strange attitude of hers. And there she handed him an old basket in which was the roast turkey, trimmed, stuffed and garnished, all prettily wrapped up in fresh green banana leaves.

"There now, there, dear husband, there's the roast turkey you've been praying for during so many long years. Take it along with you to the deepest and densest part of the woods where nobody will disturb you and where you can eat it all alone. Hurry now before the children smell it and get aware of that precious meal, for then you could not resist giving it to them. Hurry along."

He looked at her with his tired eyes and nodded. *Please* and *Thanks* were words he never used. It did not occur to him to let his wife have just one little bite of that turkey because his mind, not fit to handle more than one thought at a time, was at this instant exclusively occupied with his wife's urging to hurry and run away with his turkey lest the children get up before he could leave.

He took his time finding himself a well-hidden place deep in the woods and as he, because of so much wandering about, had become sufficiently hungry by now, he was ready to eat his turkey with genuine gusto. He made his seat on the ground very comfortable, washed his hands in a brook near by, and everything was as perfect as it should be at such a solemn occasion — that is, the fulfillment of a man's prayer said daily for an almost uncountable number of years.

With a sigh of utter happiness, he leaned his back against the hollow trunk of a heavy tree, took the turkey out of the basket, spread the huge banana leaves before him on the ground and laid the bird upon them with a gesture as if he were offering it to the gods. He had in mind to lie down after the meal and sleep the whole day through and so turn this day, his Saint's day, to a real holiday — the first in his life since he could think for himself.

On looking at the turkey so well prepared, and taking in that sweet aroma of a carefully and skillfully roasted turkey, he muttered in sheer admiration: "I must say this much of her, she's a great and wonderful cook. It is sad that she never has the chance to show her skill."

That was the most profound praise and the highest expression of thanks he could think of. His wife would have burst with pride and she would have been happy beyond words had he only once in his life said that in her presence. This, though, he would never have been able to do, for in her presence such words would simply refuse to pass his lips.

Holding the bird's breast down with his left hand, he firmly grabbed with his right one of the turkey's thick legs to tear it off.

And while he was trying to do so, he suddenly noted two feet standing right before him, hardly two yards away.

He raised his eyes up along the black, tightly fitting pants which covered low riding boots as far down as the ankles and found, to his surprise, a Charro in full dress, watching him tear off the turkey's leg.

The Charro wore a sombrero of immense size, richly trimmed with gold laces. His short leather coat was adorned with the richest gold, silver and multi-colored silk embroidery one could imagine. To the outside seams of the Charro's black trousers and reaching from the belt down to where they came to rest upon the heavy spurs of pure silver, a row of gold coins was sewn on. A slight move the Charro would make now and then while he was speaking to Macario caused these gold coins to send forth a low, sweet-sounding tinkle. He had a black moustachio, the Charro had, and a beard like a goat's. His eyes were pitch black, very narrow and piercing so that one might virtually believe them needles.

When Macario's eyes reached his face, the stranger smiled, thin-lipped and somewhat malicious. He evidently thought his smile a most charming one, by which any human, man or woman, would be enticed beyond help.

"What do you say, friend, about a fair bite of your tasty turkey for a hungry horseman," he said in a metallic voice. "See, friend, I've had a long ride all through the night and now I'm nearly starved and so, please, for hell's sake, invite me to partake of your lunch."

"It's not lunch in the first place," Macario corrected, holding on to his turkey as if he thought that bird might fly away at any moment. "And in the second place, it's my holiday dinner and I won't part with it for anybody, whoever he may be. Do you understand?"

"No, I don't. Look here, friend, I'll give you my heavy silver spurs just for that thick leg you've grabbed," the Charro bargained, moistening his lips with a thick dark red tongue which, had it been forked, might have been that of a snake.

"I have no use for spurs whether they are of iron, brass, silver or gold trimmed with diamonds all over, because I have no horse to ride on." Macario judged the value of his roast turkey as only a man would who had waited for that meal almost eighteen years.

"Well then, friend, if it is worth that much to you, I'll cut off all these gold coins which you see dangling from my trousers and I'll give them to you for a half breast of that turkey of yours. What about that?"

"That money would do me no good. If I spent only one single coin they'd clap me in jail right away and there torture me until I'd tell them where I stole it, and after that they'd chop off one hand of mine for being a thief. What could I, a woodchopper, do with one hand less when, in fact, I could use four if only the Lord had been kind enough to let me have that many."

Macario, utterly unconcerned over the Charro's insistence, once more tried to tear off the leg and started eating when the visitor interrupted him again: "See here, friend, I own these woods, the whole woods and all the woods around here, and I'll give you these woods in exchange for just one wing of your turkey and a fistful of the fillings. All these woods, think of it."

"Now you're lying, stranger. These woods are not yours, they're the Lord's, or I couldn't chop in here and provide the villagers with fuel. And if they were your woods and you'd give them to me for a gift or in payment for a part of my turkey, I wouldn't be any richer anyhow because I'd have to chop then as I do now."

Said the Charro: "Now listen, my good friend — "

"Now you listen," Macario broke in impatiently. "You aren't my good friend and I'm not your good friend and I hope I never will be your good friend as long as God saves my soul. Understand that. And now you go back to hell where you came from and let me eat my holiday dinner in peace."

The Charro made a horribly obscene grimace, swore at Macario and limped off, cursing the world and all mankind.

Macario looked after him, shook his head and said to himself: "Who'd expect to meet such funny jesters in these woods? Well, I suppose it takes all kinds of people and creatures to make it truly our Lord's world."

He sighed and laid his left hand on the turkey's breast as he had done before and with his right grasped one of the fowl's legs.

And again he noted two feet standing right before him at the same spot where, only a half minute earlier, the Charro had been standing.

Ordinary huaraches, well worn as though by a man who has wandered a long and difficult road, covered these two feet. Their owner was quite obviously very tired and weary, for his feet seemed to sag at the arches.

Macario looked up and met a very kind face, thinly bearded. The wanderer was dressed in very old, but well washed, white cotton pants and a shirt of the same stuff, and he looked not very different from the ordinary Indian peasant of the country.

The wanderer's eyes held Macario's as though by a charm and Macario became aware that in this pilgrim's heart were combined all the goodnesses and kindnesses of earth and heaven, and in each of the wanderer's eyes he saw a little golden sun, and each little golden sun seemed to be but a golden hole through which one might crawl right into heaven and see Godfather Himself in all His glory.

With a voice that sounded like a huge organ playing from a distance far away, the wanderer said: "Give unto me, my good neighbor, as I shall give unto you. I am hungry, very hungry indeed. For see, my beloved brother, I have come a long way. Pray, let me have that leg which you are holding and I shall truly and verily bless you for it. Just that leg, nothing else. It will satisfy my hunger and it will give me new strength, for very long still is my way before reaching my father's house."

"You're a very kind man, wanderer, the kindest of men that ever were, that are today, and that are to come," Macario said, as though he was praying before the image of the Holy Virgin.

"So I beg of you, my good neighbor, give me just one half of the bird's breast, you certainly will not miss it much."

"Oh, my beloved pilgrim," Macario explained as if he were speaking to the archbishop whom he had never seen and did not know but whom he belived the highest of the highest on earth. "If you, my Lord, really mean to say that I won't miss it much, I shall answer that I feel terribly hurt in my soul because I can't say anything better to you, kind man, but that you are very much mistaken. I know I should never say such a thing to you for it comes close to blasphemy, yet I can't help it, I must say it even should that cost me my right to enter heaven because your eyes and your voice make me tell the truth.

"For you see, your Lordship, I must not miss even the tiniest little morsel of this turkey. This turkey, please, oh please, do understand, my Lord, was given me as a whole and was meant to be eaten as a whole. It would no longer be a whole turkey were I to give away just a little bit not even the size of a fingernail. A whole turkey — it was what I have yearned for all my life, and not to have it now after a lifetime of praying for it would destroy all the happiness of my good and faithful wife who has sacrificed herself beyond words to make me that great gift. So, please, my Lord and Master, understand a poor sinner's mind. Please, I pray you understand."

And the wanderer looked at Macario and said unto him: "I do understand you, Macario, my noble brother and good neighbor, I verily do understand you. Be blessed for ever and ever and eat your turkey in peace. I shall go now, and on passing through your village I shall go near your hut where I shall bless your good wife and all your children. Be with the Lord. Goodbye."

Not once while he had made these speeches to the Charro and to the Wanderer had it occured to Macario, who rarely spoke more than fifty words a day, to stop to think what had made him so eloquent — why it was that he, in the depths of the wood, could speak as freely and easily as the minister in church, and used words and expressions which he had never known before. It all came to him without realizing what was happening to him.

He followed the pilgrim with his eyes until he could see him no longer.

He shook his head sadly.

"I most surely feel sorry about him. He was so very tired and hungry. But I simply could do nothing else. I would have insulted my dear wife. Besides, I cannot spare a leg or part of the breast, come what may, for it would no longer be a whole turkey then."

And again he seized the turkey's leg to tear it off and start his dinner when, again, he noted two feet standing before him and at the same spot the others had stood a while ago.

These two feet were standing in old-fashioned sandals, and Macario thought that the man must be a foreigner from far-off lands, for he had never seen sandals like these before.

He looked up and stared at the hungriest face he had ever believed possible. That face had no flesh. It was all bone. And all bone were the hands and the legs of the visitor. His eyes seemed to be but two very thick black holes hidden deep in the fleshless face. The mouth consisted of two rows of strong teeth, bared of lips.

He was dressed in a faded bluish-white flowing mantle which, as Macario noted, was neither cotton nor silk nor wool nor any fabric he knew. He held a long staff in one hand for support.

From the stranger's belt, which was rather wound around his waist, a mahogany box, scratched all over, with a clock ticking audibly inside, was dangling on a bit of string.

It was that box hanging there instead of the hour-glass which Macario had expected that confused him at first as to what the new visitor's social standing in the world might be.

The newcomer now spoke. He spoke with a voice that sounded like two sticks clattering one against the other.

"I am very hungry, compadre, very, very hungry."

"You don't need to tell me. I can see that, compadre," Macario asserted, not in the least afraid of the stranger's horrible appearance.

"Since you can see that and since you have no doubt that I need something substantial in my stomach, would you mind giving me that leg of the turkey you are holding?"

Macario gave forth a desperate groan, shrugged and lifted up his arms in utter helplessness.

"Well," he said, with mourning in his voice, "what can a poor mortal do against fate? I've been caught at last. There's no way out any more. It would have been a great adventure, the good God in heaven knows it, but fate doesn't want it that way. I shall never have a whole turkey for myself, never, never and never, so what can I do? I must give in. All right, compadre, get your belly's fill; I know what hunger is like. Sit down, hungry man, sit down. Half the turkey's yours and be welcome to it."

"Oh, compadre, that is fine, very fine," said the hungry man, sitting down on the ground opposite Macario and widening his row of teeth as if he were trying to grin.

Macario could not make out for sure what the stranger meant by the grin, whether it was an expression of thanks or a gesture of joy at having been saved from a sure death by starvation.

"I'll cut the bird in two," Macario said, in a great hurry now lest another visitor might come up and make his own part a third only. "Once I've cut the bird in two, you just look the other way and I'll lay my machete flat between the two halves and you tell which half you want, that next to the edge or that next to the back. Fair enough, Bone Man?"

"Fair enough, compadre."

So they had dinner together. And a mighty jolly dinner it was, with much clever talking on the part of the guest and with much laughter on the side of the host.

"You know, compadre," Macario presently said, "'at first I was slightly upset because you didn't fit in the picture of you I had in my mind. That box of mahogany with the clock in it, which you carry hanging from your belt, confused me quite a bit and made it hard for me to recognize you promptly. What has become of your hourglass, if it isn't a secret to know?"

"No secret at all, no secret at all. You may tell the world if it itches you to do so. You see, it was like this. There was a big battle in full swing somewhere around Europe, which is the fattest spot on earth for me next to China. And I tell you, compadre, that battle kept me on the run as if I were still a youngster. Hither and thither I had to dart-until I nearly went mad and was exhausted entirely. So, naturally, I could not take proper care of myself as I usually do to keep me fit. Well, it seems a British cannon ball fired in the wrong direction by a half-drunken limey smashed my cherished hourglass so completely that it could not be mended again by old smith Pluto who likes doing such odd jobs. I looked around and around everywhere, but I could not buy a satisfactory new one, since they are made no longer save for decoration on mantelpieces and, like all such silly knick-knacks, useless. I tried to swipe one in museums, but to my horror I discovered that they were all fakes, not a genuine instrument among them."

A chunk of tender white meat which he chewed at this instant let him forget his story for a while. Remembering that he had started to tell something without finishing it, he now asked: "Oh, well, where was I with my tale, compadre?"

"The hourglasses in all the museums were all fakes wherever you went to try one out."

"Right. Yes, now isn't it a pity that they build such wonderful great museums around things which are only fakes? Coming back to the point: there I was without a correctly adjusted hourglass, and many mistakes were bound to happen. Then it came to pass not long afterwards that I visited a captain sitting in his cabin of a ship that was rapidly sinking away under him and with the crew all off in boats. He, the captain I mean, having refused to leave his ship, had hoisted the Union Jack and was stubbornly sticking by his ship whatever might happen to her, as would become a loyal British captain. There he now sat in his cabin, writing up his log-book.

"When he saw me right before him, he smiled at me and said: 'Well, Mr. Bone Man — Sir, I mean, seems my time is up.' 'It is, skipper,' I confirmed, also smiling to make it easier for him and make him forget the dear ones he would leave behind. He looked at his chronometer and said: 'Please, sir, just allow me fifteen seconds more to jot down the actual time in my logbook.' 'Granted,' I answered. And he was all happiness that he could write in the correct time. Seeing him so very happy, I said: 'What about it, Cap'n, would you mind giving me your chronometer? I reckon you can spare it now since you won't have any use for it any longer, because aboard the ship you will sail from now on you won't have to worry about time at all. You see, Cap'n, as a matter of fact my hourglass was smashed by a British cannon ball fired by a drunken British gunner in the wrong direction, and so I think it only fair and just that I should have in exchange for my hourglass a British-made chronometer.' "

"Oh, so that's what you call that funny-looking little clock — a chronometer. I didn't know that," Macario broke in.

"Yes, that's what it is called," the hungry man admitted with a grin of his bared teeth. "The only difference is that a chronometer is a hundred times more exact in telling the correct time than an ordinary watch or a clock. Well, compadre, where was I?"

"You asked the ship's master for the chro . . . "

" . . . nometer. Exactly. So when I asked him to let me have that pretty timepiece he said: 'Now, you are asking for just the very thing, for it happens that this chronometer is my personal property and I can dispose of it any way it damn pleases me. If it were the company's I would have to deny you that beautiful companion of mine. It was perfectly adjusted a few days before we went on this rather eventful voyage and I can assure you, Mr. Bone Man, that you can rely on this instrument a hundred times better than on any of your old-fashioned glasses.' So I took it with me on leaving the rapidly sinking ship. And that's how I came to carry this chronometer instead of that shabby outdated hourglass I used to have in bygone days.

"And I can tell you one thing, compadre, this British-made gadget works so perfectly that, since I got hold of it, I have never yet missed a single date, whereas before that many a man for whom the coffin or the basket or an old sack had already been brought into the house, escaped me. And I tell you, compadre, escaping me is bad business for everybody concerned, and I lose a good lot of my reputation whenever something of this sort happens. But it won't happen anymore now."

So they talked, told one another jokes, dry ones and juicy ones, laughed a great deal together, and felt as jolly as old friends meeting each other after a long separation.

The Bone Man certainly liked the turkey, and he said a huge amount of good words in praise of the wife who had cooked the bird so tastily.

Entirely taken in by that excellent meal he, now and then, would become absent-minded and forget himself, and try to lick his lips which were not there with a tongue which he did not have.

But Macario understood that gesture and regarded it as a sure and unmistakable sign that his guest was satisfied and happy in his own unearthly way.

"You have had two visitors before today, or have you?" the Bone Man asked in the course of their conversation.

"True. How did you know, compadre?"

"How did I know? I have to know what is going on around the world. You see, I am the chief of the secret police of — of — well, you know the Big Boss. I am not allowed to mention His name. Did you know them — those two vistors, I mean?"

"Sure I did. What do you think I am, a heathen?"

"The first one was what we call our main trouble."

"The devil, I knew him all right," Macario said confidently. "That fellow can come to me in any disguise and I'd know him anywhere. This time he tried looking like a Charro, but smart as he thinks he is, he had made a few mistakes in dressing up, as foreigners are apt to do. So it wasn't hard for me to see that he was a counterfeit Charro."

"Why didn't you give him a small piece of your turkey then, since you knew who he was. That hop-about-the-world can do you a great deal of harm, you know."

"Not to me, compadre. I know all his tricks and he won't get me. Why should I give him part of my turkey? He had so much money that he had not pockets enough to put it in and so had to sew it outside on his pants. At the next inn he passes he can buy if he wishes a half dozen roast turkeys and a couple of young roast pigs besides. He didn't need a leg or a wing of my turkey."

"But the second vistor was — well, you know Whom I refer to. Did you recognize Him?"

"Who wouldn't? I am a Christian. I would know him anywere. I felt awfully sorry that I had to deny Him a little bite, for I could see that He was very hungry and terribly in need of some food. But who am I, poor sinner, to give our Lord a little part of my turkey. His father owns the whole world and all the birds because He made everything. He may give His Son as many roast turkeys as the Son wants to eat. What is more, our Lord, who can feed five thousand hungry people with two fishes and five ordinary loaves of bread all during the same afternoon, and satisfy their hunger and have still a few dozens of sacks full of crumbs left over — well, compadre, I thought that He Himself can feed well on just one little leaf of grass if He is really hungry. I would have considered it a grave sin giving Him a leg of my turkey. And another thing, He Who can turn water into wine just by saying so, can just as well cause that little ant walking here on the ground and picking up a tiny morsel, to turn into a roast turkey with all the fillings and trimmings and sauces known in heaven.

"Who am I, a poor woodchopper with eleven brats to feed, to humiliate our Lord by making Him accept a leg of my roast turkey touched with my unclean hands? I am a faithful son of the church, and as such I must respect the power and might and dignity of our Lord."

"That's an interesting philosophy, compadre," the Bone Man said. "I can see that your mind is strong, and that your brain functions perfectly in the direction of that human virtue which is strongly concerned with safeguarding one's property."

"I've never heard of that, compadre." Macario's face was a blank.

"The only thing that baffles me now is your attitude toward me, compadre." The Bone Man was cleaning up a wing bone with his strong teeth as he spoke. "What I would like to hear is why did you give me half of your turkey when just a few minutes before you had denied as little as a leg or a wing to the devil and also to our Lord."

"Ah," Macario exclaimed, throwing up both his hands to emphasize the exclamation. And "Ah," he said once more, "that's different; with you that's very different. For one thing, I'm a human being and I know what hunger is and how it feels to be starved. Besides, I've never heard as yet that you have any power to create or to perform miracles. You're just an obedient servant of the Supreme Judge. Nor have you any money to buy food with, for you have no pockets in your clothes. It's true I had the heart to deny my wife a bite of that turkey which she prepared for me with all her love put in for extra spices. I had the heart because, lean as she is, she doesn't look one tenth as hungry as you do. I was able to put up enough will power to decline my poor children, always crying for food, a few morsels of my roast turkey. Yet, no matter how hungry my children are, none of them looks one hundredth as hungry as you do."

"Now, compadre, come, come. Don't try and sell me that," the dinner guest clattered, making visible efforts to smile. "Out with the truth. I can bear it. You said, 'For one thing' when you started explaining. Now tell me the other thing as well. I can stand the truth."

"All right then," Macario said quietly. "You see, compadre, I realized the very moment I saw you standing before me that I would not have any time left to eat as little as one leg, let alone the whole turkey. So I said to myself, as long as he eats too, I will be able to eat, and so I made it fifty-fifty."

The visitor turned his deep eyeholes in great surprise upon his host. Then he started grinning and soon he broke into a thundering laughter which sounded like heavy clubs drumming a huge empty barrel. "By the great Jupiter, compadre, you are a shrewd one, indeed you are. I cannot remember having met such a clever and quick-witted man for a long time. You deserve, you truly and verily deserve to be selected by me for a little service, a little service which will make my lonely existence now and then less boresome to me. You see, compadre, I like playing jokes on men now and then as my mood will have it. Jokes that don't hurt anybody, and they amuse me and help me to feel that my job is, somehow, less unproductive, if you know what I mean."

"I guess I know how you mean it."

"Do you know what I am going to do so as to pay honestly for the dinner you offered me?"

"What, compadre? Oh, please, sir, your lordship, don't make me your assistant. Not that, please, anything else you wish, but not your helper."

"I don't need an assistant and I have never had one. No, I have another idea. I shall make you a doctor, a great doctor who will outwit all those haughty learned physicians and super-specialists who are always playing their nasty little tricks with the idea that they can put one over on me. That's what I am going to do: make you a doctor. And I promise you that your roast turkey shall be paid for a millionfold."

Speaking thus he rose, walked some twenty feet away, looked searchingly at the ground, at that time of the year dry and sandy, and called back: "Compadre, bring your *guaje* bottle over here. Yes, I mean that bottle of yours which looks as though it were of some strange variety of pumpkin. But first pour out all the water which is still in it."

Macario obeyed and came close to where his guest waited for him. The visitor spat seven times upon the dry ground, remained quiet for a few minutes and then, all of a sudden, crystal-clear water sputtered out of that sandy soil.

"Hand me your bottle," the Bone Man said.

He knelt down by the little pool just forming and with one hand spooned up the water and poured it into Macario's *guaje* bottle. This procedure took quite some time, for the mouth of the bottle was extremely small.

When the bottle, which held about a quart, was full, the Bone Man, still kneeling by the pool, tapped the soil with one hand and the water immediately disappeared from view.

"Let's go back to our eating place, compadre," the visitor suggested.

Once more they sat down together. The Bone Man handed Macario the bottle. "This liquid in your bottle will make you the greatest doctor known in the present century. One drop of this fluid will cure any sickness, and I include any sickness known as a fatal and as an incurable one. But mind, and mind well, compadre, once the last drop is gone, there will be no more of that medicine and your curing power will exist no longer."

Macario was not at all excited over that great gift. "I don't know if I should take that present from you. You see, compadre, I've been happy in my own way. True it is that I've been hungry always all through my life; always I've been tired, always been struggling with no end in view. Yet that's the way with people in my position. We accept that life because it was given us. It's for that reason that we feel happy in our way — because we always try making the best of something very bad and apparently hopeless. This turkey we ate together today has been the very peak of my life's ambition. I never wanted to go up higher in all my desires than to have one roast turkey with all the trimmings and fillings all for myself, and be allowed to eat it in peace and all alone with no hungry children's eyes counting every little bite going into my hungry stomach."

"That's just why. You didn't have your roast turkey all by yourself. You gave me half of it, and so your life's ambition is still not accomplished."

"You know, compadre, that I had no choice in that matter."

"I suppose you are right. Anyway, whatever the reason, your one and only desire in this world has not yet been satisfied. You must admit that. So, if you wish to buy another turkey without waiting for it another fifteen or twenty years, you will have to cure somebody to get the money with which to buy that turkey."

"I never thought of that," Macario muttered, as if speaking to himself. "I surely must have a whole roast turkey all for myself, come what may, or I'll die a most unhappy man."

"Of course, compadre, there are a few more things which you ought to know before we part for a while."

"Yes, what is it, tell me."

"Wherever you are called to a patient you will see me there also."

On hearing that, unprepared as he was for the catch, Macario got the shivers.

"Don't get frightened, compadre, no one else will see me; and mind you well what I am going to tell you now. If you see me standing at your patient's feet, just put one drop of your medicine into a cup or glass of fresh water, make him drink it, and before two days are gone he will be all right again, sane and sound for a good long time to come."

"I understand," Macario nodded pensively.

"But if," the Bone Man continued, "you see me standing at your patient's head, do not use the medicine; for if you see me standing thus, he will die no matter what you do and regardless of how many brilliant doctors attempt to snatch him away from me. In that case do not use the medicine I gave you because it will be wasted and be only a loss to you. You must realize, compadre, that this divine power to select the one that has to leave the world — while some other, be he old or a scoundrel, shall continue on earth — this power of selection I cannot transfer to a human being who may err or become corrupt. That's why the final decision in each particular case must remain with me, and you must obey and respect my selection."

"I won't forget that, sir," Macario answered.

"You had better not. Well, now, compadre, let us say good-bye. The dinner was excellent, exquisite I should call it, if you understand that word. I must admit, and I admit it with great pleasure, that I have had an enjoyable time in your company. By all means, that dinner you gave me will restore my strength for another hundred years. Would that when my need for another meal is as urgent as it was today, I may find as generous a host as you have been. Much obliged, compadre. A thousand thanks. Good-bye."

"Good-bye, compadre."

Macario spoke as though he were waking from a heavy dream, yet immediately he realized that he had not been dreaming.

Before him on the ground were the well-picked bones of that half turkey which his guest had eaten with so much delight.

Mechanically he cleaned up all the morsels which had dropped and stuffed them into his mouth, so that nothing should be wasted, all the while trying to find the meaning of the several adventures that were crammed into the limited space of his mind.

The thing most difficult for him to understand was how it had been possible for him to talk so much and talk what he believed was very clever as, in his opinion, only a learned man could do. But then he knew that when in the woods he always had very clever thoughts; only at home in the presence of his wife and children he had no thoughts whatever and his mouth was as if glued and it cost him much labor to get out of it one full sentence.

Soon he got tired and presently lay down under a tree to sleep the rest of the day, as he had promised himself that he would after his holiday dinner.

No fuel did he bring back that night.

His wife had not a red cent in the house with which to buy food the next day.

Yet she did not reproach him for having been lazy, as in fact she never criticized anything he did or did not. The truth was she felt immensely happy to be alive. For, during the day, and about noon, when she was busy in the yard washing the children's rags, a strange golden ray which, so it appeared, came not from the sun, but from an unknown source, had touched her whole body, while at the same time she had heard inside her heart a sweet music as if played by a huge organ from far, far above the earth.

From that moment on and all the whole day she had felt as though lifted from the ground, and her mind had been at peace as she could not remember having ever felt before. Nothing of this phenomenon did she tell her husband. She kept it to herself like a very sacred property all her own.

When she served supper there was still some reflection of that golden ray visible on her face.

Even her husband noted it on giving her a casual glance. But he said nothing, for he was still heavily occupied with his own fortunes of the day.

Before he went to sleep that night, later than usual, for he had slept well during the day out in the woods, his wife asked him timidly: "How was the turkey, dear husband?"

"What do you think was the matter with it since you ask me how it was? What do you mean? Was there something wrong with it? It was quite all right as far as I could judge, with the little experience I've had eating roast turkey."

With not a single word did he mention his visitors.

When he had turned about to go to his cot, she looked at him, watching his face sidewise and thoughtfully. Something was new in him, something had come over him. Never before had he talked that much to her at one breath.

Next day was a hungry one for the whole family. Their breakfast, including that of Macario's, was always lean. Yet this morning his wife had to make it smaller still, for it had to be stretched into two more meals.

Soon Marcario was through with the few mouthfuls of black beans seasoned with green chile and a pot of *atole* for a drink. Complain he did not because he realized that the blame was on him.

He took up his machete, his ax and his ropes and stepped out into the misty morning.

Considering the way he went about his usual hard task of chopping wood, he might as well have forgotten about the precious medicine and all that went with it.

Only a few paces had he gone when his wife called after him: "Husband, your water bottle."

This reminded him like a flash that the whole adventure of the day before might after all not have been a dream but reality. Last night, on thinking of the happenings, he had reached the conclusion that it might have been but sort of an imagination caused by a stomach not used to being filled up by a half roast turkey.

"It's still full of water," the wife said, bringing the *guaje* bottle out and shaking it. "Shall I pour the old water out and put in fresh water?" she asked, while playing with the cork cut from a corn cob.

"Yes, I know, woman, it's still full," Macario answered, not a bit afraid that his wife might be too hasty and spill the miraculous liquid away. "Yesterday I drank from the little brook. Just give me the bottle full as it is. The water is good; I got it out there in the woods."

On his way to work and some fair distance away from his hut which was the last at this side of the village, he hid the bottle in the dense brushes, partly covering it with soil.

That night he brought home one of the biggest loads of heavy fine dry fuel such as he had not delivered for many months. It was sold at three bits, a price unheard of, and was sold that same night on the first call the older boy made. So the family felt like having come into a million.

Next day Macario went about his job as usual.

On the night before he had told his wife casually that he had broken his *guaje* bottle because a heavy trunk had dropped upon it, and she had to give him another one of the several they kept in the house. These bottles cost them nothing, for the older boys discovered them growing wild in the bush somewhere.

Again he brought home that night a good load of chopped wood, yet this time he found his family in a pitiful distress.

His wife, her face swollen, her eyes red from long crying, rushed at him the moment he came in. "Reginito is dying, my poor little baby, Regino, will be gone in a half hour," and she broke into a heartbreaking lamentation, tears streaming down her face.

Helplessly and stupidly he looked at her the way he always looked if something in the house happened which was out of the gloomy routine by which this home of his was run. When his wife stepped aside, he noted that there were present several neighbors, all women, partly standing, partly squatting close to the cot on which the child had been bedded.

His was the poorest family in the village, yet they were among the best liked for their questions, their honesty, their modesty, and because of that unearned virtue that the poor are always liked better than the rich anywhere and by everybody.

Those women, in their neighborly zeal to help the so very poor Macario, and on hearing of the child's being sick, had brought with them all sorts of herbs, roots, bits of bark as used by the villagers in cases of sickness. The village had no doctor and no drug store and for that reason, perhaps, it also had no undertaker.

Every woman had brought a different kind of medicinal herb or remedy. And every one of the women made a different suggestion as to what should be done to save the child. For hours that little creature had been tortured with scores of different treatments and had been given teas brewed from roots, herbs and ground snakebones mixed with a powder obtained from charred toads.

"He ate too much," one woman said, seeing his father coming to the child's bed.

"His bowels are all twisted up, there's no help," another one corrected the first one.

"Wrong, compadre, it's an infection of the stomach, he is done for."

The one next to her observed: "We've done everything possible, he can't live another hour. One of our kids died the same way. I know it. I can see by his little shrunken face that he is winged already for his flight to heaven, little angel, poor little angel." She broke into a loud sob.

Not in the least minding the women's chatter, Macario looked at his little son whom he seemed to love best of all as he was the youngest of the bunch. He liked his innocent smile and felt happy in his way when the little tyke would now and then sit on his lap for a few minutes and play with his tiny fingers upon the man's face. Often it occurred to Macario that the only reason for being alive rested with the fact that there always would be a little baby around the house, smiling at him innocently and beating his nose and cheeks with his little fists.

The child was dying; no doubt of that. The mirror held by a woman before the baby's mouth showed no mark of breath. His heartbeat could practically no longer be noted by one or the other woman who would press her ear upon the child's chest.

The father stood there and gazed at his baby without knowing whether he ought to step closer still and touch the little face or remain where he was, or say something to his wife or to one of the other women, or talk to the children who were timidly crowded into one corner of the room where they all sat as if they were guilty of the baby's misfortune. They had had no dinner and they felt sure there would be no supper tonight as their mother was in a horrible state of mind.

Macario turned slowly about, walked to the door and went out into the darkness of the night.

Not knowing what to do or where to go since his home was all in a turmoil, tired as he was from his very hard day's labor, and feeling as though he were to sink down on his knees, he took, as if automatically, the path which led to the woods — his realm where he was sure to find the quiet of which he was so badly in need.

Arriving at the spot where, in the early morning, he had buried the *guaje* bottle, he stopped, searched for the exact place, took out the bottle, and quickly as he had not moved in many years, ran back to his hut.

"Give me a cup filled with fresh clean water," he ordered in a loud and determined voice on opening the door.

His wife hurried as if given new hope, and in a few seconds she brought an earthen cup of water.

"Now, folks, you leave the room. Get out of here, all of you, and leave me alone with that son of mine. I'll see what I can do about it."

"No use, Macario, can't you see he has only a few minutes left? You'd better kneel down and say the prayers with us while he is breathing his last, so that his soul may be saved," one of the women told him.

"You heard what I said and you do as you've been advised," he said, sharply cutting off any further protest.

Never before had his wife heard him speak in such a harsh, commanding manner. Almost afraid of him, she urged the women out of the hut.

They were all gone.

Macario closed the door behind them, turned to the cot, and when he looked up he saw his bony dinner guest standing opposite him, the cot with the child in it between the two.

The visitor stared at him out of his deep dark holes he had for eyes, hesitated, shrugged, and slowly, as though still weighing his decision, moved toward the baby's feet, remaining there for the next few seconds while the father poured a generous dose of the medicine into the cup filled with water.

Seeing his partner shaking his head in disapproval, Macario remembered that only one drop would have sufficed for the cure. Yet, it was too late now, and the liquid could not be returned to the bottle, for it was already mixed with fresh water.

Macario lifted the baby's head, forced the little mouth open and let the drink trickle into it, taking care that nothing was spilled. To his great joy he noted that the baby, once his mouth had been moistened, started to swallow voluntarily. Soon he had taken the whole to its last drop.

Hardly could the medicine have reached his stomach when the child began to breathe freely. Color returned slowly but visibly to his pale face, and he moved his head in search of better comfort.

The father waited a few minutes longer, and seeing that the baby was recovering miraculously fast, he called in his wife.

Only one look did the mother give her baby when she fell to her knees by the cot and cried out loud: "Glory be to God and the Holy Virgin. I thank you, my Lord in Heaven; my little baby will live."

Hearing the mother's excited outburst, all the women who had been waiting outdoors rushed in, and seeing what had happened while the father had been alone with his son they crossed themselves, gasped and stared at Macario as if noting his existence for the first time and as though he were a stranger in the house.

One hour later the whole village was assembled at Macario's to see with their own eyes whether it was true what the women, running about the village, were telling the people.

The baby, his cheeks rosy, his little fists pressed close to his chin, was profoundly asleep, and anybody could see that all danger was past.

Next morning Macario got up at his usual time, sat down at the table for his breakfast, looked for his machete, ax and ropes and, taciturn as always, left home to go out to the woods and there chop fuel for the villagers. The bottle with the medicine he took along with him and buried at the same spot from which he had taken it the night before.

So he went about his job for the next six weeks when one night, on returning home, he found Ramiro waiting for him. Ramiro asked him, please, to come around to his place and see what he might do about his wife who had been sick for several days and was now sinking fast.

Ramiro, the principal storekeeper and merchant of the whole community and the richest man in the municipality, explained that he had heard of Macario's curing powers and that he would like him to try his talents on his young wife.

"Fetch me a little bottle, a very little glass bottle from your store. I'll wait for you here and think over what I perhaps could do for your wife."

Ramiro brought the bottle, a medicine bottle, holding one ounce of fluid.

"What are you going to do with the bottle, Macario?"

"Leave that to me, Ramiro. You just go home and wait for me. I have to see your wife first before I can say whether or not I can save her. She'll hold on all right until I come, don't worry over that. In the meantime, I will go out in the fields and look for some herbs which I know to be good medicine."

He went into the night, searched for his bottle, filled the little crystal flask half full with the precious liquid, buried the bottle again and walked to Ramiro's who lived in one of the three one-story brick houses the village boasted.

He found the woman rapidly nearing her end, and she was as close to it as had been his little son.

Ramiro looked at Macario's eyes. Macario shrugged for an answer. After a while he said: "You'd better go out now and leave me alone with your wife."

Ramiro obeyed. Yet, extremely jealous of his young and very pretty wife, pretty even now when near her death, he peeped through a hole in the door to watch Macario's doings.

Macario, already close to the door, turned abruptly with the intention to ask for a glass of fresh water.

Ramiro, his eyes still pressed to the door, was not quick enough in getting away and so, when Macario, by a resolute pull, opened the door, Ramiro fell full length into the room.

"Not very decent of you, Ramiro," Macario said, comprehending what the jealous man had been about. "Just for that I should decline giving your young wife back to you. You don't deserve her, you know that, don't you?"

He stopped in great surprise.

He could not understand himself what had come over him this very minute. Why he, the poorest and humblest man in the village, a common woodchopper, had dared to speak to the haughtiest and richest man, the millionaire of the village, in a manner which the judge at the county court would hardly have risked. But seeing Ramiro, that mighty and powerful man, standing before him humiliated and with the gesture of a beggar trembling with fear that Macario might refuse to heal his wife, Macario had suddenly become aware that he had become a great power himself, a great doctor of whom that arrogant Ramiro expected miracles.

Very humble now, Ramiro begged Macario's forgiveness for having spied upon him, and in the most pitiful way he pleaded with him to save his wife, who was about to give him his first child in less than four months.

"How much would you ask for giving her back to me sane and healthy like she was before?"

"I do not sell my medicine for prices, I do not set prices. It's you, Ramiro, who have to make the price. Only you can know what your wife is worth to you. So name the price yourself."

"Would ten doubloons do, my dear good Macario?"

"That's what your wife is worth to you? Only ten doubloons?"

"Don't take it that way, dear Macario. Of course she means far more to me than all my money. Money I can make again any day that God will allow me to live. But once my wife is gone where would I find another one like her? Not in this world. I'll make it one hundred doubloons then, only please, save her."

Macario knew Ramiro well, only too well did he know him. Both had been born and raised in that village. Ramiro was the son of the richest merchant of the village as he himself was the richest man today — whereas Macario was the son of the poorest day laborer in the community as he himself was now the poorest woodchopper with the biggest family of the whole village to support. And as he knew Ramiro so very well, nobody would have to tell him that, once the merchant's wife was cured, her husband would try to chisel down on the one hundred doubloons as much as he possibly could and if Macario did not yield there would be a long and nasty fight between the two men for many years to come.

Realizing all that, Macario now said: "I'll take the ten doubloons which you offered me first."

"Oh, thank you, Macario, I thank you, indeed I do, and not for cutting down on the price but that you're willing to cure her. I shall never forget what you have done for us, I'm sure, I shall never forget it. I only hope that the unborn will be safe also."

"It surely will," Macario said, assured of his success since he had seen his bony dinner companion standing where he liked best to see him.

"Now, bring me a glass of fresh water," he told Ramiro.

The water was brought and Macario counseled the merchant: "Don't you dare peep in again for, mind you, if you do I might fail and it will be all your fault. So remember, no spying, no peeping. Now, leave me alone with the patient."

This time Macario was extremely careful in not spending more than exactly one drop of the valuable liquid. As hard as he could he even tried to cut that one drop into two halves. By his talk with Ramiro he had suddenly understood how much his medicine was really worth if such a proud and rich man as Ramiro would humble himself before the woodchopper for no other reason than that his wife might be cured by the poor woodman's medicine.

In realizing that, he visioned what his future might be like if he would forget about his woodchopping and stick by his medicine exclusively. Naturally enough, the quintessence of that future was an unlimited supply of roast turkeys any time he wanted them.

His one-time dinner guest, seeing him cutting the one drop in half, nodded approvingly when Macario looked at him for advice.

Two days after Ramiro's wife had recovered fully, she told her husband that she was positively sure that the baby had not been hurt in the least by her sickness, as she could feel him all right.

Ramiro in his great joy handed Macario the ten gold pieces, not only without prattling over that high price but with a hundred thanks thrown in. He invited the whole Macario family to his store where everyone, husband, wife, and all the children, was allowed to take as much home as everybody could carry in his arms. Then he threw a splendid dinner to which the Macarios were invited as his guests of honor.

Macario built a real house now for his family, bought some pieces of good land and began cultivating them, because Ramiro had loaned him one hundred doubloons at very low interest.

Ramiro had done so not solely out of gratitude. He was too shrewd a businessman to loan out money without thinking of fat gains. He realized that Macario had a great future ahead of him, and that it would be a very sound investment to keep Macario in the village and make people come here to see him, rather than have him take up his residence in a city. The more visitors the village would have on account of Macario's fame, the more important would grow Ramiro's business. In expectation of this development in the village's future, Ramiro added to his various lines in business that of banking.

He gambled fast on Macario and he won. He won far beyond his most fantastic dreams.

It was he who did all the advertising and all the propaganda to draw attention to Macario's great gift. Hardly had he sent out a few letters to business friends in the city, than sick people flocked to the village in the hope of being cured of their maladies, many having been declared uncurable by learned physicians.

Soon Macario could build himself a mansion. He bought up all the land around and converted it into gardens and parks. His children were sent to schools and universities as far as Paris and Salamanca.

As his one-time dinner guest had promised him, so it came to pass. Macario's half turkey was paid for a millionfold.

Regardless of his riches and his fame, Macario remained honest and uncorrupted. Anyone who wanted to be cured was asked how much his health was worth to him. And as Macario had done in his first case, so he did ever after in all other cases — that is, the patients or their relatives would decide the price.

A poor man or woman who had no more to offer than one silver peso or a pig or a rooster, he would heal just as well as the rich who, in many instances, had made prices as high as twenty thousand doubloons. He cured men and women of the highest nobility, many of whom had crossed the ocean and had come from Spain, Italy, Portugal, France and other countries and who had come for no other reason than to see him and consult him.

Whoever came to consult him would be told frankly that he could do nothing to save him, if Macario saw the Bone Man stand at the patient's head. Nothing did he charge for that consultation.

People, whoever they were, accepted his final verdict without discussion. No longer would they try arguing with him, once he had told them that they were beyond help.

More or less half the people consulting him were saved; the other half claimed by his partner. It happened often for weeks at a time that he would not meet one patient whom he could cure, because his dinner guest would decide differently. Such weeks the people in the land called "his low-power periods."

While at the beginning of his practice he was able to cut a drop of his precious medicine into two, he soon learned to cut each drop into eight. He acquired all devices known then by which a drop might be divided up into practically an infinite number of mites. Yet, no matter how much he cut and divided, regardless of how cleverly he administered each dose to make it as small as possible and yet retain its effectiveness, the medicine had frightfully fast become scarcer and scarcer.

He had drained the *guaje* bottle during the first month of his practice, once he had observed the true value of the liquid. He knew that a *guaje* bottle will not only soak into its walls a certain amount of any fluid it may hold, but worse, the liquid will evaporate, and rather fast, through the bottle's walls. It is for that reason that water kept in a *guaje* bottle of the kind natives use will stay always cool even should the day be very hot.

So he had taken out the medicine and poured it into bottles of dark glass, tightly sealed.

The last little bottle had been opened months ago, and one day Macario noted to his horror that there were only about two drops left. Consequently, he decided to make it known that he would retire from practice and cure nobody any longer.

By now he had become really old and felt that he had a right to spend the last few years of his life in peace.

These last two drops he meant to keep for members of his family exclusively, and especially for his beloved wife, whom he had had to cure already two times during the last ten years and whom he was afraid he might lose — a loss which would be very difficult for him to bear.

Just about that same time it so happened that the eight-year-old son of the viceroy, don Juan Marquez de Casafuerte, the highest personage of New Spain, fell sick.

The best doctors were called for help. None could do anything for the boy. The doctors admitted frankly that this boy had been stricken by a sickness not known to medical science.

The viceroy had heard of Macario. Who hadn't? But he owed

it to his dignity, education and high social and political position to consider Macario a quack, the more so since he was called thus by every doctor who had a title from an accredited university.

The child's mother, however, less given to dignity when the life of her son was at stake, made life for the viceroy so miserable that finally he saw no other way out of his dilemma than to send for Macario.

Macario disliked traveling and rarely left his village, and then only for short trips. Yet, an order given by the viceroy himself had to be obeyed under penalty of death.

So he had to go.

Brought before the viceroy he was told what was expected of him.

The viceroy, still not believing in the so-called miracles which Macario was said to have performed, spoke to him in the same way as he would have spoken to any native woodchopper.

"It was not I who called you, understand that, my good man, Her Highness, la Marquesa, insisted on bringing you here to save our son whom, so it appears, no learned medico can cure. I make it quite clear to you that in case you actually save our child, one fourth of the fortune which I hold here in New Spain shall be yours. Besides, you may ask anything you see here in my palace, whatever it is that catches your fancy and whatever its value. That will be yours also. Apart from all that, I personally will hand you a license which will entitle you to practice medicine anywhere in New Spain with the same rights and privileges as any learned medico, and you shall be given a special letter with my seal on it which will give you immunity for life against any arrest by police or soldiers, and which will safeguard you against any unjustified court action. I believe, my good man, that this is a royal payment for your service."

Macario nodded, yet said nothing.

The viceroy went on: "What I promised you in the case that you save our son follows exactly the suggestions made by Her Highness, la Marquesa, my wife, and what I promise I always keep."

The Marques stopped for a few seconds, as if waiting for Macario to say something.

Macario, however, said nothing and made no gesture.

"But now, listen to my own suggestions," the viceroy continued.

"If you should fail to save our son, I shall hand you over to the High Court of the Inquisition, charging you with the practice of witchcraft under pact with the devil, and you shall be burned alive at the stake on the Alameda and in public."

Again the viceroy stopped to see what expression his threat had made upon Macario.

Macario paled, but still said nothing.

"Have you understood in full what I have said?"

"I have, Your Highness," Macario said briefly, trembling slightly as he attempted to make an awkward bow.

"Now, I personally shall show you to our sick child. Follow me."

They entered the boy's room where two nurses were in attendance, merely watching the child's slow decline, unable to do anything save keep him comfortable. His mother was not present. She had, by the doctor's order, been confined to her room as she was close to a complete breakdown.

The boy was resting in a bed becoming his age, a light bed made of fine wood, though not looking rich.

Macario went close and looked around for a sign of his dinner guest.

Slightly, so as not to make his gesture seem suspicious, he touched a special little pocket in his trousers to be sure he had the crystal flask with the last two drops of medicine about him.

Now he said: "Will you, Your Highness, I pray, leave this room for one hour, and will Your Highness, please, give orders that everybody else will leave, too, so that I may remain alone with the young patient?"

The Marques hesitated, evidently being afraid that this ignorant peasant might do his son some harm if left alone with him.

Macario, noting that expression of uneasiness shown by the viceroy, recalled, at this very instant, his first cure of a patient not of his own family, that is, Ramiro's young wife in his native village. Ramiro had hesitated in a similar way when told to leave the room and let Macario alone with the young woman in bed.

These two cases of hesitation had been the only ones he had ever experienced during his long practice. And Macario wondered whether that might carry some significance in his destiny, that perhaps today, with only two little drops of his medicine left, he beheld the same expression of hesitancy in a person who wanted a great service done but did not trust the man who was the only one who could render that service.

He was now alone with the boy.

And suddenly there appeared his partner, taking his stand at the boy's head.

The two, Macario and the Bone Man, had never again spoken one to the other since they had had a turkey dinner together. Whenever they would meet in a sick room, they would only look at each other, yet not speak.

Macario had never asked of his partner any special favor. Never had he claimed from him any individual whom the Bone Man had decided to take. He even had let go two grandchildren of his without arguing his dinner guest's first claim.

This time everything was different. He would be burned alive at the stake as a witch doctor convicted of having signed a pact with the devil. His children, now all of them in highly honored positions, would fall into disgrace, because their father had been condemned by the Holy Inquisition to suffer the most infamous death a Christian could die. All his fortune and all his landed property, which he had meant to leave to his children and grandchildren, would be confiscated and given to the church. He did not mind losing his fortune. It had never meant much to him personally anyhow.

What he did mind above all was the happiness of his children. But more still than of his children he was, in this most terrible moment of his whole life, thinking of his beloved wife.

She would go crazy with grief on learning what had happened to him in that strange, vast city so far away from home, and she would be unable to come to his aid or even comfort him during his last hours on earth. It was for her sake, not for his own, that this time he decided to fight it out with the Bone Man.

"Give me that child," he pleaded, "give him to me for old friendship's sake. I've never asked any favor of you, not one little favor for the half turkey you ate with so much gusto when you needed a good dinner more than anything else. You gave me voluntarily what I had not asked you for. Give me that boy, and I'll pour out the last drop of your medicine and break the bottle, so that not even one little wet spot be left inside to be used for another cure. Please, oh please, give me that boy. It isn't for my sake that I ask you this. It is for my dear, faithful, loyal and beloved wife's. You know, or at least you can imagine, what it means for a Christian family if one of its members is burned at the stake alive and in public. Please, let me have the boy. I shall not take or touch the riches offered me for curing him. You found me a poor man and I was happy then in my own way. I don't mind being poor again, as I used to be. I'm willing to chop wood again for the villagers as I did when we met for the first time. Only, please, I pray, give me that boy."

The Bone Man looked at him with his deep black holes for a long time. If he had a heart he was questioning it at this moment. Now he looked down before him as though he were deliberating this case from every angle to find the most perfect solution. Obviously his orders were to take the child away. He could not express his thoughts by his eyes or his face, yet his gestures clearly showed his willingness to help a friend in dire need, for by his attitude he tried to explain that, in this particular case, he was powerless to discover a way out which would meet halfway the problems of both.

Again, for a very long while, his look rested upon the boy as though judging more carefully still Macario's plea against the child's fate, destined before he was born.

And again he looked at Macario as if pitying him and as though he felt deeply distressed.

Presently he shook his head slowly as might someone in great sadness who finds himself utterly helpless in a desperate situation.

He opened his fleshless jaws, and with a voice that sounded like heavy wooden sticks clubbed on a board he said: "I am sorry, compadre, very sorry, but in this case I can do nothing to help you out of that uncomfortable pool you have been put into. All I can say is that in few of my cases I have felt sadder than in this, believe me, compadre. I can't help it, I must take that boy."

"No, you mustn't. You mustn't. Do you hear me, you must not take that child." Macario yelled in great despair. "You must not, you cannot take him. I won't let you."

The Bone Man shook his head again, but said nothing.

And now, with a resolute jerk, Macario grabbed the boy's bed and quickly turned it round so that his partner found himself standing at the boy's feet.

Immediately the Bone Man vanished from sight for two short seconds and, like a flash, appeared at the boy's head once more.

Quickly Macario again turned the bed so that the Bone Man would stand at the feet, and again the Bone Man disappeared from the child's feet and stood at the head.

Macario, wild with madness, turned the bed round and round as if it were a wheel. Yet, whenever he stopped for taking a breath, he would see his dinner guest standing at the boy's head, and Macario would start his crazy game again by which he thought that he might cheat the claimant out of his chosen subject.

It was too much for the old man, turning that bed round and round without gaining more than two second from eternity.

If, so he thought, he could stretch these two seconds into twenty hours only and leave the capital under the viceroy's impression that the boy was cured, he might escape that horrible punishment which he had been condemned to suffer.

He was so tired now that he could not turn the bed once more. Touching, as if by a certain impulse, the little pocket in his trousers, he discovered that the crystal flask with the last two drops of the precious medicine in it had been smashed during his wild play with the bed.

Fully realizing that loss and its significance, he felt as if he had been drained of the last spark of his life's energy and that his whole life had become empty.

Vaguely, he gazed about the room as though coming out of a trance in which he had been for an uncountable number of years, centuries perhaps. He recognized that his fate was upon him and that it would be useless to fight against it any longer.

So, letting his eyes wander around the whole room, they came to touch the boy's face and he found the boy gone.

As if felled he dropped to the floor, entirely exhausted.

Lying there motionless, he heard his one-time dinner guest speaking to him, softly this time.

He heard him say: "Once more, compadre, I thank you for the half turkey which you so generously gave me and which restored my strength, then waning, for another hundred years of tedious labor. It certainly was exquisite, if you understand that word. But now, coming to where we are at this hour, see, compadre, I have no power to save you from being burned at the stake on the Alameda and in public, because that is beyond my jurisdiction. Yet, I can save you from being burned alive and from being publicly defamed. And this, compadre, I shall do for old friendship's sake, and because you have always played fair and never tried to cheat me. A royal payment you received and you honored it like a royal payment. You have lived a very great man. Good-bye, compadre."

Macario opened his eyes and, on looking backwards, he saw his one-time dinner guest standing at his head.

Macario's wife, greatly worried over her husband's not coming home, called all the men of the village next morning to help her find Macario, who might be hurt somewhere deep in the woods and unable to return without help.

After several hours of searching, he was discovered at the densest part of the woods in a section far away from the village, so far that nobody would ever dare go there alone.

He was sitting on the ground, his body comfortably snuggled in the hollow of a huge tree trunk, dead, a big beautiful smile all over his face.

Before him on the ground banana leaves were spread out, serving as a table-cloth, and on them were lying the carefully cleaned bones of a half turkey.

Directly opposite, separated by a space of about three feet, there also were, in a like manner, banana leaves spread on which the very clean bones of the other half turkey were piled up in a meticulous fashion, which could only have been done by somebody who had enjoyed his meal with the profoundest of delight and the very greatest of satisfaction.

Looking at these two piles of cleaned turkey bones, Macario's wife, thick tears welling out of her sad eyes, said: "I wonder — I just wonder who he had for dinner. Whoever he was, he must have been a fine and noble and very gentle person, or Macario wouldn't have died so very, very happy."

(From The Virginia Quarterly Review)

THE MAN IN GRAY

BY CHRISTINE WESTON

*I*N *INDIA* almost every one believes in ghosts. The heat may
have something to do with it, making people imaginative
or merely credulous in a special sort of way, or it could be
that they just enjoy frightening themselves, or being frightened.
I do know that all the time I was growing up in India the supernatural played an important part in my life and in my family's.
We were always hearing stories about haunted dāk bungalows,
sounds, voices, presences that were never explained, and that were
not meant to be explained. My parents, really quite normal people,
used to keep us entranced for hours with tales of old forts and
deserted barracks in various parts of India, where on certain his-
toric anniversaries drums were heard and sounds of battle reported
by the native villagers who lived near by. There was a house in
Monghyr, in the Province of Bihar, where some vague relative of
ours had died of hydrophobia many years before, and the neighbors swore that on hot summer nights sounds were sometimes heard
coming from the room where she had died — the choking, gurgling
noises which are said to accompany the last phase of the disease.

The stories, however, were not confined to human ghosts. An
English friend told us about a dog of his named Hubert, which
had died of distemper, and whose spirit haunted his house for
months afterwards. He used to wake at night and feel the dog's
weight lying at the foot of his bed; and when he spoke to it, it would
wag its tail in response. The odd part of this story was that the
owner never saw this ghostly pup, he merely heard it, but his

servants declared that they had seen it, and the cook even went so far as to set out scraps of food as a propitiatory gesture to the unquiet soul.

In the summer of 1915 we were living in a place called Aligarh, a civil station in what used to be the United Provinces of India, and which is now known as Uttar Pradesh. My brother and I had made friends with a young Hindu boy named Arun, whose father was a barrister, a highly educated man and a great friend of my father's. One evening when our parents were dining out Arun came to see us, as he often did at this hour. We played checkers, teased the servants, practiced on my father's typewriter, which we were forbidden to do, and then started telling each other stories. Naturally the subject turned to ghosts, and we trotted out the old favorites about ancient battlefields, the remote relative in Monghyr, and Hubert the dog. Arun had a few of his own, and when we had listened to these with undimmed and undimmable pleasure, he asked whether we had ever seen a churel. I had better explain that a churel is the spirit of a woman who has died in childbirth, and that she is unlike others in the pantheon of ghosts because she wears her head and her feet turned backward, and lives in the branches of a pipal tree. We had never seen a churel, nor, Arun admitted, had he, but there was a pipal tree in our garden, which might, with luck, contain one.

Our servants had retired to their quarters for a little peace and quiet and we had the place to ourselves. Arun led us into the garden which was dark with that heavy, almost ponderous darkness which falls over the Indian plains. The pipal tree was at the end of a graveled path that stretched from the verandah of our house to the well at the garden's foot, about two or three hundred yards. It was a beautiful tree and in the daytime its heavy shade and patriarchal character made it one of our favorite playgrounds. Tonight, thanks to Arun's stories, we approached it with somewhat different feelings. We were not, however, going to show any sign of nerves. Heroism after all is to a great extent an ambition to keep up with the Joneses, which in this case meant keeping up with our intrepid friend Arun.

Arrived at the foot of the tree where it was almost pitch dark, the periphery only a shade lighter, we gazed with maudlin affection towards our house, whose yellow lights seemed very feeble and far away. Arun bade us sit on the ground in a semicircle. He talked in whispers, and with the utmost respect, of the churel who might be listening overhead. What we were supposed to do was to remain quiet and wait for the churel, which, Arun said, would very likely come shinnying down the trunk of the tree, glide slowly past us, wailing and staring at us out of its backward-looking eyes, and would then vanish again into its native darkness.

Arun sat on my right-hand side, my brother on my left, and I could feel the latter shivering like a wet dog, though the night was very warm. I don't know how long we waited, but it seemed an interminable time, when suddenly I felt my brother raise his hand and point. "Look!" he squeaked.

All I can remember after that is the single concerted movement with which all three of us rose and fled, hardly touching the ground with our feet. Once back in our familiar, well-lighted house we turned to my brother and demanded what it was that he had seen. He said he didn't know. "But you must have! What did you say 'look' for, then?"

He repeated that he didn't know, and added helpfully: "It was something."

"But what did it look like?" persisted Arun. "Did it look like a churel?"

"How should I know?" my brother replied. "I've never seen a churel."

"Well then," said I, "if it wasn't a churel, what was it?"

"I tell you I don't know. It was something."

And that was all we got out of him then, or at any other time.

On leaving Aligarh we moved to a place called Hardoi, which was and still is a tiny station, and at the time we were there, in 1920, the European community numbered about a dozen souls, including ourselves. We'd heard a good deal about Hardoi, because my parents had lived there twenty years before, shortly after their marriage and while my father was employed as an officer in the Imperial Police. Anything that had to do with my parents' early life held a special interest for us, and both parents liked to talk about that time, my mother particularly. As a storyteller she could hold her own with our Indian friends, and the stories never palled though we'd heard them, God knows, over and over again. And just as these stories were a ceaseless form of entertainment, so were the places that we visited from time to time. I don't know why we moved about as we did on an average of once every two or three years, but I do know that as children we had no objection to that way of life — in fact we loved it. My mother had told us that Hardoi was a charming but rather unexciting spot, and she had described the house where we were going to live. Long before we set eyes on it, we knew it by heart, every room, every verandah, every nook and cranny and godown; and we had no sooner moved in it than we felt that we had never lived anywhere else. It was a typical old-fashioned Indian bungalow with a thatched roof, deep verandah, and high-studded, airy rooms. The garden was set in a compound which formed a rough square, one side bounded by a mango grove, another by a line of outbuildings which comprised the cookhouse and the servants' quarters, the third by a straggly hedge of cactus and lantana bushes, and the fourth by a broad graveled driveway bordered with beautiful trees.

On the day that we arrived at Hardoi and as our hired carriage was taking us from the station, my mother spoke suddenly and as it were into space. "I wonder," she said, "whether our friend is still here!"

"What friend?" we asked at once.

"You remember the one I told you about — the man in gray?"

At this point my father gave my mother a look, and the subject was dropped. Of late the ghost stories and their effects on our nerves had been getting a trifle out of hand, and it had apparently been laid down by my father that "this nonsense has got to stop." The story of the man in gray, though not one of our favorites, was none the less interesting, and more so now that we found ourselves, so to speak, in his domain.

Twenty years before, when my parents were living in this house, their servant, Akbar — he was, by the way, still with us, an old man now, with a white beard — Akbar had told my mother of a strange figure which he, and some of the other servants, had seen wandering through the rooms and the garden and even as far afield as the drive. No one had ever been able to pin a story on this ghost, though my mother had made exhaustive inquiries among the handful of English then stationed at Hardoi, and among the Indians themselves. Akbar's story was that on coming into the dining room one afternoon he had seen a Sahib dressed in a gray suit walk across the room and out the door into the drawing room. Thinking it must be a caller come to see my parents he had followed the stranger into the drawing room, but hadn't found him. Nor was he on the verandah beyond, nor in the garden. Akbar decided the man must have got on a bicycle and ridden away without being seen. A few days later, however, Akbar saw him again. This time, he told my mother, the Sahib — in the same gray suit — was strolling under the loquat trees near a corner of the house. He had his back to Akbar, who approached to ask for his card in order to carry it in to my parents. But the stranger turned the corner of the house and when Akbar got there he had disappeared. This, it seems, gave our faithful servant a real turn, and he told the other servants about it. Several of them thereupon confessed to having seen the strange Sahib themselves, and their descriptions of him tallied in every detail — a white Sahib of medium build, gray-haired, and wearing a gray suit. The odd thing about this story was that no one remembered seeing him face to face. According to report he was walking or standing with his back to the observer, nor did he ever turn his head to one side or another, and, although he seemed never to hurry, he invariably eluded his pursuers, sauntering from one room to the next, around corners, into the mango grove, or up the driveway, bound nobody knew whither, or why.

On finding ourselves in the identical house where this spirit of twenty years ago used to wander, we were naturally thrilled, and for the first few days we expected to encounter the man in gray wherever we went in the house or grounds, but we never did, and presently the rather fearful anticipation faded into the background of our minds. My father, too, was rather severe on the subject. He said that he was tired of having to get up at night in order to comfort children whose bad dreams were the result of their own silliness, and he didn't want to hear anything more about ghosts, gray-suited or any other.

There was plenty to amuse and interest us in our new surroundings — picnics, horseback rides, shooting parties, and the small European club where we used to play tennis and join the rest of the English community in the afternoons. There had been, my mother said, practically no change in the place or in the people since she and my father had lived here before. The friends were twenty years older, the trees cast a heavier shade, and some of the houses were painted white instead of blue, but aside from these insignificant details Hardoi remained almost exactly as it was in the winter and summer of the year 1900. The knowledge had, for me, a curious melancholy charm, and I thought of Hardoi as a fragment of mirror lying for ages untouched, reflecting in its small compass other fragments — an eye, a finger, a flash of color, and at night, perhaps, a single star.

One afternoon I rode home from the club on my bicycle to find that the rest of the family had gone to a friend's for tea, and the house was empty. I left my bicycle propped on the verandah steps and went into the drawing room, thence into the dining room, and saw the man in gray standing between me and the door which gave out on the back verandah and its view of the cook house and the quarters where our servants lived. For some reason I was not in the least surprised. I stood on the threshold of the drawing room and stared at a familiar gray-clad back and a head of clipped gray hair, and a pair of arms which hung easily at his sides. He stood still and seemed lost in thought. Then he walked across the verandah, down the steps, across the open space below, and into the cookhouse. I waited, and in a minute I saw Akbar come out of the cookhouse carrying a dishpan of dirty water which he emptied on the ground below the cookhouse steps. After that he stood wiping the inside of the pan with a dishrag. I left the house and went up to him and said: "Akbar, did you see him?"

"See who?"

"The man — the Sahib in the gray suit, with gray hair."

Akbar went on drying the dishpan and replied without looking at me:

"I don't know what you're talking about."

"He just this minute walked into the cookhouse, and you've just come out of it. He must be in there now."

"Then go in there," said Akbar, "and look for yourself."

"No, Akbar. You look."

At this moment Jalal, a slovenly boy of seventeen, a sort of assistant to Akbar, appeared from his quarters and Akbar told him to go into the kitchen and see who was there. Jalal looked from one to the other of us.

"I won't," he said.

"Perhaps," Akbar suggested, menacingly, "you would prefer a clout on the ear?"

"My father, I . . . "

"Go on, Jalal," I urged him. "What's the matter with you? Do as Akbar tells you."

Dragging his feet, Jalal slunk into the kitchen, and shot out of it again like a rabbit from its barrow. "There's a Sahib in there, standing before the stove, gazing into a pot of lentils!"

Akbar took my arm and together we went to the door and peered in. The kitchen was a black hole of a room with a single window set high on one wall. It was occupied almost entirely by an enormous primitive oven of unbaked brick and by the usual conglomeration of pots, pans, and old kerosene tins filled with water. A pot of lentils was cooking on top of the stove and there wasn't a soul in the place.

Akbar turned to Jalal and fetched him a smart slap on the ear.

"Liar," he said. "How dare you?"

Jalal burst into tears, and Akbar looked gravely at me. "Miss Baba," he said, with immense fatherliness, "you must stop this. If you do not, you will have bad dreams and lose your appetite and fall ill. You must stop it at once."

"Stop what? I tell you I saw that Sahib you've always talked about. I saw him with my own eyes."

"There is no such Sahib," Akbar replied, sternly.

"You dare to tell me that when you've seen him yourself?"

"It was a long time ago and if I saw him then, he must be dead by now."

"Ghosts don't die," I reminded him. "And besides, Jalal says he just saw him. Didn't you, Jalal?"

Once more, Akbar turned to Jalal who was wiping his nose on the end of another dish rag, one which would no doubt be used later to dry our dinner plates. "Son of a bitch," said Akbar to him, "did you or did you not see a gray Sahib in there a minute ago?"

"No," sniffed Jalal. "No, I didn't."

"Then why did you say you did?"

"I don't know. I thought you wanted me to."

Akbar made as if to strike him again, but Jalal bolted down the steps and into his own quarters, and I walked slowly back to the house. I did not, however go in. Instead, I sat on the veranda steps in sight of Akbar and the cookhouse, and there I stayed until the rest of my family came home.

For some reason, I didn't tell my parents of this occurrence, but I did confide it to my brother, who believed my story, as I knew he would. Although he was in most respects an extremely fearless boy, even rash in some things, I noticed that after hearing my account of seeing the man in gray, he kept pretty close to my side or to other members of the family, and seldom wandered off to play by himself, especially in the evenings and after darkness set in. Then one morning, a few days after the adventure in the cookhouse, my brother and I were in the garden and I saw the man in gray walking under the loquat trees near a corner of the house, exactly where Abkar had once reported having seen him years ago. "Look," I said to my brother, and pointed. "There he is — quick, look!"

My brother stared rigidly in the wrong direction. "Not there," I whispered fiercely, tugging at his arms. "Now he's walking up the driveway. There he goes!"

By the time I'd finally got my brother twisted in the right direction the figure in gray had disappeared and I said in disgust: "What's the matter with you? Why didn't you look where I told you to?"

"I did look," he answered. He had a lot of freckles and now they stood out on his white face like blisters. "I did look and I didn't see a thing."

"You didn't see a thing because you were in such a blue funk you *couldn't* see, that's what you mean!"

That night my brother refused to sleep in his room and insisted on going to my parents' room and crawling into their bed, where I shortly followed him. The next morning after breakfast my mother came to me with a look of stern and unconvincing determination on her pretty face. "What," she wanted to know, "*is* all this nonsense about seeing men in gray?"

"You told us yourself, lots of times, that you'd seen him. So has Akbar. So have the other servants. Even Jalal."

"Ghost stories," she told me, "are things to be listened to but not to be believed. How can you be so silly? And what *does* this creature look like? Tell me."

"I don't know what he looks like in front, but from the back he looks just the way the others say he does. All in gray, with gray hair."

She looked straight into my eyes, and I looked straight back into hers, and after a moment she said firmly that she didn't want to hear another word of such utter nonsense, and if I didn't stop it at once, my father would have to do something about it.

Time passed, as they say in books, and nothing more was said or heard about the man in gray until about a month after this conversation with my mother. Then one afternoon when my father and brother were out of the house and my mother was doing something to her hair in her own room, I walked from the drawing room into mine and saw a figure standing with its back to me, facing the small dressing room that separated my bedroom from the verandah at the rear. I think I gave some sort of small cry, for my mother came to me at once and for a bare second we looked at each other without speaking. Then I said: "He's gone into my dressing room and there are only two doors — this one, and the one that's on the verandah."

My mother's eyes were alight. "We've got him," she said. "Quick, I'll stay here and you go to the verandah door. Hurry!"

I sped through the house to the back verandah, where Akbar squatted on a blanket polishing silver. He did not look up as I passed, and neither of us exchanged a word. I pulled open my dressing room door and saw my mother standing in the bedroom where I had left her. We faced each other with the man in gray standing between us. He was standing quite still, his hands at his sides, his head erect, looking neither to one side or the other, and over his shoulder I met my mother's eyes and saw her forehead flush a little and the flush move upwards into her hair.

Then the man was gone, and she came slowly towards me, passing the tip of her tongue over her lower lip.

"There," I murmured, feeling my knees quiver. "Now you know. You saw him. What does he look like?"

"I couldn't say — he had his back to me."

"How could he have had his back to you? I demanded. "His back was towards *me!*"

"No it wasn't, it was towards me," my mother returned, and taking me by the hand, she led me out to the verandah.

"His back," I repeated doggedly, "his back was towards me."

"I don't," she replied, in a tone of voice which had always, in the past, clinched an argument between us, "I really don't see how that could have been so."

Well, she didn't at the time and she doesn't now — but then, neither do I .

(From Esquire)

THE INDOMITABLE BLUE

BY IRA WOLFERT

*W*HEN Wes Olmstead was a little boy growing up along the Susquehanna and wearing a tie on his Sunday shirt that knocked against his knees, his grandfather took him visiting to a nearby farm that sported a cock o' the walk, one of the breed called Arkansas Traveller.

The true gamecock always fights to the death, its opponent's or its own. Since it fights with knifelike spurs and each blow is a murderous one and literally dozens of them are exchanged in the wink of an eye, it is seldom that even the winner is good for anything after the affair is settled. The loser, of course, has its head cut off and is thrown to hands that will boil it for soup, and the winner frequently might be better off for the same fate. But there are lucky ones and, if a winner shows the trueness of its breeding, if it stands up to its death without turning tail or showing fear in any other way, it is permitted to live on — provided, that is, it can — and enjoy the company of hens and the peace of the barnyard.

That was what had happened to the Arkansas Traveller Wes Olmstead saw. It had had what is considered a very long career for a fighting chicken, winning in two mains and one hack fight, and then its owner decided it could not win any more and was letting it live out its crippled years in retirement.

At that time Wes had never even heard of gamecocks. He saw a runty little thing, weighing about four pounds, with a body that seemed to be built of rubber bands. Its feathers were a dirty-white in color and were of scant length and had no pride or sheen. Its comb was broken and one wing dragged almost to the ground and it had soured-up wrinkles in its wattles and one sour red eye, the other having turned milky in blindness.

But his grandfather warned Wes against playing in the barn-yard. He said a chicken like that could break a grown man's leg with one blow of a naked foot, and didn't enjoy anybody coming up to it or its hens, even to make friends. Keep away, and keep away from his lady friends, the old man said.

Wes listened solemnly, his blue eyes round and big. But as soon as his grandfather went into the house to talk business with the farmer, Wes began edging toward the barn. Grampa Fred never exaggerated, even for purposes of entertainment. However, Wes' father, who was Grampa Fred's son, always did and while Wes perhaps would not have gone so far as to test whether that little old bit of chicken could actually break his leg with one blow of its naked foot, he was eager to learn, out of loyalty to his father, whether it was true Grampa Fred never exaggerated or just never had been caught at it.

Wes was going to study the chicken carefully. Then, if the situation warranted, he would let himself into the yard and shoo the chicken out of it and chase it up to the house and past the window where Grampa was talking business, pretending it had got out by itself and he trying to get it back in. But the lad didn't get a chance to do any shooing. All he could do was study, for when he came around the barn and within sight of the poultry yard he saw a hound dog digging and shoving its way stealthily under the wire that fenced the chickens in.

The dog looked over its shoulder at Wes. But it didn't run. It let out a soft bloodcurdling snarl, and Wes stopped short. Shooing an angry chicken was one thing, but shooing an angry dog was another, and this was a big dog, a sixty-pound dog, trained down razor fine. Besides it had a burry coat, even around the head. That meant it was one of those killer dogs that lived wild in the hills, terrorizing deer and foxes and livestock and even bears. Wes stood motionless. He hoped only that the dog would not attack him. After a moment, the dog seemed satisfied that so meager a squirt as Wes was at the time could do it no harm, Perhaps it had some memory of playing with children on some farm somewhere in its puppyhood before it had taken to running wild. Anyway, it resumed digging.

Wes watched fearfully, and so did the hens. The boy had no confidence at all in what his grandfather had said. If he had dared to move, he would have run crying for help. But he didn't dare, and the hens didn't either. They huddled together and fluttered their feathers and squawks and drawls dribbled out of their mouths in a suppressed way as if they were afraid loud protests might make the dog more ferocious than it was, and the cock made no sound at all.

It was the cock that tore it for Wes, finally. The little battler, standing higher than the hens with its neck stretched but looking not nearly so burly, had placed himself in front of its womenfolks and kept its head turned so that its one sour red eye might remain fastened unblinkingly on the dog. But its beak opened now and then and its throat worked dryly and soundlessly and it looked so brave there and lorn that it broke Wes' heart. He turned and twitched desperately into the barn, hoping to find a pitchfork or a hoe that he might use to fend the dog off while shouting for Grampa and the farmer.

But he had hardly got into the barn when he was out of it. A terrible sound in the poultry yard had driven into his ears like a fist and had made him gasp and come running. The dog had squeezed itself under the wire and had stood a moment, picking out its dinner and gathering itself to spring upon it, and all the hens had wrung their feathers and squawked and screeched at once, making the sound that had brought Wes out of the barn barehanded.

The cock, however, remained silent. It ran forward with long, strong, limber leaps, and the dog lunged for it. They closed like lightning clashing. It was as dazzling as that. The dog was an experienced and successful killer. It lashed out more quickly than a snake, fang first, body flung sideways to block its victim's escape and bring its own powerfully trampling hind legs into play.

But the chicken was even faster. In the immeasurable instant

between the start of the dog's lunge and its completion, the cock
— running head-on to — had changed direction, side-stepped and
run completely around the dog and come up on its back. At one
moment Wes saw it disappearing in the dog's dripping white teeth
and the next he heard the dog's teeth click on empty air with a
shattering sound and saw the cock standing on the dog.

The cock seemed only to be standing there. It seemed only to
be fluffing itself out and flouncing a bit. But that was because its
legs were moving so fast that the human eye could no more see
them than it could see buckshot spraying from a gun. Watch the
target and you'll see the shot. Wes watched the target and saw it
twist and turn, first to the right and then to the left, and snap its
hindquarters in a wide, wild fling as one might snap a whip, and
he heard time after time the heart-catching sound of teeth clicking
on empty air.

There was no other sound. At the start, as the cock had run
forward, one of the hens had uttered a queer, drawling, almost
envious sigh and then had fallen silent and the others had remained
silent. The cock made no sound and only teeth spoke for the dog
as it strove to bite the soureyed little murderer off its back.

Then the dog howled and rolled over howling to squash the
chicken under it. It was sixty pounds against four, but where the
dog had gone over howling it came up shrieking. For trying to
squash that chicken was like trying to squash a bale of tight-wound
barbed wire with one's naked flesh.

Finally, the dog remembered the hole it had made under the
fence. It flung itself through it. The chicken, scraped off the dog's
back by the fence, rose into the air with an indignant squawk and
the dog ran shrieking on its two front legs. It could not run far.
Its hindquarters trailed after it like a rag. The cock had broken
its back.

The hens paid no attention to the dog's death agony. The
danger was over. They moved out of their cluster and began to
scratch the ground. The cock moved away from the fence. It
walked high on its legs and its milky eye stared blind and bland
and its red eye glared and it looked furious enough to speak. Finally it did speak. It let out a crow so ragged and squeaky that it
was like a child's imitation of one. It scowled about, as if to say:

Anybody else want to try? Then, as all roosters everywhere always have done, it began to search the ground for tidbits for the hens and when it found one it picked it up and dropped it and clucked in invitation and the hens came running and shoved him aside and, without a by-your-leave or a thank-you, ate the tidbit while the dog, brought down at last by a broken back, lay shuddering at the end of a bloody froth and waited for death.

"If a man had the strength of a gamecock," Grampa Fred told Wes on the way home, after the dog had been shot, "he could take his fist and with one blow drive it so deep into an oak tree he'd have to split the tree to get it out."

But it wasn't the strength of it that had captured Wes. It was the willingness to stand up against fear of death. There was no use telling him it was due to a lack of imagination, an inability to comprehend death. He had seen how fearful of death the hens had been. They had comprehended death very well and hens do not have any more imagination than roosters.

"It comes to them from all the way back, from the Egyptians," explained Grampa Fred. "Thousands of years ago, the Egyptians took chickens and bred it into them to be killers, and men in every generation since then have kept the strain pure."

The explanation didn't explain a thing, as far as Wes was concerned. How can you breed something "into" a living thing? You could put a bearing into a wheel. You could put steel into a ball. You could put alloys into steel. But you couldn't put anything living into a living thing. Oh, no. To do that you'd have to have the secret of the greatest mystery of all. You'd have to be able to create life.

Whatever the Egyptians had bred "into" the gamecock had had to be there all the time. It had had to be in all chickens. Breeding had just brought it out and had made it dominant in one where it had remained recessive in others.

To Wes it was a host of wonders. One wonder was what bringing out in itself a willingness to take its death had done for the fighting chicken. It had given a screechy bit of feathered fluff extraordinary strength. It had turned one of the most helpless of creatures — a creature whose place in the scheme of life was to be easy eating — into a remarkable machine.

But an even greater wonder was this: If breeding could bring out such marvelous talents in a chicken, why couldn't the chicken bring it out by itself unaided? It was there, in a Leghorn, for example, in a Plymouth Rock, a Rhode Island Red, a Buff Orpington, in any breed of chicken you could meet in any poultry yard anywhere — there, buried in the living matter, waiting to be brought out and used. Why, at the moment when a killer dog was coming for a Leghorn's throat and the Leghorn was searching in its deepest flesh for its furthest resources — why then should the Leghorn be unable to use what was in its own living matter to save its own life? But the Leghorn was unable, Wes knew. The gamecock could and the Leghorn couldn't. The gamecock brushed aside the instinct for self-preservation and so preserved himself, and the Leghorn embraced the instinct for self-preservation and so failed to preserve himself.

As Wes grew older, the question became more pressing for him. For if it was true of chickens, then it must be true of men. Who knew what resources lay buried in the living matter of living men, waiting only to be brought out and used? If nothing can be put into life but something can be brought out from it, then the whole future of man on earth must lie in him now waiting to make its appearance, as once man himself had lain waiting in the animal that stirred in the primeval slime to give him birth.

But the answers Wes got to his question about the chickens were only words without meaning. Breeding, he was told, bloodline, pure strain, stock, heredity. Finally, he stopped asking his question. But there was something there, he knew, something vast and knowable that might change the whole fate of man, that might bring man's future into the present.

Others seemed to know it, too. It was thought disgusting and even perverted or at least insensate and inhuman to breed gamecocks, but they bred them. It was illegal to fight chickens in the United States, but they fought them in every state. Children were terrified of the bloodshed, but their fathers brought them to it by easy stages, first buying them bantams who fight but cannot tear the flesh under the feathers, and getting them at last to the real thing.

In every corner of the United States, almost in every county, there

were doors that you, a stranger, could knock upon in the middle
of the night and show a chicken and find a fight. The rich would
fight you for $50,000 on the side, or five cents, whatever you had,
and the poor would fight you for whatever they had.

For, rich and poor, they all knew that there was something there,
something vast and knowable. But what it was nobody knew. Nobody that Wes ever met, anyway.

Twenty years is an exceedingly long time to keep a memory alive,
particularly when there is nothing to renew it, and Wes had
nothing. He never saw a cockfight. He hardly ever saw a live
chicken, even of the peaceful variety, and it all — the scene itself
and the great question and the meaningless answers it had provoked — faded from him and was no more than leaves that had
once fallen from a tree long since chopped down and made into
boards.

But one Saturday night he was celebrating. He was fresh
out of college then. He had come to Grand Island as a stranger,
knowing no one except his own family, which had moved there
from New York while he was still at school. Only a few days after
his arrival, while he was still wondering what to do with the remaining years of his life and filling in his time with a job in the
edge-tool firm in which his father was a partner, he suddenly discovered what he would do with his life. He would be a businessman.

It came to him as love does, in a wave that mounts sweepingly,
to crash with a storm of certainty. The firm had made an incau-
tious purchase of a carload of brass sheets and the management
could think of nothing better to do with it for the time being than
put it away in inventory. It was none of Wes' business. He was
very far from being in management, but an idea had come to him
nevertheless. If Grand Island Traction could be induced to use
tokens instead of cash fares on its streetcar lines, the brass sheets
could be turned into a profit immediately and a nice little side-
line would have been opened.

Wes had got no encouragement in his father's firm. They were
all edge-tool men there, not the least interested in the streetcar
business. The young man worked his idea out by himself in his
spare time. He learned about short rides and headways and the

riding habits in the various neighborhoods serviced by Grand Island Traction. He studied the company's rate history and rode its lines with a stop watch, noting down time lost collecting fares and making change. When he had convinced himself that Grand Island Traction would make money by selling tokens to be used as fares, he took his idea right to the top, to George Hicking himself, the company's president.

When Wes began his presentation, his legs were shaking under him. But when he finished they were not. Hicking liked the idea. He wanted to try it out on the Bellefair-Davenport Avenue line right away. From Hicking's office, Wes walked on calm legs to Sharp Street and the Chingo Iron Works. They, he had discovered, owned a Druice & Bollard coiner which could manufacture the tokens from brass sheets more cheaply than anything his father's firm owned.

It had been very difficult getting in to see George Hicking. But there was no trouble at all in getting to see John Eldred Chingo, the general manager of Chingo Iron Works. John E., as he was called, was a loud, rich, arrogant man, in the prime of his youth at thirty-two, and ordinarily it would have taken Wes ten years to reach the point where the man would have said hello to him. But now Wes was armed with the name of Hicking. He used it cleverly and John E.'s door flew open. Finally the matter was arranged, on Wes' terms. Chingo Iron Works would manufacture, Grand Island Traction would merchandise, and Wes, through his father's firm, would supply and manage.

Now all that remained was to get started. Perhaps you have seen a sub score a brilliant, unexpected touchdown. If you've watched him run eagerly to line up for the kick for the extra point and get the marvelous, thrilling game going again, you will understand how Wes felt. But there was no place to run. It was Saturday. The negotiations had lasted well into suppertime. He would have to wait to resume the gorgeous game of business until Monday morning.

Those were long hours in between. Wes decided he would waste them celebrating. He had luck. It turned out that John E. also wanted to waste the Saturday night. John E. knew the town and was a figure in its life. The two young businessmen had a grand time.

It was a struggle to carry all the liquor they took in, but their success in the struggle was one of the pleasures of the evening.

In the years since he had been paralyzed by terror of a killer dog who had not been able to frighten a chicken, Wes had grown tall and had developed a powerful body. Now there was a radiance in it. He was in love at the moment — with business, with Grand Island, with life itself and all the world that housed it. It was like a sun in him, making his presence vibrant, and wherever they went — the Hotel Plawell, Frank's, The Spa, The Chicago House — there were men who could recognize the radiance in Wes and came up to warm themselves in it. They had known such moments of love themselves. In their tired hearts they were aware they would never know them again, and they went up to John E., whom they knew, and greeted him in order to meet Wes, whom they did not know, looking at Wes as men might look at their homeland after they have been exiled from it.

It was a sad parade, but for a long time Wes had no idea it was taking place. He was too busy feeling wonderful and drinking drink for drink with John E. There was a boozy, bellowing hubbub everywhere they went. One by one, occasionally in pairs or groups, the hungering faces came steaming out of it to hang for a moment before Wes and yearn at him. But Wes was as blind as any other lover. It never occurred to him that the men were there for any other reason than to ingratiate themselves with an important personage, the general manager of the Chingo Iron Works.

Then, late, when they were in The Chicago House, a heavy-set red-faced man shouldered up to the bar where John E. and Wes were standing. John E. nodded to the man. Wes had not yet drunk so much that he couldn't notice the nod. He turned and waited with a smile to be introduced. But the man had drunk too much. The wires connecting him to his hands and feet seemed to be awash. Messages were getting garbled. Some of them were not getting through at all. He brushed right past John E. without returning the nod and took Wes' hand and began to shake it up and down.

"May I shake your hand?" the man asked.

"All right," replied Wes.

"I'd like to shake your hand," the man said.

"You are shaking it," Wes pointed out.

The man was too intent on looking at Wes' face to realize it. He kept on shaking Wes' hand up and down, and Wes kept on smiling. "I want to congratulate you," the man said at last.

"What for?"

"Because you're young."

"It was nothing at all, really. But, thank you."

A look of pain came into the man's eyes. "You're young, you're young," he cried. "That's a great thing to be," he added tremblingly.

"Always has been," said Wes.

"Always will be," the man agreed.

"Let's have a drink on that."

The man looked embarrassed. "I've had a drink, I imagine."

"Have another," suggested Wes.

The man debated with himself for a moment. "I think I will," he decided finally. "I'm entitled to it. I was young myself once."

"Who wasn't?"

"You weren't," the man said suddenly. His voice turned bitter. "What did you do to deserve that luck?"

"What luck?"

"You're young now. You've never been old."

For a moment he glared at Wes, his face baleful with envy. Then he turned to John E. They were old friends and he greeted John E. cordially, but at the same time he showed his broad, thick back to Wes with aggressive rudeness.

A cloud passed over Wes' deepest self where a moment before only a shining sun had been. *You're young, you're young.* The cry rang on in Wes. Men can't use the word "love" to each other, and that was why the man had said "young," Wes felt. *You're in love, you're in love,* the man had really said, Wes knew, *I was in love myself once.* And then he had said bitterly, *What did you do to deserve the luck of never having fallen out of love?* It had put into Wes the only sadness a lover can know. He had had an intimation of the mortality of his own love. He felt a grim, wringing pity. If love does not last forever for anybody else, perhaps it would not last forever for him either.

The man had gone away. John E., who sipped his whiskey raw from the shot glass, was lifting the glass to his lips for the hundredth time that evening.

"I want to make some money," said Wes suddenly.

"Why?" asked John E.

"Why not? It's not Sunday yet."

John E. thought a moment. He could not see what that had to do with the subject. "Have a drink," he said at last.

"I've got a drink," replied Wes.

"Have another."

"I'd rather make some money."

"Why?"

"Why not? It's not Sunday yet."

John E. stared somberly. They were back where they had started from. "What do you suggest?" he asked.

"I don't know. You know this town. You suggest."

"It's night. It's night, m'boy," said John E.

"I know. I wish it was morning."

Wes' voice was so full of gloom that John E. was touched. "It's morning," he cried. "It's morning, Wes. It's after one."

"I know, but I mean real morning. I mean Monday morning. Can't we make some money somewhere tonight?"

John E. looked thoughtful. "Well, there's the bank around the corner on Brackett Street. You might break in and rob it."

"No, no, no," cried Wes indignantly. "I mean do business. That's what I mean — do business, make money."

"Are you thinking of waking somebody up in the middle of the night and selling him a bill of goods?"

"I wouldn't mind. I wouldn't mind anything as long as it's action, it's productive, it's not just killing time."

"We could go to Mama Mamie's."

"What's there?"

"Crap, poker, roulette, blackjack, faro, anything you like."

Wes put his hand in his pocket. He had only one bill left. He didn't dare look at it. No doubt they'd cash a check for him, he thought eagerly, as they went out into the street.

In addition to the standard gambling-house equipment, Mama Mamie's maintained in its back yard a pit where mains were staged regularly every Saturday night and where those who could not afford to maintain stables of cocks to pit against other stables could bring their individual chickens and match them in hack fights when the night's main had been concluded.

The night's main was over and the hack fights had begun when Wes and John E. arrived. For, of course, the moment he learned of the pit Wes could not be held back. The whole scene of his childhood and all the questions it had provoked in him later came flooding back to him, and charged his mind so turbulently that he didn't want to delay a moment, even to cash a check. But John E. was no cock fancier. He insisted on delaying at the bar long enough to buy a bottle to take downstairs with them. "We'll need it as a chaser for the blood," he explained sourly.

Mama Mamie's, named after Mamie Stumplebock, who was known among the blades as Mamie Stopaclock, partly because of her name but chiefly because of her dour, meaty face, was across the river on the outskirts of Bellefair. It occupied a limestone house with a high stoop. The roulette and crap tables were kept on the parlor floor, and poker and whist and faro and other card games were run in individual gambling rooms on the upper floors. The cockfights were held in a shed that covered the backyard and was led to by an iron spiral staircase going down from the parlor floor.

The pit was covered over on its bare earth with a sawdust that was so dirty it was difficult to distinguish from the dirt under it. The shed was walled around with slabs of roofing tin that had once been painted white but were now scaling and rusty. The spectators bunched themselves on pine boards laid in tiers, reaching back from the pit level almost to the roof. When the two young businessmen arrived, the crowd had formed a dense, hot, rumbling mass around the pit. There was no room to sit. Everybody stood shoulder to shoulder, packed so tight in the places where a better view was offered that they were pressed sideways and, when somebody let out a yell, somebody else was sure to be pushed out of place.

The chickens awaiting their turn to fight were kept in wooden-slat crates in the open space under the stands. There Wes realized how slender are the threads binding together a man's view of what is real in the world and what he only thinks is real, what is happening and what he only thinks is happening. The chickens were making the ordinary peaceful cluckings and drawlings. In that gloomy, rocking air, pressed down with men and roofed over by their noises on the pine planks above, it seemed insane.

Then he saw something that excited him. The Arkansas Traveller, popularly called the blue, is a favorite among the American breeds and it would be hard to find a cockfight that did not feature several. But when Wes saw one in its crate, he was astounded and delighted. It was as runty as the one that had performed so heroically in his childhood. It had the same sourness in its red eyes and wattles. It might have been the same chicken, except that it had two eyes and an unbroken comb and neither of its wings dragged.

Wes was carrying the bottle John E. had bought. He pointed it at the blue. "I like that one," he announced.

"Do you like him for five?" a voice above him asked.

Wes turned. A huge man was lowering his face toward him ingratiatingly. Wes was six feet tall, but he had to look up to see the man's face. "I like him for any amount you got in mind," Wes said.

"Wait a minute," interrupted John E. "You don't know what he weighs."

"I don't care what he weighs," said Wes.

"Do you like him for fifty?" the man asked.

"He doesn't even know who he's matched against," protested John E.

"I don't give a damn if he's matched against a locomotive," said Wes.

"Give me a drink," said John E., and took back the bottle.

"A hundred?" the giant asked.

"A hundred," agreed Wes.

"Dollars?" asked the giant.

"What do you think, bees?"

"I think dollars."

Wes put his hand in his pocket. The huge man laughed. "Don't pay me now. Wait till your blue is dead."

The man went away, and John E. looked at Wes sardonically. "Have you got a hundred?" he asked.

Wes took the bill out of his pocket and looked at it. "Oh, sure," he said.

"Count again. That looks like a five to me."

"Well," explained Wes, "the rest of my money is still temporarily in that guy's pocket."

John E. took a long drink out of the bottle and handed it over to Wes. "You'd better hold on to it," he said. "Your creditor is seven feet tall."

Wes took the bottle, and laughed. "If my seven-foot creditor tries to get tough," he said, "I'll sick my chicken on him."

There were three hack fights before the blue Wes had bet on was brought into the pit. At Mama Mamie's, the chickens fought Sol McCall rules, with a referee in the pit and a handler for each cock and the gaffs on the birds' spurs round from socket to point. No cutting could be done with such gaffs, and no slashing. It was a fight to the death with ice picks.

The handlers wore heavily quilted leather gauntlets. When they released their charges, the cocks were twelve feet apart. They did not have to prod the bird or goad or urge it. They just had to hold on until time was called, and then let go. Letting go was like pulling a trigger. The chickens bounded at each other unhesitatingly.

All the thinking and maneuvering that was done took place in the time it takes a strong, long-legged chicken running at top speed to cover between seventy and eighty inches. The cocks were on each other before a man could draw a deep breath. They clashed breast to breast, necks arched, and rose into the air to bring their legs to bear in an attack called the shuffle. It was an odd name for such an attack. During a shuffle, their legs moved so fast they seemed not to be moving at all. The eye couldn't follow the movements. But something in each chicken seemed to follow them, estimating each movement, predicting its course and measuring its consequences, parrying, feinting, thrusting.

Wes got a clear look at the first of the fights. The chickens ran at each other, leaped, hung in the air for an instant, and then came down. The fight was over. One chicken had come down dead and the other had come down to strut in a circle around it, and flap its wings and crow.

Wes' eyes blinked. They couldn't stop blinking. "By God," he said, "what happened?"

John E. shrugged disdainfully. This was not for him. It was too gamy for his taste.

"You see the whole thing," said Wes. "But you have to think back over it and piece it together to find out what you saw."

"Aah." John E. made a gesture of contempt. "It's just reflex action."

There was a pause between matches to enable the crowd to get its bets down. There were no bookmakers. The spectators bet among themselves, scurrying to watch the chickens weighed and armed and hooded, and then running out from under the stands to get a vantage place around the pit, waving money over their heads or waving their empty hands and crying out the amount of their wagers. Through it all Wes stood lost in the sight he had seen.

He remembered how the chickens had gone for each other. His mind had stopped over that sight a long time, he realized now — now that the fight was over. But while the fight had been taking place, Wes had been living in ordinary time and the fight had rocketed through it in a nearly single blast of speed. But something in him, as in the chickens, had not been living in ordinary time, had kept step with that nearly single blast of speed. During the fight, he had felt like a man standing on a platform and watching a train hurtle by too fast to be anything but a blur of light. But there had been another man in him, he understood now, who had ridden along beside the train, slowing its motion by that act, transforming its motion into another extraordinary kind of time.

For the sight of the chickens going for each other had stopped Wes' mind for a long time. Both chickens had run in the same way — eager, utterly silent, wide-legged, spurring the earth under them in their long, strong, limber leaps, their fierce eyes calculating relentlessly, their necks stretched forward malignantly, their beaks out like faces held for a kiss. What had stopped Wes' mind was that not only were the two cocks acting alike, but each was acting like the blue he had seen destroy a dog and it had seemed to him that they were one thing and had always been one thing, without change, chicken succeeding chicken, breed succeeding breed, land succeeding land, century succeeding century, all without change in any important particular. In the thousands of years since the Egyptians had first started breeding them, there had been billions of gamecocks. But it had struck Wes that somehow, in some unfathomable way, they had all really been only one. It was a very queer notion and it had made him feel very queer.

The chickens, Wes remembered, had been feinting each other on the way in. He could remember having seen the feinting. Then they had leaped, breast to breast, each trying to get above the other, but not too far above.

The leap had had to be calculated precisely. That, no doubt, was what the feinting on the way in had been about. If one could be induced to leap too soon, the other could get under it, and the one on top would have only back feathers to stab while the one underneath would have the heart. But if there was too long a delay in leaping, if the timing was a thousandth or a hundred thousandth of a second off, that would be fatal, too. The chicken that had leaped first could plummet its weight down from above and knock its opponent off its feet. It would be the equivalent of breaking a swordsman's arms before killing him. But the prize both strove for was to jump just high enough to have the enemy's head at the other's feet — where the gaffs were.

There was no way to count how many separate ruses each cock had tried on the way in to get the other to miscalculate the timing and direction and height of its upward leap. But Wes had a sensation of having witnessed hundreds of separate little slippery shifting twists, as numerous as bubbles in a seethe and as uncountable. Yet something in each of the chickens had counted the bubbles and measured and judged them and acted in response to the judgment arrived at, and, when they had leaped, they were equal. They rose to the shuffle simultaneously. Neither had been able to outwit the other.

But the ruses had continued during the rise. That was when the fatal move had been made. One chicken had made a slight turn during the rise, providing an opening. The other had pounced. But it had pounced into a trap. The pounce had brought it too close to the first chicken's wing. Apparently the first chicken had calculated on that, for it was waiting. In mid-air, rising to shuffle, it was waiting, and it brought its wing down on its opponent, depressing its opponent's rise and accelerating its own, and when it passed its opponent's head it drove the gaffs into the brain.

What had happened in a split flash took a long time of careful recollection for Wes to piece together. He looked at John E. John E. was drinking from the bottle. Wes waited until John E. put the bottle down before he asked his question.

"What was that you called it?"

"What do you mean — what was what I called what?" growled John E.

"Reflexes?"

"What else?"

"I don't know what else," Wes said.

"Reflexes," said John E. "That's all it is, only reflexes."

"I've got reflexes, too," said Wes shyly.

"Chickens got no brains," said John E. "Only reflexes."

Chickens were fighting again, but Wes did not see them. Nor did he see the fight after that. Too many men had closed in around and in front of him and he didn't bother to crane over their heads, or shove an opening through their shoulders. It wasn't that the deaths in the pit had disturbed him. Chickens dying were just meat on the table to him. Besides, if all is one and one is all, then one cannot die. Its death cannot have the meaning of death. Nor can its torment have the meaning of torment.

No. He did not look because the fight he had seen was still alive in him. It seemed to him to have an enormous significance. But what that significance was he could not say. It lay just out of reach in his mind. The reflexes in the chickens were the same as in all chickens. They were the same as in a highly trained, skillful fighting man. The same reflexes were buried in him, as in all chickens, as in all men. The same freedom from the instinct for survival lay buried in him. The only difference was that it had been brought out into the consciousness of the gamecock while in him, as in all other chickens and all other men, it had remained smothered in the unconscious, blind, mute flesh.

Freedom from the instinct for survival. It was the future. It was eternal life. For this freedom could not come to a mortal creature unless it also had freedom from death. The gamecock had it. It was aware that all life is one and one life is all and that therefore there can be no death for one unless there is death for all. Wes had it, too. All men had it. The difference was that the gamecock had its freedom from fear in its consciousness where it could use it to command its energies, while men had it buried in them, waiting, waiting, waiting for some interminably delayed future in which by some mysterious process it would be brought out.

Suddenly the men in front of Wes stooped forward and remained that way, bowed and breathless. Wes could see the pit. "You blue there," he heard. "Come on, you blue." Far down, below the rows of bowed, breathless shoulders was a bronze-colored Pierce Shuffler and opposite it was the Arkansas Traveller on which Wes had bet the giant man a hundred dollars he did not have.

It was apparent that the first shuffle was over. One of the bronze's eyes was a red blear, and the other was hanging down its cheek on a string. The blinded chicken did not back up. It stood turning its head from side to side, maneuvering to poke a way through the sudden dense darkness that had fallen upon it and striving to discover where the agony within its flesh was coming from.

The Pierce Shuffler's maneuvers were confusing the blue. It stood, watching tensely, trying to make up its mind what nature of attack this could be. Then it became uncertain whether to strut or make an attack of its own. The bronze was not attacking. Therefore the fight was over, and an instinct clamored within the blue to make a victory strut around its fallen foe. But another instinct was clamoring within the blue at the same time, a warning that the fight was not over yet and that it might be fatal to strut.

There was no instinct of death in either bird, and the bronze kept trying to maneuver out of its blindness and the blue Wes had bet on kept shifting tensely from one posture to the other, from the strut position to the attack position and back again, all in flicks and twitches so rapid they were blurred.

"I lose."

The words in Wes' ear were hardly more than a grunt. Wes turned his head. The huge man was standing beside him, staring at the pit. He had worked his way through the crowd to get near Wes and make sure his hundred dollars wouldn't escape, but now he saw that he would have to pay. "That dog," he muttered, "that lemon." Suddenly he put his head back and roared at the bronze who had been continuing to try to poke a way through its dead eyes. "The hell with your eyes. Use your legs, you stupid son of a bitch."

It shocked Wes, but he looked away. The chickens had made a move. The blue had begun dreadfully to move forward. It had made up its mind to attack. It came circling.

Then, even more dreadfully, the bronze made up its mind to attack, too. It was helpless and hopeless. But if one is all and all is one and death has no meaning, helplessness has no meaning either, nor does hopelessness, and stubbornly, with infinite care, the bronze turned to get at the blue, gauging the blue's movements by the slight, feathering sounds it was making. As the bronze turned, it gathered its legs under it stealthily, feinting all the while, now this way, now that way, now with its head, now with its wings and shoulders, now with its feet. Its head swung from side to side. The eye hanging out on a string swished against its cheek. The crowd had become so still that the little swishing sound could be heard.

The blue swung hard. The bronze heard and started to rise, and the blue pulled back. Frantically, the bronze realized it had been outmaneuvered and tried to pull back. The blue had calculated the bronze would do precisely that. When it saw it happening, the blue rose. The bronze was pulling back and the blue had no trouble getting above it. It exploded its buckshot legs against the bronze's head.

A great terror seized Wes. It came from awe. The bronze was down on its side. A nerve in the back of its head had been severed, and it was paralyzed. It couldn't even move away from its own blood. Its tongue had fallen out. The tongue lay in the clotted dirt of the pit, and the bird couldn't even put its own tongue back into its own mouth.

The bronze's handler thought it was dead and came forward, knife ready to cut off its head. Then he saw the bird was not dead, and he withdrew. That was the rule of it.

No animal took its death unless trapped. But the fighting chicken had to. It had to show men that it could be done. The fighting chicken could not be pushed into a fight, or goaded into it, or attacked into it. It had to seek it out. Otherwise men could not be sure that the gamecock, in its normal conscious self, had prevailed over the instinct for self-preservation.

Nor could the cock allow any of its other instincts to divert it from its meaning to men. If it had been kept away from hens until emaciated for one — as it usually is when in training for a fight — and was then given the choice between a hen in rut and a cock, it had to choose the cock. If it was starved for food, and was given a choice between corn and a cock, it had to choose the cock.

Not a bull nor a lion nor any man who surrenders to his own instincts will stand up to something that has taught him by inflicting pain that it is stronger than he is. It will do so in madness, but not in resolution. When retreat is open, the bull, the lion and the man, however unwillingly, must turn tail and retreat. But the gamecock must not. Otherwise it could not show its meaning to men.

It is a spirit in them. The true gamecock guards its spirit as a mother guards her young, at all costs, at the cost of its own life. The mother guards her young because she knows in some inscrutable way that, individual though she herself may be, still in some inscrutable way her children are her only future. So with the gamecock. It had learned in some inscrutable way that its spirit was its future and must be protected as young are protected. And when it demonstrates this so that men who see may know, its owner can know that he himself has a place among the long line of knowers, a line stretching back through the generations for more than three thousand years when men first bent themselves to keep the spirit of the gamecock supreme above the instincts of its flesh.

So the handler withdrew his knife and backed up when he saw that the blinded and paralyzed bronze was still alive. He wanted the owner's place on the line of men stretching back to the time of the Pharaohs.

It made the giant man come out of a despair, and clutch at hope. "Come on, you bronze bum," he bellowed.

The bellow struck Wes like a blow. But he couldn't loosen the terrifying grip of awe in him, and he couldn't take his eyes off the pit. The blue had begun its victory strut. It put one wing down and made a circle around the fallen body of its opponent. The bronze lay with its tongue in its blood, and the blue's wing dragged through the stillness with a scratching, fluttering sound. Its legs dug and scraped and flurried the earth of the pit. Its chest swelled like that of a man in triumph, and, like a man in triumph, it was about to stretch its arms and beat its chest and roar, and glare from its sour little red eyes.

But Wes could look only at the bronze. It wasn't surrendering. There was no death, so there was nothing to surrender to. It was paralyzed, but something in it wasn't. Staring, his eyes stretched with the awe that was like a terror in him, Wes felt he could almost make this something out. It was faint and blurred, but it was there — under the feathers, under the skin, deep, crouched in a jungle of exhausted, wildly bleeding organs and looking calculatingly through the bronze's blind eyes at the blue strutting around it. Suddenly it sprang. Wes could see it. It was the spirit of the cock. It dragged with it the paralyzed flesh in which it crouched, and aimed for the blue's heart.

Oh God, thought Wes, and closed his eyes.

A shout went up, and he opened them. The bronze was dead, spitted on the blue's gaffs. The blue was standing stuck in the bronze's heart, puzzled by its inability to strut. With a swift, bitter gesture, the handler pulled the bronze free and cut its head off and threw the body to the hangers-on who would boil it for soup.

Wes stood stunned. The irony of it had spitted him. The birds had torn themselves to pieces so that men who saw might know the greatness that lay buried in themselves. The one instinct that stood most intractably in the way of man's highest aspirations, that accounted for his meanest meannesses, his greatest greeds, his most destructive selfishnesses, that accounted for his fears, his hates, his lusts, his wars, for everything that stood in the way of his own future on earth, was his instinct for self-preservation. The chicken had destroyed itself to show that the instinct could be conquered.

The huge man was riffling through a roll of bills with one thumb. He was looking among fives and tens and fifties for a hundred. When he found it, he held it out to Wes.

Wes didn't take it. "You'd better keep it," he said.

"Didn't I have a bet with you?" the giant asked.

"You did," said Wes.

"Well, take it. I lost."

"You seem to need the money an awful lot."

It must be, Wes decided tremulously. The chickens had shown this man and he had looked, but he hadn't seen. He had seen nothing. The blue had torn the bronze to pieces for nothing. All the man had seen was himself winning or losing $100.

"That's all right," the huge man said. He still held the bill extended. "Won't be long before I'll get it back. Who do you like for the next one?"

"Put that money in your pocket," said Wes, "or I'll stuff it down your throat."

The giant looked at Wes, puzzled. "What's the matter with you?" he asked, and Wes struck out violently with a wild, roundhouse right.

But there was no room to swing. John E. had been cradling the bottle in his arms. He was jostled as people jumped to hold Wes and to hold the giant. The bottle fell and there was a loud crash, and John E. crashed with it, and another man slipped with a scream through the pine planks into the chicken crates below.

In the tangle, the giant could not be seen. "Where's that big guy?" Wes cried. "Where did he go?" He wanted to kill the man. If man couldn't see the way to his future even when it was tearing itself to pieces to show itself to him, how could anybody ever achieve it? He tried to bull his way forward through the crowd, and someone said, "Throw them in the pit," and a voice cried, "Gentlemen! Gentlemen!" and another cried, "Kick him in the shorthairs."

Mamie Stopaclock was running down the spiral staircase, a sawed-off baseball bat in her hands, and two men with cauliflowered ears ran behind her. "Pay the man his money, and throw the bum out," she shouted and the $100 bill was snatched from somewhere and lifted high to pass over a crowd of heads and stuffed into Wes' pocket while he bulled and thrashed and cried, "Where'd that dog go?"

He couldn't move. There were a dozen hands on him, holding

him fast. "He's the enemy," he shouted. "He's the enemy of all human progress."

"You'll make progress," said Mamie Stopaclock, and the hands that had been pinning Wes lifted him and hustled him over the planks and up the spiral stairway and ran him, on legs that touched the floor only every now and then, through the roulette room and through the foyer and there they clapped his hat on his head and pushed him through the door.

"Don't come back, you troublemaker," Mamie said, and the door slammed in Wes' face.

"I'll sick my chicken on you!" he shouted through the door.

Then a policeman had hold of his arm and was preventing him from throwing a rock through Mama Mamie's front window.

"Now, sonny," the policeman was saying, "if you don't do that, I won't do anything either.

"If you're quiet, sonny," the policeman was saying, "I can be quiet, too. Otherwise I'll have to make plenty of noise on your head."

Wes let go of the brick, making sure it would fall on the policeman's foot. The policeman hopped up into the air, and Wes walked away.

(From Quarto)

THE ROCK

BY VURRELL YENTZEN

THERE WERE ROCKS on the beach, some sharp enough to make clean cuts. The bones of the trees the waves had cast were littered here. Paul sighed, watching a tiny crab which sulked in a pool of tears the weeping sea had left. And his lips moved as he rehearsed again what he must tell his wife Alzade.

He looked at her with pity, lying there on the blanket beside him, swollen and grotesque from the child that was heavy within her.

. . . I spoke to Bruce this morning and we looked at the X-rays he took yesterday while you were in Port Arthur . . . what can I say? . . . the child that is dreaming within you has floated out of normal delivery position because it is malformed . . . it's a hydrocephalic baby . . . it will not live . . .

She grunted softly as she mopped at the sweat that glazed her flesh. The brownness of her skin was without erotic appeal, he mused, as nakedness in itself has no appeal . . . a brown, solid coolness, Alzade was, and even as Veeda had been . . .

It was ironic to think how serene and contented he had felt now that he had finished interning and settled down to practicing in Port Arthur, Texas. There was much in Port Arthur which reminded him of Louisiana; French was heard more frequently than English on the streets. And hearing was like feeling pleasure without pain . . .

Somewhere the shouts of children playing came, but he did not turn his head to listen.

. . . how would you tell her that . . . how could he say bluntly
. . . Alzade, this child kicking within you, dreaming warm and
contented, is not going to live . . . this pitiful, little animal, your
son and my son, awaits birth to find death . . .

He sighed again, feeling all this tenderness for women involved
in fertility . . . always he felt hurt somehow when a woman came
in, annoyed, irritated, even sometimes cursing that she was preg-
nant . . . he wondered sometimes if it were possible for the child
feeding within the dark womb to perceive that he was unwanted
. . . but then, of course . . . that was impossible.

He could see her press her hand suddenly against her stomach
as if she would quiet the child that had moved within her. Paul
put out his hand to feel the solidness and the enormousness that
her pregnancy gave her. With pity, he touched her, ready then
to tell her.

She turned her head sharply. "For Christ's sake! Stop pawing
at me. God! It's hot."

. . . it had been hot, too, in the Philippines when Lester and
he had landed on Samar the fifth day of the Battle for Leyte Gulf
to pick out a spot for the epidemiology team. The PT base was
on the side of a steep hill. Water from frequent showers during
the last days had drained to the new road, bogging it, until no
jeep would pass. But that was unimportant; there was no stretch
more than three hundred feet where a jeep could travel. And
they walked around the base area, the mud sucking at their feet.

A sailor said Monta was the Chief Master of Arms and made
tent platform assignments. Bogging through the mud, they found
Monta's tent on the hillside. Paul called and, presently, a brute
appeared at the edge of the platform over their heads, completely
naked except for muddy boots. To Paul, he was obscene, man
was naked enough when caught unexpectedly, but a view from
below was shocking in its strangeness.

It embarrassed Lester and he reddened, but he blushed easily;
he was still young emotionally.

"Take the three tents on the far side," Monta said, pointing to
the left after Paul had explained what they needed.

When they left him, Lester said, "That was revolting."

"Perhaps we caught him unaware, say sleeping or changing clothes," Paul said, ready to excuse him.

"With rubber boots? Nonsense."

Yet the explanation was simple. Later, when Paul knew Monta better, he reminded him of the incident. And Monta grinned, saying he had with him only the clothes he wore. He had slipped in the mud, so he had washed his clothes and was waiting for them to dry.

But washing hadn't been a problem for Paul after the first few days. Veeda came to the tent begging for washing. Out of pity for her poverty — she was barefooted and was wearing a dress made of a coarsely woven fabric dyed a dull brown — he had hunted up some dirty clothes to give her. He had felt this immense dignity within her even then. She was not asking for favors; she was asking for work.

There was a clean, animal look about her which animated her plainness until, at times, he thought her beautiful. But then he guessed he never saw her distinctly. Even now, he couldn't remember her clearly, as if she were some intangible vision. He remembered more those kindnesses and the smile that showed her white teeth. And more than anything else — the solidity within her.

They were both solid women — Veeda and Alzade. Sometimes he had thought he would tell Alzade about Veeda, but she would never understand. She would exclaim, "How revolting! Really, Paul, can't you keep those things to yourself?"

He looked again to the rock.

Seeing his glance, Alzade said, "Paul, get the portable out of the car." She sighed heavily from her discomfort. "I suppose I should go in, but it's so warm and comfortable here."

When he brought the portable radio to her, she found some music. He stretched out on the blanket again and listened casually, studying the rock on the beach.

How was he going to tell her?

He dreaded telling her, knowing her unhappiness would be his unhappiness. It was as if he found in all these pregnancies

a chain, linking one generation to another . . . a mystery and a
hope which he clung to, almost desperately, finding in them some
faith which explained the reason for man's existence . . . and
sometimes he felt that unless he could rid himself of the emotional
attachment he felt for each of these pregnancies, he should give
up his profession. But he gave up all of this now to find . . .
what? What frightened him? Because he could not believe in
a life after death, he must find here a mode of living which would
give him satisfaction . . .

Like he thought once he had found with Veeda.

Cobayen . . . and it seemed the memories he remembered most
were fragments, like white bones from the trees out of the sea . . .
the white lilies in the field he crossed . . . he could recall how
sweet the fragrance, almost overpowering when he walked through
them . . . and after that, the rough old rice fields with the carabao
wallows, where sometimes an old pig of a cow wallowed with her
calf, muddily caked . . . their hides rough and cracked . . .

Over the small streams where the pathway was an old rotten
log and sometimes he didn't make it and stepped off into the
stagnant water, knee deep, and on through the village and the
smoke of fires where meals cooked or clothes boiled.

And always the coconut fronds overhead . . .

Everything just a little sad . . . like a quiet interlude in music,
and on through to Veeda's shack to stretch out on the split-bamboo
floor while she fried a tough little cockerel in coconut butter and
cooked unpolished rice.

And later, eating with his fingers, relishing food because he
was hungry, and going down to the stream in the bushes to urinate because there wasn't an outhouse — these people didn't know
or care about sanitation, except what he taught Veeda and insisted
that she tell her neighbors.

There was always the laughter in the dusk of the houses. Her
teeth were white and strong and when she carried the child, it was
carried high. He loved to see her walk, because the dignity now
was heightened.

She was a trader, that woman!

From the clothes and the money he gave her she was building
security for herself and her coming child. When he would lie

on the bamboo floor, listening to her voice when the women would gather in the first dark, she talking and laughing in Visayen which sounded so musical, like French, almost the nostalgia became too much.

He would be there in his trunks, barefooted, while they, aware and yet not aware of him, gossiped like the women at home. And sometimes when he would be filled with the sickness for home, he would tell of the States and Veeda would interpret for him, proud of her thin knowledge of English.

Somehow the stories were always unbelievable, like the time he tried to explain snow and they were not aware of coldness. Chillness perhaps. How could he give the impression of a coldness they never felt? Yet they had tried to understand. They listened intently to him when he spoke and to Veeda when she explained. But then it didn't matter. It was a tale of a wonderful land where everybody was rich. And he would tell Veeda it was not that; it was not that at all.

He would ask, what is a house but a place to keep the rain from your head! And what is food, but something to feed our bodies? And bathrooms, which she couldn't visualize, in fact, said were unimportant; no one in the village had one.

How could she want what she didn't know?

She had been more interested in the small stove he had made for her from the five-gallon tin so she could build her little fire in it for cooking. The women had come and admired. He had been forced to find many flour tins so that they, too could have these little stoves.

And more, too, he did.

He brought medicine, especially atabrine and aspirin. Veeda always said she wanted medicine. And he would lecture to her, telling her what she must explain to her people. But he wondered sometimes if she hadn't sold the medicine instead of giving it.

When he knew the child was coming, he told Veeda he would deliver it. She must send for him at the first sign of labor; he didn't want this child delivered by a native midwife.

Planning, then, that he would deliver her although he was only a pharmacist's mate at the time, he made up the surgical packs and sterilized them in the autoclave in the lab. Methodically he stole the instruments he would need. Lester, seeing him, said, "My God, what do you plan to do? Move a hospital to that shack?"

After packing the surgical packs in a small box, he walked to Veeda's shack and said to her, "I've tied this box securely. You must not open. When you will give birth, you will send for me and I will be here and need this."

And she put the box away carefully in the bottom of the sea chest that held some of his clothes.

But for all his planning Veeda delivered the child without him.

Lester, who had been out on a larval survey, came to him, saying, "Veeda has her baby. You lucky dog! It's very white."

He had gone to see her immediately. She kept the baby in a hammock in one corner. Heavy netting and blankets darkened the corner to keep away the flies. Until his navel was healed, she explained.

"Damn it, Veeda," he said. "Why didn't you send for me?"

"It is old Filipino custom a woman gives birth in her way," she said meekly. "I will bring you the son."

Almost dismayingly came the vision of childbirth in the Philippines . . . the woman in labor crouching from the increasing pains of the rhythmic contractions, the midwife kneeling beside her, massaging and pressing the bulging stomach, until the child is dropped into a layer of wood ashes which experience has taught have some antiseptic value. The eyes and throat of the child are cleared of mucus, but the white ashes, clinging like powder, sterilizing man's entry into primitive society, remains protectively for the first week . . .

This, he wanted to avoid with Veeda; he had wanted to bring some of the refinements that man had developed in childbirth.

Veeda brought the child to him, wrapped securely in cloth.

"I must see what you've done with him." Laying the baby on the floor, he unwrapped him.

"See, we have tied with the rattan," she said, pointing to his navel.

"There isn't much to be done now," he said, reluctantly. "Get me the package I brought you."

And when he opened it, he painted the navel with merthiolate.

"Now look," he said. "This is a belly band." She repeated his words after him. "You must keep him tied like this for a few days." She watched carefully. And more he told her, knowing that it was somehow futile. Then, she wrapped up the child and returned it to the hammock in the corner. "You shouldn't be stirring around so much either," he said. "You must rest."

She looked surprised. "I do not feel sick," she said with dignity.

He didn't live in big chunks of experience in the Philippines . . . it was like music in a low key, tearing at his heart and his compassion . . . when he would help these people he was taken by the futility of the help; it was a temporary respite . . . when he was gone, they would return to their worms and their fevers and their diarrheas and their infant mortality and their superstitions.

"We must give him a name," Veeda said. He named several possible names, but she shook her head. Finally he said, "Let's call him Norman."

She was taken with the sound of the name although she had never heard it before. "Where comes this name?" she asked.

"It's in the family. It's my father's name."

It pleased her. "We name him Norman. Write on a paper so I can take the priest to baptize. Soon I go to Tenoquin and pray to the gods."

He smiled at her indulgently, watching little Norman nurse at her ample breasts. "I'm going to send you to the States," he said.

It alarmed her. "I do not want to go to America."

"But you will be happy there. I will teach you the many customs."

"In America they will not like me. I do not want to go where they do not like the black people."

He was disturbed. "Veeda! Where have you heard this?"

"The black Americans they come to the village and force some girls and they say, 'In America, Filipinos, too, are black.' I do not want to go where I am black. I do not like this."

"Veeda!" He was angry now. "Has anyone tried to harm you."

"No." Then she laughed. "I take the knife and say, 'Go way. I do not like. I will cut.' And they laugh and do not touch. Maybe because they see I am big with child."

"You must go to the States," he insisted. "I wish I could go back with you now. But I have orders for China duty. But my family will take care of you until I return. You will like it in Louisiana."

She was silent for several minutes. "I do not like this. I will stay. I have made much already with the clothes and the goods and the money you give me. I make trade. See? We have boat already from Catabologen to Tacloben. Soon we have two boats. You must come to Catabologen. I have there one house and many coconut trees."

"But, Veeda. In the States I can do so much more. Here there is so little for my training. Besides I must learn to become a doctor. You must come to the States with me and we will have there, too, a big house. And we will make of this son a big man." He looked at the child and she, seeing his glance, hugged Norman protectively.

She would not listen.

And when he returned, she was gone.

Where? No one could or would tell him. She had left, the natives said vaguely.

Lester Teller helped Paul wangle two weeks leave and delay in orders from the base commander. Paul managed to get to Catabologen on a native craft, but he could not find Veeda there. Hopefully, he waited for her, waiting as long as he could, thinking even of deserting. But he returned to the base, to China and later to the States, promising always he would return to the Philippines and find Veeda.

But two years passed before he was out of the service, two years of writing to the Consulate and working through the Red Cross without a trace. Veeda and his son disappeared into the people of the world.

He excused himself, finally, thinking she would get along. The solidity she had in her was the mark of the matriarch . . .

the rock on the beach with blind eyes . . .

the resigned eyes, begging for compassion and sometime catching a glance somewhere over the heads of people and seeing there at once understanding, an awareness of a common feeling . . . and what if through Alzade he was cut off from generations to come . . . what would he live for now? The melancholy of a lonely life, contemplating man as an animal which still crawls within the shadow of the human to come. If in the church he had found what he wanted those many years ago in the dim days of his remembered youth, willingly he would have given himself . . . but he could not become a priest without faith . . .

poverty . . .

humility . . .

chastity . . .

there had been a time when he thought he had a vocation for the church . . . it happened in New Orleans. He reflected later it must have been moral incrimination, still, at the time he felt good and noble. He had talked to the Jesuit priest at Loyola and the Jesuit was certain Paul had a vocation. In him, Paul found a gentleness and serenity which was quietening.

He had gone to see the Monsignor and talked, pouring out all he felt, trying to explain, to say what he felt, as if he could put into words a kind of belongingness.

But the Monsignor, "You're too old. We usually start training in grammar school. However, we will take you as a brother and feed and clothe you."

It was not food and clothing he was seeking. "I don't want to become a brother. I want to become a priest," he said doggedly.

The Monsignor had looked at him critically; Paul had felt like a lost blood cell. "Another Order may take you," the Master said. "Others don't have strict requirements as the Jesuits. However, we will be glad to have you if you want to become a brother. I will let you speak with Brother Alfonso before you leave. He will answer any questions you have."

Brother Alfonso came and Paul was repulsed by the sight of him. There was avarice in his face and something in his manner, some softness, what, he wasn't sure — a kind of worldliness. Anyway, he was repulsed and there weren't many questions he could think to ask, he was that disappointed. The way he felt, he was sure he was destined to become a priest.

He was led into a closed classroom, heavily paneled, with the appearance of age. A mustiness filled his nostrils . . . an odor of old wood rotting submerged in stagnant water . . . decay . . .

The brother talked cheerfully and persuasively, but Paul was unmoved. Finally, Paul said, "I must go."

The brother said he should return anytime and talk with him. He would be glad to answer any questions.

But even that hadn't hurt the feeling of humility he had within him and he would spend long hours in the Cathedral in Vieux Carré, praying, but largely he was contented to sit quietly in a pew, feeling contented . . . there was a feeling of awareness, more of continuity, as if in the Sanctuary was the beginning and the end . . . here, perhaps, was what he was seeking . . . eternal life. For a lifetime he would have been contented to reflect on the goodness within man . . . and that he was man himself, not so perfect, but capable of good . . . of god.

The days passed, marking passage by the sleep he needed and the food he wanted. He was serene and secure because he had found God. And if he who walked in His name on the face of the earth had taken him by the hand and led him away, he would have lived his life adoring the Mystery.

But the passing days made his return home more and more urgent and finally he left the Cathedral and returned to the land where he was born. Then the rawness of a practical life began to encroach into his tranquillity. When he would go to Mass each morning, he did not find the contentment that he had known in the Cathedral and he tried to deny this to himself, he would refuse to think, as he refused then to think of impure thoughts by saying a Hail Mary or an Our Father . . . but the waters ate away at the sands beneath the tower of his contentment and the day came when it was gone. It was as simple as that.

It had been like a spell or a sickness.

And almost frightened, he had returned to the Cathedral in New Orleans and each day he would sit in the pew and try to recapture his faith, but it was gone . . . and thinking about it, he decided that his rationalism had eaten away at the mystery; where he thought he had found God, he had found the organized Church.

And he thought, churches should be the biggest in the world. They should tower to the sky. They should dwarf man into minuteness and insignificance, so that when the Church asked, "Man, who is your Master?" he would look to the tallest spire and say, "You, O Lord."

And though he was sad that the contentment was gone — it was as if God had died, like a dear friend, like his mother . . . still, through his unhappiness seeped the consolation that never again would he be concerned with dying and going to hell. It gave him a soaring relief, as if he had been released from death . . . and there was no longer a veil before his face as there was between Alzade and him.

Somehow he must reach through and explain.

The children on the beach were playing nearby now and three, chasing a ball, almost ran over them, kicking sand on the blankets.

"Look at these kids," Paul said to Alzade. "They don't know how unhappy they will become."

She was looking at him intently as she did when she was thinking about him. "Paul, what is the matter with you? You've been so quiet."

A tiny girl had found the crab in the pool of water and was now methodically pulling off its claws.

"Childhood is the happy time," he said watching the child. "Then, we're content with so little."

"I don't like you when you're like this. It's too depressing. What are you trying to be, Jesus Christ?"

He laughed, as if it were a joke. "Tell me, Alzade, are we happy because we know so much or because we know so little?"

She was silent then, as she was when he asked something he knew she didn't want to think about.

"Paul, I was thinking," she said finally. "We should open the Carter addition now. We could run up a group of twenty houses there. I hate to wait any longer."

He frowned slightly; he had never approved of this real estate business she was developing. "I thought you were going to wait until you were straightened out again." He looked again at the bigness of her and he wondered in the child dreaming within her . . . well, *knew*.

"I know. But I'm afraid we'll miss out if we wait any longer."

He looked at her then, sitting round and heavy, her arms on her knees, giving an impression of permanency.

"You love money, don't you Alzade?"

"It's not that," she said candidly. "It's the wonderful power of it and the respect it brings to you." And almost respectfully, she touched her stomach, like making the sign of the cross, "And for your family." Then, sighing, almost grunting, she lay back on the blanket.

He was filled with pity for her; he wished he did not have to tell her what he knew.

"Alzade," he said quietly, "Sometimes these pregnancies don't always work out."

"Are you thinking of Frances and Bill? Well, I'm not worried." There was contentment in her voice. She touched her stomach firmly. "My child is going to be sound and healthy."

He felt then, as if he were going to stab her. "Alzade. Not every baby is a good one. They don't always turn out the way we plan." There was an awkwardness in his voice and a pity he had tried to prevent coming through.

She turned her head sharply. For a moment, she studied his face. "Paul. What are you trying to tell me?"

He reached for her hand and squeezed it firmly. "I'm sorry, baby. Bruce called me about the X-ray plates. The child is defective, a hydrocephalic. That's the reason the child had turned from normal delivery position. That's why Bruce spoke of a breech delivery."

He could see the child moving within her. With panic she pressed at her stomach as if now pain, too, was there. "I don't believe it. It's not true." But already there was a mistiness in her eyes.

He pressed her hand again.

"Don't," she said, jerking her hand out of his. She rolled over on her side clumsily, but carefully, away from him. For a few moments sobs shuddered through her.

He wondered if the child within her wept with self-pity . . . it is unconsolable . . . finding in itself neither a sexlessness nor a consolation which will still the tears that seep forth from his blind eyes . . . it's face is formless with the amorphous enlargement of the embryo . . . within the dark warmth, it's sightless eyes gaze upon a wall . . . it knows nothing; it can but feel . . . recoiling with terror at the cold blast of disapproval . . .

soon . . . he will be dead . . . gasping for the last load of air carried by some tiny red blood cell like a tiny crab, soon to lay dreaming in a bluish-red pool . . . an instance of stillness in a lake of nothingness . . . soon . . . there will be weeping . . . even before the last clod falls with thudding silence upon ears that hear no more, the last instance of now will become then . . . blood on white paper . . .

regret that the red fragrance of the white lily sleeps in the seed of tomorrow . . .

"Alzade?"

"Yes." She did not turn towards him.

"It's just one of those unfortunate mishaps, baby. We can go on to a good baby later."

"I don't want to talk about it." There was bitterness in her voice.

. . . I cannot tell you Alzade, which is the beginning or the end . . . neither where today was yesterday, or when the night comes with the brightness of a silent word, sweeping aside the veils of dreams . . . of a red bird . . .

in a cool brown rock.

When Paul looked at the rock again, he saw into it and through it. Doubting his eyes, he touched it, trying to find in it's coolness and texture, an assurance of solidarity, but it was as glass.

He listened again to the low, sweet music . . . the low, sweet music of humanity, one of the poets had written.

Looking through the rock, he could see upon the beach, seeing there the bones of the trees that the waters had cast.

He turned to Alzade, puzzled, and said, "Look to the rock and tell me what you see."

"It's a plain, ordinary rock," she said. "Is that enough?"

"Tell me what you see." There was a persistent tone in his voice, as if he wanted her, too, to see what he could see.

"It's just a rock. A goddamn, bitchy rock. I cut my foot there last week."

"I tell you that if you can see, you will look not to the rock, but in the rock and through the rock to the beach beyond."

She stood up wearily, cutting short the explanation he would have given her. "It's too hot for anagrams. It's just a goddamn rock. I'm returning to Port Arthur tonight, Paul. In the morning I'm letting out the contracts for the houses."

Taking her blanket she walked beyond the rock to lie on the beach among the bones of the trees. Pressing her heaviness into the cool, damp sand, she began to weep.

BIOGRAPHICAL NOTES

BUSH, GEOFFREY. Mr. Bush was born in Minneapolis, Minnesota, in 1929 but has lived most of his life in Cambridge, Massachusetts. He graduated from Harvard University in 1950, *summa cum laude*, in Greek and English literature. He also studied for two years at Oxford University on a Rhodes Scholarship and took a B. Litt. there. Mr. Bush is now at Harvard again, doing research and writing as a member of the Society of Fellows of Harvard University. His father is a professor of English at Harvard and his mother has had a story published in *The Virginia Quarterly Review*. He states, "I should say, perhaps, that "A Great Reckoning in a Little Room" corresponds, in part, to one or two existing documents, but that most of it is made up." He has had other short stories in *Harper's Bazaar*, *Charm*, and *The Hopkins Review*.

CLAY, RICHARD. Mr. Clay was born in Philadelphia in 1915, went to school there and in Switzerland and spent the last five years before college at St. George's School in Newport, Rhode Island. He studied for a short time at Princeton and Harvard, worked in the oil business in California and the advertising business in New York. He says: "As a boy I loved to make model airplanes and often went over to Willow Grove airport to watch the Pitcairn autogyros in the late twenties. After my stint in the advertising business I decided to go back to school and learn aviation. This has been my career ever since 1940. I first worked as a civilian employee of the Air Force and for the last ten years have been employed by Sikorsky Aircraft, a manufacturer of helicopters in Bridgeport, Connecticut. I began writing when I was in school, but put it aside when more pressing problems of marriage and career intruded. Recently I found I could spend some time on it again and, more important, that I had some things I wanted to say. His first short story, "Very Sharp for Jagging," was published in *The Hudson Review* and reprinted in the O. Henry *Prize Stories* for 1954. Two other short stories, including "A Beautiful Night for Orion," have been printed in *The Hudson Review* and two more have been accepted for future publication. Mr. Clay is living at present with his family in Westport, Connecticut.

DEMOTT, BENJAMIN. Before entering college in 1946, Mr. DeMott spent seven years in a variety of jobs in downtown New York, downtown Baltimore, in the United States Infantry and in Washington, D.C., where he worked as a newspaperman and free lance writer. His fiction has appeared in *The Partisan Review*, which published his first short story, in *New Directions Thirteen*, *New Mexico Quarterly*, *The Atlantic Monthly* and the *Western Review*. Work of his is forthcoming in two paper-bound volumes, *More Stories in the Modern Manner* and *Modern Writing*, both published by Avon.

DORRANCE, WARD. Mr. Dorrance was born in 1904, of Southern antecedents, in Jefferson City, Missouri. At present he divides his time between Sussex in England and Virginia in the United States. He was educated at the University of Missouri (A.B., A.M., Ph.D.) and at Columbia University and the Sorbonne. He has been variously surveyor's assistant, bank runner ("but neither fast nor far!" he adds), schoolteacher and officer in the Coast Guard. The books he has written include *The Sundowners*, done while he held a Guggenheim Fellowship in 1942. Since the war, which he spent in the Arctic, he has devoted himself to short stories. He has contributed to *The Hudson Review*, *The Sewanee Review*, *The Atlantic Monthly* and to various textbooks and anthologies.

410

DOUGHTY, LEGARDE S. Born in Augusta, Georgia, Mr. Doughty completed his education at Belmont College, North Carolina. "The fact is," he explains, "I applied myself not at all in school and what comprehension I have come to has been got the hard way." He has been employed as Texas representative of the *New York Cotton Broker*, an administrative analyst in the Civil Service and as a proofreader. His writing embraces poetry, fiction, essays and criticism which has been published in many magazines, mostly quarterlies, in the United States and in England and Australia. He is the author of a novel, *The Music Is Gone*, published in 1945. He is technical editor of *The Humanist*, the bi-monthly publication of The Humanist Association. He emphasizes, "I am a liberal in all things, political, societal, literary, etc."

ENRIGHT, ELIZABETH. She was born in Chicago but has lived in New York ever since she was a year and a half old, except for an interval when she studied in Paris at the School of Applied Art. She is married and has three sons. Her work has appeared in *Cosmopolitan*, *Collier's*, *Ladies' Home Journal*, *Mademoiselle*, *The New Yorker*, *Harper's Magazine*, *Yale Review* and *The Virginia Quarterly*. She has written many children's books, one of which, *Thimble Summer*, received the Newberry Medal in 1939. A collection of her short stories, entitled *Borrowed Summer*, was published by Rinehart and Company in 1946 and another collection is to be published in the fall of 1954.

FRAZEE, STEVE. Mr. Frazee was born in Salida, Colorado, about ten blocks away from his present residence there. He attended Western State College at Gunnison, Colorado, from which he was graduated during the depression. Among his occupations have been newspaper work, road construction and hard-rock mining, all mixed with fiction writing over a period of twenty years. After the last war, he concentrated entirely on fiction. He is married and has two children. His work includes a great many short stories and five paper-bound volumes, mainly with western backgrounds. He is the author of a historical novel, *Shining Mountains*, and an adventure-mystery, *The Sky-Block*. He has also written various articles ranging in subject matter from crooked gambling to fly fishing. Forthcoming books by him are a Doubleday Western, a Macmillan Western and an historical novel, *Excalibur Six*, which will be published by Rinehart and Company.

GOLD, IVAN. Mr. Gold was born in 1932 and lives in New York City. He was graduated in 1953 from Columbia College, where he was an editor of the student humor magazine, *Jester*, and a frequent contributor to *The Columbia Review*. His short story, "A Change of Air," won first prize in a contest conducted by the latter magazine. Mr. Gold has worked variously as a shipping clerk for a textile firm, a coach cleaner on the Pennsylvania Railroad, a typist, a post office clerk and a soda bottler for a soft drink firm. He recently completed his first novel and presently is in the Army.

HEATH, PRISCILLA. She was born in Manchester, New Hampshire, and attended public schools there and Bates College in Maine. She says, "I was active in intercollegiate debating as well as contributing verse and a story to the undergraduate magazine and I was graduated with high honors in sociology and economics. This hindered my literary education but saved me from accumulating a burden of literary notions which I would have had to discard later. Graduate study becoming impossible for financial reasons, I worked at temporary and part-time jobs, most of them with relief or social welfare organizations, until I became associated with the National Youth Administration in 1937. During the next four years I was everything from 'non-relief youth worker' on a local project to Chief of Project Control in the State Office where I was also in charge of publicity and did various kinds of ghost writing." In 1941 she was married and for two winters taught liberal arts subjects in a small business college. In 1948 she attended the first session of the Kenyon School of English. Since then stories of hers have appeared in *The Western Review* and *The Kenyon Review* and she is now working on a novel. She is the mother of two children. Her husband teaches English and American literature at Kenyon College in Gambier, Ohio.

HÉBERT, ANNE. She was born in Quebec City, Province of Quebec, Canada. A volume of her poems, *Les Songes en Equilibre*, won the Prix de la Province de Quebec in 1943 and a play,

L'Arche de Midi, won the same award in 1951. A book of her short stories was published under the title of *Le Torrent* in 1951. She is the author of many radio scripts and is presently working with the National Film Board of Canada as a script writer.

HOLWERDA, FRANK. Mr. Holwerda was born in 1908 in Manhattan and explains, "Most of the time I do not add that this Manhattan is in Montana but it is." He attended college for a year, then took various extension courses but feels that the main part of his education was received in public libraries from Boston to San Francisco. From infancy on, he has traveled a great deal. Before the outbreak of the last war, he worked in the foreign service of a large American firm in Netherlands Guiana, British Guiana and the Dominican Republic as well as in the Canal Zone of Panama where he met his wife. He served in the Army and after the war returned to Central America in the exporting business. From there he went to Alaska for a gold-mining company. With his wife and seven-year-old son, he now lives in Renton, Washington. He was published for the first time in 1953 when Fiction House accepted a book he had written, *Family Circle*, an article, and *Accent* and *Cosmopolitan* two of his short stories.

JARRELL, RANDALL. Mr. Jarrell was born in Nashville, Tennessee, in 1914. Since leaving Vanderbilt University where he took his M.A. degree and did two years of graduate work in English and psychology, he has been combining the professions of teaching and writing. He has taught at Kenyon College, the University of Texas, Sarah Lawrence, the Salzburg Seminar in American Civilization and the School of Letters of Indiana University. He is now an Associate Professor of English at the Woman's College of the University of North Carolina. Recently he has been a visiting professor at the University of Illinois, and has been, at Princeton, a Fellow in Creative Writing and a lecturer in the Seminars in Literary Criticism. After serving in the Army Air Force from 1942 to 1946, Mr. Jarrell was for one year literary editor of *The Nation*. Since the publication of his first book of poetry, *Blood for a Stranger*, three others have followed: *Little Friend, Little Friend* (1945) *Losses* (1948) and *The Seven-League Crutches* (1951). His poetry has won him many honors, including an award of a thousand dollars from the National Institute of Arts and Letters. *Poetry and the Age* is his first book of criticism. *Pictures from an Institution* is his newest work.

JENKS, ALMET. Mr. Jenks was born in Brooklyn, New York, in 1892. He attended Brooklyn Latin School and was graduated from Hotchkiss School in 1910 and Yale College in 1914. While at Columbia Law School, he was an editor of the *Columbia Law Review* until his graduation in 1917. He served with the New York National Guard on the Mexican border in 1916. He also served with the A.E.F. in France in the First World War and with the Army of Occupation in Germany. From 1919 to 1927 he practiced law in New York. His first short story, "The Funeral Guest" was published in *Harper's Magazine* in 1926 and he has written many short stories for *The Saturday Evening Post* since. He was Historical Officer with the Third Amphibious Corps covering the Okinawa operation in the last war. With his wife he now lives at Little Compton, Rhode Island.

LOVERIDGE, GEORGE. Mr. Loveridge was born in Waterbury, Connecticut, in 1904. He attended public schools there and later graduated from Brown University in 1926. He has worked since for the *Providence Journal* in various capacities as writer, city editor, news broadcaster and music reviewer. He is the author of several published short stories and a novel, *No One's Kindness*. He is married and has two sons. His home is in Providence, Rhode Island.

PATTON, FRANCES GRAY. Mrs. Patton was born of a long line of North Carolinians in Raleigh, North Carolina, in 1906. From very early childhood she has been interested in writing. Her first "poem" was written when she was three years old. She attended Trinity College (now Duke University) and the University of North Carolina. During her student years, her writing won her many honors and awards. In 1927 she was married to Lewis Patton of the English department of Duke University. After her marriage, Mrs. Patton did very little writing until 1944 when she resumed it at her husband's insistence. Her first story, "A Piece of Bread," won second prize in a *Kenyon Review* Short Story Contest and appeared in the *O. Henry Memorial Award Prize Stories*. Since 1946 thirty of her short stories have been published in *The New Yorker*, *Ladies' Home Journal*, *Harper's Magazine*, *McCall's Magazine* and *Collier's*. In 1951 a collection of Mrs. Patton's stories was published under the title of *The Finer Things of Life* by Dodd, Mead and Company. Last year she received the Sir Walter Raleigh Award presented by the North Carolina Literary and Historical Society for the best writing by a native of that state since 1950. She is the mother of three children.

PAYNE, ROBERT. Mr. Payne was born in Saltash, Cornwall, England, in 1911. He studied at the Universities of Cape Town, Munich and Liverpool. He worked as a shipwright apprentice in Birkenhead and for a while as an Assistant Inspector of Taxes at Guildford. He visited Java, Bali and Malaya after journeys through Europe and Spain during the Civil War. In 1941 he was put in charge of camouflage and made assistant armament officer at the Singapore Naval Base. After the war began in the Pacific he was sent to Chungking as cultural liaison officer and occasional London *Times* correspondent. He was appointed Professor of English Poetry at Fuhtan University, and again at Lienta in Kunming, acting also as a lecturer in Naval Architecture. After a prolonged visit to India at the end of the war, he came to the United States. He is the author of *Forever China*, *China Awake*, *The Revolt of Asia*, *The White Pony* and biographies of General Marshall, Mao Tse-tung and Charles Chaplin. He also has written two volumes of poems and a number of novels. He is now Professor of English and Author-in-Residence at Alabama College, Montevallo, Alabama.

ROBINSON, ROSANNE SMITH. Mrs. Robinson was born in Cleveland, Ohio, but spent her early childhood in St. Petersburg, Florida. She attended high school in Indianapolis, Indiana, and graduated from Northwestern University in Evanston, Illinois. The following summer she went to work for *The New Yorker* where she was a reporter for *The Talk of the Town* for five years. She later worked as a copy writer for a woman's home magazine. She began writing fiction three years ago by taking short story courses at Columbia University. Stories by Mrs. Robinson have been published in *Harper's Bazaar* and *Charm*. She recently completed a novel, *No Wider Than the Heart*. She has a seven-year-old son, Roderick, and lives in Whately, Massachusetts.

SHAW, IRWIN. Mr. Shaw is a native New Yorker, having been born in Brooklyn. His writing career began in high school; at Brooklyn College he was involved simultaneously in playwriting and football. Upon graduation, he began to write serial dramatizations of comic strips for radio, the success of which gave him the necessary leisure to write two plays. One of them was the memorable *Bury the Dead*, produced on Broadway in 1936 when the author was only twenty-three. Since then, in addition to writing occasional motion pictures for Hollywood, he has written several more plays, among them *Salute*, *Siege*, *The Gentle People*, *Sons and Soldiers*, and *The Assassin*. His short stories have appeared in many magazines but most frequently in *The New Yorker*. He has been represented in previous volumes of *The Best American Short Stories* and in a number of other anthologies. Three collections of his short stories have been published by Random House — *Sailor Off the Bremen*, *Welcome to the City* and *Act of Faith*. He also is the author of two novels, *The Young Lions* and *The Troubled Air*. During World War II, Mr. Shaw saw service in Africa, England, France and Germany, first as a private and later as a warrant officer. He is now living in Europe.

STAFFORD, JEAN. Miss Stafford was born in Covina, California, in 1915. She was educated at the University of California and at Heidelberg, Germany. She later taught school for a year in Missouri, worked for *The Southern Review* in Louisiana, and lived for various periods of time in Massachusetts, New York, Tennessee, Connecticut and Maine. She is the author of three novels, *Boston Adventure*, *The Mountain Lion*, and *The Catherine Wheel*, the last published early in 1952. Her short stories have appeared in *The Kenyon Review*, *The New Yorker*, *Harper's Magazine*, *Harper's Bazaar*, *Mademoiselle* and *The Sewanee Review*. In 1945, she received an Academy of Arts and Letters Award and was granted two Guggenheim

Fellowships in 1945, and 1948. Her work has been represented in five previous volumes of *The Best American Short Stories* and in other anthologies. She is living in New York.

TAYLOR, KRESSMANN. Mrs. Kathrine Kressmann Taylor was born in Portland, Oregon. She was educated in journalism and the liberal arts at the University of Oregon. Before her marriage to Elliott Taylor in 1928, she wrote advertising and publicity in San Francisco. The Taylors moved from farm to city and back to farm in California, Oregon, New York and Pennsylvania where Mr. Taylor died last year and where Mrs. Taylor has a farm near Gettysburg. There are a daughter and three sons. Mrs. Taylor is at present Assistant Professor of English at Gettysburg College, where she conducts a course in Creative Writing. Her short story, "Address Unknown" won her great fame in the nineteen-thirties and later was published in a book with that title by Simon and Schuster. A second novel, *Until That Day*, was published by Duell, Sloan and Pearce in 1942. A number of her short stories have been published in various periodicals.

TRAVEN, B. Mr. Traven lives in such seclusion in Mexico that little is known publicly about him apart from his novels and short stories and he has been called "the mystery author." To close friends, however, he has confided that he originally came from Illinois. His best-known book is *Treasure of the Sierra Madre*, which was made into an award-winning moving picture. His latest book is *Rebellion of the Hanged*. Other of his novels include *The Death Ship* and *The Bridge in the Jungle*. He is also the author of many short stories and novellas. His work has been translated into many languages.

WESTON, CHRISTINE. Mrs. Weston was born in Unao, India, forty-nine years ago, but has been an American citizen since 1928. Her father was French, her mother English; both their families had been in India for several generations, her father's as indigo planters, her mother's in the British Army Service. Much of the material in Mrs. Weston's widely read novel, *Indigo*, was taken from her family's history. Her formal education comprised a couple of years in a Catholic convent in Naini Tal, India, but she writes that she "made up the deficit under my father's tutelage at home, and my own voracious reading." In 1923, she married an American and came to the United States where she and her husband lived in Maine for almost twenty-eight years. In 1951, she was divorced and for a short time lived in New York City. Her short stories have appeared in several magazines and she is the author of five novels and one juvenile book. Mrs. Weston is on an extended visit to India for the purpose of writing a book.

WOLFERT, IRA. Mr. Wolfert was born in New York City in 1908 and graduated from the Columbia University School of Journalism in 1930. He became a sports writer for a New York newspaper and later joined the North American Newspaper Alliance for which he has worked since 1929. During the last war he was a correspondent in the South Pacific and later covered the invasion of Normandy and was with the 1st and 3d Armies in France, Belgium and Germany. In 1943 he received the Pulitzer Award for his telegraphic reporting on world affairs. He is the author of *Battle for the Solomons* (1943); *Tucker's People* (1943); *Torpedo Eight* (1943); *One Man Air Force* (with Captain Don Gentile, in 1944; *American Guerrilla in the Philippines* (1945); *Act of Love* (1948); *Married Men* (1953). His short stories and articles have appeared in *Harper's Magazine, Collier's, Esquire, Redbook, The Saturday Evening Post* and other magazines.

YENTZEN, VURRELL. Mr. Yentzen was born in Nederland, Texas, in 1919. He studied for a degree in agriculture at Texas A & M and received a B.S. in 1946. Before settling down to writing, he engaged in several occupations such as construction work and farm service. Since 1951 he has been in New York, studying at Columbia University. His first novel, *A Feast for the Forgiven*, was published this year by Appleton-Century-Crofts. He is now working on a new novel which also is about the Cajuns of Bayou du Sang in Louisiana. His home is in South Nyack, New York.

THE YEARBOOK OF THE
AMERICAN SHORT STORY

JANUARY 1 TO DECEMBER 31, 1953

ROLL OF HONOR

1953

I. *American Authors*

ANGELL, ROGER
    Children at the Shore. New Yorker.

ATWELL, LESTER
    But That Was Yesterday. Today's Woman.

BABB, SANORA
    William Shakespeare. Kansas Magazine.
    The Larger Cage. Antioch Review.

BARTH, LAWRENCE
    Out from My Brain. Shenandoah.

BELLOW, SAUL
    Mintouchian. Hudson Review, Summer.

BISHOP, ELIZABETH
    In the Village. New Yorker.

BLACKWELL, LOUISE
    Big Buster. Hopkins Review.

BONHAM, MARGARET
    What's Wrong with Our Child? Saturday Evening Post.

BOURNEUF, AGNES
    Do Not Worry for the Customs. Town and Country.

BRADBURY, RAY
    Sun and Shadow. The Reporter.
    And the Rock Cried Out. Manhunt.

BUECHNER, FREDERIC
    The Tiger. New Yorker.

BUSH, GEOFFREY
    A Great Reckoning in a Little Room. The Atlantic.

CALISHER, HORTENSE
    So Many Rings to the Show. New Yorker.

CALLAGHAN, MORLEY
    The Way It Ended. Canadian Home Journal

CHEEVER, JOHN
    The National Pastime. New Yorker.

CHIDCHESTER, ANN
    The Outcasts. Canadian Home Journal.

CLAY, RICHARD

A Beautiful Night for Orion. Hudson Review.

DAVIS, WESLEY FORD
    A Piney Woods Idyll. New Mexico Quarterly.

DEAL, BORDEN
    A Variety of Porches. Prairie Schooner.

DEASY, MARY
    The Lovers. Virginia Quarterly Review.

DEMING, BARBARA
    A Giro. New Yorker.

DEMOTT, BENJAMIN
    The Sense That in the Scene Delights. Partisan Review.

DIVINE, ELINOR
    The Onlooker. Mademoiselle.

DORRANCE, WARD
    A Stop on the Way to Texas. Atlantic.

DOUGHTY, LEGARDE S.
    The Firebird. Prairie Schooner.
    Shadow of London Gaol. Shenandoah.

DUCKETT, MARGARET
    God, the Father. Arizona Quarterly.

EATON, CHARLES EDWARD
    Brasil Moreno. University of Kansas City Review.
    Bird of Paradise. Shenandoah.

ENRIGHT, ELIZABETH
    Apple Seed and Apple Thorn. Mademoiselle.

FOOTE, SHELBY
    Child by Fever. New World Writing.

FRANCIS, H. E.
    An Anchor in the Land. Prairie Schooner.

FRAZEE, STEVE
    My Brother Down There. Ellery Queen's Mystery Magazine.

FUCHS, DANIEL

417

Twilight in Southern California. New Yorker.

GIRDNER, AUDRIE
Andrew, Edith, Edith Andrew. Prairie Schooner.
GOLD, HERBERT
The Witch. Yale Review.
GOLD, IVAN
A Change of Air. New World Writing.
GOYEN, WILLIAM
The Enchanted Nurse. Southwest Review.
GRAU, SHIRLEY
Fine Girl, White Girl. New World Writing.

HEATH, PRISCILLA
Farewell, Sweet Love. Western Review.
HEBERT, ANNE
The House on the Esplanade. Queens Quarterly.
HERBERT, F. HUGH
The Binghams Came to Blows. MacLean's.
HERNDON, BOOTON
Giddy-Giddy Gout. Park East.
HINRICHS, NOEL
The Sign Shooter. Harper's Bazaar.
HOLWERDA, FRANK
Char on Raven's Bench. Accent.
HOROWITZ, MORT M.
Summertime Heartbreak. Saturday Evening Post.
HUGHES, ELEANOR RUFUS
Mrs. Emily Gebhardt. Kenyon Review.
HUTCHINSON, ROBERT
Drug Store: Sunday Noon. Harper's Magazine.

IVERSON, WILLIAM
Every Minute a Mermaid. Cosmopolitan.

JACKSON, CHARLES
A Mother's Day Story. Today's Woman.
JARRELL, RANDALL
Constance and the Rosenbaums. Accent.
Gertrude and Sidney. Sewanee Review.
Pictures from an Institution. Kenyon Review.
JENKS, ALMET
No Way Down. Saturday Evening Post.
JOHNSON, VERA
The Way Is Hard and Weary. Canadian Forum.
JUMPER, WILL C.
The Giant Eye. Pacific Spectator.

KARGES, JOANN
The Steep Climb to Summer. Pacific Spectator.
KILEY, FREDERICK S.
Old Darkness. Epoch.
KRONMAN, RUTH
Moment of Meeting. Charm.

LOVERIDGE, GEORGE
The Latter End. Yale Review.

MASTERS, CHARLIE
When a Saint Leaves His Niche. Arizona Quarterly.
McCULLERS, CARSON
The Pestle. Mademoiselle.

NORRIS, HOKE
Mirror on the Wall. Prairie Schooner.

PATTON, FRANCES GRAY
The Game. New Yorker.
PAYNE, ROBERT
The Red Mountain. Harper's Magazine.
PITTENGER, TED
Sayonara. Atlantic.
PORTER, KATHERINE ANNE
The Seducers. Harper's Magazine.
POWERS, J. F.
The Presence of Grace. Accent.

REID, BEN
Papa Haydn's Dead and Gone. Hudson Review.
ROBIN, RALPH
Jumping Bean Season. Yale Review.
ROBINSON, ROSANNE SMITH
The Mango Tree. Harper's Bazaar.
RUGEL, MIRIAM
The Flower. Harper's Magazine.

SALINGER, J. D.
Teddy. New Yorker.
SALISBURY, RALPH
Summer Death. Perspective.
SCHUYLER, WILLIAM
Back Again. Pacific Spectator.
SHAW, IRWIN
In the French Style. New Yorker.
The Sunny Banks of the River Lethe. New Yorker.
STAFFORD, JEAN
The Shorn Lamb. New Yorker.
In the Zoo. New Yorker.

STEGNER, WALLACE
 Impasse. Woman's Day.
STUART, JESSE
 The Greatest Short Story in the World.
 Georgia Review.

TAYLOR, KRESSMANN
 The Pale Green Fishes. Woman's Day.
TRAVEN, B.
 The Third Guest. Fantastic.

WEST, JESSAMYN
 Breach of Promise. Harper's Magazine.
WESTON, CHRISTINE
 A Man Has No Choice. New Yorker.

The Man in Gray. Virginia Quarterly Review.
WHITMORE, STANFORD
 Bontemps. Pacific Spectator.
WILSON, WILLIAM E.
 Coach. Colorado Quarterly.
 The Snow and the Sun. University of Kansas City Review.
WOLFERT, IRA
 The Indomitable Blue. Esquire.
WORTHINGTON, REX
 A Kind of Scandal. Accent.

YENTZEN, VURRELL
 The Rock. Spring.

II. *Foreign Authors*

AHMAD, IQBAL
 The Opium Eater. Atlantic.

BATES, H. E.
 The Water Cress Girl. Mademoiselle.
BUZZATI, DINO
 The Bewitched Businessman. Harper's Bazaar.

COLETTE
 The Hidden Woman. Harper's Bazaar.
COPPARD, A. E.
 Lucy in Her Pink Jacket. Esquire.

DAHL, ROALD
 Galloping Foxley. Town and Country.

GRADE, CHAIM
 My War with Hersh Rasseyner. Commentary.

HARA, TAMIKI
 Summer Flower. Pacific Spectator.

JACOBSON, DAN
 Dutchman, Jew, Piccanin. Commentary.
JOAQUIN, NICK
 The Woman Who Had Two Navels. Partisan Review.

O'CONNOR, FRANK
 Adventure. Atlantic.
 The Martyr. Harper's Magazine.
 The Little Mother. Harper's Bazaar.

PRATOLINI, VASCO
 Vanda. Mademoiselle.

SALINAS, PEDRO
 The Breakfast. Hopkins Review.
SVEVO, ITALO
 Father and Son. Hudson Review.

THOMAS, DYLAN
 A Story. Harper's Bazaar.

DISTINCTIVE VOLUMES OF SHORT STORIES

Published in the United States

1953

BRADBURY, RAY
Fahrenheit 451. Ballantine Books, Inc.
The Golden Apples of the Sun. Doubleday and Company.

BROOKS, CLEANTH and WARREN, ROBERT PENN, Editors
An Anthology of Stories from the Southern Review. State University Press.

BROPHY, BRIGID
The Crown Princess and Other Stories. Viking Press.

BURNETT, WHIT and BURNETT, HALLIE SOUTHGATE, Editors
Story Number Four. A. A. Wyn.

BURRELL, JOHN ANGUS and CERF, BENNETT, Editors
An Anthology of Famous American Stories. Modern Library.

CALDWELL, ERSKINE
The Complete Stories of Erskine Caldwell. Little Brown and Company.

CHEEVER, JOHN
The Enormous Radio and Other Stories. Funk and Wagnalls.

CONKLIN, GROFF, Editor
Science Fiction Adventures in Dimension. Vanguard Press.

CONKLIN, GROFF and CONKLIN, LUCY, Editors
The Supernatural Reader. Lippincott and Company.

DAHL, ROALD
Someone Like You. Alfred A. Knopf.

DAVENPORT, BASIL, Editor
Tales to Be Told in the Dark. Dodd, Mead and Company.

DAVIS, H. L.
Team Bells Woke Me and Other Stories. William Morrow Company.

DAY, ARTHUR GROVE, Editor

The Greatest American Short Stories. Mc-Graw-Hill.

FOLEY, MARTHA, Editor
The Best American Short Stories, 1953. Houghton Mifflin and Company.

GELLHORN, MARTHA
The Honeyed Peace. Doubleday and Company.

GREENE, JOSEPH and ABELL, ELIZABETH, Editors
Stories of Sudden Truth. Ballantine Books, Inc.

GUERNEY, BERNARD GUILBERT, Editor
New Russian Stories. Translated by the Editor. New Directions.

HEARN, LAFCADIO
Tales Out of the East. Story Classics.

HOPKINS, J. G. E., Introduction
The Scribner Treasury. Charles Scribner and Sons.

HUGHES, LANGSTON
Simple Takes a Wife. Simon and Schuster.

HUMPHREY, WILLIAM
The Lost Husband and Other Stories. William A. Morrow and Company.

JACKSON, CHARLES
Earthly Creatures. Farrar, Straus and Young.

MAUGHAM, W. SOMERSET, Editor
Maugham's Selection of Kipling's Best. Doubleday and Company.

POHL, FREDERICK JULIUS, Editor
Star Science Fiction Stories. Ballantine Books, Inc.

SALINGER, J. D.
Nine Stories. Little, Brown and Company.

SITWELL, SIR OSBERT
 Collected Stories. Harper and Brothers.
STAFFORD, JEAN
 Children Are Bored on Sunday. Harcourt,
 Brace and Company.

TENN, WILLIAM, Editor
 Children of Wonder. Simon and Schuster.

VAN DOREN, MARK
 Nobody Say a Word and Other Stories.
 Henry Holt and Company.

WEAVER, ROBERT, and JAMES, HELEN, Editors
 Canadian Short Stories. Oxford University
 Press.

DISTINCTIVE SHORT STORIES IN AMERICAN MAGAZINES

1953

I. *American Authors*

ABBOTT, DELMAS W.
 Rabbits Flee the Burning Sedge Grass.
 Northern Review, Oct.–Nov.
ABRAHAMS, WILLIAM
 The Poison Typewriter. Ellery Queen's
 Mystery Magazine, Dec.
ANGELL, ROGER
 Children at the Shore. New Yorker, Aug.
 15.
ANGOFF, CHARLES
 Perjury. University of Kansas City Review, Winter.
ARD, WILLIAM
 The Baby-Sitter Mystery. Today's
 Woman, June.
ARMSTRONG, CHARLOTTE
 Laugh It Off. Ellery Queen's Mystery
 Magazine, Oct.
ATKINSON, LAURIE
 The Connoisseur of Legs. Husk, Oct.
ATWELL, LESTER
 But That Was Yesterday. Today's Woman,
 June.

BABB, SANORA
 William Shakespeare. Kansas Magazine.
 The Larger Cage. Antioch Review, Summer.
BAIZER, ASHUR
 The Proposition. Commentary, Jan.
BAKER, BARBARA ANN
 Wilderness. Montevallo Review, Summer.
BALLENGER, WALTER
 The Unbreakable. Argosy, April.

BARRON, EVE
 The Beautician. Phylon, First Quarter.
BARTH, LAWRENCE
 Out from My Brain. Shenandoah, Winter.
BELLOW, SAUL
 The Eagle. Harper's Bazaar, Feb.
 Mintouchian. Hudson Review, Summer.
BEMELMANS, LUDWIG
 The Dog That Traveled Incognito. Collier's, Jan. 10.
BENCHLEY, NATHANIEL
 Silent Night. Cosmopolitan, Dec.
 An Hour for Lunch. Esquire, Dec.
BENTLEY, E. C.
 The Feeble Folk. Ellery Queen's Mystery
 Magazine, March.
BERKEBILE, FRED D.
 Swamp Bushranger. Woman's Day, May.
BERKMAN, SYLVIA
 Blackberry Wilderness. Harper's Bazaar,
 July.
BERNSTEIN, HILLEL
 The Biter Bit. New Yorker, June 6.
BETTS, DORIS
 Mr. Shawn and Father Scott. Mademoiselle, Aug.
BINNEY, JAMES
 Afternoon. University of Kansas City Review, Winter.
BIRNEY, EARL
 Enigma in Ebony. MacLean's, Oct.
BISHOP, BERT W.
 Exorcism. Prairie Schooner, Summer.
BISHOP, ELIZABETH
 Gwendolyn. New Yorker, June 27.
 In the Village. New Yorker, Dec. 19.

DAVIS, HARRY
The Narrow Season. Quarterly Review of Literature, Vol. VII, No. 8.

DAVIS, WESLEY FORD
A Piney Woods Idyll. New Mexico Quarterly Review, Autumn.

DEAL, BORDEN
A Variety of Porches. Prairie Schooner, Summer.
Hunt the Stranger. Prairie Schooner, Winter.

DEASY, MARY
The Lovers. Virginia Quarterly Review, Summer.

DEJONG, DAVID CORNEL
I Have a Brother. Southwest Review, Summer.

DEMING, BARBARA
A Giro. New Yorker, Aug. 8.

DEMOTT, BENJAMIN
The Sense That in the Scene Delights. Partisan Review, Jan.–Feb.
The Sunflower Seeds. New Mexico Quarterly, Spring.
The Uses of the Rothermans. New Mexico Quarterly, Autumn.

DEMPSEY, DAVID
Mr. Hertzing's Wonderful Clock. Charm, Oct.

DERLETH, AUGUST
Monie. Prairie Schooner, Fall.

DE VRIES, PETER
Fall Guy. New Yorker, May 2.
Swell Egg. New Yorker, Oct. 17.

DICKER, HAROLD
The Piano. Prairie Schooner, Summer.

DIVINE, ELINOR
The Onlooker. Madmoiselle, Aug.

DORRANCE, WARD
A Stop on the Way to Texas. Atlantic, June.

DOUGHTY, LEGARDE S.
The Firebird. Prairie Schooner, Spring.
The Plaque. Arizona Quarterly, Summer.
Antique Snuffbox. University of Kansas City Review, Winter.
Shadow of London Gaol. Shenandoah, Winter.
Uncanonized Saint. Decade, Vol. XI, No. 4.

DREW, MABEL E.
The Sandbanks. New Liberty Magazine, June.

DUCKETT, MARGARET
God, the Father. Arizona Quarterly, Winter.

DUGANNE, PHYLLIS
The Children's Secret. Saturday Evening Post, Oct. 24.

EATON, CHARLES EDWARD
Brasil Moreno. University of Kansas City Review, Summer.
A Passion for Emeralds. Prairie Schooner, Fall.
Bird of Paradise. Shenandoah, Winter.

ELLIOTT, GEORGE P.
A Family Matter. Quarterly Review of Literature, Vol. VII, No. 2.

ENRIGHT, ELIZABETH
One for the Collection. Harper's Magazine, May.
Apple Seed and Apple Thorn. Mademoiselle, Sept.

ESY, HILDA COLE
Don't Be Like Me. Collier's, Sept. 18.

FARRELL, JAMES T.
I'm Dancing Frances. University of Kansas City Review, Summer.

FINN, LARRY
When Do We Kill? MacLean's, Nov. 15.

FITZGERALD, JIMMIE HODGES
The Auction. Kansas Magazine.

FOGELQUIST, HELEN
Friday Afternoon. Kansas Magazine.

FONTAINE, ROBERT
The Chair Flower. Chatelaine, Oct.

FOOTE, SHELBY
Child by Fever. New World Writing, 4th Mentor Selection.

FORD, COREY
The Boy Who Was Born Again. Collier's, Dec. 25.

FOSTER, MICHAEL
Fugitive from Broadway. Saturday Evening Post, May 30.

FRANCIS, H. E.
The Darkness Is So Big. Prairie Schooner, Spring.
An Anchor in the Land. Prairie Schooner, Winter.

FRANCIS, HERBERT A.
The Thankful Heart. Collier's, Nov. 27.

FRAZEE, STEVE
My Brother Down There. Ellery Queen's Mystery Magazine, April.

FRIEDMAN, BRUCE JAY
Wonderful Golden Rule Days. New Yorker, Oct. 31.

FUCHS, DANIEL
Ecossaise, Berceuse, Polonaise. New Yorker, Aug. 1.

Twilight in Southern California. New Yorker, Oct. 3.

GALLANT, MAVIS
The Other Paris. New Yorker, April 11.
A Day Like Any Other. New Yorker, Nov. 7.

GHINGER, ARNOLD
The Welders. Contemporary Reader. March.

GIBSON, WILLIAM
The Man Upstairs. Argosy, Aug.

GIRDNER, AUDRIE
Andrew, Edith, Edith Andrew. Prairie Schooner, Fall.

GLAZE, ANDREW
A Slightly Different Story. New World Writing, 4th Mentor Selection.

GLEN, EMILIE
Beggar by Name. Prairie Schooner, Summer.
Bamboo at the Grave. Prairie Schooner, Winter.

GLEN, JOHN
The Victim. Northern Review, Feb.-Mar.

GOLD, HERBERT
The Witch. Yale Review, Summer.

GOLD, IVAN
A Change of Air. New World Writing, 4th Mentor Selection.

GOLDKNOPF, DAVID
Christmas Twice. Harper's Magazine, Jan.

GORDON, ETHEL EDISON
A Rose in Her Hair. Collier's, May 23.

GOYEN, WILLIAM
The Horse and the Day Moth. Mademoiselle, Jan.
The Enchanted Nurse. Southwest Review, Summer.
The Armadillo Basket. Harper's Magazine, Dec.

GRAF, NANETTE
The Reunion. Prairie Schooner, Winter.

GRAU, SHIRLEY ANN
The Sound of Silver. New Mexico Quarterly, Summer.
Fine Girl, White Girl. New World Writing, 4th Mentor Selection.

GUSTAFSON, RALPH
In Point of Fact. Queen's Quarterly, Autumn.

HAGEN, ESPA
The Road to Espa. Woman's Day, June.

HALL, JAMES B.
An Assault in the Park. Western Review, Autumn.

HAMNER, EARL, Jr.
Snake. New World Writing, 4th Mentor Selection.

HARDWICK, ELIZABETH
Two Recent Travelers. Kenyon Review, Summer.

HARRIS, ROSEMARY
The Pay-Off. Charm, Jan.
Wine of Life. Canadian Home Journal, Sept.

HARSHBERGER, KARL
Del. Atlantic, Sept.

HATVARY, GEORGE EGON
The Mask. University of Kansas City Review, Autumn.

HAWKINS, JOHN and WARD
We Won't Be Any Trouble. Collier's, Nov. 13.

HAWLEY, CAMERON
River of Flames. Saturday Evening Post, Sept. 19.

HAYNES, JOAN
Felice. Prairie Schooner, Winter.

HEATH, PRISCILLA
Farewell, Sweet Love. Western Review, Summer.

HÉBERT, ANNE
The House on the Esplanade. Queen's Quarterly, Summer.

HENDERSON, ROBERT
The Platform Rocker. New Yorker, Nov. 14.

HENDERSON, ZENNA
Loo Ree. Fantasy-Science Fiction, Feb.

HENSEL, JAMES
A Quiet Afternoon. Redbook, Oct.

HERBERT, EMILY
Voices in the Air. Canadian Forum, Oct.

HERBERT, F. HUGH
The Binghams Came to Blows. MacLean's, July 1.

HERNDON, BOOTON
Giddy-Giddy Gout. Park East, April.

HINRICHS, NOEL
The Sign Shooters. Harper's Bazaar, Aug.

HINTZE, NAOMI A.
The Happiest Years. Woman's Home Companion, Oct.

HOFER, ERNEST H.
Dinner at All Souls. New Yorker, Oct. 17.

HOLSON, WILLIAM
The Worst Thing in the World. Prairie Schooner, Fall.

LIVESAY, DOROTHY
    Matt. Canadian Forum, Jan.
LOVERIDGE, GEORGE
    The Latter End. Yale Review, Spring.
LULL, RODERICK
    The Gallant Liar. Saturday Evening Post,
        Sept. 12.
    A Fighting Chance. Collier's, Oct. 16.
LUNN, DICK
    The Relic. Northern Review, Feb.-March.
LYNCH, JOHN A.
    Ebb. Four Quarters, Nov.

MACDONALD, JOHN D.
    The Trouble with Erica. Cosmopolitan,
        Sept.
MACEWEN, JOHN A.
    The Sandcastle. Canadian Forum, July.
MACLEOD, WILLIAM A.
    Letter Home. Blue Book, Oct.
McCARTHY, MARY
    The Figures in the Clock. New Yorker,
        Feb. 28.
McCLEARY, DOROTHY
    The Letter. Virginia Quarterly Review,
        Spring.
McCOY, ESTHER
    The Pepper Tree. California Quarterly,
        Autumn.
    Daga at Four-Ten. Kansas Magazine.
McCULLERS, CARSON
    The Pestle. Mademoiselle, July.
    The Discovery of Christmas. Mademoi-
        selle, Dec.
McFADDEN, FRANCES
    A Classic Affair. New Yorker, Feb. 14.
McKNIGHT, JOHN P.
    Death and the Rock. Charm, Feb.
McNAMEE, JAMES
    Two Ways to Hook a Sucker. MacLean's,
        Aug. 15.
    Give the Bride a Kiss, George. MacLean's,
        Sept. 15.
McNULTY, JOHN
    You Can't Tell How You'll Get Clobbed.
        New Yorker, Oct. 31.
MADDEN, HARRY T.
    First Holdup. Saturday Evening Post,
        Dec. 5.
MAINO, JEAN GOULD
    The Good Cry. Prairie Schooner, Spring.
    Cruise. Prairie Schooner, Fall.
MALAMUD, BERNARD
    The Girl of My Dreams. American Mercury,
        Jan.

MARSHALL, LELA
    The Dress. Prairie Schooner, Summer.
MARTIN, ERIK
    The Game. Park East, Jan.
MASTERS, CHARLIE
    When a Saint Leaves His Niche. Arizona
        Quarterly, Autumn.
MATTHEWS, JACK
    Dime. Western Review, Spring.
MAULDIN, BILL
    The Affair of the Wayward Jeep. Saturday
        Evening Post, June 27.
MAXWELL, JAMES A.
    Fighter. Collier's, Jan. 10.
MAYHALL, JANE
    Pride and Uncle Schofield. Perspective,
        Spring.
MENASHE, SAMUEL
    The Ring. Quarterly Review of Literature,
        Vol. VII, No. 3.
MILLER, JAMES E., JR.
    The Rabbit Hunt. Prairie Schooner, Win-
        ter.
MILLER, MERLE
    Wedding March. Redbook, June.
    December Song. Esquire, Dec.
MILLER, MILTON
    Barren. New Mexico Quarterly, Winter.
MILLER, WARREN
    Manita. Masses and Mainstream, June.
MUHEIM, HARRY
    The Typical Touch. Esquire, Nov.
    The Way Things Are. Colorado Quarterly,
        Winter.
MURPHY, ROBERT
    The Magnificent Mating. Saturday Eve-
        ning Post, Sept. 19.
MURRAY, DON
    The Bowl of Fruit. New Liberty Mag-
        azine, Jan.
MURRAY, PHILIP
    Adam and Eve and Several Apples. Georgia
        Review, Summer.

NABOKOV, VLADIMIR
    Prin. New Yorker, Nov. 28.
NEVILLE, KRIS
    The Man with the Fine Mind. Fantastic,
        Jan.-Feb.
NIMS, JOHN FREDERICK
    Monte. Colorado Review, Winter.
NORRIS, HOKE
    Mirror on the Wall. Prairie Schooner,
        Winter.

O'CONNOR, FLANNERY
  The Life You Save May Be Your Own. Kenyon Review, Spring.
  A Stroke of Good Fortune. Shenandoah, Spring.
  A Late Encounter with the Enemy. Harper's Bazaar, Sept.
ORNSTEIN, WILLIAM
  The Man Who Spoke to Himself. American Jewish Times-Outlook, Sept.
  Curiosity on a Mission. Kansas Magazine.
  The Only Pebble on the Beach. Kansas Magazine.
O'REILLY, NAN
  In a Manger. Canadian Home Journal, Dec.

PAEPCKE, MADELINE
  Donna. Montevallo Review, Summer.
PAREDES, AMERICO
  Over the Waves Is Out. New Mexico Quarterly, Summer.
PARSONS, ELIZABETH
  The Stilly Night. Virginia Quarterly Review, Winter.
PATTEN, LEWIS B.
  The Winter of His Life. Colorado Quarterly, Spring.
PATTON, FRANCES GRAY
  The Game. New Yorker, May 9.
PAYNE, ROBERT
  The Red Mountain. Harper's Magazine, Feb.
  Zutko. Prairie Schooner, Summer.
PETER, ROBERTA ENGLE
  The Defender. Woman's Day. Nov.
PHILLIPS, WILLIAM
  The Fox and the Grape. Partisan Review, Nov.–Dec.
PITTENGER, TED
  Sayonara. Atlantic, Sept.
PORTER, KATHERINE ANNE
  The Seducers. Harper's Magazine, Nov.
POWERS, J. F.
  The Presence of Grace. Accent, Autumn.

RAINE, NORMAN REILLY
  Dangerous Derelict. Saturday Evening Post, Sept. 26.
RAVEN, MARK
  Jonas, My Old Friend. Commentary, Aug.
REID, BEN
  Papa Haydn's Dead and Gone. Hudson Review, Summer.

REYNOLDS, JAMES
  The Muted Harp. Atlantic, Aug.
ROBERTS, MARY-CARTER
  One Is Deadly. Harper's Bazaar, Jan.
ROBIN, RALPH
  Jumping Bean Season. Yale Review, Autumn.
ROBINSON, ROSANNE SMITH
  The Mango Tree. Harper's Bazaar, May.
ROEDOCKER, LOUISE
  The Gift. Today's Woman, Dec.
ROHMANN, PAUL H.
  The Gaugin Syndrome. Antioch Review, Fall.
ROSS, DANFORTH
  The Cloud. Sewanee Review, Spring.
RUBINSTEIN, S. LEONARD
  World, Barbed-Wire. Western Review, Winter.
RUGEL, MIRIAM
  The Flower. Harper's Magazine, July.

SALINGER, J. D.
  Teddy. New Yorker, Jan. 31.
SALISBURY, RALPH
  Dawn. Perspective, Spring.
  Summer Death. Perspective, Spring.
SANDER, JOSEPH
  Cross on the Moon. Contemporary Reader, March.
SARTON, MAY
  The Screen. Harper's Bazaar, Oct.
SCHUYLER, WILLIAM
  Back Again. Pacific Spectator, Winter.
SELLARS, MARY
  A Man Called Spike. Blue Book, May.
SHAW, IRWIN
  In the French Style. New Yorker, Jan. 17.
  The Sunny Banks of the River Lethe. New Yorker, Feb. 7.
SHERBURNE, ZOA
  From Mother — With Love. Seventeen, Dec.
SHERWOOD, WILLIAM
  The Edge of Night. Prairie Schooner, Winter.
SLIFE, GENE
  A Piece of Paper. Kansas Magazine.
SMITH, H. ALLEN
  The Admirable Avery. Esquire, Dec.
SMITH, JOHN CAMPBELL
  Departure. Collier's, July 4.
SMITH, MARINOBEL
  The Golden Chain. Colorado Quarterly, Summer.

WOLF, PATRICIA
  After the Assyrians.   Western Review,
  Autumn.
WOLFERT, IRA
  Moses on Canal Street.   Atlantic, April.
  The Indomitable Blue.   Esquire, Dec.
WOOD, CHRISTOPHER
  The Enemy.   Fantasy and Science Fiction,
  Feb.

WOODFORD, BRUCE P.
  A Young Hunter.   Decade, Vol. XI, No. 4.
WOODLEY, J. B.
  With a Vengeance.   Galaxy, Oct.
WORTHINGTON, REX
  A Kind of Scandal.   Accent, Winter.

II. *Foreign Authors*

ABE, YOSHIO
  Son's Way.   Masses and Mainstream, June.
ABSE, DANNIE
  Glory Be to God for Dappled Things.   Com-
  mentary, Oct.
AHMAD, IQBAL
  The Opium Eater.   Atlantic, Oct.
ANAUD, MULK RAY
  The Barber's Trade Union.   Atlantic, Oct.

BATES, H. E.
  The Treasure Game.   Atlantic, July.
  The Water-Cress Girl.   Mademoiselle, Nov.
BENTLEY, E. C.
  The Foolish Folk.   Ellery Queen's Mystery
  Magazine, March.
BERKOWITZ, J. D.
  The Heart of a Chauffeur.   Commentary.
  Feb.
BOSE, BUDDHADEVA
  Despair.   Pacific Spectator, Spring.
BROPHY, BRIGID
  His Wife Survived Him.   Mademoiselle,
  July.
BUZZATI, DINO
  The Bewitched Businessman.   Harper's
  Bazaar, July.

CHEKHOV, ANTON
  The Boa Constrictor and the Rabbit.   Har-
  per's Bazaar, Dec.
CICELLIS, KAY
  Open House.   New Mexico Quarterly,
  Winter.
COLETTE
  The Hidden Woman.   Harper's Bazaar,
  July.
  Respite.   Mademoiselle, July.
COPE, JACK
  The Tame Ox.   Harper's Magazine, April.
COPPARD, A. E.
  Lucy in Her Pink Jacket.   Esquire, Dec.

DAHL, ROALD
  Lamb to the Slaughter.   Harper's Maga-
  zine, Sept.
  Edward the Conqueror.   New Yorker,
  Oct. 31.
  Galloping Foxley.   Town and Country,
  Nov.
DUNSANY, LORD
  Told Under Oath.   Town and Country, Jan.

GODDEN, RUMER
  The Tightrope.   Ladies' Home Journal, Oct.
GORDIMER, NADINE
  Six Feet of the Country.   New Yorker,
  May 23.
  Believe the Heart.   Mademoiselle, Oct.
GRADE, CHAIM
  My War with Hersh Rasseyner.   Com-
  mentary, Nov.

HAMILTON, WILMER
  The Pen Friend.   Harper's Magazine, Nov.
HARA, TAMIKI
  Summer Flower, Pacific Spectator.

ISHAKH, ALEXANDER
  "Bar Mitzvah."   Commentary, Oct.
ISHIKAWA, TATSUZO
  Thoughts in the Dark.   New World Writ-
  ing, 4th Mentor Selection.

JACOBSON, DAN
  Dutchman, Jew, Piccanin.   Commentary,
  Sept.
JOAQUIN, NICK
  The Woman Who Had Two Navels.   Par-
  tisan Review, July–Aug.

LAGERKVIST, PAR
  The Marriage Feast.   Harper's Bazaar,
  May.

LAVERTY, MAURA
  Here Comes Christmas. Today's Woman,
    Dec.
LEWIS, WYNDHAM
  The Rebellious Patient. Shenandoah, Sum-
    mer-Autumn.
LOFTS, NORAH
  Heaven in Your Hand. Charm, Feb.

McNULTY, FAITH
  A Man's Country. New Yorker, June 27.
MOELJONO, JOKE
  The Crickets. Pacific Spectator, Winter.
MORTIMER, JOHN
  The Pugilist. Harper's Bazaar, Sept.

NAKAJIMA, ATUSHI
  The Best Archer in the World. Quarterly
    Review of Literature, Vol. VII. No. 2.

O'BRIAN, PATRICK
  The Walker. Harper's Bazaar, Oct.
O'CONNOR, FRANK
  Adventure. Atlantic, Jan.
  This Mortal Coil. American Mercury, Jan.
  The Martyr. Harper's Magazine, Feb.
  The Little Mother. Harper's Bazaar, July.
O'FAOLAIN, SEAN
  An Enduring Friendship. Commonweal,
    Jan.
O'FLAHERTY, LIAM
  The Mirror. Esquire, Nov.
  The Fanatic. Esquire, Dec.

PRATOLINI, VASCO
  Vanda. Mademoiselle, July.
PRITCHETT, V. S.
  Passing the Ball. New Yorker, Sept. 5.

RAO, RAJA
  Javni. Atlantic, Oct.

SALINAS, PEDRO
  The Breakfast. Hopkins Review, Spring.
SANSOM, WILLIAM
  The Big Stick. Harper's Bazaar, July.
  A World of Glass. Atlantic Monthly, Oct.
  The Girl on the Bus. Atlantic, Nov.
  Woman in a Cupboard. New World Writ-
    ing, 4th Mentor Selection.
SILONE, IGNAZIO
  Along Dusty Roads and Behind Hedges.
    Harper's Bazaar, June.
ST. JOHN, WYLLY FOLK
  The Man Who Got Away. Everywoman's,
    Sept.
SVEVO, ITALO
  Father and Son. Hudson Review, Summer.

TAYLOR, ELIZABETH
  Swan-Moving. New Yorker, Dec. 26.
TEMPLE, WILLARD F.
  The Whispering Gallery. Fantastic Uni-
    verse, Aug–Sept.
THOMAS, DYLAN
  A Story. Harper's Bazaar, Dec.
TODRIN, BORIS
  The Caged Ones. Ladies' Home Journal,
    Sept.

WAKEFIELD, H. RUSSELL
  The Sepulchre of Jasper Sarasen. Fan-
    tastic Universe, Aug.–Sept.
WARNER, SYLVIA TOWNSEND
  A Kitchen Knife. New Yorker, June 13.
  Shadwell. New Yorker, Oct. 17.
WARREN, JOYCE
  Time Lucy Went. New Yorker, Nov. 14.
WHIPPLE, DOROTHY
  Saturday Afternoon. New Yorker, Sept.
    26.
WILLIAMS, WINIFRED
  A Nice Young Man. Woman's Day, June.

ADDRESSES OF AMERICAN AND CANADIAN MAGAZINES PUBLISHING SHORT STORIES

Accent, Box 102, University Station, Urbana, Illinois
Adventure, 205 East 42nd Street, New York City
American Jewish Times Outlook, 603–4 Southeastern Bldg., Greensboro, North Carolina
American Magazine, 250 Park Avenue, New York City
American Mercury, 251 West 42nd Street, New York City
Antioch Review, 212 Xenia Avenue, Yellow Springs, Ohio
Argosy, 205 East 42nd Street, New York City
Arizona Quarterly, University of Arizona, Tucson, Arizona
Armenian Review, 212 Stuart Street, Boston, Massachusetts
Atlantic Monthly, 8 Arlington Street, Boston, Massachusetts
Beyond, 421 Hudson Street, New York City
Blue Book, 444 Madison Avenue, New York City
California Quarterly, 7070 Hollywood Boulevard, Los Angeles, California
Canadian Forum, 16 Huntley Street, Toronto, Ontario, Canada
Canadian Home Journal, Richmond and Sheppard Streets, Toronto, Ontario, Canada
Catholic World, 411 West 59th Street, New York City
Charm, 575 Madison Avenue, New York City
Chatelaine, 481 University Avenue, Toronto, Ontario, Canada
Collier's, 640 Fifth Avenue, New York City
Colorado Quarterly, University of Colorado, Boulder, Colorado
Commentary, 34 West 33rd Street, New York City
Commonweal, 386 Fourth Avenue, New York City
Cosmopolitan, 57th Street and Eighth Avenue, New York City
Country Gentleman, Independence Square, Philadelphia, Pennsylvania
Discovery, Pocket Books, Inc., 630 Fifth Avenue, New York City
Ellery Queen's Mystery Magazine, 570 Lexington Avenue, New York City
Epoch, 252 Goldwin Smith Hall, Cornell University, Ithaca, New York
Esquire, 366 Madison Avenue, New York City
Everywoman's, 31 West 47th Street, New York City
Family Circle, 25 West 45th Street, New York City
Fantastic, 366 Madison Avenue, New York City
Fantastic Universe, 471 Park Avenue, New York City
Fantasy, 175 Fifth Avenue, New York City
Fantasy and Science Fiction, 570 Lexington Avenue, New York City
Folio, English Bldg. Indiana University, Bloomington, Indiana
Four Quarters, La Salle College, Philadelphia, Pennsylvania
Four Winds, 3 Liberty Street, Gloucester, Massachusetts
Galaxy, 421 Hudson Street, New York City
Georgia Review, University of Georgia, Athens, Georgia
Good Housekeeping, 57th Street and Eighth Avenue, New York City
Hairenik Weekly, 212 Stuart Street, Boston, Massachusetts
Harper's Bazaar, 572 Madison Avenue, New York City
Harper's Magazine, 49 East 33rd Street, New York City
Hudson Review, 439 West Street, New York City

Interim, Box 24, Parrington Hall, University of Washington, Seattle, Washington
Jewish Forum, 305 Broadway, New York City
Jewish Horizon, 154 Nassau Street, New York City
Kansas Magazine, Box 237, Kansas State College, Manhattan, Kansas
Kenyon Review, Kenyon College, Gambier, Ohio
Ladies' Home Journal, Independence Square, Philadelphia, Pennsylvania
MacLean's, 481 University Avenue, Toronto, Ontario, Canada
Mademoiselle, 575 Madison Avenue, New York City
Masses and Mainstream, 832 Broadway, New York City
McCall's, 230 Park Avenue, New York City
Montevallo Review, Alabama College, Montevallo, Alabama
New Mexico Quarterly, Box 85, University of New Mexico, Albuquerque
New World Writing, 501 Madison Avenue, New York City
New Yorker, 25 West 43rd Street, New York City
Northern Review, 2475 Van Horne Avenue, Montreal, Quebec, Canada
New Liberty Magazine, Toronto, Ontario, Canada
Pacific Spectator, Box 1948, Stanford, California
Park East, 220 East 42nd Street, New York City
Perspective, Washington University Post Office, St. Louis, Missouri
Phylon, Atlanta University, Atlanta, Georgia
Prairie Schooner, 12th and R Streets, Lincoln, Nebraska
Quarterly Review of Literature, Box 287, Bard College, Annandale-on-Hudson, New York
Quarto, 801 Business, Columbia University, New York City
Queen's Quarterly, Queens University, Kingston, Ontario, Canada
Redbook, 230 Park Avenue, New York City
Saturday Evening Post, Independence Square, Philadelphia, Pennsylvania
Seventeen, 488 Madison Avenue, New York City
Sewanee Review, The University of the South, Sewanee, Tennessee
Shenandoah, Box 722, Washington and Lee University, Lexington, Virginia
Southwest Review, Southern Methodist University, Dallas, Texas
This Week, 420 Lexington Avenue, New York City
Today's Family, 295 Madison Avenue, New York City
Town and Country, 572 Madison Avenue, New York City
University of Kansas City Review, University of Kansas City, Kansas City, Kansas
Upstream, 1539 Tennessee, Lawrence, Kansas
Virginia Quarterly Review, One West Range, Charlottesville, Virginia
Western Review, State University of Iowa, Iowa City, Iowa